"We have to get out of here," David said. "Addison's fighting for an air strike. Something like this will make it happen."

"Something like what?" Jamie insisted. "What's to notice? Nobody's dead."

"Exactly." David turned to her with the oldest eyes Rocky had ever seen. "I need you to tell Mom and Dad what happened, Jamie, and that we need to get out of town."

"Out of town?" She pushed David away. "Now? Where to?"

"I don't know, yet," David said. "I need to buy some time to think. Go get the family. Meet us at the dock. Bring as little as possible. We aren't coming back."

"Jesus Christ," Barry muttered. "Are you serious?"

David nodded once. The sound of the sirens drew too close for comfort. The shadier characters had slipped into the shadows. A third siren joined the chorus. David was right. They needed to move.

"John was lucky. . ." Jamie made a noise of disgust. "Okay, *really* lucky, and someone must be watching out for him, but why would Addison care about that?"

"Dozens of people saw what happened." David waved at the dispersing crowd. "They recorded everything. It's already on the net."

"So what?" Jamie looked from face to face.

No one replied.

"All this talk about Addison and secret government plots and blasted air strikes." Jamie's face grew red as she shouted. "Why would anyone care about you? Or John? Why would anyone give a crap about what happened here?" She panted angry breaths. "What should I *tell* Mom and Dad? What do you think happened here?"

The sirens screamed too ruddy close. A handful of people waited, ready to run, but Rocky could tell they wanted answers. Fine. He'd seen it himself.

"He was dead, Jamie," Rocky said. "John was dead, and David brought him back to life."

Available or forthcoming from John Robert Mack

Tales of Mystery and Woe
Supernatural / Sci Fi Universe
Tales of Mystery and Woe: a comedy
Tango with a Twist
Whiskey Tango Foxtrot
No Tengo Tango

A Consequence of Folly

Danny Decker and the
Horribly Unlikely Space Adventure

Superhero Universe
Call Me Angel
Übermen
(Forthcoming)

Third Testament
The Gospel of John
The Acts of St. Michael
(Forthcoming)

Avalon Redux
Once a Future King

Several characters appear in both timelines of the TOMAWAC multiverse. Names like Elizabeth Turner, Morrison James, and Sam Madera appear in both timelines. Rest assured that to avoid universal collapse, these characters may share names, but they are completely different people who never meet. All thanks go to Maestro who travelled from 200 years in the future to keep slavers from invading Earth in 1961. Unfortunately, time doesn't work like that. Now we have multiple timelines.

THIRD TESTAMENT
THE GOSPEL OF JOHN

SECOND EDITON

JOHN ROBERT MACK

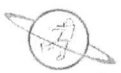

Zen Monster Press

The Gospel of John

For my brother,
who has been there from the beginning.

When goodness grows weak,
When evil increases,
I make myself a body.

In every age I come back
To deliver the holy,
To destroy the sin of the sinner,
To establish righteousness.

—The Song of God
(Bhagavad-Gita)

John and David tore across a deserted roof, feet pounding and arms pumping. They pushed off the ledge and soared though empty space to the next crumbling building where John landed light as a ninja. Gravel crunched just behind him, and David huffed a breath. Must've slipped. Ha! John leapt over the tattered furniture and ducked under the laundry flapping in his path.

His cousin closed the gap, but John reached the next ledge two steps ahead. He pulled his feet together and prepped his leap. . . but where was the scaffold on the other side?

"Fuck!" Too late to stop.

Pigeons surged into the empty space.

"John!" David's hand snagged John's waistband, jerking him to a halt.

John shut his eyes and froze. He had to be nearly parallel to the street below. Thank God his cousin had his back.

"When did they pull down the platforms?" John asked.

"Yesterday." David adjusted his weight and sucked in a ragged breath. John eased into his knees, bringing his center closer to the building.

He opened his eyes. Yowsa. Straight down.

"I missed the memo." John resisted the urge to let his arms hang.

"Really? Hadn't guessed." David squatted with his feet wide apart inside the ledge, one hand latched onto John's pants and the other holding a clothesline pole, counterbalancing his weight.

According to the readout in John's freshly stolen goggles, the rat crawling across a pile of garbage on the street below was precisely 55.6 feet away. The crow picking at a dead dog had a wingspan of 36.3 inches. The temperature was 93.2 degrees Fahrenheit, and the date was March 5, 2086.

"Good thing my pants are stretchy." John lifted his chin to send his weight backward. It was all the help he could give as David tugged him to safety. After running the rooftops for three years, they'd saved each other from dozens of boneheaded maneuvers.

"And you told me clothes made a crummy present for the big one-eight." David grunted with effort.

John kept his eyes up and let his cousin do the work, trusting David to know his center. The smoggy night sky glowed orange. Twin beams of light from a helicopter slashed the fog overhead, but no sound of rotors met John's ears.

Only Dicks had silent copters!

"Shit!" The moment John caught his balance, he twisted, grabbed David, and dragged him down, pushing him against the garbage cans near the ledge and covering him in case someone opened fire. Dressed head to toe in black and with dark skin and hair, they should look like one more pile of trash.

John kept his eyes down so the copter wouldn't see a flash from the lenses. Huh. Used condoms and a rush drive. Someone had had a party. At least they played safe.

Lights raced across the blowing gravel, splashing over broken furniture and fluttering, patched laundry. The copter itself ran silent.

The local cops might have roughed them up a little, but anyone picked up by the federal Dicks vanished forever. They'd made a sweep right after graduation, busting windows and grabbing people, friends of John's who'd been looking for work on the other side of the bridge that day. That's when John and David had resigned themselves to working in the family shop.

"What are they doing out tonight?" John whispered. "They haven't hassled the Ghetto in months."

"You think they know we're searching Venice?" David breathed light and fast.

"Let's hope not. That kind of attention we do not need."

The wind from the blades chuffed quietly.

John held his breath and clutched David a little tighter.

"We're okay, coz," David whispered, but his heart beat as fast as John's, so he was worried, too.

The lights moved off, thank God.

"I have the world's worst wedgie." John released David and turned to catch a glimpse of the copter as it moved up the coast. He rose and adjusted his pants.

"Better than the alternative, right?" David reached over and messed up John's hair.

John elbowed his cousin. "I say you set the whole thing up so you'd have a chance to grab my ass."

"In your dreams." David snorted.

John bristled. Dreams weren't a joke. David knew that, damn it. John's last nightmare had been the worst—

Who are they after, now? a voice said in John's head. He spun and dropped into a crouch. A middle-aged, Black woman poked her head through an open window across the street, searching the sky. Mrs. Delaney. He'd heard her words as plain as day in his mind. He shook his head. Damn it. That kept happening more often, too.

The woman closed her window.

"How are we supposed to cross that without the scaffolding?" John rose and stepped closer to the ledge, hoping David hadn't noticed anything weird. Would he buy the redirect?

"You had a nightmare again, didn't you?" David asked quietly. "One of those visions. And with that woman, you. . . heard something."

David always knew what was in John's head. Sharing a room for eighteen years did that. David didn't need to be a freak like John.

"I'm sorry. You don't want to talk about it." David pointed up at a zip line that crossed the alley. Well, that answered John's question about how they'd cross.

But he didn't want to talk about his stupid dreams. He'd told David first thing when the nightmares had started, just like he told him everything. Then, when John had started guessing what people thought, it'd seemed like a funny coincidence. But it wasn't. Not after today. Now John knew he was a blasted freak.

David climbed onto the crates below the line, looked down at John, and nodded at the rig attached to the cable. He wasn't going to push. He never did, which was one of the reasons John inevitably spilled.

"That building that collapsed today?" John climbed up beside his cousin. "Out near Venice."

"They say the foundation destabilized in the last quake." David made room.

John tested the rig, fiddling one thumb against it. The spring seemed tight.

"I dreamed it this morning." He could almost see it again, the crumbling walls, the screaming faces. That had clinched it. It wasn't make-believe.

"What?" David grabbed John's arm. "Why didn't you tell me?"

Because saying it out loud made it real.

"I just did." John released the catch and took three bounding steps, hurtling through the air. The wind blew hot against his face.

Too hot. It burned.

A roiling wall of fire surged through the tunnels, a searing blast that roasted John's skin as he soared through the old subway system.

People ran screaming at the head of the burning plasma. It crested and rolled over them, incinerating them so fast their blood boiled to steam.

Featureless faces screamed at him in pain. People he knew burned so hot they melted. The stench filled his lungs, and the blaze boiled through the tunnels like a hunting animal, following the twists and turns, seeking out any living thing. Killing. Destroying.

A familiar pair of men stood back-to-back as the plasma hit them from both sides. They vaporized. Who?

John hit a rooftop couch at top speed and bounced over it, rolling across the gravel. Flames covered him. He cried out, but the inferno vanished. In a crouch, he searched the darkness for fire.

"Blast it and burn it!" He yanked the goggles from his face.

David grabbed John's hands, and the contact pulled him back to the real world, but his heart still raced. He tasted smoke.

"John?"

He had to pull it together. What he'd seen wasn't real. But that smell! That's what human flesh smelled like when it burned? Like a sweet barbecue? He raced to the nearest corner and puked.

David's hand rubbed his back. Well, he'd sat Shiva while John threw up before.

"Now I see shit when I'm awake?" John punched the wall. "I have, what? Seizures? How can I do anything for Makabee like this? I'll get someone killed."

The errands Makabee sent them might be minor set against the larger dissident acts he organized, but John and his friends were moving up; the map Makabee had given David's sister Jamie proved that. But if John freaked out in the middle of a mission, he could get someone killed. And if his friends found out about the mind reading. . . who'd want to be anywhere near someone who got glimpses into their heads?

Hell, Jamie was only sixteen, but she already had Makabee's ear.

What use was a freak like John?

"Fuck!" He punched the wall again.

A nearby crow called back to him.

"What did you see?" David asked, as if it were the most normal question on the planet.

"It sucked, coz. I don't want—" No. He had to calm down. Other than helping Makabee close the ghettos for good, what future did he have? He shook out his hand and met David's gaze.

No accusation there. No pity. Just concern. They'd figure it out together. David would never abandon him.

"I'm fine." John rolled his shoulders a few times.

"You're bleeding," David said, pointing.

"Damn." The sleeve had ripped through in the fall, so John attached his goggles to a clip and yanked off his shirt. He wiggled a finger in the hole. "This was my favorite covert ops shirt."

David chuckled. "Covert ops?"

"We're working our way up." John jabbed David's arm.

"Today controversial graffiti, tomorrow we assassinate the president." David opened a first aid kit.

"It could happen." John ran his hands over his head to smooth out his hair. Thank God his cousin knew when to let something go.

"Don't worry, coz, your new *Casablanca* haircut is still pretty." David dabbed alcohol onto a pad and clucked his tongue. He'd been giving John grief about the new do all day.

"You're just jealous because you have Q-tip head," John said.

"Not me." David cleaned the abrasion on John's shoulder. "I like the hair of my ancestors." Tension drained away with David's gentle touch. Fine. John could deal with it. Whatever the hell *it* was.

"It's like they're really happening," John said. But that didn't feel quite right. "Or like it's going to happen?" Those words felt true. "Like it's going to happen."

"What did you see?" David shook a can of adhesive bandage.

"I saw fire in the tunnels this time. And people burning. . . our friends. . . burning."

"Our friends?"

The crow on the chair preened itself.

"I don't know who," John said. "I saw people without faces but I knew them." He shivered, and not just from the chilly adhesive. "And the smell. . ." He swallowed to keep from puking again.

David handed over a water bottle.

"Thanks." John didn't know whose faces had been blackened and twisted, but he could smell the corpses? What the hell was that? "I think it's really going to happen."

"Should we cancel tonight's search?" As simple as that, David accepted his story. The gentle way he fussed over John's injury calmed him further.

"Barry's already waiting for us." John tested the shoulder to see if the adhesive had set. "I can't give up on Makabee because of one stupid vision, or whatever the what." He ground his teeth. "I'm such a freak."

"I don't think so."

"You don't count." John shook himself all over. Let it go. Change the subject. "How can I be so skinny?" He worked his arm more and struck body builder poses. "We spend all day searching Venice and dragging junk back for your dad's wacky furniture." He held his arms away from his sides and could count his own ribs. "And most nights we run the rooftops or swim around looking for the air pockets on Makabee's map. I should be a god."

"Nice redirection, Mr. Vanity." David collected the first aid supplies. "You don't look so bad."

"I look like Tonto," John said, "in the video."

"You say that like it's a bad thing."

"I have these blasted visions." John shrugged. "I'm the only Indian in the Ghetto. . ."

"You'd rather be in Texas with the rest of the Indian Nation?"

"No. But it'd be nice if someone around here looked like me." Pulling his shirt on, John followed David. They reached a ladder and climbed up. "You look Jewish, just like your dad. It gives you a connection."

"I look Jewish? What is that?"

"Oh, come on. . . you do!"

The boys ran. The next roof had a new patio set.

"Do I say you look gay?" David swung on a pipe.

"Nobody looks gay."

"Bruce the Florist?"

"That's just stereotyping." John cuffed him.

"So was yours." David smacked him back.

"You know what I mean." John dropped onto his stomach near a ledge. Voices reached him from below.

David lay down and whispered close to John's ear. "You may not look much like me, hotshot, but you're still my brother."

"Cousin," John corrected.

"Technically, second cousin." David made a disgusted noise and crawled over John to the ledge.

John did the math. "Whatever."

An elbow to the ribs startled him. David glared at him then shook his head and turned away. Blast. David was trying to help John feel better, and there he was acting like it wasn't good enough.

"I am an asshole," John said.

"Yes, you are."

"I'm sorry."

David adjusted his goggles and said nothing. Still pissed, then.

"Coz," John began, "thanks for not thinking I'm a freak."

"Who said you weren't a freak?" Well, that was David's petulant voice.

John kicked his cousin's foot.

"If there's a copter out, Dicks must be on the streets, too." David scowled then finally shook his head and kind of, almost smiled. Good. "We'll need to be careful." He fiddled with his goggles and turned his attention to the street below. "Wacky!"

John touched his eyewear and night turned to daylight. "Absolutely wacky." The new equipment had much better night vision. "Thank you, Barry." Their friend Barry, who was likely waiting for them, oversaw equipment acquisition.

In the alley below, two small girls dug through a pile of garbage. They wore matching dresses that might have been pink several years and owners ago. Now they seemed nearly grey with bright yellow patches to cover the holes.

One girl shrieked and kicked at a rat that scurried away.

The other girl laughed, but it turned to coughing.

"Serves you right," her sister said.

The other girl ignored her and kept digging.

More and more of the littlest kids had fallen sick. Old people, too.

"They shouldn't be eating from the garbage," David said. "I think Makabee's right. The rats have been infected on purpose."

"Sometimes garbage is all they have to eat." John's family was lucky. Uncle Bo had a few wealthy customers who kept food on their plates, so John rolled onto his back and shoved his hand into his pants pocket. He pulled out his last few bills and held a hand out to David.

"*We're* only a day or two away from dumpster diving," David said.

"Uncle Bo has a delivery for us tomorrow. Lincoln." Lincoln was the new Hamptons since the original had drowned, so any delivery out there meant a long train ride but serious cash.

David's eyes grew big. "When did he tell you that?"

John lost his smile. He hadn't been told. He'd just heard it in Uncle Bo's mind.

"Oh." David handed over his cash.

"He wants to surprise us." John rolled up the bills. "So act surprised." He wrapped it with a thick rubber band, then flipped onto his stomach.

He whistled.

The girls looked up.

"For food." John tossed the money down to them. "Stay away from the blasted rats."

The girls scrambled for the little bundle and ripped it open. One girl gasped, and the other looked up.

"Thank you." She tugged on her sister's sleeve. *I don't know what those men want in return, but we better leave vapor trails.*

John shook her thought out of his head. Damn it.

"It's happening, isn't it?" An old man wandered into the alley, shirtless, his pants held up with a rope. "It's starting now. He sees it." He nodded vigorously. "He must see it, because it's coming!"

The man peered up at John, smiled a manic, toothless smile and waved both hands.

"Jesus, is that me in a few years?" A chill ran across John's back.

"No, it's not," David whispered.

"It's coming!" The old man shouted abruptly. His waving turned frantic.

John waved back, and the old man resumed his erratic journey.

"A seven-headed dinosaur and ten top hats can't be wrong."

Stupid old man.

Something tapped John's calf! He twisted around, knife up and ready.

"I love doing that." Barry crouched at his feet, unfazed by the blade. He grabbed the toe of John's boot and wiggled it.

"*So* not funny." John relaxed and sheathed his knife.

Barry was an expert at theft. He wore the same style of black clothes as John, his long, dark hair hidden under a knit cap.

"Greetings and salutations, hep cats and cool rats." Barry grabbed first David and then John in fierce hugs and kissed them both on the cheek. "Barir bin Saeed Al-Hadi at your service." He flourished one hand and bowed.

"I hope you don't introduce yourself like that on the other side of the bridge." John punched him lightly in the kidney for surprising them.

"And waste my mother's off-the-hook genes?" Barry placed one hand on his chest and posed like a Greek statue. As long as no one scanned his ID chip, Barry passed as cracker outside the Ghetto. "You cut me to the quick, coz." And he spent way too much time trying to sound as hep as the latest net series.

"I thought we were meeting at the bank," David said.

"Fifteen minutes ago." Barry tapped the goggles on his forehead. "I got bored."

"Attention span of a tachyon." John shook his head and scanned the street again.

"We saw a copter," David said.

Barry did a double take.

John nodded.

Barry gave a low whistle.

Something moved on the street below!

John stifled his friend with one hand.

The old crazy stared directly at two men standing side-by-side under a streetlight. They wore similar suits cut so well they had to be expensive. Their fedoras were the real deal, too, not cheap knockoffs like John and his friends wore to parties.

"A seven-headed dinosaur and ten top hats can't be wrong?"

The kind-of-hunky guy's arm came up so fast John barely registered the movement. The muzzle flared, but no sound reached John's ears. The silencer did it's job as well as the copter had.

The old crazy's head snapped back, and a dark ribbon of blood unfurled behind him. Then he dropped like a stone.

Barry and David clamped their arms around John before he realized he was moving. He lunged forward, sucking desperate breaths around the hand David fastened over his mouth. Barry swung a leg over John's hips to keep him down.

"There's nothing we can do," David whispered so close to John's ear he felt the moving air. "It's too late."

Nothing they could do? They could keep that fucking cracker from killing one of their own again. They could. . . They could get themselves killed. That guy was trained for it.

John wasn't. Not yet.

"I know." He jerked his head away from David's hand.

A black halo of blood formed around the dead man.

"That may have been premature." The older agent lowered the younger man's gun arm with a single finger.

"Sorry, Mr. Addison." The younger man doffed his fedora and wiped his forehead with one arm. He was blond and attractive in a scary cracker kind of way. "Shades of prophesy, what he said?" His voice held a trace of a Southern accent.

"I hope that was a joke, Pierce." The older man, Addison, lit a cigarette. He turned his back to his associate, but John noticed the trembling of his hands.

"Of course, sir."

"The whole damn street smells like piss," Addison said. "Double check my vaccine schedule in case anything new's been introduced. I don't want to catch shit." He kicked the melted tire of a burned out, broken car. "We'll need to spend some extra time here. Get a hotel across the bridge." He held up a hand. "Wait, make it a motel. We'll need to come and go without some desk clerk recording our every move."

"Why this ghetto?" Pierce opened a holo screen over his cell and worked it.

"There are a hundred ghettos. . ." Addison scanned the dark windows and turned slowly.

John had never really noticed the streaks of black that covered the buildings from fire and smoke, but watching this man scrutinize his home, he saw them plainly. Half the windows were boarded over on street level. No one could afford to replace the glass after the police raids.

". . .but in this particular ghetto, a few months ago, a mouthy kid in a synagogue really torqued off a rabbi." Addison completed a circle.

Wait. Mouthy cat in a synagogue? That could be David. He dragged John all over the Ghetto asking questions and pissing off church elders wherever they went.

"There's a lot of mouthy young men out there these days." Pierce kept working the holo.

"A mouthy teenager in a synagogue?" The older man gave him a sidelong sneer. "How old is our science project now, and what exactly do you suppose that fanatical mother of his would have him doing?"

What the hell? What did that even mean?

Pulling out his cell, Addison tapped it. A small holographic screen winked into existence. He swiped the screen, sending it to Pierce.

"Oh yeah, that could be him, sir." Pierce scrolled, but his damn big shoulders blocked the hologram from John's view. "Timing's right, too. This was the first ghetto, right after HIV went airborne. . . so lots of 'Muslim terrorists' here, of course."

Wait, the way he said that. Even the Dicks knew blaming the Muslims had been a scam?

"Blacks, gays. . . lots of Hispanics. The whole enchilada." Pierce scrolled and scrolled. "A lot of Jews who wouldn't convert to the UCA."

"Well, it is New York, after all," Addison said.

David tugged at John's arm. He wanted to go? Fine. John glanced down as they leapt to the next rooftop.

Pierce ducked. His gun flashed out and swept the street. He must have heard.

Officer Jonas King froze at the corner of Luther and Jerome: two crackers scanned the rooftops with a bloody corpse at their feet. A couple of shadows leapt between two buildings. It was always the rooftops. The stench and heat drove everyone upward where they might find a breeze.

"Put the damn gun away," the older of the two men said. "One body is enough. The punks in this ghetto wouldn't dare jump us."

Jonas pulled out his weapon and headed onto the scene. He wasn't quite sure what to do with two homicidal crackers on his beat, but he had a meeting scheduled hereabouts with an agent from Dickerson Incorporated, and he'd be blighted before he'd let some petty shooting ruin a conference that could mean a promotion.

"You there!" Jonas called.

The young guy pulled his piece so fast, Jonas almost pissed himself. Holy shit! They stood with weapons drawn and aimed. What next? What would happen if he shot a couple of crackers?

"Do we look like locals?" The older man gestured at his fancy suit. "I think you're the one who should holster his weapon, Officer King."

Jonas' cell buzzed. He grabbed it with one hand but kept his gun level. He raised the cell into his line of sight and activated the hologram. Holy mother of the Apocalypse! These men had higher clearance than God! Addison and Pierce. Dickerson agents. Jonas did the math: the older man had to be his contact.

"I'm sorry, sir." Jonas holstered his weapon and hustled forward, adjusting his too-small uniform. The extra jogging wasn't doing anything to trim his waist. "What happened here?"

"Looks like someone killed a homeless guy." The man named Addison took a drag from his cigarette. "Nothing important."

Jonas glanced at the corpse then bounced between Addison and his assistant, Pierce.

"Officer Jonas King." He held out a hand. "I'll send someone out to clean up the body."

"Whatever." Addison ignored the hand.

Was there any way Jonas would survive this meeting? No wonder Randall had insisted he was too busy to attend. Damn cracker.

"Have you seen either of these people?" Addison held out his cell.

Two faces appeared. Jonas peered closer to the hologram of a very familiar couple. The man, Bo, was a Jewish friend. His wife was Ruth, a pretty White woman with dark hair and blue eyes just like the hologram. They had three kids, and the oldest, David was tight with Jonas' oldest boy. Why the hell were the DIs interested in them?

"What are their names?" Jonas asked.

"Mary and Joe," Addison told him. "But I doubt they'd use those names."

"Mary and Joseph? Like in the Bible?" Jonas needed to stall while he worked it out. Now that he thought about it, Ruth did kind of look like the White folks' Mary. What the hell?

"The names are a coincidence, I assure you," Addison said. "The photos have been age-progressed, so they might look differently."

"Lots of Jew men here in the Ghetto, sir. Lots of pretty women." Whenever he met federal agents, Jonas used a bit of his folksy, none-too-bright civil servant act. The private contractors with Dickerson Incorporated were the worst: untouchable and they knew it. The kids called them Dicks with good reason.

"But likely not a lot of pretty White women." The agent tapped the screen. "They might be with this fugitive, as well."

And that was definitely Ruth's cousin, Naomi. Her son spent so much time with Jonas' oldest boy, Noah, it was like having another mouth to feed, not that Jonas minded. John and David were a good influence. Without them, who knew how Noah would've ended up? Most likely the same as Rocky, who spent more time jacked into some net drug than in the real world.

"And they'd have this young man with them." Addison tapped the screen. "He'd be eighteen or so."

Well, that certainly was David. The image didn't seem doctored at all, although his hair was shorter than Jonas had ever seen it.

"Can I see the two women again?" Jonas had to stall. "They sure are pretty." He chuckled. "I have to be honest, sir. All the White folks and Jews kind of look alike to me. Tell you what, send them to my cell, and I'll make sure all the men get copies."

"No. Never mind." Addison closed the hologram. Uh-oh, was he suspicious? Had he seen through Jonas' front?

"I want you to be our eyes and ears, officer." The agent stepped closer. "Look around. Let me know if you see them. I can't risk them finding out I'm here. They'll run."

"What did they do?"

"They killed a man," Addison said.

What the hell? Jonas felt like he'd been hit by a brick. How in the world could anyone in that family have committed a crime like that?

"Must've been a pretty important man," Jonas prompted, scrambling.

"They also stole classified government property," Addison said. "They're terrorists."

"I see," Jonas said. Folks threw that word around so much. "In that case, I'll let you know the second I learn anything."

"Good man." The agent looked Jonas up and down. "Until we need you again."

Jonas extended a hand. The agent ignored it. Dick.

"Good to meet you." Jonas turned and left. Giving them his back made his skin itch. Would his cracker partner find two corpses laying in the street when he finally brought his spineless cracker ass downtown?

Half a block. An entire block. And... around the corner. Jonas breathed a sigh of relief. Those DIs had already left one body to clean up. He hitched his pants and picked up his pace.

What the hell had Bo and his wife gotten themselves into? They seemed like the most God-fearing, quiet folks in the Ghetto, them and their whole family. Murder? Jonas could see straight-laced Naomi killing someone almost as easily as he could see Jesus himself committing murder. And David? Well, Jonas' own son Noah was more likely to perpetrate a crime.

And what about the other boy, John. Why didn't the DIs have photos of him? It just didn't ring true to Jonas. He might not be some fancy-ass DI, but his instincts were as good as anybody's, and right now shit smelled wrong. Still, Jonas had kids of his own to think about. He couldn't outright defy that cold-blooded bastard, but he didn't need to rat out folks he'd known for years, either.

Not unless he had to.

Addison waited until the lying son of a bitch walked around the corner then lit a cigarette. He'd made a quick decision to keep the images from the rest of the local cops. There'd be too many people to follow, and someone was bound to warn the fugitives.

"He's lying, sir," Piece said.

"No shit. He recognized both parents and the cousin." Addison started down the street toward the bridge. "His pupils dilated when he saw the photo of our science project. He fucking knows the little bastard."

"So the families are still together."

"Exactly. That makes it easier." Addison sucked on his cigarette. "And they're all here somewhere, in this God damned ghetto." Finally, after so many years, he was close enough to taste victory. "We need to get a trace on the cop's chip. See if he goes to warn them."

"Already done, sir."

"Can we predict what the half-breed kid would look like? I don't want to buy gum from him at the mini mart and walk away."

"We can, sir, but it's hard to say which parent he'll favor more." Pierce played with his screen. "We do have his DNA on record, so we might be able to get close. Good idea, sir."

"You think Mary had more kids?" As close as Addison was to success, he needed to find a way to hone in tighter.

"Worried about her perpetual virginity?"

Addison backhanded Pierce before he'd consciously registered his anger. Fucking ouch. Was that man's jaw made of metal?

Without a word, Pierce returned to work on the hologram.

"Don't get biblical on me, for fuck's sake." Addison rubbed his knuckles. Had they augmented Pierce's skull? Possibly. They'd done a lot to his assistant back in the day. "Our science project's a clone from the bloody crust on a two-thousand-year-old piece of wood. That's it." Addison shoved his hand in a pocket to hide the shakes. "You know I trust you to do your job but keep getting snarky with me, and I'll eat your balls in a fondue."

"Why did you ask about the kids, sir?"

"If she ever had more kids," Addison pointed out, "there might be a birth record. We need to search the DNA database for anything that could be related."

"Will do." A bright red mark had blossomed on Pierce's cheek.

"How old are you?" Addison was glad his assistant had learned to accept anything he dished out, but he sometimes wondered about it.

"Thirty-eight."

Unbe-fucking-lievable. Addison focused so obsessively on his goal, he often lost track of the years. "Why the hell are you still on this job?"

"I have an option?" Pierce kept his nose in the hologram as he walked.

"Not really, I guess." Addison squashed the cigarette butt under his foot. The damn things didn't work as well, anymore.

John couldn't force his heart to slow down. From the top of Regent Tower, he scanned the drowning borough nick-named Venice. Taller than anything else in the Ghetto, the Regent provided a view all the way to the Atlantic. It also held an earthquake-fractured vault that opened into the subways, the safest route to Venice with copters in the air.

Those Dicks had blown that old man away and carried on with their conversation over his bleeding corpse as if he didn't matter. Fine. Maybe John couldn't do anything to *them*, but he would do his best to help the Pipeline search Venice. No one knew what Makabee wanted there, but the map he'd given Jamie pointed to several specific locations.

David hadn't spoken all the way across town. He stared out over the city now, his eyes unfocused, not really looking at anything. His silence made sense. When it came down to it, the conversation they'd overheard was worse than what they'd seen.

"You think they were talking about you?" Barry asked. "Mouthy cat in a synagogue?"

David held his silence.

The Dick's body had blocked a clear look at the hologram of the suspect. But who else? And why would a couple of Dicks care that David torqued off a Rabbi? David torqued off a lot of Rabbis. And priests and ministers.

Once Pastor Su had grown tired of David's endless questions and politely asked him to stop raising his hand in the middle of her sermons, he'd started a tour of the Ghetto. John tagged along for moral support.

"Synagogues. . . Chapels. . . Mosques. . . ha-cha-cha-cha." Barry's perpetual solution to any problem: crack a joke. "A rabbi, a priest, and a minister all walk into a whorehouse. Only the priest comes out."

John snorted.

"You'd think you were sent here to raise Hob, coz." Barry nudged David.

"I just ask questions." But he almost smiled.

Of course, asking questions got people arrested, but John knew better than to point that out.

"How do I zoom?" He didn't want Barry to crack more jokes. His friend directed John's fingers to a dial around the right lens. The old levee popped into view beyond the drowning buildings. "Whoa!"

Even in the dead of night, the remaining shards of the old seawall stood clearly as a broken line low in the water. With the new goggles, John could make out the salt stains on the buildings that marked high tide. Every year, the water swallowed another block, forcing the Ghetto rats living there to squeeze in with friends or relatives who would have them. Water lapped at the windows of John's old elementary school, but the flooded neighborhood seemed deserted.

"Looks safe to me," he declared.

"I'm guessing your mom would not consider 'safe' an appropriate word," Barry said.

"The way you suck up to her—" John continued his scan.

"Just because I choose to act the gentleman..." Barry sniffed loudly.

"Gentleman?" John elbowed him. "The way you make it with anyone in a skirt under thirty years old?"

"Forty." Barry grinned, nudging him back. "Don't be ageist."

John led the way from the roof to a maze of fractured stairwells and crumbled marble into the belly of the abandoned bank. Water dripped down the walls, and rat pellets dusted the stairs.

"Ever since Joanne told us about the rats, the blasted things creep me out." Barry kicked one down the steps.

"Because they were cuddly and loveable before we thought someone infected them with disease?" John held up a heavy hatch while the others crawled through. "Next you'll claim the HIV mutation was a government plot to frame the Muslims and force the rest of us into ghettos like Joanne says."

"Well?" Barry passed through but must have missed the sarcasm. "You heard what that Dick said."

"And Joanne does get closer to politicians than any of us," John added, pointing out the obvious.

"I wouldn't mind getting closer to Joanne." Barry clicked his tongue.

"Not cool. It's Joanne, she's like family."

"And this ain't Kentucky." Barry's voice echoed in the stairwell.

"Besides which, there's no way you could afford her." Hm. David's tone seemed a bit *too* casual. Did *he* have a crush on Joanne?

"I hear that, old soft." Barry chucked David's shoulder.

They slipped through the vault cracks into a pitch-black service tunnel after strapping flashlights to their foreheads. By the time they crossed Atlas Drive, water sloshed at their ankles. They crawled onto a rusty catwalk and followed that until it ended where the tunnel sloped sharply down into the water. Strapping their lights to a nearby pipe, they stripped and hauled gear out of their packs.

David checked the bandage on John's shoulder. "Wouldn't want to get that infected." He added a bit more spray.

"What happened?" Barry asked.

"Oh, I decided to dig out my chip so I can come and go as I please." John winked at Barry. "It didn't go well."

"Wow." Barry snorted. "If only we could plant that for truth without bringing down a battalion of Dicks. Can you rez it, coz?"

John pulled on his trunks and slipped an oxygen mask over his mouth and nose. He attached it to a small canister of compressed oxygen and a rebreather at the back of his neck.

Barry was quite good at theft.

Fully fitted, with a pack around his waist and a light strapped to his forehead, John checked David's equipment. They stuffed their larger packs behind an access panel for safekeeping and locked arms for luck.

John smiled and gave David a shove that toppled him off the walkway.

"I was named for John the Baptist," he joked over the com unit in the mask, then stepped off the ledge into the water. The cold shock of the subterranean river caught his breath. He floated for a few seconds, letting his breathing slow and regularize. The sensation of water on his skin, the womblike embrace. . . John felt more at home in the water than on land.

He opened his eyes.

David gave him the finger.

John returned the gesture with a grin. He swept the familiar debris with his light. A thin fuzz of algae grew over pipes and rocks and subway cars alike. He relaxed as he navigated the twisting and turning underwater tunnels. Schools of silvery fish darted away when the light touched them. Visibility seemed lower than usual. Someone had passed this way recently.

Several wrecked trains lay like slain whales on the floor of the first subway station. The doors—most of which had been forced with crowbars and blowtorches—gaped like blackened wounds in the trains' sides. Disaster crews had cleared all the bodies right after the Quake.

Any dangerous wreckage had long since drifted to the floor, so the young men swam among the trains in relative safety. Nonetheless, adrenaline pumped through John's veins. Trips into Venice, always a part of their work on the Pipeline, meant he belonged to something larger than the day-to-day life in the Ghetto. Something important. Something that also connected David— *Spear!*

"Look out!" John grabbed Barry's arm and pulled him close.

"What the what?"

A two-foot steel spear shot through the water an inch from Barry's head. It embedded itself halfway into the concrete wall.

"Lights out," David said.

The tunnel dropped into complete darkness, and the trio ducked behind the nearest subway car. As John's eyes adjusted, subtle lights rippled across the algae-crusted tunnel, cars, and rails.

"Who's trying to kill us?" Barry whispered.

John peered over the lower edge of the window, careful of the broken glass. A corpse floated into view on the other side of the car. A spear protruded from his right eye and the spiderwebbed plastic of the mask he wore. Blood floated in a halo around him.

"Holy wow." David touched John's arm.

Barry pointed through the gloomy, shifting water beyond the floating corpse. Three women in expensive dive suits faced a lone man in a cheap getup with enormous tanks who swam away from them in a frenzied panic, but he wasn't fast enough.

The smallest woman took aim and a twin of the spear that had almost killed Barry shot all the way through the tank, the man's back, and out his chest. His body arched. Foom! The tank exploded, and air rushed in a fountain of bubbles to the roof. The man folded forward.

The women swam down to a pair of large metal boxes with biohazard labels on them. They futzed with the boxes and flotation jets ignited, raising the boxes a few feet from the tunnel floor. The women swam off, and the boxes followed, leaving two corpses floating in the water.

"Organ pirates," Barry murmured.

"Holy shit," John said. "It was just a stray spear." The corpse on the other side of the subway car drifted out of sight. "Must've been shooting at that poor guy."

"You saved my damn life, coz." Barry squeezed John's arm. "How'd you even see that?"

"Good peripheral vision?" John hadn't *seen* anything.

"I guess." Barry moved to the next window, shining his light on another corpse. "Looks like three."

David's eyes accused John.

John raised his hands. What should he have said? He'd just *known*. David shrugged broadly: maybe not everything about freakiness sucked.

"Okay, boys." Barry returned. "Let's leave vapor trails."

"What about them?" John pointed. The lights on the dead bodies slowly swept the tunnel as they settled to the floor. Creepy.

"They were stupid enough to think they could sell body parts

on the black market, down in the tunnels in the middle of the night."
Barry moved off. "Dead's too good for 'em."

"Coz… rough." John swam through the subway car. "I'm
going to tag them." He couldn't leave them there to rot and feed the
fish. They had mothers and fathers and brothers. Someone should
retrieve the bodies.

Barry sighed loudly over the com. "Do you have any idea how
hard it is for me to steal those damn things?"

"I'll only leave the one." John pulled a hypo from his pouch
and shot a tracker into the nearest corpse. "Good enough?"

"Blah, blah, blah." But Barry's tease seemed good-natured.
They all knew that if *they* died down there one day, they'd want
someone to tag their bodies so they'd be recovered. No one wanted
to disappear. It happened too often, and the waiting hurt too much.

"It does settle one question," Barry offered while John worked.
"If the ultrarich really have giant banks of clones somewhere for
harvesting body parts, why would they bother with black market deals
like this?"

John set the beacon to start transmitting four hours later—long
after he and the others would be home.

"There's ultrarich," David said, "and then there's 'owning your
own bank of clones to harvest body parts' rich. Might not be the same
thing."

"True words."

Checking for survivors, John found five bodies, young and
cracker. From the look of their equipment, they'd been poor. Not all
the crackers on the other side of the bridge could afford the nicer
things.

"No one we know," John said. "Five dead. Probably interns in
a hospital or clinic." He considered collecting sundries to return to
their families, but would they even talk to a Ghetto rat? They might
have been poor, but White was White. Well, nothing John could do
about it.

"Must've figured safety in numbers." Barry moved aside as
John swam through the subway car to rejoin his friends.

"They figured wrong," John said.

"At least their people will know." David met his eyes in the gloom.

Ugh. Too much to think about. People died in the Ghetto all the time. If they weren't your people, you couldn't lose yourself in shock or grief or you'd live that way every damn second of every damn day. John had work to do, and it was important work, work that might one day put an end to the constant tragedies.

David's mouth set in a firm line, and he nodded.

"Jesus, will you two kiss and get it over with?" Barry laughed. "I wanna go look for buried treasure."

"Okay, that's it Al-Hadi, you're the next corpse." John grabbed for his friend, who whooped and swam off.

John wanted to move out in any case. Someone might come looking. He also wanted to wash away the traces of DNA he might've picked up from the dispersing blood.

He led the way up the tunnel, which angled toward the surface. As the water grew warmer, John switched off his light. No reason to announce their arrival. The others followed suit, and they navigated the last few yards in darkness.

The tunnel widened until it opened onto the street, fifty feet under water. Murky moonlight showed them the subway entrance and the tumble of cars and trucks that filled the street. They swam to the corner of an old insurance building and surfaced.

The air was balmy, the moon full. The clouds had cleared off.

John hovered in the shadows, treading water and scanning the buildings for snipers. All the windows appeared empty.

"How do you do infrared?" John followed Barry's lead to switch modes. His friends burst into bright shades of red, yellow, and orange.

"Holy wow," John exclaimed. "Wacky."

All visible buildings showed cold. No snipers. Some birds high up.

John led the way deeper into Venice. Crumbling buildings loomed over them like old monsters covered with black, sightless eyes. As John swam in the moonlight, the enormous figures carved in granite seemed like gargoyles leering down from rooftops and staring defiantly at the encroaching ocean while the neighborhood slowly drowned. Against the glowing backdrop of the city lights, the rusted girders jutted out from the tops of buildings like dead branches.

"Uncle Bo would love this place," John said, still over the com. He thought so every time they explored.

David nodded.

"Oh yeah," Barry said. "It always reminds me of that crazy Deco stuff he makes."

Uncle Bo talked about the place all the time. The buildings had been built right after Staten Island surrounded itself with a levee back in the 60s. The city had been so confident of its safety from the rising ocean, they'd redone everything in granite and glass and covered the island with carved figures and decorations based on old Art Deco models. Then the Quake destroyed the levees and destabilized the entire island.

"Hey, John," Barry said, "you ever ask your uncle if he wants to swim out here with us? I'd love to hear his words about all the wacky artistic insanity."

"My mom would have an absolute coronary if she ever found out he came here with us." That alone would make it worthwhile. John loved his mom, but she did everything she could to keep him a little kid. Not that her attempts worked.

"Those are true words," Barry said. "Uncle Bo's ultra wacky."

All their friends loved David's dad. When John could be honest with himself, he had to admit he was closer to David's parents than his own mom. He could tell Uncle Bo anything. Absolutely anything. His mom acted as though he'd become a terrorist in training if he sneezed in church.

What would his own dad have thought of his work on the Pipeline? Uncle Bo supported it. He'd told John more than once that his father would be proud of him. So why wasn't his mom? John checked the monuments overhead. His neck prickled as if the cold, dead stone watched him, but the goggles showed nothing except for a couple of birds.

Michael perched high above the water on the head of an enormous gargoyle. An imposing dark figure wearing jeans and a black, leather vest, he watched the young men swimming below with eyes that smoldered a deep, watery green. While David was his personal responsibility, Michael couldn't help that his attention wandered frequently to John. The pair seemed inseparable.

Raphael manifested beside Michael, who rose and crossed his massive arms but otherwise ignored his brother's sudden presence. The smaller, ancient-seeming Asian man watched his companion more than the young men in the water.

"You seem much interested in him these days." Raphael inspected Michael with the eye not covered by a black patch.

"It's almost his time."

"That has been said many times throughout history." His Fu Manchu moustache wobbling as he chuckled, Raphael turned his attention to the activity below.

"This time it's true." Michael ran a hand through his straight black hair and pulled it away from his face.

"That has been said almost as much."

"You doubt that he's really the One?" Michael shifted to a different rooftop so he could continue to observe the swimmers' progress.

"Which one?" Raphael had followed. "You thought the nun mystic was *the One*. . . and the Middle Eastern shepherd. There have been so many that I wonder at your use of *the One*."

"This time is different." Michael's eyes flared brighter. "And I know what you're going to say. I have said that as many times as I have said any of the other things."

"We will see." The corners of Raphael's lips curved in a hint of a smile. "We always do." He looked Michael up and down with an appraising gaze. "And I was going to say that your outfit is a cliché, *kimosabe*."

Michael smiled, making no comments on the slate blue robes of his companion.

"My question is different." Gabriel appeared on a slightly higher perch. "I'm curious to know which one you're actually watching." She fanned herself with a bright white fedora that matched her suit. Her ginger curls moved in the breeze as if under water.

"David," Michael said. "I have always been his guardian." He crouched, perched on a naked girder that stuck out from the crumbling building like an exposed broken bone.

"You know it's nearly John's time as well, don't you?" Gabriel's eyes flared red. "His death can't be avoided."

"I know that." Michael's jaw clenched. But was it almost John's time? Was that really their Father's wish?

"All signs say it is inevitable." Raphael sounded almost smug. He saw more and farther than any of them, but his confidence in his ability reeked of ego.

"I'm concerned over the impact his death will have on David." Hmm. Michael could lie more easily than he'd thought. "My charge will be devastated."

"As far as we can tell, that's the entire point." Even Raphael remained uncertain then.

None of them had heard from the Father in so long, how could any of them be confident about anything?

Far below, John treaded water. A police siren sounded in the distance. He switched his goggles back to basic magnification and searched the sky for lights. Nothing.

"What should we try this time?" he asked.

"St. Matthew's?" David floated beside him.

"Still hoping for relics?" Barry asked.

David splashed him. "Makabee's map shows an air pocket under the sanctuary, and no one can find it."

"We'd be the ultimate hep cats if we found it," Barry pointed out.

"We've been there five times," John teased. "And that place is far more interesting during the day."

Sunlight transfigured the church into an amazing work of art when filtered through stained glass windows that had miraculously survived two decades of the worst natural disasters in US history.

"St. Matthew's it is." David dove and swam toward the church.

John followed, his light sweeping an erratic beam across the roof. The street lay about forty feet below that and dropped farther in a steep hill beyond. John had only gone that deep once. Their friend Noah had a grandfather with an old fishing boat and professional scuba equipment.

John's light illuminated David's dark, sleek body as he sliced through the murky water. The buildings rose up around them, and the dim glow of the moon couldn't reach that deep. Three beams of light swept the rotting clay shingles and converged on a broken hole in the roof. They swam through single file.

Gooseflesh rippled across John's skin as he hovered in the sanctuary. David sank to the floor, exploring the rubble. Barry swam to the choir loft.

John's light swept across the life-size statues that stood watch in recessed alcoves high in the walls. Algae softened their marble features. He floated a few feet away from the statue of St. John the Baptist. The statue's head bowed, watching the floor where churchgoers had not stepped in a decade. What idiot had carved the statue to look Anglo? The actual man had probably looked more like David and Uncle Bo.

A muffled clatter from below drew John's attention the same moment someone shouted over the com. Who? The loud noise distorted the sound too much for John to recognize the voice.

"What's wrong?" John asked. A dark gray shape slid effortlessly through his light. A bright eye glinted a reflection. A shark!

"Holy shit!" John's heart thundered in his chest. Was any of the blood from the bodies still on him? Was his shoulder bleeding?

"Go, go, go, go, go, *go*!" David brushed past, grabbing John's arm and dragging him along.

The giant fish turned its nose their way and raced toward them. How the hell did a fish have teeth that large?

A light flashed in John's eyes, blinding him. Was that Barry's lamp? What the what? Another flash… So bright…

So much light!

Sunlight filled the sanctuary with color. Beams filtered through stained glass rippled in the bright, dusty air. Rows of shiny, dark pews filled the floor below. The statue of John the Baptist watched the floor with sharp, clear features.

The doors creaked open, and two men hurried up the central aisle. John knew them. He'd just seen them on the street.

"This girl was practically born for the Project." The attractive man scrolled through images as they walked. He seemed younger. "She's perfect, Mr. Addison. Eighteen, sweet as a turtle dove, and about as bright."

"You've got to be kidding me." Addison snatched the tablet. "Mary?" He stopped and regarded the other man as if he suspected some kind of sophomoric joke. "Her name's Mary?"

"The Lord works in mysterious ways, sir." His voice held a trace of a Southern accent.

The sanctuary swirled and changed. The two men sat in chairs facing a girl in the first pew, a girl who looked like David's sister Jamie— No. David's mother. She had to be Aunt Ruth, but so much younger. She held a pair of vials, one in each hand.

"I am the Lord's servant," teenaged Aunt Ruth said. "Will I be allowed to go home first, or will I fly directly to Nevada from here?"

The smile on Addison's face reminded John of a shark.

Shark! What had happened to the shark?

Arms enfolded John. A heart beating almost as fast as his own pressed against his back. David held him, now, crammed behind the statue of John the Baptist. A huge mouth flew at his face.

"Blast!"

The shark hit a narrow gap between the statue and the alcove wall, shaking the statue. Voices screamed over the com unit, too confused and overlapping to understand.

The shark rammed forward again. It thrashed in a frenzy trying to squeeze into the alcove, trying to reach John.

"Are you back?" David's voice reached him over the chaos. His arms held John close, as far from the shark as possible. He must have pulled John to safety when— Damn it! He'd almost gotten them both killed with what? A vision? A seizure?

The shark rammed the statue again, and stone scraped on stone. John the Baptist moved half an inch. There'd be time to yell at himself later. Right now, John had to think, to find a way to save himself and his cousin. Okay. He and David were crammed behind a statue with a shark ramming it in a frenzy. What could they do?

"I'm back," John insisted.

"What the hell is going on?" Barry shouted high and terrified.

"We're fine," John called to shut him up. "Stay away from us. There's a shark up here. You'll just get killed. Please shut up so we can talk. We're safe."

"A shark? Sweet Baby Jebus!"

The shark slammed the side of its body against the statue. The stone slid another inch.

"For now, anyway."

The shark swam a short distance away.

"Any ideas?" John asked.

It rammed the statue again. Stone scraped stone. . . and something clicked. It wasn't over the com, though. The sound had originated behind them. But what. . . ?

The wall behind them swung open. A secret door behind the statue?

"Stay away for a minute, Barry," John said. "I think we found a secret passage."

"Excelsior!" Barry exclaimed with delight. "Really? I wanna. . ."

"Get a closed door between you and the blasted shark!" John

and David hurried into a little room hidden behind the statue of John the Baptist. "As soon as this monster realizes we're gone, he's going to come looking for you."

"Oh, cheese it."

The inside of the door had a handle that turned, and John checked to make sure the deadlatch worked before closing it between them and over two tons of hungry fish. He followed David to the far wall. They held onto one another by childish reflex, and John, for one, was not about to let go because they were too grown up to huddle together like kids.

John kept his light trained on the closed door long after the sounds of the shark's attack ended. David's light swept the room, little more than a closet.

"What happened?" Barry asked over the com.

John turned to David. What should they say? That John had some kind of seizure during a shark attack, so they'd both nearly died?

"John smacked his head trying to get away from the shark," David said. "He lost consciousness for a couple of seconds."

John nodded his thanks for the cover story. In truth, David had dragged him away in the nick of time during another blasted seizure. Was this the new normal? Seizures under stress? How could he admit that to anyone, even Barry? He never lied to Barry.

"Your fish friend's circling the sanctuary," Barry said.

That was one problem with an open com. John had no way to talk to David privately about his vision. Had it been the past? Had that really happened? What had Aunt Ruth agreed to do?

"Either of you see one of those things before?" Wonder filled Barry's voice.

"No way," John said. "Only in videos."

"Me neither. Noah told me about a few he saw after the Quake when bodies were still in the subways." Barry spoke so gently. "How'd you find that room?" After John explained, Barry whistled. "What's a secret room doing thirty feet in the air?"

David patted John's arm and drew his attention to a tiny red light on a control panel and a small vault-style handle built into the wall behind them. The control panel held a standard keypad and two LEDs. A red light was lit. The other LED was dark. The way the thing worked seemed obvious: enter the correct code, the dark light would come on, spin the handle, and the door would open.

Holy wow!

John's excitement dimmed. Without the correct code, they'd never go farther. He looked to David. Maybe he had an idea.

His cousin shrugged and started tapping numbers, then hit "enter." The panel whined. Wrong number. David punched another set of numbers.

"Hey, Barry?" John watched David work. "I think we found another way out of this room."

The machine whined at them a second time.

"Holy mackerel! Okay, shark's gone. I'm on my way."

David punched numbers while they waited for Barry.

"Maybe we should try hitting every number from zero until we manage to find the right code." John opened the outside door and waved Barry over with his light.

"Our tanks only have enough oxygen for a couple of days, coz." Barry greeted John with the obligatory squeeze. "I'm glad you weren't snacks for the sushi. And a secret door? Straight up."

They moved into the room where David kept tapping numbers and hitting the enter key.

A faint "ding" startled John. What the what? The second light blinked green. The red light had gone dark.

"How did you manage that?" John stared at the blinking light.

Barry reached for the handle, but David pressed an arm across his chest. His caution made sense.

"What's wrong?" Barry asked.

"Double door system?" John pointed at the outside door. "It screams airlock. If it's airtight on the other side, something very bad might happen with both doors open at once."

"Wait, you think this leads down to Makabee's air pocket?"

"The power's still on." John pushed the outer door shut. "Anything's possible"

"How'd ya find the right code ya lucky bast-id?" Barry punched David's arm.

"Luke 11:10."

"Knock and the door shall be opened," John said. "Excellent. We're dealing with priests here, not world-class spies."

Barry spun the handle, and the door slammed open away from them. Holy wow and what! A cyclone sucked John through and tossed him head over heels. The roaring of a waterfall and the muffled shouts of his friends ripped apart the silence of the murky depths. He hit walls and stairs, bumped solidly into someone, held on, and slid to a standstill at the bottom of a flight of steps, tangled in a heap with the others.

The water washed away into the darkness. So a landing, not the bottom. John had lost his light in the fall, but the others flashed theirs around. No one seemed hurt.

"You okay?" David passed John his mislaid light.

"Yeah, fine."

"If you get your flipper out of my crotch, I'll be great," Barry complained. "That was so intense."

A short flight of stairs led to the open door above them. Below, stairs continued down and turned at another landing like the one that had prevented them from washing all the way to the bottom. Water soaked the steps, but the upper walls and ceiling remained dry, so the passage had been dry as a bone until they'd stumbled across it.

"Good thing you thought to close the outside door." Barry untangled himself and rose to his feet. "We'd have been a wreck on a raft all the way down." He peeled the oxygen mask from his face and took a hesitant breath. "Air's fine."

John removed his mask. The air tasted musty but seemed breathable. They slung their flippers on their backs and crept down the stairs, which wound deeper and deeper.

"Jesus," John whispered, "we must be below the building by now."

David's face glowed with excitement as he nodded silently. They'd found it. One of the air pockets Makabee wanted most.

"Go ahead," Barry prompted. "You told us so."

"I would never." David ducked his head. "But I so did tell you so."

"It's probably just going to lead to a vat of sacramental wine," John teased. "The good stuff the priests hid for themselves."

David gave him a sour look.

Barry punched him in the arm.

A thick, dark, wooden door with no apparent lock stood at the bottom of the staircase. A blackened iron handle seemed ready to open.

"I guess if you get this far, you belong here," John suggested.

David grabbed the long ornate handle and pulled.

The door slid open with a high-pitched squeal.

John held his breath.

"Hello-o?" Barry called softly. "Anybody home?"

"You have a visitor." The motel system woke Addison from a sound sleep. He slid his pistol from under the pillow and strode to the door, navigating in the dim light. He tapped the locking panel, and Pierce's face appeared on the screen.

"Someone found the office under St. Matthew's." His assistant didn't flinch or blink.

What the fuck? Addison waved the door open, lowered his gun, and stood aside. Pierce hurried into the room and sparked up a cell.

"That isn't fucking possible." Addison grabbed a robe from the back of the door. "That place is under a hundred feet of water."

"An alarm signaled me that the lock disengaged." Pierce opened a screen and worked it.

"More likely the energy supply finally ran out." Addison set the gun aside and lit a cigarette while Pierce worked. The assistant had been right to wake him, anyway.

"Someone keyed in the right passcode."

"How the fuck is that possible?" Addison tied the bathrobe closed and stood on the opposite side of the hologram. "Is there any chance the cameras are still working?"

"Accessing them now."

"Could that fucking place still be airtight?"

Pierce froze. His eyes met Addison's through the translucent screen.

"Well?"

"Yes," Pierce said. "And yes."

Video played. The room had been perfectly preserved. Amazing. Addison's desk filled it more than he remembered. The picture was hazy, but two, no, three men moved around it. Trunks. Flippers. Dripping wet. They'd obviously had to swim to reach the room.

"Who the hell—?"

One young man looked directly into the camera.

Addison gasped so hard he choked on his cigarette. By the time he stopped coughing, static filled the screen. "What the hell happened? Bring it back," he demanded. "Did I fucking see what I thought I saw?"

"The camera cut out." Pierce waved a hand through the screen. "Someone must have spotted it."

The image replayed. The familiar face looked into the camera again.

"Pause that," Addison said.

The image froze.

"It's him." Addison stepped closer. "Son of a bitch. It's our fucking science project." And he was in St. Matthew's where it all started. What were the fucking chances? "Get a team..." He stopped because Pierce had opened another screen already.

The man in charge of the local DIs seemed none too pleased to be awakened at whatever-the-fuck o'clock in the morning. Too fucking bad. What was his name again?

"McCarthy" appeared in red letters in one corner of the screen.

It was the little things Pierce did to help that kept him alive.

An antique mahogany desk dominated the center of the foul-smelling room. It reeked of stale smoke, most likely from a fire after the Quake. John crouched beside the desk, staring in shock at the contents of one drawer: half a dozen glass vials exactly like the ones he'd seen Aunt Ruth holding in his vision. He picked one at random. It held little black chunks. *It looks very old.*

John shook his head. The sounds of Barry and David rifling the room returned.

"We're going to have company." David stood over John holding something. "I found a camera. It was running."

"That's not possible," Barry crowded close as John rose.

"Really?" David glanced around the room skeptically. "A working camera is where you draw the line here?"

The situation involved too many coincidences for John's comfort. The shark? Not common, but not unknown. But then he'd had a vision of Aunt Ruth there in the church with the two men they'd just seen. And David had guessed the code so easily. Then he found a camera? Could it be coincidence?

Barry loaded things into his backpack, apparently unconcerned.

"You okay?" David touched John's arm. His eyes were so innocent and open. Why would John suspect him of anything bad?

"I'm fine." John shook himself. "Thanks."

David nodded and turned away, but John stopped him.

"Thank you." He put as much sincerity into his voice as he could. David had saved his damn life.

Another nod. "We'll talk topside."

"What're these?" Barry set a box on the desk and held up a glass sphere the size of a peach. He tossed it to John.

"No idea." It caught the rays from John's light and refracted them. Some sort of prism, then. "Wacky, though. Uncle Bo would love 'em."

He tossed it to David who held it to a light.

"I don't see any reason Makabee would want them." John turned back to Barry. "Bag 'em up for Uncle Bo?"

"As you wish, *kimosabe*." Barry stuffed it into a pack.

John grabbed the vials. They might be important, especially since they'd been in his vision. He yanked drawers out of the desk and dropped them to the floor. Damn, they'd made furniture solid back in the day.

"We should hurry, guys." David rifled a sideboard. "Whoa!"

John looked over.

"You think this is real gold?" David held up a candlestick.

"Is the Pope Catholic?" Barry rushed over. "Jackpot, gentlemen." He opened all the doors. "There's only a few pieces, though." He helped David load them into a pack they'd found. "Still worth the price of admission."

John stayed with the desk. Makabee most likely had little interest in treasure, and this place held a permanent spot near the top of his list. What would he be looking for? John pulled out the last drawer. Nothing but staplers and pens. Hm. He'd played plenty of spy games in his time. He dropped onto his back and scooted under the desk. The light strapped to his head picked up a glint of metal. An old-fashioned data drive.

"Bingo!" John peeled it from where the drawers had been.

"What did you find?" David peered under the desk at John's left knee.

"A wad of cash?" Barry crouched at his right.

"This is the kind of thing Makabee might want." He held the drive out to them. "Looks almost as old as we are. Should we look for more?"

"That camera makes me nervous." David held a hand to John and helped him to his feet. "I think we should leave vapor trails."

They grabbed a few things at random, helped each other arrange the newly found packs, and ran up the stairs, fitting their masks in place. Once in the air lock, Barry closed the door.

"Stay there." David hurried to the outer door, yanking it open. "No time for finesse."

"That's going to—" Barry shouted.

The onslaught of water plastered John against the wall. Oh yeah, that hurt, but John ignored the pain.

Blast. Trouble. Colored lights flashed in the sanctuary. Someone lurked outside the church. Dicks? The water stabilized, and John led the way out, pausing behind the statue.

"As soon as we can," John said over the com, "go down, not up, and stay hidden."

Bright light flooded the space from above and outside, flickering in the water and colored by the stained glass.

"That's actually pretty," Barry whispered.

Muffled shots sounded strange underwater. What kind of weapons did they have? Were they shooting at John and his friends?

No. The shark had returned. It thrashed a couple of times before swimming directly to the light streaming through the hole in the roof. A line of blood trailed behind as it rushed into another spat of weapon fire.

"That's ginchin' lucky," Barry said. "It'll slow them down."

"Let's go." John didn't want to waste an opportunity. He hurried to the floor. "Radio silence. Lights out." He had no way of knowing whether their visitors could hijack their frequency, and light filled the sanctuary.

The church had several exits, and a few only opened from the inside. Anyone trying to bypass the enormous shark near the roof would be unlikely to test a door with no handle on the outside. John led the way to an exit near the back of the sanctuary and slowly opened the door onto darkness. He switched to infrared. The only warm bodies were less than a foot long and hurried away at his movement. Good. The fact that fish swam there meant no Dicks patrolled the area.

He switched his goggles to low light, and the bleed-off from the searchlights high above worked just fine. He led his friends away from the church and into a nearby alley. As well as John knew Venice, no way a bunch of Dicks could find them.

Addison braced himself for disappointment.

Several holographic screens showed the DIs swimming into St. Matthew's and searching the place, but they'd taken far too long to get to the site. Although he'd already had copters patrolling the Ghetto, the teams hadn't been prepped for underwater action. They'd had to fly all the way back to base to refit.

Addison wanted to kill someone for incompetency, but there'd been no fucking way to foresee that particular development.

Pierce watched the videos from the other side of a holo screen. His eyes flicked rapidly from one image to another. He never seemed worried that Addison would shoot him. Interesting.

"They're gone, sir." A single pasty face filled the main screen. "We can widen the search parameters—"

"Don't bother," Addison said. "Those Ghetto rats know that place better than any of your men. What did you find in the room?"

"Office supplies." McCarthy shook his head. "The infiltrators shook it down. Was something valuable in there?"

Addison caught Pierce's eye.

His assistant closed all the screens with a wave of his hand.

"Was there?" Addison reached for a cigarette. He'd run out.

Pierce pulled a pack from his own pocket. He held out a cigarette without a word. Hm. Something had to be wrong.

"I'm not going to shoot you, Pierce." He took the cigarette.

"I can't be certain, sir." Pierce lit the cigarette. "We moved out of that office in a hurry." His voice trembled.

"I haven't killed you in twenty years, for Christ's sake." He inhaled the sweet smoke. "What the fuck is bothering you?"

"Remember data spheres?" Pierce's hands went to his pockets.

"Obsolete technology that was all the rage for about two years. I hated them. Why?"

"I wouldn't even worry about it, except that he was there. And that has to mean something, doesn't it?" The fact that he kept his hands in his pockets meant they'd be shaking otherwise. "When we moved out, I shredded all the papers and wiped all the drives. I did it all myself as usual. I oversaw all the packing myself."

"Except?" Addison hated exceptions.

"Except a box of data spheres." He met Addison's gaze evenly. "We were in a hurry, and the data had been transferred. I wiped them clean, but I asked Father Patrick to smash them all with a hammer and dump them."

Because that was why they'd been all the rage for only two years. They had unbelievably massive storage potential, but once the information was encoded in the crystals, no matter how hard you wiped them, they carried a trace of it.

"Do you have any reason to believe he didn't carry out your request?" Addison asked.

"None at all, sir, but. . . but why else would *he* be there?"

It was hard to say. For all they knew their science project was just looking into his roots.

"What was on them?" Addison demanded.

"Most of them were empty. A few had medical records of the girls."

"Just the medical records? And just the girls?"

"Yes, sir."

Addison breathed easier. He snubbed out his cigarette. He patted Pierce's shoulder. They had nothing to worry about. The younger man flinched then his eyes registered surprise. Had Addison ever touched his assistant before? Hard to say.

"The reason you're still alive after all these years is that you obsess over details like this." Addison moved to the windows. "So someone finds out what a doctor said about a couple of hundred girls who pissed in a cup. I don't care."

In the reflection, Pierce relaxed visibly.

"You're sure there wasn't anything else on those spheres?"

"Positive, sir." Pierce almost came to attention.

Addison needed to make sure this leniency wasn't used as an excuse to get sloppy. He turned to look his assistant in the eye.

"This is, remarkably, the only thing you've fucked up in twenty years, so I'm giving you a pass. I remember those stupid things, and I don't recall uploading anything sensitive." He'd hated them from the beginning. Too trendy. "Anyone else would already be cooling and staining the ugly shag carpeting."

He wandered over to the enormous spa tub in one corner of his motel room. He kicked it. "Real marble." The bar against the wall was mahogany with steel trim. The liquor stocked there was all top shelf. "Why is this place so familiar to me?" Something about the Art Deco doodads on every piece of built-in furniture nagged at his memory.

"The room's an exact duplicate of the motel in *Singin' in the Rain*, sir." Pierce called up several scenes from the new video. "You can't go online without seeing the preview."

"I could give a shit what the place looks like." He snubbed his cigarette in the ashtray.

"I know, sir. It's all I could get on short notice." He waved the images away and called his files up again. "They had a couple of last-minute cancellations."

"This is your one free pass." Addison moved to the window. Trees and shrubbery filled the motel grounds. Far too many places for someone to hide. "It means the next time you fuck up, I kill you, twenty years on the job or not." He closed the drapes. "Everyone is replaceable on this project."

"Except you, sir," Pierce returned too quickly.

"Don't suck up." Addison slipped out of his suit coat. "Keep me updated."

"Of course, sir." His assistant turned on his heel and left.

"Fucking military training." Addison reached for the pack Pierce had left on the counter. "After all these years."

Pierce hurried down the hall to his room. He keyed himself in and barely made it to the toilet before puking violently. If Addison found out he'd lied. . . Another round of vomiting left him dizzy and weak. He flushed the toilet and sat back against the tub to catch his breath. If Addison ever found out what had been on those data spheres, Pierce would die in an instant.

He ran a sleeve over his mouth. Father Patrick must have destroyed them. Why wouldn't he? Pierce had already looked him up and found out the old man died in the Quake. He had no way to verify whether he'd shattered them. But he must have.

He *must* have

John checked his shoulder in the dresser's cracked mirror. The bandage hadn't deteriorated in the water, so he dropped the can of adhesive next to the single glass sphere he'd kept as a memento.

David lay on his mattress with his back to John, ready for sleep. It'd been a hell of a night.

John pulled the chain on the single bare bulb that lit the room. When the light went out, the glow-in-the-dark bullseye he'd painted ten years ago shone a dim green.

"I'm still worried about you." David's voice was quiet and undemanding. John could ignore it if he chose. He could slip into bed and pretend nothing had happened.

"How'd you know the door code for the door?" John led with the least of his concerns because he didn't want to think about what really scared him. He leaned against the old dresser and crossed ankles and arms.

"It wasn't brain surgery." David sat up.

"There's more than one verse about knocking on a door." As John's eyes adjusted to the light from the open window, the confusion in his cousin's face showed clearly.

"And what worked was the third one I typed in," David explained.

Oh. That made it less mysterious. John's question sounded a little foolish, now.

"How'd you find that camera?" If John was going to fess up, he may as well say it all. "How'd you know where it was? And why have you been so insistent on St. Matthew's? Did you know what we'd find there?"

"Makabee gave that location priority." David's face relaxed but in a way that John knew it took effort. "What's going on?" He rose and crossed to sit on the window seat. "Did I do something wrong?"

John's breath caught in his throat. He thought back over the night. So many things felt wrong. That vision had almost killed them.

"Seriously, John, what the hell is going on?"

They'd shared a bed until they were twelve years old, for Christ's sake. If anyone knew John, David did. If John trusted anyone, he trusted David. Maybe for the rest of the world, he wanted to be an adult, ready to face whatever he met, but with David? He wanted that one place that was safe, that was always his home.

"Those Dicks tonight?" John had to say it. He couldn't keep it to himself. "Looking for a mouthy Jew? I had a vision about them."

"When the shark attacked?" So he knew.

"When I almost got us killed, yeah," John said. "I saw them in St. Matthew's." He closed his eyes to picture it again. "It was years ago. Before the Quake. They talked about a project." He opened his eyes and met David's gaze. "They were talking to your mom, but she was our age, maybe younger. That's how I knew it had to be the past. Your mom had these vials." He turned to the dresser and pulled one out of a drawer. "And I found some exactly like it in that room."

David held out a hand, and John passed him the vial.

"So you think I was looking for this," David said, "because you saw my mom as a girl in your vision right before that shark opened the secret door for us, and I figured out the code."

When he said it like that it sounded stupid.

"Never mind," John said. "Let's just get some sleep."

"No, wait. I'm not being a jerk. I'm serious." David held the vial in the light from the window. "Any idea what it is?"

"No."

"So." What the hell was David thinking? He tossed the vial once and grabbed it in a fist. "I'm what then? A government agent? A Dick?"

"God damn it, David. I don't know what any of it means, but these visions… they have to mean something, don't they? If not…" If not he was just as insane as the crazy old man in the street, the one who'd been blown away like he didn't matter at all.

"I don't know what to think." John swallowed hard.

"Can I try?" David waited for John to nod. "There *is* a connection between the Dicks and St. Matthew's. There must be. That's why Makabee is so interested in it and why all those Dicks showed up when we opened the door. It's also why you had the vision then and there. You'd just seen those guys. You were in a place important to them, so when the adrenaline hit from the shark attack, some part of you connected the dots and you had that vision." He tossed the vial back to John. "For my mom to be there is way too big to be a coincidence, so that has to mean something, too."

"You make it sound like the most normal thing in the world." John could hardly believe it. "But it's. . ." What was it? "It's utterly declassed." But he really *wanted* David to accept it… on his side… not involved somehow.

"And?" The weird light through the window made the bones in David's chest and shoulders stand out. "Look, I'm trying to be extra casual because you're upset, but really, how do I know the stuff *I* know?"

"What?"

"I've always been able to find stuff you lost," David said. "I know stuff. I sense stuff. I see auras. You treat it like it's normal because I've always done it. And my mom, how does she always know where we are? Whether we're here at home or out somewhere? She always knows if we're okay. People think that's weird, too." He opened his arms wide. "We're all freaks in this house, coz. You're just a late bloomer."

Wow. Could he be right?

"What's really wrong?" David asked quietly. "I know this stuff tonight freaks you out, but what's really going on?"

He wanted to know the truth? Fine. The truth.

"Do you want to help your dad in his workshop your whole life?" John met David's eyes. "I love your dad, but that isn't what I want for my life. We can't go to college. We can't get a job outside the Ghetto, and what the hell is there here?" He waved a hand at David. "You have your teaching. You're great with the kids in Sunday school, and no one really expects a teacher to have a college degree here, so you'll eventually get a regular teaching job. And I end up making furniture my whole life?" He shook his head. "That's not what I want."

"That's why the things we do for Makabee are so important," David insisted. "We can change all that. *He* can change all that."

"Can I?" John snapped.

David jumped at the volume.

"Working on the Pipeline is the one thing I have." John forced himself to speak quietly. "The one thing I knew we'd always do together, you, me, Jamie. . . our friends." But mostly him and David. "Now? I almost got you killed. Who the hell's going to want me tagging along now?" He swallowed the lump in his throat.

"I will never turn my back on you." David's face stayed so calm.

"You say that now—"

"Shut the fuck up, John." David rarely swore like that. "I stabbed myself in the back of the hand when I was five years old. Remember that?" He grew quiet. "Why do you think I did that?"

John remembered. It was the scariest thing he'd ever seen: David screaming with a scissors stuck all the way through his hand. But it'd been an accident. . . or. . . something. . .

"I did it because I figured out how much of a freak I am." He sat in the window again. "I was scared, terrified. You and me, we had a fight. Remember?"

John did, but only vaguely. All memory of the argument had faded behind the image of the scissors in David's hand. And his screams.

"I didn't understand why you were so mad at me." He met John's eyes. "I realized there's a lot I don't understand." He leaned closer. "And a lot of people don't really get *me*… but you never once let me think there's anything wrong with me. You're always there." His eyes were so sad. "How can I do less for you?" He pulled one bare knee up to his chest. "And that thing with the shark was bad. . . but you saved Barry's life before that." He rolled his eyes. "Peripheral vision my finely tanned butt. It's not all bad, coz."

John's heart beat so hard it hurt. His eyes burned. He'd been so scared, so worried that his issues would be too much even for David. He worked through the little things, the things David had mentioned, the things *he* could do. John wiped a hand across his face in case he was crying.

"I don't see myself as a carpenter, you know. You neither." David quirked a smile. "You can't hit a nail straight to save your life."

John couldn't let himself laugh. If he did, he'd start crying. Blast, he was tired.

"We're going to make this work with Makabee," David said. "Somehow. Somewhere."

"I can't live here my whole life, Dave," John said. "I'll fucking die."

Emotion hit David's face out of nowhere and his eyes teared up. He took a second before he could speak.

"Sorry. Long day." He wiped a hand over his face. "We'll just have to find someplace more suited to your highly refined sense of fashion and architecture. You and me."

John choked out a laugh.

"You realize we have no choice but to hug it out." David rose and opened his arms.

John closed the space between them.

David held him close.

John swallowed hard to keep the lump down. With David's arms around him, his fears seemed stupid. He was safe there. Home. He could cry if he needed, and David wouldn't tease him. Which meant he didn't need to cry, after all. How could he have thought that

David would desert him, that David was hiding something from him? It was stupid.

He sucked in one deep breath. David even smelled like home.

"Uh-oh." David pulled a bit away. "Your cell."

John turned in David's arms. An emergency icon flashed above his cell where it lay on the dresser. Noah.

"Accept call." John hurried over.

"John?" Noah appeared in the hologram. His eyes glanced up and down. "Shit. You were already in bed."

"Nope. Doesn't matter, anyway. What do you need?"

"It's Rocky, man. He's completely rushed out over here at the Temporary Building, and I can't wake him up. I'd carry his ass home as usual, but there's fucking Dicks everywhere, and I don't think I can get him across the rooftops on my own." He took a quick breath. "I tried calling Barry, but his cell's off."

"What the what, Noah? You can call any time," John insisted. Barry and Noah were tighter, sure, but they were both family. "We're on the way. Get him to the playground on the roof, the usual place where we jump across. We'll be on the other side with a rope so you can send him over."

"Thanks, coz." Noah's image flooded with relief. "I owe you."

"No worries, now turn off your damn cell."

All cells broadcast constantly to Dickerson's satellites. No one had figured out how to turn off the signal without killing the cell. Noah shouldn't even have had his at the Temporary Building.

By the time John disconnected, David already hung out the window throwing loose bits of mortar at Barry's bedroom window across the alley. John shoved the dresser out of the way and lifted the floorboard where they stashed their work clothes. He grabbed David's pack and held it up, but David didn't take it immediately. He stared at John with a smirk.

"What?" John asked.

"You're a beat bash." David took his pack. "You're terrified our friends will find out your secret, but the moment one of them needs us, you're on your way without a second thought."

"And?" John pulled on his shirt and dug around for pants.

"It's like you were born to fight the good fight, coz. You just can't help yourself." He dug out his own covert ops uniform.

"What can I say?" Adrenaline had already hit John's system, tearing away the fatigue and distress. "You make a hell of a shrink." And having someone to help allowed John to push all his other worries into the background.

John, David, and Barry crossed the Ghetto in silence. John saw two copters before they reached the roof next to the Temporary Building. Were they looking for the cats who'd broken into St. Matthew's? No way to know.

"What took so long?" Noah's voice called across the gap between buildings. "The Dicks are searching downstairs." He stepped into the light from the street below. Rocky lay in a heap at his feet.

"Sorry, coz. Crazy night." John unwound the rope around his waist. "How is he?"

"He's a rushed-out junkie, how do you suppose he is?" Noah had reason to be bitter. Rocky sparked up a lot, and Noah often had to save his ass. "The Dicks are still scouting the lower floors, so it'll take them a hot minute to reach us."

The lower floors of the Temporary Building were pretty much intact and inhabited by families with nowhere else to go. The Dicks would have to search apartments door to door. The walls of the upper floors, where the parties happened, were little more than broken frames and support beams. Easier to search.

John held out one arm and aimed at the usual I-beam. He released a catch in his palm, and a grapnel shot through the air from his wrist. It hit the beam and secured itself.

He tugged on the line to make sure it was solid then fixed the wrist shot to a clothesline pole.

The gap between buildings was narrow enough to jump across

on a good day, but an unconscious brother would need to be sent across in a sling.

The sound of rapid, booted feet echoed up from below.

"Shit, they must've found the party." Noah reached out. "Throw me the harness."

Barry tossed it over. Not the first time they'd needed to bring an unconscious friend to safety.

Dozens of young people poured into the open space two stories below them. The highest floors were nothing but two walls and steel girders, scaffolding, with a jungle gym of ladders and slides that John and his friends used for exercise and training.

Noah wrapped his unconscious brother in a blanket and snapped him into the harness.

"One advantage to the fact that he's a rush head," Barry muttered. "He's skinny." He stepped into position to help John catch.

"Incoming." As the partygoers swarmed the scaffolding below, Noah threw his brother. Rocky slid toward them, swinging all the way. A spotlight picked out his unconscious form.

"This is Dickerson Incorporated," a voice called out over a speaker. "You are out after curfew and will be detained under the authority of President Clement."

A gun fired.

John and Barry caught the blanketed bundle.

The smell of urine hit John as soon as he took a breath.

"Je-bus." Barry gasped. "No wonder he used a blanket."

"Here comes the hot Black man." Noah stripped off his shirt, threw it over the rope and flew across the space to them. The spotlight followed him. Shots rang out. Someone had a semi-auto.

Noah didn't flinch.

David steadied him as he hit the roof, and John and Barry gave Rocky into his hands as soon as the older brother landed and pulled his shirt on.

"Leave the rope and throw the harness across," Noah said.

People swarmed the girders and boards behind him. Some were already jumping the space, but a few would need the rope to cross.

More shots rang out. Noah threw Rocky over one shoulder and led the way across the roof.

"What's the plan?" John knew what he'd do, but this was Noah's brother so it should be Noah's plan.

"Do not leave the building," the Dick called out.

Before Noah could speak, Rocky groaned and woke up abruptly, throwing his brother off balance. They fell to the roof together and Rocky puked voluminously. Noah managed to shove him away in time.

"Blighted junkie," Noah muttered as other folks raced past. At least they'd be a diversion for the Dicks.

A pattering of automatic rifle fire rang out, followed by screams and weeping.

John scanned the street below. Dozens of people fanned out through the streets. Several knelt on the road with their hands behind their heads. A handful of bodies sprawled awkwardly in pools of blood. The Dicks ran ragged with so many targets to chase.

Rocky was awake now, but too groggy to stay ahead of the Dicks. Maybe he didn't need that, though. The rooftop furniture served many uses, and everyone escaping spent zero time so close to the party. With so many Dicks around the building, they had zero chance of getting Rocky away, even with extra hands.

"Over here." John hurried to a nearby couch and waved his friends closer. The cushions lifted easily, attached to a hinged plywood board. It would be a tight fit, since Noah was big.

"Be grateful your brother's skinny." John gestured into the hiding space. "Hide out here for half an hour. By then the Dicks will be long gone. They're not going to spend any time looking this tight to the festivities since everyone is scattering."

Rocky hobbled over, but Noah hesitated. "I really hate you sometimes." They climbed in and John closed the box. As angry as Noah was, he would never leave his brother unprotected in this condition.

"Hey." The cushions lifted, and Noah's face peered out. "I'm sorry I snapped at you, John. Seriously. Thanks, you guys."

"Stay safe." John pushed the cushions down so they could make their own escape. They raced to the eastern ledge and leapt the narrow space between buildings.

A single shot rang out. A sniper.

Barry grunted and muffed his landing. He rolled and lay on his back.

Oh God, let him not be dead. Not like that.

"Where?" John landed lightly and had hands on Barry in an instant.

"My shoulder." Barry sat up. "Just a graze."

Thank God.

"Hey look, we're twins," John said.

"Are you nuts? My mug's way too—"

More gunshots rang out and more screams of pain and terror.

David dug into his first aid kit, but Barry waved it off.

"You can take care of me once we get home." At least he stopped talking like a video star when things got serious.

Jonas headed home. The sun rose, and the DIs vanished to wherever DIs holed up when they weren't making life in the Ghetto miserable. They had fifty kids in custody, nearly all of them with injuries. Ten dead. Thank God no one had caught *his* boys... or their friends. Would the kids the DIs captured ever be seen again?

He made the last turn toward his house and spotted two older boys climbing down the side of a building. Ah hell. He'd been looking forward to a little shut eye.

The boys hunkered down a second then ran off. Must have spotted Jonas.

"Stop where you are," he called. "Police."

The boys ran faster, so Jonas fired his weapon into the air. They stopped, hands up. Well, at least they weren't so stupid he'd have to shoot them. He scanned their chips: Rocky and Noah.

"Ah, hell, boys, are you trying to get yourselves killed?" He holstered his gun and closed the space.

His boys hung their heads and stared at the concrete. How could Jonas make sure they stayed home at night when his job was to keep all the other kids off the streets?

The stink of urine stopped Jonas several feet away. Better and better. He glanced around, but they had the street to themselves. Good. An audience they did not need.

"Which one of you pissed himself," he asked.

Neither spoke, but Rocky shrank a bit.

"Were you out rushing again?' Jonas asked. "Do you have any idea what will happen to this family if you're caught? I'll lose my damn job, and then where will any of you be?"

Rocky didn't respond.

"How do you pay for that stuff?"

Rocky held his silence.

"I expect you to answer me, boy." Jonas stepped closer despite the smell. "Where are you getting the money? Stealing? Hooking?"

"No." Rocky looked up for a second, desperation in his dark-rimmed eyes. Then his face dropped again. "No, sir. I find odd jobs around."

Jonas doubted that. "Well, then you're luckier than most, and you're just stuffing it into that data port you call a brain?"

Noah stifled a laugh. Data port had a sexual connotation with the kids.

"And what about you?" He cuffed his eldest son, but gently. "You out drinking and whoring around with that gypsy friend of yours?"

Noah looked up with fire in his eyes, but he kept his silence. He didn't seem able to keep from glancing at his brother, though.

"So you found him rushed out of his mind and had to carry his ass home over the rooftops," Jonas said.

Noah's eyes opened wide, then he dropped his gaze to the ground.

"I may be old…" Jonas hitched at his belt. "But I'm not a total *fuddy duddy*, or whatever you kids call us old folks these days." What to do with them? "Rocky, you will come home directly after school, and you will not leave this house until school in the morning."

"How long?" Rocky muttered.

"As long as I say, and it just doubled."

Rocky looked up but seemed to know better than to mouth off. "Yes, sir." He ducked his head.

"And Noah. You'll go to Mrs. Darcy and help her clean out that cat-infested apartment tomorrow, and you will not charge her."

"But that's. . ." Noah glanced at his brother with venom in his eyes then shut his mouth and stared at the ground.

Since he'd graduated high school, Noah made money cleaning apartments for some of the elderly residents who still had a few dollars tucked away. The money sucked, but with jobs scarce and no chance of college for a Ghetto rat, Noah and his friends had to find work where they could. At least it was honest pay.

"I doubt you went searching for your brother out of the goodness of your heart." Jonas adjusted his belt again. He would not pay for a larger uniform; he needed to jog more. "So I imagine whatever you were doing when you stumbled on him was almost as stupid."

Noah kept his silence.

"And just so you both know, if I ever catch you out after curfew again, I will run you in without a second thought." He stepped closer for emphasis but hardly loomed over Noah as he once had. "I will not lose the only serious income in the family because my sons are punk-ass kids."

"I'm *not* a kid, anymore." Noah spat.

"And the way you said that proves it, don't it?" Well, Jonas knew what he had to do next. "Noah get me the hose. Rocky strip off those clothes."

Noah jumped to his task in obvious delight.

"What?" Rocky glanced around. "Right here on the street? Are you cheesed?"

"You are not walking into our home smelling like piss. Your mother would kill me." Jonas stepped away. "You don't have the good sense to pull down your pants before taking a leak, you have no right to complain about stripping on the street to clean off."

Noah returned with the hose before Rocky had hauled his shirt over his head.

"Get your brother a blanket, boy," Jonas said. "This water is damn cold."

By the time John slid their dresser into place again, no more than a couple of hours remained until they had to get up for work. If only he could sleep through. If only he could have one night without nightmares.

"Bunk with me tonight." David lay down and patted his mattress. "You always sleep through that way."

On another night, John might have cracked a joke. They were grown men now, weren't they? But David was right. John always slept better when they shared a bed like they had when they were kids. Just a couple of hours without dreams would help so much. He grabbed his pillow, dropped onto his back with a groan and pulled the sheet over his legs.

He dozed in seconds.

"Did you notice?" David whispered.

"What?"

"We managed to rescue Rocky, no problems."

"Huh, maybe there's hope for me, yet." John rolled onto his side and snuggled down.

"I wouldn't go *that* far." David settled in, his back to John's.

"Why are you bothering me?" Addison closed his bathrobe. Clement would wait for the honorific, wouldn't he? Fine. "Mr. President."

"I was just calling to say, 'hello.'" The shiny, pasty man feigned offense. Fucking asshole.

"Hello." Addison sent as much invective into his voice as possible. Lack of sleep made him irritable. Clement's thin lips, when they smiled, reminded Addison of an alligator.

"Now, that's just not friendly," the president complained. "Why don't you tell me how things are going? You know, at the Project in Nevada that we're all expecting to change the entire God damned world while you're *fucking off* in New York."

The two-word scream reminded Addison just how close to insanity Clement lived. Well, the man in the hologram was not only the president; he was also the almighty leader of the United Church of America and the most powerful man on the planet: the one who paid Addison's considerable salary.

"If I were fucking off you'd see my dick inside someone, wouldn't you?" Addison tightened his robe. "I'm just trying to get shit done."

"This obsession of yours is going to cause all of us trouble, Stuart." Clement took a sip from his martini. "Let it go. We don't need Subject Zero anymore, do we?"

Really? That was his takeaway? Fine. Fuck him.

"I found him," Addison said in his softest voice.

The alligator froze mid-sip. He set down the martini and leaned in. "Well. That's good news." Simon feigned disinterest.

Addison had him. Perfect.

"I assume you'd rather not have my 'obsession' wander into the room when the cameras are rolling for the unveiling of the new phase of the Project." Addison slipped his pawn into check.

"And you're certain you can eliminate him this time?" Clement reclaimed his martini and drained it.

His obvious attempt to prod Addison misfired. Simon had been able to gaslight Addison when they'd been kids, but now? No fucking way.

"Well, if all else fails…" Addison spoke as nonchalantly as his cousin had. "I can firebomb the God damned city, can't I? It's a fenced-off island sinking into the ocean, for Christ's sake."

"And Nevada?"

What a prick. Phase Two had been Simon's idea. He'd never let go of that bone. Fucking mongrel dog.

"Nevada is in capable hands." Addison fantasized about eviscerating his cousin. "I am in contact with them every two hours."

"And who *are* you fucking these days?"

Asshole. Addison cut the line

An alarm woke Bo from dreams of the past: he and Ruth had played with their newborn son in a cold spring in the Nevada desert. They'd been so innocent back then: Bo's name had been Joe, his wife, a girl named Mary. Their son's name. . . well, they'd just called him Jesus.

So much had changed.

As the clock chimed, Bo scrambled back to reality almost twenty years later. His wife was Ruth. His son was David. They had two daughters, Jamie and Layla. And then there was John, who would have been like a son if his mother Naomi allowed it. Her name had been Sally in the life before.

Bo groaned and slapped the toggle on the clock. It clattered to the floor.

"Oops." Bo rolled onto his back. His arm fell across Ruth's waist.

An animated hologram of the solar system floated over the bed with tiny planets, moons, and asteroids orbiting a vibrant sun that David and John had programmed in sixth grade.

Jamie's snakelike double helix circled the bed with reptilian movement she'd invented.

Layla's precocious contribution had been added just a year earlier: the signs of the eastern zodiac hung in one corner of the room, the western in the other. They lobbed holographic fireballs at one another.

The animated solar system mesmerized Bo. In so many ways, he saw John as his own son: he'd changed his diapers, taught him to ride a bike, held him when he cried because he'd fallen off the bike. But Naomi remained adamant: John's father was Zack... and Zack had died.

Bo understood that she didn't want John to lose a connection with his father. Christ, Bo had loved Zack, too, and would never want John to lose his love of that amazing man... but the boy could use a living dad, and Bo was more than willing to fill the role. Hell, biologically, David wasn't his boy, either, was he?

Boys? Hell... men. They'd both turned eighteen. They were adults.

Maybe the words didn't matter. Bo was the person they found when they needed to talk. Maybe that should be enough.

"Did you break another clock?" His wife's pillow muffled her voice.

Bo rolled over and retrieved the clock from the floor. The crooked second hand moved once, twice... and a delayed third time.

"Nope. Still ticking away the morning."

Ruth hummed an approving sound.

"You kept me up pretty late last night." Bo's whole body felt tired. Satisfied... but tired.

Ruth made her contented sound again.

"Okay." Bo stood up, scratched his chest, noticed a few more gray hairs, and yawned loudly. "If we open the store late, you get to deal with Naomi."

"I'm awake." Ruth turned over and looked up with bleary eyes. Her dark hair spilled across the pillow like a halo. She still took his breath away, even half asleep and without makeup. With her dark hair and brown eyes, she was his very own da Vinci Madonna.

"Remember when we did that all night and went on with the day as if we'd had eight hours of sleep?" She stretched and yawned.

Well, maybe not *quite* a Madonna.

"I guess we aren't kids, anymore." Bo kissed her.

"I'll be up in a minute, old man."

He pulled on boxers, headed through the door to his workroom while slipping into a tank top, and he flicked on a light. Splashes of paint in every color covered the floor. Vibrant bric-a-brac filled the shelves and tables: broken pottery and mirrors, old lawn ornaments, signs, and toys... anything colorful that might decorate a lamp or a chair.

That was the boys' job... finding raw materials, as well as providing the occasional extra pair of hands and making deliveries. Work was scarce in the Ghetto and Bo's shop had always paid the bills, so both boys had jumped in. Bo and Ruth had been thrilled to have them involved in the family business. The fact that they made deliveries and scavenged raw materials freed Bo to spend his days building furniture. More product to sell meant more money for the family, so their help truly created an advantage.

Wait a minute. A wooden crate sat in the middle of the floor. It hadn't been there the night before, so Bo scanned the shop. Had someone broken in? As cluttered as everything seemed, Bo would have noticed a wooden crate in the middle of his workshop. He approached it carefully.

Wait another minute. He recognized the crate. He'd used it before. It sat half-full of plum-sized glass globes. The interior crystals caught the light and refracted it into rainbows. Nice. What were they? Old-fashioned glass doorknobs? Maybe paper weights.

How had they ended up in his shop? He selected one, but it slipped out of his hand. Wet? Oh. The boys must've found them on another expedition into Venice, but the globes were in almost perfect condition. No algae. They couldn't have been underwater for ten years.

One mystery solved and another one raised.

Well, they'd make a festive addition to some piece of furniture. Bo hoisted the crate onto a shoulder and carried it into a corner where he could go through it later. Naomi shouldn't see it until the globes dried. She didn't approve of the boys' late-night excursions.

Bo understood, though. Eighteen was the age a young man was supposed to go off on his own, to start his adult life. The virus mutation had changed all that. No one in the Ghetto attended college and few saw the point, anyway. No one would give a Ghetto rat a job… even with a degree.

In the Ghetto, they had high schools… but beyond that life was medieval. Kids worked for their parents, or, if they were lucky, found someone outside the family to take them in and teach them a trade. New cases of HIV were a rarity, but no one on the other side of the bridge wanted the system to change. The system worked for them.

Bo reached the door to the store that Ruth and Naomi ran. With the light off on the other side, the glass showed his reflection. Not bad for an old carpenter closing in on forty. Keeping up with four kids helped: wrestling with the boys, stickball with Jamie and her friends, tag with Layla and hers.

Most kids in the Ghetto hated their parents, saw them as failures. Clement did a fine job of twisting the truth around and pitting the generations against one another. Bo knew the older kids worked on the Pipeline for Makabee, whoever that might be. They told Bo everything. Sometimes too much, but the minor raids the boys made and the vague net piracy that was Jamie's specialty seemed little more than harmless ways to vent frustration.

If Naomi found out though, she'd have a stroke. Anything that might alert Addison and his cronies sent her into fits. But all that had been so many years ago. Maybe it was just a bad memory.

Bo stepped into the store, turned on a light, and made his way to the stairs. Naomi had the room at the top so she could hear the kids coming and going, not that it helped much. All of them but Layla, who was only eight, after all, found ways to sneak out.

"Time to get up, ladies!" His first stop was the girls' room. "School in an hour. You better hurry if your hair is going to be stylin' for all those boys."

"Da-ad!" Layla's voice was blurry with sleep.

He'd stopped just stepping into the room after Jamie had

turned twelve and discovered modesty. Layla still asked why Daddy needed to knock.

"Girls?"

"We're awake!" Jamie's voice, as usual, sounded impatient.

Bo moved on to the boys' room.

Jamie held her breath until her father knocked on the guys' room. Then she turned back to the black-clad ninja with a watery halo surrounding his body. Geek. Chances were, the actual man behind the hologram was middle-aged, overweight, and bald. The identification badge on his avatar's shoulder read Masanari. If he were Japanese, he'd have known better.

"I'm so sorry, Masanari," Jamie said with respect. "That won't happen again."

"What was that, Justice?" he demanded. "Are you alone?"

"Of course, sir. A minor interruption. Please continue."

Masanari might be a geek, but he worked higher up on the Pipeline than Jamie had ever hoped to reach. Respect was the word of the day.

Layla sat on the window ledge swinging her feet and bumping her heels on the wall. She crossed her eyes and stuck out her tongue.

Jamie gave her sister an angry glance. She'd keep her mouth shut if she wanted to see her ninth birthday.

Layla rolled her eyes. With that one, precocious was an understatement.

"Was that your *father*?" The water around Masanari swirled faster to mirror the emotion in his voice. "How old are you?"

Blast it and boil it! Should she lie? No. Not in the long run.

"Sixteen, sir," she said quickly, "but the agents who found the device were working on Makabee's map, the one you gave us. I've been on the Pipeline for three years. I know I'm young, but this intelligence is real, I assure you."

"How old do you think I am, Justice?" The avatar smiled and the movement of his halo slowed down. Something about the movement seemed creepy. "I wasn't asking because a young woman is a bad thing."

Oh, swell. So it was like that. Jamie forced herself not to react.

Layla hopped down from the window ledge and rolled her eyes again. She grabbed her towel and left the room quietly.

"So you're interested in my device. . . the device that we found in Venice, the data drive." Suddenly, everything she said would sound like innuendo, blast it.

"We are. We need to see the actual data, but are you certain this is a secure line?"

"I wouldn't be talking to you on it if it weren't." She glanced down at the drive John had given her. "But I don't think I can scan the data."

The avatar chuckled. "*You* don't trust *me*?"

"No! Not that." She didn't want to offend him. "I mean, it's old. It needs a data port. From the research I've done, this kind of port hasn't been used in years."

"So just scan it with your table."

"I. . ." Jamie's heart rate shot up. What if she couldn't get the data to them? Who the hell in the Ghetto could afford a data table? And they were way too big to steal. "I don't have a table."

"I'm sorry." The halo of water turned red. "That was elitist of me. Sorry. Can you scan an image of the physical device so I can see what sort of port it has?"

"Yes." Thank God. She clicked a photo of it, manipulated it to render a 3D image, and sent it to Masanari. "On its way."

Another screen showed her the routes the signal followed to prevent it from being tracked. If her parents ever noticed the elaborate system Barry had stolen for her, they'd ground her for eternity.

"And it was found where?" Masinari asked.

"In a church out in Venice," she said. "St. Matthew's. It's high on Mackabee's priority list." How to say it? "The operatives I know found a dry room in an air bubble. The data drive was there. From all appearances no one has been in that room since before the Quake."

The guys had so lucked out on their discovery. She'd found the drive halfway under her door that morning and almost screamed when she read the note. If she hadn't been asleep, she'd have been with them on that dive, blast it. If the information was everything they hoped, it could mean bypassing years of junk missions way below her ability. Jamie might be sixteen, but she spent every spare moment studying the net.

"Hm." The watery halo settled into a blank rhythm. "I'll pass this information up the Pipeline. If it's anything important, we'll contact you for a physical drop off."

Yes! They wanted it. They had to!

"Of course, sir. Thank you for your time."

"You know. . ." His voice changed into a not-so-subtle tone.

"Yes, Masanari? Are there further details on the exchange of this device you wish to discuss on a line that's frequently recorded by Makabee himself?" It was a risk. Angering Makabee's flunky could ruin everything, but Jamie didn't want to give this worm an inch. Ugh.

"No." The watery halo disappeared entirely. "You'll be contacted. . . if we decide this thing has any value."

His avatar vanished. Blast! Had she ruined it all?

Something pinged.

She glanced at the tracking screen. A message popped up.

You will be contacted. I guarantee it. The ID badge in the corner displayed a hammer.

Jamie gasped. Makabee? The man himself?

Masanari is a prick. You handled him correctly.

All her screens derezzed. The system shut down.

Jamie grabbed her cell and turned it back on, but the exchange hadn't been recorded. As far as the net was concerned, it hadn't happened.

"Jumpin' Jiminy Cricket," she whispered. "It was him." It *had* to be.

Bo reached the boys' room. John had installed a dead bolt a year earlier, so Bo was free to walk in as long as the door wasn't secured. The lock bothered Naomi tremendously but so did anything connected to the fact that they'd grown up. They always told Bo almost everything going on behind that door. . . and there were a few things he'd rather not discover when one of the boys was in there alone.

Shit. *Men*. Young men? That sounded so formal.

"Damn it, Naomi," he muttered under his breath. "If I could just call them my sons, everything would be easier."

Wait. Guys? That could work. The guys. Bo stared at the door. How had he grown old enough to have an eighteen-year-old son? Or two.

"Wake-up call." He knocked, opened the door, and smelled seawater. Yep, the guys had been out to Venice. He shut the door quickly so Naomi couldn't stick her head in and notice the odor.

Two tousled heads looked up from David's mattress on the floor. When they crashed together, they looked like bear cubs. Cute, but they'd kill him if he snapped a photo.

"Time to get up, guys." Bo hunkered down and rubbed David's head. "Nightmares? Or just out too late?"

"Both." John forced a smile.

"You've got an hour 'til work. . ." Bo rubbed his head, too. "And thanks for the glass globes."

The guys glanced at each other with a grin.

"How illegal was their acquisition?" Bo asked.

They pushed and shoved their way to sitting positions.

"Not at all, Uncle Bo," John said. "We found them in Venice, and everything out there is practically public property these days."

"Nice speech." But it still didn't fit. "They don't look like they've been under water for ten years."

"They weren't." David grinned. He nudged John.

"Okay Uncle Bo, you have to promise to keep this to yourself," John said.

"I promise." Bo sat on the bed with them.

The guys made room.

"So Jamie got us this map." John pulled out a cell and activated the hologram. "It's a sat map of all the buildings completely submerged out there."

"What are those?" Bo pointed at several obvious white areas.

"Air pockets." John grinned.

Ah, that explained the doorknobs.

"We're going out there and cataloging every one we can find." David pushed closer, and Bo threw an arm around him. His son pointed at several spots.

"Where'd Jamie get the map?"

"See that?" John scooted around to Bo's other side and pointed at the map over his shoulder.

"Makabee?" Bo recognized the stylized hammer symbol. "The real one?"

"Jamie swears up and down it's the real thing." John grabbed Bo's shoulders and shook him.

"Why does one of the most important revolutionaries in the country give Jamie a map?" Bo asked. "Nothing against her, but she's a sixteen-year-old girl."

"Have you not been listening to all the missions we've done for him, old man?" John shook him again.

Oh crap. That had been Zack's voice. John's father exactly.

Bo had to swallow. He wiped a hand over his face.

"What?" John asked. "What did I say?"

"Nothing wrong, son." Bo gave John a one-armed hug. "You just sounded exactly like your father for a second there."

"Yeah?" John's eyes opened wide.

"He and I had a few adventures of our own," Bo admitted. "If not for that, I'd have put a stop to all this—" He turned back to the map and waved at it. "A long time ago."

"Yeah?"

"Yes, and one day very soon I will tell you all about our adventures." Bo patted John's knee. "Your father was. . . a good man." He gestured at the map to distract the guys. "Where'd you find the globes?"

John manipulated the hologram to zoom in on a church.

"Okay," Bo asked, "Jamie is certain this is the real Makabee and not some Dicks trying to trap you?"

John ran the hologram through some hurdles that Bo didn't pretend to understand. Instead, he caught David's eye while John worked and raised an eyebrow.

David nodded rapidly and silently mouthed, "It's okay."

Bo sighed. If David said it was okay, then who was he to argue? David was the real reason Bo hadn't stopped their role in the Pipeline.

"John and I take care of each other." David rolled his eyes as if reading Bo's thoughts.

"You should come with us some time, Uncle Bo." John waved the hologram away and fell back onto the mattress. "It is so-o-o amazing out there, especially in the moonlight. You'd love it." He hooked a thumb under the elastic of his briefs and stared up at the glow-in-the-dark bull's-eye on the ceiling. "Barry said so, too."

"I may have had all the adventures I need for one lifetime." Bo patted John's knee. He kissed David's forehead. Salt. "But thanks for the invitation." How many other parents would get an invitation like that? "Besides which, scavenging the raw materials is your job. I just make stuff." He forced John to sit up so he could kiss his head, too. "Thanks again for the glass. I'll find something extra stellar to make."

The boys exchanged a pained glance.

"Wacky, Dad. Say wacky." David shook his head. "Stellar makes you sound old."

"And whacked," John added with a wry grin.

"The two of you should think about getting a shower before coffee and breakfast" Bo pushed up from the mattress. "You smell like salt."

"Wow. Your mom's going to have a fit, isn't she?" David sniffed his arm, then looked up at Bo, his dark eyes mischievous.

"We'll be in the kitchen when you're ready." Bo forced himself to break eye contact with David and headed out of the room. As he closed the door, a yelp sounded. Most likely the boys wrestling.

Not boys. Men. Sort of. Bo shook his head and chuckled.

Ruth stood in the kitchen, making breakfast as promised.

"What did they bring you this time?" Her voice stayed quiet so Naomi wouldn't hear.

"A box of glass doorknobs or something." The linoleum felt cool under Bo's feet. He sat in one of the chairs he'd made for the dining room set. The backs of the chairs and the top of the table were inset with small tiles, a dark blue background with colorful fish.

Coffee perked happily in the pot on the counter. It was a luxury he never took for granted.

"And I suppose you didn't tell them they shouldn't be going down to Venice?" Ruth's voice might have been annoyed and might not. She stirred the oatmeal.

"If I do, they'll just stop telling me that they are. They're adults, now."

"I just don't want it to become a habit." Ruth's face told him she wasn't criticizing. "You know what happens if David gets arrested."

"Arrested doing what?" Jamie made her way to the counter and spooned oatmeal into a bowl.

In the privacy of her room, Naomi wept. Did they have no idea how thin the walls were? Did they really think she wouldn't overhear? The boys had been out in Venice scavenging for Bo? She needed to put a stop to that. John should not fool around those broken buildings and tunnels. It was all well and good for David, but had everyone forgotten the mass graves after the Quake? The rotting, half-eaten corpses pulled out of the water?

And if her son were caught by the DIs, what would happen to

him then? Addison had his DNA on file because she'd been stupid enough to believe he'd wanted to help her with such a difficult pregnancy. They'd stayed hidden for so long because they were careful. They didn't cause trouble.

Things were easy enough for Ruth and Bo. David had a marvelous destiny to fulfill. Naomi couldn't watch him for five minutes these days without noticing exactly who he was. And when he spoke to the three of them alone? Talked to them with that voice he reserved for the adults? How long before everyone knew who he was?

She sat on the chair at her dressing table and gazed at the image in the mirror. She was an old woman already. So many years trying to find a way to save her son had taken their toll. But he was a miracle. A gift from God to parents who would never have conceived on their own. Even Addison had failed.

Then Gabriel had told her she'd have a son. And she'd spoken the truth. But the whole truth? Naomi should have seen it. She should have understood her role immediately, but she was so thrilled that she and Zack would have a child of their own.

Then Zack had been blown out of the sky so they could escape.

That's when she'd known. In that moment, the very instant she'd shielded her infant son from the glare of a giant fireball, she'd understood her role in the story. She'd realized her son's fate. John was destined to be no more than a voice in the desert, cut short so David could... could what? Save the human race? It sounded ridiculous in black and white like that. Was it sinful of her to wish the boys' roles could be reversed?

She felt nauseous every time she saw a painting of the head of John the Baptist on a silver platter. She'd been so elated at the miracle of her pregnancy, she'd missed the parallels. How could she have been so ignorant?

She opened a drawer and slipped out the only photos she had of Zack. She'd discovered them stuck behind the lining of her pack a year after they fled Nevada. They were her secret: a strip of photos Zack and Bo had taken in a booth just before Zack was killed.

Naomi wiped her face with the sleeve of her robe. She and Zack had gone skinny-dipping that night while everyone else slept.

"He's just like you, Zack," she whispered, "just like we both used to be." Her husband had been such a handsome daredevil. "I've changed so much." The hand holding the photo trembled. "You'd hardly recognize me." She smiled at the two young men making monkey faces for the camera. "You weren't even thirty."

Bo saw Zack as a big brother and wanted to help. Naomi knew that, but she couldn't stop thinking that Bo had lived, and Zack had died. If she let things happen, sooner or later, John would be dead, and David would live. It would happen all over again.

No. She wouldn't let it.

Her son thought she was a spiteful old shrew? Fine. She could handle that as long as her strict rules kept him alive. Bo thought her strong hand cut into his male bonding time with her son? Fine. She could handle that, too. John had a father. His name was Zack. He might be dead, but he was still John's father.

Why couldn't one of those angels come down to remind her of all the wonderful things her son would bring about? He might die young, but he'd be the start of it all, wouldn't he? Wouldn't he? She'd talked with angels for a year, but where had they been in all the years since? Had she imagined all those talks with Gabriel? Had it been a horrible hoax? Had they all been a little insane?

"Please, God…" She prayed with all her might. "I had guidance every step of the way once upon a time. Where are my angels, now?"

When she opened her eyes and looked into the mirror, Gabriel smiled back at her.

Naomi gasped.

"Hello, Naomi." The angel pulled off her white fedora and shook out her fierce red hair.

Naomi dropped the little strip of photos. Was it possible? Had she gone really, truly insane?

As always, Gabriel's suit glowed bright, bright white.

Naomi spun on her seat.

The angel was there, really and truly there.

"You're right, you know." Gabriel's smile erased all the pain in Naomi's heart. "It has been too long." Naomi had forgotten about the British accent.

Gabriel stepped to one side.

Zack stood behind her.

Naomi covered her mouth with a hand to stifle any noise. A huge sob broke through her reserve. He was so handsome, so strong. He was exactly as she remembered him. The years hadn't touched him at all.

"Don't worry, love," he said in the deep voice she hadn't heard in so long. "They won't hear a thing." His voice made it real. He was really there. That's what he'd said every time they'd made love in the compound in Nevada where the walls were oh so thin.

Like a young girl, Naomi leapt from her seat and threw her arms around her husband. He was real! He was solid!

Twenty years fell off her shoulders.

"If I was sneaking into Venice at three o'clock in the morning, you'd have a fit, wouldn't you?" In the kitchen, Bo's eldest daughter gave her parents the third degree.

Bo breathed and exchanged a look with Ruth, letting her take the ball on this one.

"Jamie. . ." Ruth started, then stopped. What could she be thinking? "Your father might disagree with me, but if you were with David we'd be okay with it. We'd rather not have you out there on your own."

"Because I'm too young or because I'm a girl, or both?"

"It's neither, honey." Ruth reached across the table and laid a hand on Jamie's wrist. "You and your brother are not the same person. David would know what to do if something bad happened, if someone got hurt. You know how calm he can be in emergencies. We're just afraid you wouldn't know what to do."

Jamie chewed the information over with her oatmeal. She was so unpredictable. She could blow up over something one day and laugh about it the next. Adolescence was like that. Finally, she nodded.

"At least you're honest about it," she said. "I guess you're right. I need to get CPR training." She rose and moved to the stove for more oatmeal. "Do we have honey?" She flipped her straight brown hair off her shoulders.

"Sorry, no." Ruth's hands drifted into her lap. "And thanks for understanding."

The glance she gave Bo had to be her way of reminding him the time to tell Jamie and John—and probably Layla, as well—the truth about David was fast approaching. Their children were entirely too perceptive.

Bo couldn't imagine how they were going to broach the subject. *Hey, David, raise someone from the dead so the others believe you're the Son of God.*

Could David even perform miracles? Bo didn't know. He hadn't seen any. His son just knew so much.

Layla wandered into the kitchen, her long, dark curls still wet from the shower. She shuffled to the table and sat at her usual place beside Jamie.

"I'm going to flunk Sunday school," Layla announced.

"It's not Sunday," Jamie said.

"I know it's not Sunday." Layla favored her sister with a withered glance.

"Then why are you worried about Sunday school?"

"Well, regular school isn't a problem, is it?" Layla asked. "It's way easier. Have you read the Bible?"

Bo smiled as his daughters bickered quietly over breakfast. As usual, Layla held her own. For a girl of eight, she'd built a very sophisticated vocabulary.

"Oh, don't bring Paul into it." Layla shoveled oatmeal from her bowl as she argued. "Jesus would have slapped that man."

"You know Ms. Schimmel's going to use Paul." Jamie waved

her spoon at her sister to emphasize the point. "She's in love with him."

"What are you ladies talking about anyway?" Bo sat with them.

"I have a test this weekend in Sunday school, and Ms. Schimmel thinks Paul is the answer to every question in the Bible." Layla sighed a deep, exasperated sigh. "I think he's an idiot; therefore, I'm going to flunk Sunday school."

"How do you flunk Sunday school?" John's voice rang through the air as the guys, still in their briefs, hair wet, rushed into the kitchen.

"I'll never get into college, now."

"No one is going to flunk Sunday school," Ruth insisted.

"How *do* you flunk Sunday school?" John jumped onto the counter with his bowl.

"She must be disdespecting Paul again." David leaned against the counter beside his cousin, using John's knee as a table for his own bowl.

Layla rolled her eyes. "I've known how to pronounce *disrespecting* since I was five."

"You couldn't make it into college, anyway," Jamie teased.

"Could so."

"No way."

"Uh-huh."

Ruth's hand slipped around Bo's waist. Today the teasing stayed playful. David quietly ate and threw in the odd shot, but he mostly listened. John shoveled his food, reaching across David for more oatmeal as he took Jamie's side in the debate, both guys as uninhibited as Adam these days. Jamie had lost some of her adolescent modesty, as well, but she still wore a robe when the boys were around. She ate as fast as John.

Watching John and Jamie, Bo noticed how similar the two of them had become: strong, opinionated, easily excitable.

Layla was more like David: quiet and unflappable. She even *looked* like her brother. Layla's dark curls hung down past her shoulders and David's stayed in a curly mass around his head, but they looked so much like brother and sister no one would ever guess that, biologically, they weren't even related. Welcome to the nuclear family of the twenty-first century.

The room fell quiet.

Bo looked up. Everyone faced the door.

Naomi stood there, her bathrobe pulled tightly around her.

Oh damn.

"Do you boys need to wander around in your underwear in front of the girls?" Something was different. Could she be joking?

"I thought the body was the temple of God?" John didn't look up. "Why should we be ashamed of God's temple?"

Here we go. Bo wasn't wearing much more than the guys.

But Naomi didn't snap back. She leaned against the doorframe and smiled. "And you have a beautiful temple, John." Which was not what Bo had expected. "But perhaps you shouldn't let everyone who wanders by worship at your altar. Have you ever asked whether it makes the girls uncomfortable?"

"No." John's answer was quiet. He seemed to be waiting for the other shoe to drop.

"And there you are." Naomi adjusted her robe. "Don't forget how you were at eight."

"I don't mind if the guys are in their shorts, Aunt Naomi." Layla's voice was muffled around her oatmeal. "I think it's funny."

"Well, as long as you think it's funny, then." Naomi wandered to the coffee pot and poured herself a cup.

Bo could tell how carefully she weighed every single word.

John and David exchanged puzzled glances.

"Are you okay, Mom?" John stared at his mother.

"Um-hm." Naomi sipped her coffee then looked around. "Does anyone need to use the shower before I take it over?"

"I will." Jamie jumped up in an obvious escape to the hallway.

"What seems to be the problem with Paul?" Naomi took Jamie's place at the table. "Maybe I can give you some ammunition for that test."

"Really?" Layla's eyes lit up. "That would be great! I think Paul's a dork."

"Me, too, baby." Naomi patted Layla's hand. "Me, too."

While Layla explained her problem, John nudged David and the two of them headed to the door.

"John?" Naomi took a deep breath and squeezed Layla's hand.

The guys stopped and turned. John folded his arms across his chest.

"I know where you were last night." Before John could interrupt, she held up one hand. "Wait. I don't think it's safe there. . . and I would like you to tell someone when you go so we know where to look if you don't come back."

John pulled an annoyed teenager face and opened his mouth to speak, but she pre-empted him again.

"Please. I'm not going to stop you. I just want to know where to send the Calvary in case of emergency. . . and I want the two of you to look out for each other." Her eyes, for the last point, stared directly at David.

"We do." David placed a hand on John's shoulder. "We do."

"Can you at least leave a note?" She surprised them all by smiling.

John glanced from his mother to David and back to Naomi. He nodded, his arms relaxing at his sides.

"Thank you." She took a sip of her coffee and turned her attention away from the guys, who left quietly. When the door to their room closed, Naomi let out a deep breath. She turned to Bo and Ruth.

"I'm trying," she said quietly.

Bo nodded. What had just changed?

"We should get dressed." Ruth gave Bo a squeeze.

Bo shook himself out of his trance.

"Bo?" As he passed her, Naomi touched his arm. "I'm sorry. I'd like to talk tonight. We need to work together on all this."

"Sounds like a good idea." He squeezed her hand.

"Can we get back to Paul now?" Layla asked. "Please?"

"What's Beatrice saying about that dork these days?" Naomi rested her head on her hand and her elbow on the table.

Bo followed Ruth down the hall. What had changed?

Addison flipped through several video feeds of the cop, who'd definitely recognized the science project. Apparently, King simply had no intention of telling the family about it. Hm, so much for the much-vaunted Ghetto rat loyalty.

"He has to be the most boring human being ever." Pierce had the chore of following the feeds from the cop's apartment. "He does his job, then sits at home watching TV and eating."

"That's ninety-five percent of the human race." Addison turned his attention to another screen where a facial recognition app ran through local cameras, comparing surveillance video against known images of Mary's family. The equipment in this third-world camp was so antiquated, his apps could barely integrate. Well, he could exercise patience. After eighteen years, he nearly had them. Better to be certain than rush in and risk tipping them off.

"What about the cop's kids?" Addison moved to the window. The shrubs outside his room still bothered him.

"The older masturbates excessively…" Pierce gestured and brought up feeds in two bedrooms. "And the younger spends most of his time in two-bit theft to support a pretty severe white noise habit." Another gesture brought up another screen. "Watching the eldest kid's time online, apart from the porn, he's definitely part of the Pipeline. Minor league stuff." He turned to Addison. "Want me to run a list of known contacts?"

"Don't waste your time." Addison smoked his cigarette. "The cop's a dead end. Too self-centered to let people know they're in trouble. Chances are his brats are the same."

A young couple crossed the garden.

"We should take a photo of the science project to the area schools," Addison said. "See if anyone recognizes him."

"Should I send it to the DIs?"

"No. We can use the exercise. The fewer people who have those photos, the better." He turned to watch the couple again. "And let's find a way to eliminate the cop. Nothing too obvious."

"The Dicks start a riot every few weeks, it seems." Pierce flicked through several screens. "Shouldn't be too hard to make sure he's caught in the crossfire. What about his kids?"

"Who gives a shit about the kids?"

"Sorry, sir." But something seemed to bug him.

"You pissed you had to watch the darkie jerk off?"

"I. . ." Pierce cringed. "It's all part of the job, sir."

"I didn't say being pissed was a bad thing."

The couple sneaked behind a bush, probably to fuck.

"If it helps you sleep better," Addison said, "we can eliminate the kid, too."

"Thank you, sir."

For Addison, the whole thing was a job from start to finish. Pierce, though? He was sincerely a racist. A squirrely one, at that.

"There's a couple of love birds fucking in the bushes out there. Please scare the shit out of them for me and arrange to have all the shrubs near my window removed."

"Yes, sir." Pierce closed all the screens. "Is that all, sir?"

John fidgeted while David closed the top button of his shirt. Uncle Bo had suggested they wear suits for the delivery to Lincoln. They'd get stares and insults, anyway, but there'd likely be fewer parents who dragged their kids away in fear if they dressed up.

"Blasted *suits* in this heat." John stretched his neck and rolled that odd glass sphere across his fingers.

"Stand still." David flicked his ear. "You know you'll be happy you're wearing the suit if Eric Hernandez is out cleaning windows."

John felt his face flush. Eric rarely wore a shirt when he worked.

"If he starts flirting with you again," David insisted, "I am *not* going to rescue you."

"Maybe I don't want rescuing?" John insisted. "He's a stick of buttah."

"Now you sound like Barry." He tipped John's chin up for more room to tie the tie. "And you have worse taste than I thought."

"At least I never went out with Amelia Haberdasher."

"We went out twice." David pulled the knot of John's tie more firmly than necessary.

"And you didn't even get to first base." John braced himself for the next tug. When it was over, he resumed staring at the ceiling.

"Maybe I'm just not a manwhore like you."

"Oh, my God." John brushed David away. "I act like a normal guy once, *one time*, and you will never let me hear the end of it."

But David smiled. He waited patiently while John glanced down.

The tie was untied again, damn it.

John stepped closer and closed his eyes while David went back to work.

"We didn't even have sex," John muttered. It was the only time John had had any action. "It was a blow job. . . and I was really drunk."

He barely remembered it. Unlike some of his friends, John wanted to wait until he found someone he cared about. Noah teased him for being old-fashioned. It's not like he needed to be married, but the one time he'd let his inhibitions down had felt completely empty. He'd enjoyed it, sure, but afterward he'd just felt lonely. He didn't want to feel like that again.

David slid the knot into place in the middle of John's collar, wiggled it until it lay even. "Manwhore."

John quirked him a half-grin.

"You know you're never going to fall in love as long as you have me to tie your ties for you." David smoothed the tie down John's chest. "I'm far less drama than a boyfriend." John laughed and threw an arm around his cousin's shoulders, steering him toward the door.

"Wait." John stopped.

David waited.

"Total subject change."

David nodded.

"My mom. . ."

David smiled. He'd obviously been waiting for it.

"You think everything's okay?" John asked. "I'm still freaked out by her lack of bitchiness."

"Why are you asking me?"

"Because you always know this kind of fewmet."

"I meant, why aren't you asking your mother?" David held his gaze evenly.

"Honestly?"

David never expected anything else.

"I'm afraid to. Something. . . she reminded me of how she used to be. . . when we were little. I almost forgot she used to be different. It's easier to stay mad." He shook his head and looked down. "It doesn't make sense."

"Talk to your mom!" With one quick movement, David pulled the shirttail from the back of John's pants and bolted from the room, thundering down the hallway.

John cursed under his breath and ran after his cousin, dropping the glass doodad on his bed.

Jamie hooked her bra and pulled her blouse out of the locker.

Tracey wrapped herself in a towel and spent her usual ridiculous amount of time on makeup. She was so damn pretty, she hardly needed it.

If only Jamie knew how to do all that. No. She knew how to do all that, she just couldn't find it in herself to care. Boys rarely did more than trim their eyebrows and maybe put on a little eyeliner. Why did girls let themselves get dragged back into the middle of the twentieth century by a bunch of melodramatic videos?

"I can lend you my makeup." Apparently, Tracey had caught her staring. In the mirror, she smiled. "The glosses and stuff, anyway. You try to put on blackface in this neighborhood someone's likely to take you out." She shook her head and blotted her lips. "As much as you say all this is bullshit, I catch you watching me work my magic."

"Such a Betty Boop you are." Jamie pulled on her slacks. "Who has time for all that? Some of us have more important things to worry about than whether our lipstick matches our nail polish."

"I'm not being fresh, coz." She dropped the towel and pulled on clothes. "If you don't like it, that's fine. But if you don't, why do you watch me layer it on?"

Jamie did up her belt and tie while she thought about it. Tracey was her best friend, and she wanted to be honest with her.

"Most of the time, I don't even worry about it." Jamie watched her friend slide into her hose. She even made that look sexy, blast it. "But every now and again, I think it would be fun to go out to Babylon looking like Marlene Dietrich."

"Oh my God, have you seen the new *Heaven's Gate*? She is the absolute cat's meow!"

"Have you seen the bloopers where the capture derezzed and they accidently showed the actor underneath the Dietrich avatar? Big fat dude!" Jamie had seen every episode.

"What?"

"Scout's honor, it was a live broadcast, and the whole system shook for five seconds, and there stood this big, fat guy in green screen tights."

"Goes to show you, *mija*." A woman appeared around the locker. "Never judge a woman by how well she does her makeup." The stranger stood tall and immaculate. Her skirt suit professional, her hair pulled up in a bun, and she wore wide glasses tinted just enough to obscure her eyes.

"Can I help you?" Even though fully dressed, something about being approached in a locker room made Jamie feel naked.

The woman raised an eyebrow. She didn't speak, but the movement of one foot drew Jamie's attention.

Six-inch, blood red stilettos?

Oh, dear God, it couldn't be. Jamie looked into the woman's eyes again. "Joanne?"

Tracey gasped.

"I'm so sorry." Jamie moved closer. "I didn't recognize you with clothes on." Her face burned. Blast it!

Joanne smiled.

"I mean. . . God, I am so sorry I said that."

"Don't be." Joanne waved Jamie's concern away. "You usually see me naked in a cage at Babylon, *mija*. I wore the power suit in case I bumped into anyone else who knew me professionally."

"At the high school?" Tracey closed her locker. "Who would be a client here?"

Joanne raised an eyebrow. "*You've* both seen me there."

"Oh, right." Tracey hurried closer. "But is anyone an actual client? Principal Skinner?"

"You look wonderful, Joanne." Jamie pushed Tracey aside. "Absolutely Fortune 500."

High-pitched giggling shattered the air, echoing on the ceramic tiles. A group of seniors, *seniors* no less, careened around the corner, flapping towels at each other. The leader slid to a stop when she saw Joanne, and the other girls piled into her.

"Sorry, ma'am," the leader said. Someone giggled. The rest held their cool for two seconds, then they shrieked and ran off.

"Holy mackerel." Jamie palmed her face. "It's like a lesbian scene in some stupid porn video for guys."

"Without the bad music." Joanne drew the two girls around a corner to a towel room. "As much as I enjoy reliving my own high school trauma," she said with enough sarcasm to make the point obvious, "I'm here for a reason."

Jamie couldn't even imagine why Joanne might be there. They were friends, yes, but they'd only spent time together outside the tunnel parties once, when a whole group had spent the day at a beach. While everyone else played in the ocean, Jamie had hung out with Joanne on the littered sand.

"What reason?" Jamie asked. "And why in the locker room?"

"Creepy, I know, but it's the one place in the school without cameras." She closed the towel room door. "You were told to expect a contact." She removed her glasses and tucked them in a pocket.

What in the world did that mean?

Joanne raised an eyebrow.

"Makabee, stupid." Tracey nudged her.

Jamie gasped. Joanne worked for Makabee?

"Not just a cheap call girl, you know." Joanne smiled.

"It's not that." Jamie almost choked. Okay, pull it together. "Besides which, I know what you charge."

"Touché." Joanne nodded. "Do you have the data drive?"

"Yes, of course." She dug in a pocket. "But how have you been working for Makabee all this time, and we didn't know it?"

"You don't have clearance." She crossed her arms. The whole professional, business look changed Joanne's appearance completely. "No offense, but there is an entire side of me you do not know."

"Oh, my God." How had Jamie not thought of it before? "Up in your dance cage over the biggest party on the East Coast, you draw in clients who are the most important businessmen—"

"Businesspeople," Joanne interrupted. "Politicians, as well. I am very nicely placed. I hear more gossip than bartenders or hairdressers."

Impressed didn't cover it. Jamie worshipped this woman. She pulled the data drive out of a pocket.

"Wait." Jamie looked Joanne square in the eyes. Her heart beat hard and fast. If she'd suddenly shown this hidden persona, couldn't there be others hiding in there? How did she know Joanne worked for Makabee and not for the Dicks? Her job would cover for that agency just as well.

Joanne smiled. "Check your messages."

Okay. Good. There must be some kind of connection there.

"Make sure you back up your drive online before you open it," Joanne suggested.

It. What would "it" be?

Jamie opened a holo screen, backed everything to her drive at home, then checked her messages. There it was. A hammer. *The* hammer.

She tapped the icon. A scroll appeared in the air over her cell. The image resolved larger and a higher resolution than her device should've been able to generate. But there it was.

The scroll opened, and Joanne's face smiled out at Jamie. The hologram flashed once, then died. The cell beeped. It vibrated and shut down.

"He makes sure to erase all traces of his presence whenever he contacts someone." She gestured at the dead cell. "Once you get home and plug it in, your cell will recover completely."

That was exactly what had happened before… But was that enough? Was that something the Dicks could do?

"Good." Joanne smiled. "You're starting to think the right way. You should be suspicious." She crossed her arms. "What would I need to do to convince you I'm here for Makabee?"

Jamie's thoughts raced. How could Joanne prove her loyalties?

"It's a conundrum, isn't it?" Joanne asked. "How do secret agents contact one another? Who do you trust?" Joanne turned her attention to Tracey. "I need you to wait for us outside. Please don't be offended, but if Jamie told you about that drive, you know how important this is."

Tracey glanced from one to the other, then nodded. "Should I wait or just head home?"

"Good girl." Joanne touched her arm as Tracey passed. "Just wait for a minute or two. And thank you. This can't be easy."

Tracey glanced at Jamie and left the room.

"So here we are." Joanne was the world's baddest bitch. "Remember the beach?"

Jamie did. Joanne had asked Jamie to sit with her because she couldn't swim. Her years as a rush junkie had left her with a compromised nervous system and a seizure disorder. She couldn't risk seizing in the ocean but didn't want all their friends to know.

Joanne had told her about a husband who'd died in the

Mexican-American riots and a daughter she hadn't been able to support on her own, not with her addiction and not in the hellscape of the early days of the Ghetto. She'd eventually sold her daughter, hoping that someone with that kind of wealth would provide the child with a better life than Joanne ever could.

Jamie met her friend's gaze evenly.

"I ask you to trust me because we're friends," Joanne said at last. "Because you know I could never help the government. With all I have lost, I want nothing more than to assassinate Clement and hand this nation over to someone who isn't insane."

Jamie's heart pounded.

She was a sixteen-year-old girl. She liked to think of herself as more mature than most, but the real world had just come knocking at her door. This wasn't a game. This was espionage on a global scale where people lived and died based on the kind of information on the drive she held in her sweating hand.

Might someone die because of what she held? Could she live with that? Did she trust that Joanne fought on the right side?

Did she trust that *Makabee* fought on the right side?

She opened her hand and stared at the little drive that might hold the key to toppling a nation.

"Holy crap, Joanne," she whispered. "I just jumped into the shark tank with both eyes closed, didn't I?"

"May I?" Joanne closed the distance and opened her arms wide.

Jamie nodded, and Joanne wrapped her arms around her. They held each other like that for a few moments, then Jamie sucked in a deep breath. No. She wouldn't be afraid. She knew what she did was right. She stepped out of Joanne's embrace.

"I lucked out, didn't I?" she said. "You vouched for me. If I was just some Ghetto rat, Makabee would never have given me the map in the first place." It all made sense. "This has nothing to do with whether I trust you. It's all about the fact that you trust me."

Joanne nodded.

"Why?" Jamie asked.

"The beach." Joanne held out a hand. "I laid it all out for you.

My deepest, darkest sins. Hell, Jamie, I told you I sold my daughter on the black market."

Jamie shook her head and shrugged.

"You never told a soul."

Jamie held out the flash drive.

"If I can't trust you, I can't trust anyone." Joanne took the drive and slipped it into a pocket.

"Can I ask a favor?" Jamie hoped to God she wouldn't ruin the moment.

Joanne simply smiled.

"Can you teach me how to look as fucking badass as you do right now?"

Joanne raised an eyebrow.

"And not just the makeup and the suit." Jamie waved a hand to include Joanne's entire body. "I mean the entire persona. How the heck do you do that?"

"Welcome to Joanne's finishing school for badass dames." Joanne threw an arm around Jamie and led her to the door

The line at the bridge was insane, and crossing the checkpoint would take hours. Blast it. John and David had work passes from Uncle Bo, so, normally, all they had to do was walk the bridge and the station automatically detected the permits on their cells.

What was the hold up?

"Some bullshit about photos and swabs," a man in line said. "A lot of us had our data wiped in the Makabee virus years ago, and they pick today of all days to update their database?"

John caught David's gaze as they rolled their cargo carrier a few feet forward. The sudden interest in data could be the result of the mouthy Jewish cat or the raid at St. Mathew's. In either case, John didn't want to get his chip updated. The only person in the family with a full profile was Layla. The rest only had their names registered.

"Noah said he owes us a favor." David kept his voice low.

"And distraction is kind of a specialty for him and Barry." John sent a message.

Noah replied almost instantly. They were on the way.

Relieved, John turned his attention to the crowd. Everyone was on foot, of course, since only the Dicks were permitted to cross in vehicles. John had only been in a car a handful of times in his life. No one he knew even owned one. Power stations for them weren't allowed on the island, anyway. Clement claimed they could be weaponized. They all walked it or biked.

A few buses ran from time to time, but they were erratic which made deliveries a pain, so John and David had to roll their package through the Ghetto on a heavy cart, wheel it across the bridge, and load it onto the train on the other side.

Fortunately, someone would meet them at the station out in Lincoln. The awkward, heavy crate contained a set of cast iron patio chairs.

"Too bad your dad's not a jeweler." John leaned against the crate in the shade it cast.

"Amen to that." David leaned beside him.

"Is that my favorite family?" The voice seemed familiar, but not the tall cracker in blue coveralls and baseball cap.

"Hey there, Billy," David said immediately. He approached the man and hugged him.

John noticed his blue eyes. "Oh my God, I didn't recognize you with your clothes on!"

Billy made a face. "Why not say that a little louder with all these Dicks around."

"Sorry." John cringed. "You know what I mean." He hugged Billy as well. "I can't see your blond hair."

Billy bartended at parties in the subway and rarely wore more than a pair of briefs. For the most part, the events floated, but one station was known to have the best parties on the Eastern seaboard.

"Is there a party at Babylon coming up?" John asked, realizing that Billy's uniform must mean he was getting supplies.

Billy just smiled.

"Tonight?"

Billy shrugged and made a noncommittal face, but it was obvious he meant "yes."

"Wacky." Since all of Uncle Bo's customers paid cash, John would have money for the party.

"Hey there." Noah ran up with Barry right behind. "Billy? Is that what you look like with clothes on?"

"Seriously?" The bartender rolled his eyes. "First of all, it's not like I run around completely naked. . ." No one spoke. "Okay, maybe once or twice, but how many blue-eyed men live in the Ghetto?" He opened his arms. "Anyway, you guys know I love you, but I hope you aren't planning to let all your friends join you in the line ahead of me."

John leaned closer. "They're just keeping us company while we wait, and. . . trust me, the line will move much faster when we get closer to the check point."

"Oh." Billy took in Noah's grin and Barry's exaggerated innocence.

Barry held a surreptitious hand down at arm's length.

Noah tapped it with one finger.

"Just try not to get yourselves killed." Billy pulled up a hologram of what looked like order forms. "You two actually tip pretty well." He glanced through the translucent screen at John. "Not as well as some, of course." He winked. "But pretty well."

John's face flushed, and he headed back to the crate to move it forward.

"Oooh." Barry hopped up behind John and smacked the back of his head. "That's right. John has a crush on a married man, boo-boo-be-doo."

What a bastard. Anything John said would sound pathetic, so he ignored the rest of the razzing. He didn't really have a crush on Billy exactly, but the man was sex on a cracker, worked in his underwear and always had a hug and a kiss for John when he bought a drink.

Of course, he tipped well.

"I figured you'd have a massive goose egg." Noah took John's chin to lift it.

"From?" John shook him off.

"Smacking your head on a concrete statue?" Barry said.

What? Oh! In St. Matthew's. The lie!

The face Noah pulled told John he'd just lost all credibility.

"Okay, fine." Shit. John hated lying to his friends. "David covered for me."

His cousin raised a curious eyebrow. Would John tell them about the visions? Should he?

"I freaked out when I saw the shark. Absolutely froze." Lying shouldn't be so easy. "David saved my bacon."

"Geez, coz." Noah tapped his shoulder. "If I'd seen a flippin' shark up in my mug? I'd have pissed myself."

"Really?" John breathed a sigh of relief.

"S'okay." Barry threw an arm around him and kissed the top of his head. "We all know I'm the brave one."

"Stupid one is more like it," Noah said. "The chances you take just to show off? You'll be lucky if you don't get blown up before your next birthday."

"Speaking of which, I think that's our cue." Barry laughed and danced away.

"Four Dicks. Should be easy." Noah skulked closer to the front of the line. He made a point of acting shifty and jittery. "What they doin' up there?" He jumped a couple of times as if to get a better view. "They taggin' chips, man?" His legendary impersonation of every Black Ghetto rat in videos slid into place effortlessly. "Why they do that? Why today, man?"

He slid back and forth as if deciding whether to run for it.

"Get back in line, boy," a Dick ordered.

People murmured at that. The Dick should know better than to call someone "boy" on his home turf. The Dick's partner shook his head, although John couldn't tell if his disgust was directed at the Dick's ignorance or the Ghetto rats' sensitivity.

Noah made a dash for the barrier.

The insensitive Dick called out and ran toward him, his partner a step behind. They both had guns drawn, and the crowd hit the ground in silence. They knew the drill. One shot rang out before Noah swerved and ran to the bridge railing, planted one hand on it and vaulted easily.

The Dicks leaned over the railing for a better view.

At exactly that moment, Barry ran up to the already nervous pair left at the sentry point. He held a hand over his mouth.

"You have to let me through," he said loudly through his hand.

"Just move away." The sentry stepped back and held up a gun.

"You don't get it. I'm going to. . ." Barry threw up at the sentry, spewing more than John could credit. How did he do that on cue?

The sentries jumped back.

Barry glanced down at his own vomit.

The sentries followed his gaze to a scattering of bright green data chips that lay strewn across the pavement in the puddle at his feet.

"Drugs!" One sentry already had his weapon out, but Barry hightailed it toward the opposite railing. The sentries followed.

"Let's just get through," John said to the man who'd originally answered his questions when they'd hit the line. "Nothing illegal about wandering through an unmanned sentry station."

"True words," said a professionally dressed woman ahead of John. "Let's move, people, before they end up keeping us here all day." And that's all that the crowd needed. As one, they surged forward, eager to take advantage of the distraction. The best part was that anyone asked would say a tall, redheaded White woman had led the rush.

John and David maneuvered the box through the sentry station and turned up the street. They'd need to detour to the train station to avoid any possible Dicks who might decide to round up stragglers.

John's cell beeped with a message. Barry.

You owe me a new pair of shoes. He and Noah had already met up in the tunnels off the river.

I'll pick something up in Lincoln, John sent back.

Jazzy!
And I'll never again give you crap about carrying a rebreather at all times.
Ha!

Michael perched high atop the sentry tower. The narrow bridge shifted with the movement of so many pedestrians. What would it take to destabilize it? He closed his eyes and sifted through the possible futures. Well, a minor quake wouldn't do it. Wait. Apparently, a bundle of C4 would, also.

Michael needed to stop peeking. He never liked what he saw.

His charge moved quickly through the no man's land on the other side of the bridge, derelict buildings and the broken remains of the levee that had been piled on the shore to slow down any Ghetto rats attempting to sneak through without authorization. The young men reached the final wall and hurried through the open gate into the train station beyond.

Gabriel's presence brought a smile to Michael's face.

"That was silly," he said.

"Silly?"

"You know what Raph would say."

"I would say willful and foolish." His appearance drove Michael's smile away.

"I didn't really change anything important." She flipped her hair behind her shoulders.

"Then why do it?" Raphael's voice dripped with superiority.

"To annoy you."

Gabriel smiled at Michael. He smiled back.

"Children." Raphael's eyes flashed a bright, angry blue. He fled in a huff that Michael felt as a showy gust of wind.

"Why'd you really do it?" Michael asked.

Gabriel sighed. She touched Michael's wrist.

Noah kicked his shoes off a couple of feet under the water. He took a second to reorient himself before he spotted the tunnel to safety.

Above him, the sentry pulled a shock grenade from his belt and tossed into an unruly mob of Ghetto rats, it'd give them enough of a shock to stun them without any permanent damage. But the damn thing bounced badly and missed the crowd entirely. It hit the water and detonated, releasing a high voltage shock that struck Noah, paralyzing him. He sucked in lungfuls of water and sank to the bottom, eyes staring blindly until they popped.

"Oh." Michael drew his hand away. "The commotion distracted the sentry."

"It wasn't Noah's time." Gabriel rose. "Not yet. Not like this."

The Staten Island Station was, literally, the end of the line. The buildings near the SIS were slapdash, the platforms poorly maintained. Only the holographic billboards competing for attention proved that the station wasn't actually in the Ghetto. Even in the morning light they shone brilliantly, flashing images quickly enough that John couldn't stop his eyes from glancing. They promised hundreds of wonderful things they could buy in New York that weren't available in the Ghetto.

The preview for the new *Tonto* video caught John's eye. There stood the star himself, staring down at John larger than life. He pointed it out to David.

"Can you believe it's at an actual theater out there?" John said.

"Hey, anything that makes them money."

"True words."

John had been in the station before. Often the delivery just needed loading on an outbound train. Occasionally, he and David had a chance to travel with the cargo which gave them a glimpse of the city beyond. But even then, their work pass typically allowed just enough time to transfer the cargo to the customer's vehicle and suck in a breath of air before they had to board the train back to the Ghetto.

Today's pass allowed a two-hour drop-off time in Lincoln.

Maybe they'd get the package to the client fast enough they could race to the beach. A real beach! With sand and without trash and dead fish.

"Which platform?" John asked.

David held up his cell with the boarding ticket floating above it. Ugh. They were headed for the farthest platform. Great. At least they had plenty of time before the train departed, so they didn't need to rush.

"Notice anything odd?" David asked, holding the cell out to John.

"No train changes? That's weird."

Why would anyone pay extra for a direct ride from the Ghetto to Lincoln? Well, that made the entire process easier. They wouldn't need to move their cargo between trains. The walkway opened onto the final platform.

Nobody there.

What the hell? The train sat empty and unattended as far as John could tell. By far the cleanest and most modern they'd ever ridden, it fairly gleamed. A glass canopy opened the cars to the sky. Inside, rows of empty seats and tables waited, widely spaced and inviting.

"Are we on the right platform?" John shifted nervously. If they were lost, they might miss their actual ride.

The ticket above David's cell blinked green, which meant that someone had registered it. John looked around.

"About damn time." An obese young man in a porter's uniform tromped in their direction. "We have a schedule to keep. Get your box loaded." He pointed at the cargo car.

"We're twenty minutes early," David said far more politely than John would've managed.

"What did you say to me, boy?" The pale face showed angry shock. "I don't care who convinced the company to send this train out to the ninth circle of Hell for your package." He pulled himself up. "If I say you never showed up, who do you think they're going to believe?"

Before John could lay him flat with one punch, David's

shoulder touched his. He needed to cool it. They weren't in the Ghetto anymore.

"That's what I thought," the porter said, turning his back. "Get your shit loaded and get your asses on my train." He walked away.

His train? Ass pony.

"Aren't porters supposed to help load our shit?" John said quietly enough so that only David could possibly hear him.

"Coz, look at that train. This is going to be the best trip we've ever had." David pushed John into place to move the crate. "Someone likes Dad's stuff enough to charter an amazing frickin' train to come get it? Can you imagine the kind of tip they might give us? You might even be able to buy that pair of shoes for Barry in Lincoln after all."

John snorted a laugh and pulled his side of the cart. No tip would be big enough for a pair of shoes in Lincoln.

They loaded the cargo and hurried to the third passenger car. The ticket actually reserved spots on a certain car! It was surreal. Usually, they had to elbow their way aboard and ended up standing the entire first leg of the journey out.

John hopped up the last step into a blissfully air-conditioned car. The carpet was clean and the glass overhead sparkled. The view would be amazing!

"Well, coz, do you think we'll find a seat for ourselves?" John asked.

David chuckled. The car stood empty.

As the door slid closed with a quiet hiss, their ticket flashed green again. The door at the end of the car opened and a pretty brunette hurried toward them as David started to seat himself at one of the tables.

"I'm sorry. That table's reserved." She stopped a few feet away, a fake smiled plastered across her face. "Your seat is back here." She lifted a hand to gesture behind John.

John turned to the end of the car. None of the seats back there had tables. So it was like that. Well, she seemed friendlier than the porter.

"The ticket doesn't seem to indicate assigned seating," John said. "Just an assigned car."

"I know it looks like we're running light, but as soon as we hit the real stations, we'll fill up quickly." The fake smile widened. God forbid the real passengers rub elbows with Ghetto rats. "I'm sure you know how it is." She waved politely but with emphasis.

Yeah. John knew how it was.

David's face begged him not to make a stink about it. When would they have a chance to ride in a glass-covered luxury train again?

Fine. John smiled. "I bet ours is the presidential seat back there so we can have an undisturbed view of the entire car."

Oh, thank God, she thought. "I just knew you'd understand."

John pushed her out of his head. He understood. Back of the bus.

When they'd settled in, David nudged him.

"They're bastards," he said. "Okay fine. But how often do we get out of the Ghetto? I mean, way out of the Ghetto? Just think how fine that sand is going to feel and how jealous everyone will be when we tell them about it." He wore that same peaceful face he used on the kids in his Sunday school class. He really wanted John to relax.

"This trip must be damn important to you if you're going to Sunday school me."

"Uh-oh, busted." David settled back as the train moved.

"So was it going to be the 'God gives you what you need' lesson or 'Be grateful for what you have'?"

"Neither." David leaned back and closed his eyes. "Who is to say what is good or bad?"

"Oooh, sneaky." John leaned over David so he could watch the platform slide past. "Using Taoism so I don't realize it's a Sunday school lesson." Once the train started off, all sense of motion ceased. "Holy crap, we're on a mag lev."

"No way." David crowded closer and strained his neck.

The train rounded a curve. Sure enough.

"I didn't even know we *had* a monorail at the SIS." David leaned back a bit to give John a better view, draping an arm across

John's bent shoulders. "And there's really no difference between Taoism and the original stories in the Bible."

John glanced at David's face before staring out the window again. It was the kind of thing David said all the time. John knew his expected response: "And you'd know of course, because you were there."

David grinned. He patted John's back.

Okay, fine. Ignore the crackers and their shit. Who knew how long it might be before Makabee broke open the ghettos? Enjoy the moment.

The attendant had nailed it. When the doors opened at the very next stop, a sizable number of passengers boarded. All ages, men and women, all of them White. Blond hair. Brunette. A couple of redheads. They all dressed well, in clean, expensive clothes, the men in suits and the ladies in fashionable dresses. None of the women wore suits like the stars in the videos and the women in the Ghetto.

The crackers all displayed big smiles and chatted with each other as they shuffled into the tabled seats. None of them seemed to notice the dark young men in the back.

"It's like they're controlled by aliens," David whispered.

John snorted.

Every face turned in their direction as if shocked that someone would hide in the back of the car.

An older gentleman in an ice cream white suit opened his mouth and raised a hand in their direction, but the moment he actually focused on them, his mouth closed, and his hand fell to his side. His eyes narrowed as if he couldn't believe what he saw.

"Sorry," John mumbled, embarrassed at the noise he'd made.

Slowly, the other passengers returned to their conversations, but the mood had changed. The smiles all seemed a bit more forced.

One woman switched seats with her daughter so the little girl would be on the inside, away from the aisle. She flagged down the attendant. From the way she glanced at the back of the car as she spoke, John had no doubt he knew her concerns.

The attendant seemed to work hard to avoid looking at John and his cousin. John wanted to moon the lot of them.

"Keep your pants on," David muttered.

"How do you do that?" John turned to him in surprise.

David rolled his eyes. "Whenever you think someone is being rude, you want to flash your ass."

It was true. He did.

Music played over the PA. Neo-swing. Great tune. The passengers smiled and laughed again, pointedly keeping their backs to the Ghetto rats.

"We didn't get music," John muttered.

David nudged him, and John prepared for a lecture, but David pointed out the glass canopy with a huge grin. Enormous leafy trees filled the view as the train passed through a thick forest. They blocked out the sky, as if the train rocketed through an arboreal cave. Holy wow! The Ghetto had a couple of parks, but nothing like this.

"That alone is worth the price of admission." David sighed and sat back in his seat.

The trees fell away, and the view opened over a grassy field dotted with goats.

"Coz. Goats!" John leaned closer. People kept goats in fields this close to the Ghetto? People had *fields* this close to the Ghetto, for that matter? All of their other trips had taken them into the center of New York, the city itself, where overcrowding made the air thick. John had never seen farmland.

The field dropped away into a pond, or maybe it was a lake. What was the difference? The water sparkled a perfect shade of blue, and a flock of ducks jetted across the surface past a man and a boy in a fishing boat. The boy waved at the passing train. On impulse, John waved back, even though he likely traveled too fast for the child to see him.

The world filled the view, wide and open, green and blue.

A lifetime's worth of stress slid off John's shoulders.

"We were meant for open spaces," David whispered, and John understood exactly what he meant.

They pulled into another station and the car filled. A young mother and her boy made their way to the seats across from John, the last seats in the car.

The young woman's hat lifted from her face as she looked up to say hello, and John flashed her his best smile.

Hers shattered and died. She glanced up and down the length of the car in desperation, then gave John a forced smile, more like a grimace, and shoved her son into the seat first.

"Are those Ghetto rats, Mommy? I wanna talk at the Ghetto rats."

The woman grabbed the boy's arm and shook him.

"Ow!"

David grabbed John's knee. It was a plea.

John sucked in a deep breath and released it. He was in a magical land of trees and goats. It was worth the price of admission.

"Here comes the candy lady!" The boy pointed up the aisle. "I wanna ice cream anna soda anna candy bar."

"Hush. Let's just start with what's included in the ticket."

Included? John hadn't heard of such a thing. He glanced at David who already had his cell out.

"Sodas included," David said. "Snacks are—holy wow."

The prices listed doubled what John had tossed to the little girls in pink dresses. A casual nibble on a luxury car could feed those girls for a week. John's stomach twisted.

When the attendant maneuvered her cart to the end of the car and spoke to mother and son, she kept her back to John and passed sodas and sandwiches across the aisle.

"We appreciate your understanding," she said quietly.

John seethed.

Then she started up the aisle again.

"Excuse me," John said.

She kept walking.

"Excuse me, miss," he said louder. A glance at David gave him permission on this one.

Her shoulders sagged a moment, before she turned to him with her painfully fake smile.

"Our tickets include a beverage, too, if I'm not mistaken." John used his lightest, friendliest tone.

David held the cell forward, the hologram carefully zoomed in on the price of the ticket.

"I'm so sorry." The woman shook her head and touched a hand to her chest. "I don't know where my head must be."

David's knee nudged John before he could tell her it was likely lodged up her ass. She passed two glass bottles of soda to John with her fake smile, then turned away.

John stared at the bottles. He'd never seen soda in glass bottles before. They were a retro fad he'd heard about, but in the Ghetto, soda came in plastic. He turned to David, who shrugged.

The bottles had metal caps. John tested the cap, but it seemed awfully tight. Didn't they need some kind of bottle opener for these things?

"Excuse me again." His face burned as the attendant turned back to him. "How do we open these?"

The condescending smile appeared. "Just twist the cap."

Someone ahead of them giggled.

John's heart raced. He twisted the cap harder, and it popped off.

The bottle chilled in his hand.

"Whoa." John handed the other bottle to David, who grinned when the bottle frosted up.

Blast. Having to ask something as basic as that? If John couldn't open a crummy bottle of soda, how the hell would he make it outside the Ghetto?

"To adventures." David clinked his bottle to John's.

"Adventures." John forced a smile.

The houses along the rail grew larger and more opulent. Pillars and expansive porches fronted each and every one. The yards full of trees and shrubbery dwarfed any park in the Ghetto. They had to be hotels or something. They couldn't be single family homes.

But they were. Pale-skinned parents watched a child or two on playground equipment more extravagant than John's school had had. Small clusters of pasty White people lounged around enormous swimming pools. Not one of them swam in the sparkling water.

"They must use a heckuva lot of sunscreen," David murmured.

"They don't want to risk looking like us."

The boy across the aisle screamed.

John almost dropped his bottle reaching for the knife that wasn't at his waist. Was someone killing the kid? His scream rang with the panic of murder.

"I wanna ice cream, not a stupid sammich!" The sandwich in question flopped onto the floor in the aisle. The kid screamed again. His mother slapped him firmly.

John almost dropped his soda again.

"You will eat what I give you." She hid her harsh voice beneath the sound of the swing band.

The kid whimpered but stopped screaming.

John couldn't move. She'd hit the boy so hard.

When the mother turned and saw him staring, she glanced down at the discarded sandwich. "You can have that if you want it."

What the hell?

She turned away before David grabbed John to prevent him from launching himself across the aisle. He forced John to turn away.

"There's a reason for this." David released him but kept a hand on his shoulder. His eyes held John. They did that a lot recently.

"She thinks we're animals," John muttered.

"And you want to prove her right?" David squeezed his shoulder.

Damn. Double damn.

"No." John sucked in a deep breath.

"All right then." David released the arm. The city sped by behind David, too fast for John to make out. . . until a single building rose out of the ground to touch the very sky itself. Holy. wow.

David smiled. "I wondered when you'd notice that."

A glass tower. It rose far above the rest of the buildings. It had to be miles tall, an enormous bullet of glass and steel.

"Holy shit." John had seen holos of the new headquarters for the United Church of America, but he hadn't conceived the scale. They called it The Tower of the Bible. Makabee called it The Tower of Babel.

John bent over David's lap, pressed close to the canopy so he could see the top. Well, so he could try to see the top. Did it reach the clouds?

"How tall is that thing?" John asked.

"Tall enough I'm glad our house isn't within a mile of it." David draped his arm over John's back.

"True words."

A soft chuckle drew John's attention to a seat a few rows ahead.

"See, Barbara, that's what happens when you let the monkeys out of the zoo." A middle-aged cracker chuckled behind his hand. "They gawk as if it were one of the seven wonders." Ass pony.

David pulled his feet up quickly. Huh? He'd had enough, now? He slipped off his shoes and crawled onto the seat to crouch in John's lap, straddling one leg. He pawed and poked at John's hair, pretending to eat lice. He even hooted monkey sounds.

"Monkey like pretty train." David spoke loudly enough to carry. "Oo!" He bared his teeth at the couple staring in shock.

Holy wow! David *never* acted out like that.

"Okay, coz," John murmured. Nearly the entire car stared at the spectacle, and some of the stares seemed decidedly unfriendly. "Careful of the twig and berries there," he added as the foot between his legs shifted.

His cousin tumbled back into his seat, grabbed John around the neck and pulled him close while he pointed at the Tower of the Bible.

"First thing to go when the shit hits the fan." He kissed John's head. "Just you wait."

"From your lips to God's ears."

And seeing David act like a monkey in public? Definitely worth the price of admission.

The final station tested John's patience yet again. Although he and David hurried to the cargo car, the porter made them wait and wait and wait. John glanced at his cell. They'd been standing almost an hour, which meant they were late to meet their client, and, more importantly, they'd used up half of their beach time.

"We did load on first," David pointed out.

The porter chatted with someone as if he had nothing better to do.

"Yeah, that's why we're waiting." John strode over to the porter and cleared his throat. "Excuse me, sir, but I think our crate is the only thing left on the train. Any chance we can just get it ourselves?"

"You ain't ever getting in that car, boy." The cracker glared at John as if he'd asked to rape his sister.

"Excuse me, but what seems to be the delay?" A quiet woman's voice startled John.

He spun, expecting to be hassled further. A small Asian woman with white hair regarded him peacefully. The flowing beige and rose kaftan she wore indicated she wasn't a train employee.

"Everything's been offloaded except our cargo." John had had enough. "And this guy won't let us get our property because we're from the Ghetto."

"Can't be too careful nowadays, can I?" The porter folded his arms and smiled a big smug grin. "Never know what kind of trash has crawled out of that garbage heap."

John clenched his fists at his sides.

"David and John, I presume?" The woman raised an eyebrow. Oh! She had to be their contact.

"Yes, were you sent here by Dr. Sung to meet us?" John gave

her his full attention. Surely someone sent by a prominent doctor could move things along.

She smiled a little strangely. "Yes, in a way, I was."

"I'm sorry we're late." John allowed himself to glare at the porter.

"Well, ma'am," the porter declared, swiping his holo screen to his companion and nodding in the direction of the train. "You should know better than to do business with the Ghetto. This is what happens. We can't let them start getting ideas."

The woman drew herself up and set her chin. Her flowing dress did nothing to soften her sudden steely demeanor. The porter flinched under her aggressive stare.

"Really?" She folded her arms. "I was under the impression they only lived there as part of a quarantine for illness, not as any sort of punishment.

"So you're some kind of tree-hugging liberal, huh?" The porter rolled his eyes.

"Well, that is how I usually vote on the Senate floor, yes."

Whoa. The porter's eyes bulged, and he coughed. He pulled out his cell the same time David held his out to John. The ticket now read, "Shipment claimed by Senator Amanda Sato."

A Senator?

"I am so sorry, ma'am," the porter stammered.

"I kept my name with my second marriage," she said to John quietly as the porter hurried to help his coworker with the crate. "And my husband, Dr. Sung, bought the chairs as a sort of favor to me, so I thought it would be rude to ask him to drive out here to claim them."

A Senator drove out to the train station to meet them herself? Crazy. She ignored the porter's attempts to placate her, simply directed John and David to follow her with the crate on their cart.

"I adore your father's furniture," she said. "If I could entice him to work a little faster, I might even buy more of it." She winked at John. "Those creative types. What can we do?"

As she turned her attention away, John glanced at David.

Holy wow!

David smiled and nodded. Hm. He didn't seem surprised enough.

"Here we are." She presented a van with the wave of one hand.

"Fuck me." The words left John's mouth before he could stop them. The van was a floater. An honest to God *floater.* "Ma'am, I am so sorry."

"Are you kidding?" She laughed. "That sort of reaction is exactly why my husband wasted so much money on a cargo van."

The van itself wasn't anything special, but it hovered about two feet from the ground. John had no idea how it worked. He'd seen them in videos but had long suspected they were just made with special effects. He'd never in his life expected to see one in person.

"Go ahead," she said. "You know you want to look under it."

John grinned at her, then at David, whose eyes were huge. They dropped onto their stomachs, in spite of wearing their only suits, to see if they could tell how the thing worked. The space under the van rippled, like air over hot concrete. There was no movement, no slight waver of the vehicle. Blue coils glowed with an eerie radiance.

"I recommend you refrain from sticking a hand under it to see what will happen." The fact that she could be so delighted by her toy made her seem like a young girl, despite her white hair.

"What'll happen?" John asked. He glanced at David, who shrugged.

"The van exerts enough pressure into the pavement to keep a two-ton van hovering in the air." She smiled. "You seem smart. Do the math."

"Wow." Not wanting to be rude, John jumped up and offered a hand to David. "How does it work?" He brushed off his suit once David was on his feet.

"I press start, and it lifts into the air." She shrugged and pointed her cell at the cargo door in the back. "I left it running because raising and lowering the thing uses the most energy, apparently."

The back end of the van opened so John and David could load the crate.

"Do you have staff to unload at the other end?" If they hurried, he and David might still squeeze in a few minutes at the beach.

"I do." She folded her hands. "But I've heard so much about you two from your father, that I was hoping I might talk you into a tour of my home and maybe a martini or two." She held up a quick hand. "And of course, I'll pay you for your time. Cash."

"Uncle Bo talks about us?" What the what?

"Oh, yes, I'm sorry." She clapped her hands once. "The way he speaks, it's like you're both his sons. I forget that he's your uncle."

Uncle Bo talked about him like that?

"It's okay, Senator," David said into the silence. "We all think of John that way." He seemed to notice John's surprise. "Dad's thought of you as his own since you could walk. Is it really a shock?"

"He's always been like a dad to me, Senator." Wow. Not something he'd have thought to discuss in front of a total stranger. "I just. . . my mom is a little fussy about the details, so I'm careful to use the words she likes."

And while the beach would be fun, how often would they be invited for martinis at a Senator's house in Lincoln? David's face told John his thoughts matched exactly. Except. . .

"I'm sorry, Senator. . ." John turned to her. "Our passes only allow us outside the Ghetto until the train leaves again in less than an hour."

"Is that really the only hesitation?" She pulled out her cell. "Be honest with me and stop calling me Senator. My name is Amanda. All that Senator business makes me feel like I should be wearing a suit."

John's curiosity devoured him. How well did Uncle Bo know her? What must her home be like if she owned a floater? How amazing would it be for Makabee if John and David got to know a Senator? It might be the perfect connection to overcome John's freaky vision problems.

David's face said "duh" in three different expressions.

"If there's a way around the curfew, ma'am," John said, "we'd be delighted to help you with the shipment."

"Done." She tapped the phone with a flourish. "You can stay

as long as you like, and as soon as you're ready to go, I'll arrange a ride back to the bridge."

Wacky! John followed David into seats behind the Senator, and the van drove off. It moved with absolutely no vibration or sound at all. It just glided along.

As the van pulled onto the roadway, Amanda spun her seat to face John. "It drives itself," she said.

"How do you know Uncle Bo, ma'am?" John felt like Alice in Wonderland.

"I'm his best friend's mother." She waved a hand. "Well, one of his best friends. The three of them grew up like brothers."

"Dave *Sato!*" John couldn't believe it. "You're Dave Sato's mother." He looked at his cousin. "That's who they named you after." David still didn't seem nearly as freaked out as John. What the hell? John shook his head. "I can't believe it. Have you been in touch all this time?" Hadn't they lost contact with all those friends long ago?

"Goodness no." She tucked a strand of hair behind one ear. "It's a bizarre coincidence, if you must know. I was canvassing closer to the coast, meeting with people to trick them into voting for me." She winked. "I sat at a table all covered in mosaics. There were three symbols arranged in a triangle. An open circle, a Jewish Chai, and a fish, which meant as little to the woman who owned the table as it does to you, but those were three symbols my son, your father, and their friend Joey had used when they were boys. They signed all sorts of secret notes with those, marked places they thought us old folks didn't know." She smiled and sat back. "I had to know where she'd found that table. When your parents left Wisconsin in such a hurry, well, Dave needed a long time to recover the loss of his best friend." She smirked. "Of course, your *mother's* best friend went a long way to consoling him."

"Oh my God. You knew Aunt Ruth too?" John demanded.

"My son's wife, Vonna, was her best friend."

John recognized the name. Vaguely. They were married? Why hadn't Uncle Bo mentioned anything?

The van slowed to a halt.

"Did you know my dad?" John blurted out. "His name was Zack."

"A bit." She waved a hand in a so-so gesture. The doors slid open, and she exited the van. "Your parents were ten years older, so they didn't 'hang out' with the younger kids so much. The boys idolized Zack though." She touched John's shoulder. "Even though your dad had been best friends with Joey and Dave his whole life, he asked Zack to be his best man."

That John had known. He also knew part of the reason was that his dad had been older and could help Uncle Bo with the wedding plans. Talking to someone about their past rocked John's world. Their parents never talked about it, and never with outsiders.

Wow. The word 'outsiders' sounded so unfriendly.

Once John and David off-loaded the crate, Amanda gestured for them to back away. Slowly, the van lowered itself to the driveway and a small vibration, a hum that John only now realized had existed, ceased. He felt like a five-year-old on Christmas!

They dragged the crate around the van and John froze. Her house was incredible. Set into the side of a hill, the glass, steel, and raw wood home seemed more like an extension of the hillside than an intrusion. Trees and shrubs blocked the private rooms, but John could see into most of it.

He glanced around. Woods filled the property. Everywhere he looked, he saw trees. Why not live in a house of glass when your nearest neighbor lived a mile away on the other side of a forest?

"I'm glad you like it," she said. "The neighbors say it's so small it brings down the property values." She shrugged. "You can take the girl out of the Shinto. You can't take the Shinto out of the girl."

John nearly dropped the crate. She must have joined the UCA along with the rest of the Asians. She must have, or she'd be stuck in the Ghetto, too. But she'd dropped that proclamation about her religion as if it were the least interesting comment in the world.

"Just leave the crate there." She waved to one side. "I still need to decide where the set will live." She winked at John again. "I assume I don't need to hide my beliefs from the two of you, do I?"

The guys settled the crate where she'd indicated. John found David's eyes. Okay. Finally, he seemed a bit nonplused by the entire situation. Good.

"Well?" Amanda regarded John levelly.

What had been the question? Oh, yeah. "No ma'am. No need to hide anything, really."

"Good." She gathered her hair and held it in place with two chopsticks as she led them into the light, airy foyer. "Home security?"

Something beeped.

"Take a break, Annabelle." She glanced up at a corner of the room. "In fact, take the rest of the day. Include all security. All cameras off, too" She sighed a deep sigh and folded her hands. "Your father was like a son to me for any number of years. Dave is in Canada with his own family now."

"Canada?"

"His wife is Puerto Rican." She waved a hand. "When I was a little girl, we were Confucian at public functions, Buddhist when we worshipped, and Shinto whenever we needed a break from the formality. Adding in a membership to the UCA wasn't problematic for me. My son didn't have that option. They chose not to submit to the ghettos and fled with their son." It all made sense. If she ever wanted to see her son again, the country needed to change.

"What has Uncle Bo told you?" John asked.

She regarded him for several seconds.

"I need to wait ten minutes to answer you. At that point my security personnel will have left the building." A huge smile lit her face. "Tour?"

The forest filled the views through the glass walls. The living room rose a few steps to the kitchen and dining area, but the entire space lay open. Amanda led them to the back of the house, where a glass door slid aside to allow them onto a patio.

John nearly gasped. The hillside swept down to the beach, but a concrete patio held a bar, several wooden lounges, and a pool that defied logic. It hung over the empty space with the water held in place as if it were a solid object.

John dashed to the edge. David stopped at his side, grinning.

Okay. A million times better than the beach.

"How does the water hold its shape?" John asked.

"Nothing fancy, really. Glass walls. The water spills over into a second pool. The basement opens onto a patio down there as well." She laughed. "If I'd had a place like this when Dave was a boy, he'd have spent all day diving from that glass wall and giving me fits." She turned to John. "I hope one day Gardner is able to give me fits that way." She smiled. "My grandson."

"There's always hope, ma'am," John assured her.

"Indeed." She waved her hands. "Not too shabby?"

John grinned. "It's absolutely wacky, ma'am."

"And that means good, I take it." She laughed.

"The best." John glanced to the side, where David leaned against his shoulder. Yeah. Wow. Blue sky. A crystal-clear pool drained off into the air. In the background, a pristine white beach and bright blue ocean. John had died and gone to Heaven.

Naomi sat beside Bo on the stoop in front of the little shop. The sign over the door read, "Furniture." They'd been afraid to register any kind of company name that might be sent into national databases, so the sign simply read, "Furniture." It waved a bit, creaking in the breeze that created their only relief from the constant heat.

The sun set behind the buildings across the street. Dark shadows blanketed the road and sidewalk, covering the pedestrians in twilight. The wind picked up every day at sunset as the land cooled faster than the water, drawing people out onto porches, into the streets, and up onto the rooftops.

The sky shone pink, the buildings brown, and the pedestrians—mostly young people trying to get to parties before curfew—wore gray and charcoal with accents of burgundy, ochre, and hunter green. The remake of *Casablanca* had everyone under the age of thirty, even the Ghetto youth who could hardly afford the expense, dressing in pressed slacks with suspenders, starched shirts, jackets, and fedoras.

Knots of teenagers rushed through the streets laughing and shadowboxing each other, young men and women alike tipping their hats to Bo and Naomi as they sat on the stoop, him in shorts and a t-shirt, her in a plain sun dress, her arms bare and dark.

The greetings were, in fact, meant for Bo. He knew their children's friends, many of them by name. Naomi knew only a few. As they passed, she asked Bo for their names and tried her best to say a friendly "hello." Invariably, her words drew guarded glances before she received any greeting in return. Her son's friends seemed afraid of her. If only she could honestly wonder why.

"They just don't know you as well," Bo offered during a lull in the traffic.

"They just think I'm an insufferable old woman." Naomi enjoyed Bo's shock more than she likely should have. "I know what people think of me. I looked into the mirror this morning and finally saw what I've become."

Bo kept his silence, watching her face in the fading light. She wanted to tell him everything Zack and Gabriel had told her, but Bo shouldn't know those things, yet. What could she say?

"Things were so different when we were kids," she started. "Our parents were the ones running around half-naked and painting their hair green."

"*Our* parents?" Bo leaned back on his hands.

"Okay... *your* parents." Naomi gave him a sidelong glance. "My parents, too... my biological parents." Her biological parents had died when she was a teenager, and she'd lived with Mary's family afterward. She always talked about *that* family as her family. Bo sometimes forgot that she'd had other parents.

"My folks were like yours: hippies and rebels." Naomi watched their neighbors pass. "Mary's parents were either a throwback or a leap forward. Our world went to Hell in a hand basket before your generation made its mind which way to go... and now? Now the kids are wearing suits and crew cuts, embarrassed by the tattoos and piercings their grandparents have left over from days gone by."

An older couple passed across the street, Adam and Cerci from church. Naomi waved, and they waved back. Silver glinted from the threads sewn from his wrist to his elbow. Studs sparkled in his cheeks.

"See," Naomi whispered.

Bo chuckled but maintained his silence. It was one of the things the kids loved about him. He'd sit there and listen, patiently waiting until someone made their point.

"What's going on here is bigger than any of us, Bo... even us, even with all we know." *Even with all I know,* she added to herself. "We don't have the luxury of being selfish. Not us. Not now." A mangy German shepherd wandered past during the pause. "Not me."

She took Bo's hand. His skin was rough and worn from his work, the nails ragged. Once upon a time, they'd been the soft hands of an artist. Fortunately, he'd learned to turn his talent into something they could sell.

The eyebrow he raised at her touch softened into a smile. He wouldn't want her to see his surprise. She squeezed his hand. He was such a good man, and she had completely forgotten. Fortunately, Zack had reminded her. They'd been good friends, too.

"Good evening, folks." The deep voice startled Naomi. Even Bo jumped. Recognizing the policeman, Jonas King, Naomi bristled but tried to hide her reaction. The big man standing over them in sweatpants and a t-shirt was obviously out for exercise and not on official business.

"Officer," Bo offered.

"I'm not in uniform, Bo." The policeman waved a hand dismissively. "I'm just plain old Jonas, right now. I don't go on duty for hours!"

"Nice night for a walk." Naomi felt more comfortable with the neighborhood adults, even collaborators like the policemen. She saw them in church and knew how to make polite conversation. "Wasn't it a lovely sermon last Sunday?"

Bo winced. But why?

"We're just doing a job, Naomi." Jonas' voice took on an angry edge. "We're no different than Bo here. He makes a good living from the doctors and lawyers on the other side of the bridge."

Oh dear… how embarrassing. The sermon had been about the first century Jewish historian, Josephus, who collaborated with the Romans. The minister had turned the story into a not-so-subtle jab at the local city workers who collaborated with the government.

"I am so sorry, Jonas." How could Naomi possibly recover from that? "I was with the little ones on Sunday. We had a separate story time… we heard about the Garden." She glanced frantically from one man to the other. "Was there something wrong with the adult service?"

Bo winked, and the policeman seemed mollified.

"Pastor Su felt the need to heap a little judgment on the hard-working folks who keep this city running," he said.

"You know we're your friends, Jonas." Bo painted his face with a humble expression. "Hell, our boys are practically brothers. You know that." He rose to his feet to meet the other man's eyes. "I am extremely grateful for the good fortune I have with the sales I make." He held out a hand. "I don't know why Su feels the need to stir up trouble like that."

"From your lips to her ears, Bo." The policeman shook Bo's hand, then adjusted the waistband of his sweatpants.

"Is Rocky doing any better these days?" Bo might pretend to simply ask out of concern, but Naomi knew that topic would move the policeman along.

A complicated series of shrugs and clothing adjustments indicated that Bo had hit the target. Rocky wasn't doing well, and his rush habit embarrassed the policeman. That boy was on Naomi's daily prayer list.

"He's doing fine. Thanks for asking." He brightened with a fake smile. "Noah volunteered to help old Mrs. Darcy clean out her place. For free. He's always helping out, that one."

"You should be very proud of him." Naomi rose to join the men. "Of both your boys."

"Well, this thing won't run itself off." The policeman patted his ample stomach. "Good to see you both."

They said their good-byes, and off he jogged.

"Nice save." Bo took her hand.

"I can't believe I had to." As much as she agreed with the pastor's opinion of people like the policeman, she couldn't afford to make enemies. "I need to be more careful."

They grew still. Naomi may not have known a whole lot about her son's life, but she knew his friend Noah hated his father for cooperating with the government. At least John didn't hate her like that.

Bo squeezed her hand. He was such a good man.

"He's always there for the boy," Zack had said to her that morning. "You should let him *be* there for the boy."

And, of course, he'd been right. John would need his Uncle. And Ruth. The entire family for that matter. The decisions had been taken from Naomi's hands.

"We need to work together." She tugged Bo's hand to draw him down to the stoop. "My boy needs..." Her voice faltered and caught. She had just seen Zack. Death had not taken him from her forever. "He needs a father. He needs you... and he needs Ruth." She gripped his hand tightly. "*I* need you. I need your help with my boy. I need you to look after him. I need you to help me convince him that I love him."

With the words out in the air, a calmness settled around her like a shawl. She gazed over the buildings at the darkening sky, at the young people bustling down the street in excitement for the night's adventures.

"Your children are good children... all of the children... *our* children are good children." She met his gaze. He listened so patiently. "Our children are *good* children. I need you to help me listen to them." She already felt better. "You're good at that. At listening."

Bo allowed her to talk it out. So much of the fear drained out of her as she stared over the tops of the buildings. He wanted to speak, to tell her he was overjoyed to help with John, that he was honored she had asked, that he and Ruth could use her help with their children, too. So many decisions would need to be made soon. Bo was afraid, too.

He wanted to tell her all these things, but he wasn't sure how to say them. He watched the years fall away from her face as the sun set. When she spoke again, her voice was almost the voice of the young woman he had first met thirty years earlier.

"Remember when we'd all sit together on the top of a mountain and watch the setting sun?" she whispered. "The sky was enormous in New Mexico, bigger than anything I'd ever seen and filled with so many colors I thought it would make me blind. And sometimes, we wouldn't say a word. We'd just sit and watch the sky change colors, grow dark and turn into a giant canopy of stars." She drew in a deep breath and exhaled. "I miss the mountains, Bo. God help me, I even miss the desert. I haven't been outside this Ghetto in so long." She fell silent.

"Maybe we all need to go on a trip together," Bo said, spinning hope. "It's just a short ride to the Appalachians from here."

A short drive and innumerable insurmountable barriers.

"Yes," Naomi said. "That would be nice."

Her head dropped onto his shoulder. He lay his arm around her shoulders, and they watched the sky grow dark.

Ruth stood at the edge of one plate glass window, hands clasped together and pressed against her lips in a silent prayer of thanks. Her husband and her cousin sitting together like that—friendlier than she'd seen them in years? Maybe the worst had passed. If they worked together, everything would be so much easier.

"We should have told her years ago." From a shadowy perch on the roof across the street, Michael watched the quiet pair with the vaguest hint of a wistful smile. "She would have been a better mother. She would have been happier."

"If she'd been a better mother, John would be a different man." Gabriel stood behind him. "If she were happier, he might not be so close to Joseph or David, and you have to know that I wish him nothing but happiness."

"Michael is convinced this supposed messiah is going to accomplish what all the others have failed to do." Raphael's chuckle seemed as sincere as it was surprising.

"Not all the others failed," Michael insisted.

"Didn't they?" Raphael glanced around. "I don't see the Father's Kingdom here on Earth. What else is a messiah supposed to accomplish?"

"We never know what a messiah is supposed to accomplish, do we?" Michael glanced sidelong at Gabriel. "Do we?"

"Rumors of war and rumors of rumors. The planet destroyed. Eden returned." She straightened her jacket in a gesture that meant she was perturbed. "Servants do as we're told, and we don't need more information than necessary to complete our services."

"Hosanna in the highest," Raphael said dutifully.

"Hosanna, hosanna, hosanna." Gabriel made no attempt to hide her annoyance.

The angels watched as the pedestrians moved through their short, haphazard lives. Raphael smoothed out his robes and vanished. The pedestrians thinned as the darkness grew more tangible. Joseph and Sally retreated into the shop. Mary had moved upstairs some time earlier.

"You want to talk to the boy." Gabriel's voice seemed soft and caring. "You must know what harm *that* would do, at least."

What could Michael say? Of course, he wished to speak to

John. The young man was his son, but Michael knew his duty. The fate of humankind rested in the balance.

"David *is* the one," Michael said. "He will succeed. He must." He met his sister's eyes. Their eyes glowed with angelic radiance. "There's too much to lose this time."

"What do you know, Michael?" She shivered, which was something that hadn't happened in centuries, had it?

"I know nothing," Michael said. "But do any of us understand as much as we think we know? Is the future really set in stone as we believe?"

"I don't know," she admitted. "All lines seem to end with John's sacrifice. After that?" She touched Michael's arm. "I was a mother. I understand."

But did she? Did she really?

John sat in a lounge chair beside a pristine swimming pool with a martini in one hand. His jacket and tie lay neatly folded on the table beside him. David sat in the next chair, eyes closed, face peaceful.

"You know…" Senator Amanda Sato stood nearby, sipping her own martini. She lifted her glass in the direction of the nearly finished Tower of the Bible. "Every time I see that thing scraping the atmosphere, I'm glad my house is more than a mile away from it, so I don't get hit when it comes crashing down."

John nearly spit out his drink.

David opened his eyes and smiled.

"I see you agree with me." She set her glass on a table. So much for John's assumption about the evils of the entire wealthy class.

A young woman approached, the first non-White John had seen since boarding the train. Her skin glowed a deep chestnut. She nodded at John, whispered in the Senator's ear, and withdrew.

"She's lovely, yes?" The Senator smiled at John as the woman left.

"Well, yes, but that's not. . ." He felt his cheeks heat up. "I just. . ."

"Go ahead and say it." Amanda's face became serious. "All my talk of equal rights and yet my servants hale from the Ghetto."

Which was exactly what John had wondered.

"It's a predicament, as is so much in this world." Her eyes wrinkled in concern. "All the jobs I offer are subordinate positions, yet they're the only ones I'm able to offer. They're also the only jobs my people could get outside the Ghetto. I provide health care for them and tutors for their children." She lifted the martini pitcher and carried it to John and David. "I fear it's the best I can do at the moment." She held the decanter toward John. "There's a bill on my desk giving me ulcers, and I'd like to ask your opinion if I may."

"Of course." John offered his glass. Best. cosmo. ever. Billy made a mean drink, but the vodka in this pitcher went down so smoothly John didn't want to think about how much it must've cost.

"Clement wants the UCA to put a church in every ghetto." The Senator moved to David's side with the decanter. "Everyone who converts will receive special dispensation through the church regardless of ethnicity or sexual orientation. They can leave the ghettos. . . after five years with the church."

John spit his drink. "They're making five-year plans assuming the ghettos will still exist? But HIV has been almost eradicated."

"I always knew grouping the health risks with the terrorist risks and the religious dissidents would cause us trouble." She set the pitcher on the table. "But I'm just one person. Now they point at things like Makabee's Pipeline as evidence that terrorist fever has caught in the ghettos. They seem to think that all residents are, by definition, national security risks."

"We wouldn't be risks if they treated us like American citizens." John rose from his chair, fists clenched.

"Preaching to the choir." She held up a hand. "Here's my dilemma: I vote for this bill, I send a signal I approve the assumption that the ghettos are here indefinitely, at least another five years. If I vote against it, I help kill a potential escape for folks just like you if we aren't able to close them." She folded her hands. "Which is worse? Setting a bad precedent or voting against a potential boon?"

John finished his drink in one swallow. How would they ever get out of the Ghetto if the president got his way? David's face remained fastidiously blank, but frustration niggled at the corners of his eyes. No. Makabee would make a difference. He'd do it without the politicians.

"If we say we're willing to wait," John said, "it tells the world our situation must not be so bad."

"You look so much like your father right now. Like Zack." The senator raised her glass to him. "He'd get that same intense look in his eyes."

John's throat tightened.

"He'd be very proud of you."

"For what?" John scoffed. "Being an excellent delivery boy?"

"Don't disrespect your uncle." She raised a finger. "His work is excellent and helping him does you credit."

"You're right." John ducked his head. "I'm sorry."

"But that's not what I meant." She settled into one hip and regarded one young man then the other. "I mean your other work."

"What other work?" John swallowed hard.

"Bo asked me one day, hypothetically of course, what would happen to teenagers helping Makabee once they turned eighteen and could be tried as adults." She smiled tightly. "He did his best to keep it a general conversation, but I'm too smart for him." She smiled. "Don't worry. Your secret, whatever it might be, is safe with me. But your father. . ." She glanced at David. "Both of your fathers have every reason to be proud."

John forced that lump back down again.

"I need to tell you something, though." Her demeanor became formal. "There's another agency taking an interest in the Ghetto."

The suit looking for a mouthy teenage guy? Could she mean him?

"I don't know much about the man in charge, but he's dangerous and he answers only to Clement." Her eyes bore into John's. "You might want to keep your heads down for a few days." *Especially David.*

John blinked, and the voice in his head faded. Had she done that on purpose? No. John had just picked up her intensity.

"Thank you, ma'am," he said. "We'll be careful."

Amanda relaxed and a decade dropped off her as she smiled.

"The woman out here earlier? She informed me of a call I need to return. But I'm enjoying our conversation." She moved toward the house, stepping slowly backward. "I'd love for you to stay a while longer. I don't know, maybe I can think of some embarrassing stories about your parents when they were your age and causing trouble." She stopped moving away and laughed. "Like the time the boys all streaked across the school grounds after the swim team won State."

"Wha-a-at?" Uncle Bo? Streaking? Wacky.

David nodded and shrugged. He sipped the martini, emphasizing that they really didn't have much else to do that day. Then his eyes narrowed. They could also really use an ally like the Senator if they ever did get caught working for Makabee.

"Of course, ma'am," John said. "We'll wait right here."

"Good." She clapped once. "I'll have Burton bring out more drinks." She headed to the door. "And please feel free to jump in the pool. It doesn't get used nearly as much as it should. Burton will bring towels." She paused in the doorway. "I'll have him bring trunks as well."

John rose and stepped to the edge of the pool. David's shoulder touched his lightly.

"So much better than the ocean," David said.

"Way worth the price of admission."

They clinked glasses.

Amanda Sato closed the door to one of the few rooms in her home with no windows. She leaned against her desk, crossed her ankles, and folded her hands in her lap. She drew the chopsticks out of her hair, and shook it out, brushing it behind her shoulders for good measure. She tapped the desktop, and a screen popped up in front of her.

Hm. Whom should she call first? Dave. She needed to make sure he wasn't involved with his old friend before she called the Pipeline.

She'd been genuinely shocked when she'd first seen the inlaid table, absolutely certain of its origin. But what were the odds? Slim to none, unless someone was manipulating behind the scenes.

Could Dave be involved? Could he have reconnected with Joey and his family? Sato's connections in both the US government and the Pipeline came up empty.

As far as she could tell, it was simply a bizarre coincidence. Well, she'd only need a short call to her son to determine whether he, at least, was involved. She tapped the icon for her son's number, pasting her best motherly smile in place. His image appeared almost immediately. He wore a thin tank top, dark with perspiration. Working out again.

"Hello, Son, am I interrupting?" She kept her tone light and innocent.

"Are you kidding?" He grinned and wiped his face with one arm. "This is just the break I needed to keep your grandson from kicking my ass."

"Again," Gardner added in the background. He pushed his way into the image with his father. "Hey, Gram!"

"Hello, Milligram. Are you teaching your father a lesson for me?"

He snorted. "Don't I always?"

His father grabbed him around the neck, and Gardner seemed to let him do that these days. With a sixteen-year-old, who could say?

"Any chance you can give Centigram a reprieve?" she asked.

"Okay, but if he paid you to do this, I expect a big birthday present."

Sato smiled. "You'll get a big present regardless, won't you?"

"That's 'cause I'm so adorable."

"Hit the showers, son." His father pushed him away affectionately. "You have Spanish homework tonight, don't you?"

"Aw, man," Gardner called off screen.

"You'd think the genes would help." Dave shook his head. "What can I do for you, Mom?"

"You'll never guess who I've run into recently." She studied him for any changes. "Joey."

"Joey?" The double take seemed sincere. "What's he doing in New York? Last I heard, his boss had him pulling doubles in Milwaukee."

"Not him. The other Joey."

Confusion covered her son's face, then abject astonishment. She might as well have told him she'd seen the risen Christ, although that was a poor choice of metaphor. . .

"Joey One? In New York? Oh my God, Mom; how is he?" His surprise had to be genuine. He couldn't fool his mother.

"He's fine, Son. Making furniture, if you can believe it. Mary's with him, and Sally. They're all fine." She tapped the cell to send a photo of the inlaid table. "Here's how I found him."

The joy on her son's face tightened Sato's throat.

His eyes teared up. He didn't speak.

"Their boys are right here, swimming in my pool," she told him, straining to keep her tone light. "Right now."

"Oh my God, Mom." Dave coughed.

She'd exaggerated her contact with Joey to the boys. They'd messaged back and forth a bit, and when she'd asked for details about the boys, the kind of thing any grandmother might ask about someone's sons, Joey had been very complimentary. But she'd used her husband's contact and had never revealed her identity.

"They look *just* like their fathers." She gave her comment a huge smile to sell it.

"Wow, mom. That's. . . unbelievable." Ah. There it was. The slightest twitch of his eyebrows that said he knew about the Project, that David wasn't biologically Joey's son, so any resemblance had to be a coincidence.

"Isn't it?" She hadn't been certain. When she'd stumbled onto that mosaic table, she'd been convinced the entire scenario had to be a setup of some kind. But by whom? She'd prayed her son hadn't been a part of whatever game was being played, that he wasn't part of whoever was playing her... but it was obvious he hadn't been in contact with his Joey recently. His shock was too real.

"Can I talk to them?" Dave bounced on his heels.

"I'm not sure that's wise... under the circumstances." She furrowed her brow and glanced to the side.

"Circumstances?" The smile drained from his face. He was working hard to keep his thoughts from her, but what child could fool his mother?

"Well, with this Addison fellow snooping around." She met his gaze. "Joey's pretty nervous."

"Jesus, Mom, is this a secure line?" Dave glanced in every direction and hunkered closer to his cell. "You can't just... Joey told you about. . . about *Addison*?"

Of course, he hadn't. She hadn't even seen Joey face to face.

"Well, I am a Senator, Dave. Sometimes people confide in me for help." Would he believe her?

A thousand thoughts scrolled across her son's face. He was thrilled to hear that Joey was still alive, that his best friend's family was okay. He didn't understand how his mother knew all this delicate information. He wanted to pursue it further but was afraid of spilling more information than he should.

"I don't have words." The biggest grin she'd seen in years broke across his face. "You have to give me his contact."

"I can't." She pinched her face again. "I mean, it's been how long since he's seen you?"

"Eighteen years." His eyes grew wistful again. "I haven't seen him since..." Most likely he was about to say since Joey's parents died in that car crash.

So the situation was exactly as she had predicted. Thank God.

"What if I give him your contact, and he can call you if he chooses?" she said. "I'm certain he'll call, but this coincidence stretched credulity for him." And for her as well. "If we let him make the next move, it looks a lot less suspicious."

"Of course. Yes." He nodded. "Jesus, anything to get him to call me." He ran his hands through his damp hair. "Oh my God, Mom! Joey's all right! I can't. . . Oh my God!"

That's all she'd needed to know.

"Oh damn." She waved her hands randomly, pretending to manipulate her screen. "That's the president on my other line. I'm so sorry, but I need to take it or some poor, third world country might get bombed."

"No, I get it." He raised both hands. "Save the world. And Mom?" His eyes filled with water again. "Thanks."

"You were such good boys." She smiled and cut the line.

The smiled dropped from her face. She picked up the chopsticks, coiled her hair on top of her head and set it. Her son wasn't involved. Was that good or bad? Hard to say.

She touched the other icon on her screen, the Hammer

John blew out his air so he'd remain at the bottom of the pool for a few extra seconds, staring out through the glass wall that helped the pool hang in space. The distorted view through the cool, refreshing water showed him the shoreline and the ocean. That was the only view unobstructed by the forest.

He pushed to the surface and sucked in a deep breath.

David walked along the glass wall where the water slid over into the second pool. His suit, like John's, had been a gift from the Senator. Her servant had insisted the guys were meant to keep them.

"No offense," Burton had said with a grin, "but who's going to want to wear them after they cupped your twig and berries?"

John had liked the guy instantly.

"Look at me, I'm walking on water!" David held his arms out to his sides and closed his eyes.

That's exactly what it looked like, too. How funny. Well, the opportunity pulled John closer.

"Then allow me to baptize you, Savior." He grabbed David's ankle with one hand, his calf with the other hand, and he pulled hard.

With a yelp, David splashed into the water. Knowing his cousin, John sucked in a lungful of air. Yep. Both arms locked around John's torso and yanked him under.

The water felt cool and wonderful. It also provided a rare opportunity.

"Handstands?" John asked once he'd surfaced.

"Perfect." David held out his hands.

John lowered into his knees and took David's hands as his cousin stepped onto a thigh, climbing John's body to his shoulders. David stood up, and John held his calves for support.

"Tell me when you're ready." David lowered into a crouch and held his hands out again.

"Okay." John took them, sucking in a deep breath. He stabilized his arms by connecting his elbows to his sides.

David's weight adjusted, and John pushed as hard as he could. David shifted his weight forward until John held most of it. Then all of it. If all was working, David was extending his legs until he stood in a handstand in John's hands. From the amount of weight that shifted from his shoulders to his hands, David nailed it.

"Got it," David said.

Okay, John needed to reset his center and press up. Then David would be in a full handstand above him with John's arms fully extended.

He pressed up. And he pressed up.

"Sorry, coz," John said. "Not going to happen."

David's weight shifted, and John pushed as hard as he could to send David away. He hit the water with a splash.

"At least in a pool, it's fun to fall out of it," David said after he surfaced. "We almost had it."

"Excuse me." Burton stood at the side of the pool with a plate of martinis. "I'm very sorry to bother you." His voice carried a hint of a Puerto Rican accent.

"No bother." John swam to the side of the pool. "What can we do for you?"

"I'm afraid the Senator has been called away." The servant set the tray on a nearby table. "She's asked me to extend her most humble apologies and an invitation to remain as her guests as long as you like. Anything you need, I can get for you."

John turned to David. Playing in the pool rocked the world, but staying without her there felt like an abuse of her hospitality.

David nodded.

"I hope she's all right." John pulled himself onto the deck. "And that we haven't offended."

"Nothing like that." The servant waved both hands. "She just has to prevent the world from ending or something." He grinned then seemed to realize he shouldn't do that. "You're welcome to stay."

"I'm David." David pulled up beside John and extended a hand. "We haven't really been introduced."

"Burton." The servant took David's hand. "Nice to meet you."

"I'm John." He shook Burton's hand as well.

The servant extended the plate holding two full martini glasses. John and his cousin took the glasses, and Burton tucked the silver platter under an arm.

"Wouldn't want to waste them." John extended the glass to Burton. "I'm already buzzing. You should try this."

"I'm really not supposed to." Burton glanced around.

"Security cameras are off, right?" John pointed at the supposedly defunct camera.

"These are nice." Burton took the glass and sipped. "Thank you."

Excellent. The Senator had really turned off the cameras, then, and she trusted them. Burton extended the drink, but John held up a hand.

"I can share with David. We've had enough anyway."

David passed him his glass.

"How is it to work here, if it's okay to ask?" John sipped.

"Ask away." Burton raised his glass. "I love it here. Work's not hard. I'm getting my degree online, which would never happen without the doctor's help." He shrugged. "I'm studying medicine, and the genetic manipulation of the Y-chromosome is giving me nightmares."

John had no idea what he'd just said.

"My point exactly," Burton said. "But Dr. Sung is tutoring me himself."

"How do you work here—?" John looked around at the most amazing place he'd ever seen in his life. "And then go home to the Ghetto at night?" He handed the martini to David, who finished it.

"I don't. We all live here in apartments." He pointed across the yard. "Just behind those trees."

"Whoa. You get to live here? Outside the Ghetto." John passed David a towel and dried off.

Burton finished his drink and set it, with the platter, beside David's empty glass. Just how orchestrated was this conversation?

"I know, right?" Burton settled into one hip and stuck his hands into his pockets. He glanced around. "It's not perfect."

John gave him a curious look, moving to his neatly folded suit. He picked out his shorts and socks, hoping Burton would elaborate if allowed the time.

"Don't get me wrong," Burton insisted, "it's great here. A million times what we'd have in the Ghetto, but sometimes it's hard just to run out and get a loaf of bread."

John thought about their encounters on the luxury train and extrapolated that kind of hassle to a daily basis. What a nightmare.

"So we all stick pretty close to the house." Burton opened his arms to include the yard and house. "But it's not like that's a hardship."

"True words." David held up his wet trunks.

"Seriously. Yours." Burton pulled plastic gallon-sized baggies out of a pocket. "Here. For the trip back."

Burton looked like a man with more on his mind, so John closed his eyes and listened.

They'd be a hoot to work with, Burton thought.

Holy wow. It worked.

"How many positions does she have available?" John decided to try the direct approach. "Is this conversation part of the interview, too?" He left his shirt untucked.

Burton's eyes opened wider then narrowed.

"Busted. The Senator said you two were smart." He shrugged. "She's thinking of expanding the staff. When she bumped into your dad, she decided she'd offer you jobs here if that was something you wanted."

"What jobs?" He pulled on his shoes but left them untied.

"Not sure." He led the way into the amazing home. "I'm her assistant, but she doesn't tell me everything."

"So we'd live here, too?" John shrugged into his jacket as they passed out of the house and onto the drive.

"Of course. The train ticket alone would be worth more than you'd make in a day," Burton told them.

The snacks on the train probably cost more than John would make in a day.

"It's a big decision," Burton said. "Your dad has a few more pieces he's building for the Senator. She'll probably ask to have the two of you deliver them yourselves, and she'll likely send a van to meet you at the bridge."

"The floater?" John asked as they passed the van.

"Probably not." Burton barked one sharp laugh. "The roads out that way are pretty rough."

He led them to a car worth more than John was likely to earn in his lifetime. As they piled into it, John and David exchanged looks. If she planned to send a van for them in the future, she must have had them ride the train for a reason. Why? To give them a glimpse of the life they could have working for her? To expose them to the wider cracker world so they saw how much nicer she was than anyone else was likely to be?

The panel between the seats slid down and Burton watched them buckle in.

"She's doing all this because she thinks of your dad as family." He turned to start the car but made a point of glancing at them in the mirror. "I'd heard all kinds of stories before she even bumped into him." He grinned. "Dave, her son, has a million stories about growing up with his best friends."

As the car moved down the drive, John stared at the passing trees. He'd never in his life seen so much space and beauty. Even the beaches at the edges of the Ghetto were cramped, dirty, and concrete. And the Senator wanted to offer them jobs out here?

His stomach tightened. Would he be any less of a prisoner? It was a beautiful prison, granted, but wasn't a prison a prison no matter how lovely? Would he be able to do any of his work for Makabee? If the president had no intention of closing the Ghettos any time soon, wasn't the Pipeline that much more important?

David nudged him with a knee. From the serious expression on David's face, his thoughts ran along similar lines. John glanced out the window. The Tower of the Bible loomed over the landscape.

Clusters of folks wandered over the bridge into the Ghetto. No one checked passes for people returning. Who would sneak *into* the Ghetto? And who cared? A sleek black car created a momentary excitement, but after John and David exited, and it drove away, the crowd lost interest. The pair were just two more Ghetto rats headed for home.

John stopped near the bridge. Everyone's skin seemed so dark. Almost everyone had brown eyes. Outside the Ghetto, all the skin had been so pale, almost porcelain. And there had been so many blue eyes with blond hair. Certainly, some of those were artificial. It had seemed like a foreign country.

Everything he'd learned about their parents left him unsettled.

They knew a Senator. Somehow, David had known about her. But how?

"Why so quiet?" David spoke in little more than a whisper.

"You knew," John said.

"What?"

"You knew that Senator Sato knew our parents."

"Yes." Thank God David didn't try to lie.

"Why didn't you tell me?" John asked.

"I don't know." He watched people crossing the bridge. "Because. . ." His face showed John his worry. "How do I know any of the things I know? When you heard that Dad wanted to send us out to Lincoln, you didn't tell me right away."

"I didn't even know if I should believe it," John admitted.

"Exactly."

But it wasn't the same thing; he had to know that.

"Please don't get mad at me." David's face was lined with concern. "I'm trying."

John settled himself and gestured for David to continue.

"I don't hear things the way you do, but sometimes I just know stuff." David watched the pedestrians. "When you told me where we were going, I knew who was there. When I met the Senator, I knew about her son. But it's not my place to talk about it. I mean, I know things about Mom and Dad's sex life I really wish I didn't know. Should I tell you that?"

"Whoa. No. Not even a little."

"Exactly. So if there's stuff I don't tell you, it's because I think it's someone else's privacy, or I think you don't want to know it. I'm going to make mistakes about that sometimes." He met John's eyes. "I told you I'm a freak, too."

John understood, but how much did David know about John? Did he understand what was happening, why he had those visions?

"And that's the reason I haven't said anything about any of this before." David seemed so sad. "Because the moment you know I see stuff, you're going to wonder what I know about you, what I see about you, and you'll always want to know."

"What *do* you know?"

"More than you can possibly imagine." David chuckled and shook his head.

"Fine," John said, "you're Nostradamus." As the sun hid behind the tops of the buildings, more and more people showed up to cross.

"Nostradamus was a wuss," David said.

"So we're both freaks. We don't belong in here and no one wants us out there."

David didn't disagree. The Senator might like them, but no one else out there did, and that damn tower would be a constant reminder, leering down at them wherever they went.

"There's another reason I didn't tell you about the Senator and her son," David murmured. "I feel guilty because I have my dad, and your mom doesn't want you to think of him as your dad, no matter how much he wants you to think of him that way, and so here's this connection to his past that points out the fact that yours is dead. And that kind of sucks." He took a deep breath. "I didn't know how to say that without it sounding like bragging or something. Or... it just sounds stupid now that I'm trying to explain it. I figured however it went down out there, well, that's just the way it would be. I was afraid I'd mess things up no matter what I told you."

David's explanation was the truth, and that helped, but, somehow, just a little bit, it wasn't the truth. John didn't like that. He didn't like that at all.

"Let's go home." John headed toward the bridge.

"Wait." David touched his arm. "You know as far as I'm concerned, he's your dad. As far as he's concerned, too."

"I know... I know." And the thought helped... a little. Maybe. But John still didn't want to live out his life as a carpenter's son.

He also didn't want to live in a beautiful prison with glass walls, looking out on a world that hated him.

What did that leave him?

Crossing the bridge into the Ghetto hurt. It physically hurt. Living there day after day, John had grown used to it. It was normal.

And the other deliveries, any of them that went that deep into cracker land, the customer always sent someone to pick it up at whatever train station.

Seeing the world through the small filthy windows of a crowded train wasn't much different than living in the Ghetto. The only parts of the outside world John had experienced had been almost as overcrowded and grimy. But that mag lev with its glass canopy? And being there in her house, smelling rich people's air, swimming in a rich person's pool, drinking her vodka? John's life seemed pathetic and horrible by comparison.

The worst part? The truth was that, in some ways, John's family was privileged. They always had food. He could afford to throw bills at less fortunate girls digging for scraps. Sure, the power went out sometimes but not for lack of paying the bill. When it came down to it, in that other world he was just a Ghetto rat like all the others, but here in the Ghetto, if he started making trips out to Senator Sato's house and drinking her booze and swimming in her pool, was he any better than Noah's dad?

He had money in his pocket. For anyone in the Ghetto, it was a lot of money. Because Uncle Bo was friends with a Senator's son.

John stopped in the middle of the bridge. The smell of garbage hit him hard. A pair of rats crawled along one railing. Compared to the fine suits and well-pressed pleats in the skirts of the crackers, the hand-me-down clothes around him seemed sad. But these were his people. These were the folks he saw every day of his life, and he'd never noticed the thread-bare elbows and worn knees before.

"What's wrong?" David asked.

"I don't think I can go back."

"Why not?"

"To the Senator's house, I mean. I can't go back there."

"I knew what you meant. Why not?"

All of these people worked hard; they struggled from day to day to survive. They did what they could to stay alive, and, most importantly, they helped each other. They were his people. To a degree, they were *all* his family.

"You know why not."

The river of travelers broke around them as if they were an island.

"Of course, I do," David said, "but I also know you need to say it out loud."

On the other side of the bridge, maybe they had better clothes, and sodas that chilled themselves, but...

"Because we'll never belong out there," John said. "Never. And pretending we will, that one day we'll change the world and somehow, they'll accept us? It's pathetic. It's fucking mental. And we can go play at being rich with the nice lady who buys dad's furniture because she pities us and not because he's an amazing artist, which he *is*. . . and that will just make us the worst kind of pathetic. Because. . ."

Because it would be so much easier. Because life would be so amazing for them with a rich lady's job and a rich lady's apartment in the woods.

"Because you want it too badly," David said.

"I do." John could hardly breathe. "I want it so bad it kills me."

"And it'll hurt too much to give it up every time we visit home."

"And we won't fit in, anymore. Barry and Noah, they'll want us to find them jobs out there, or they'll want us to steal booze for them, and they'll be right. We *should* do that for them because they're our *family*... they are our family... but—"

"But she'd be a nice lady doing nice things for us because she's loyal to Dad, and she's not some evil cracker living out there who deserves to be ripped off."

And that was it. Not all of them were evil. Not all of them hated the Ghetto rats. At least one woman, one Senator for Christ's sake, wanted to help, wanted to do what she could, was willing to listen to the true words of John and David, two Ghetto rats in suits bought third hand on the cheap.

"Am I wrong?" He faced David, grabbed his arms for emphasis. "Can we change it? Will Makabee fix everything?"

A long pause stretched out. A very long pause.

Would David ever answer?

"I don't know," David finally said. And there it was. The truth. Not what John had wanted to hear, but maybe the reality?

How the hell could anything change? Who could possibly change things enough for it to matter?

"Wow, coz," John said, "that is so not the answer I wanted to hear."

"Would you rather I lied?"

"No. Never that." John looked up as the sky continued to darken. "I'm tired of feeling like an outsider. I just want to belong somewhere."

"I have an idea." David's tone helped. He had an idea. A great idea, maybe.

"Lay it on me." He released David's arms.

"Let's go to Babylon tonight and get blind stinking drunk with the people who always make us feel like we belong. We'll call Barry and Noah, who have known us since we crapped our diapers, and we'll bring Jamie and Tracey, who have watched us do a million stupid and idiotic things and still love us. I'm sure we'll see Joanne there and Billy, who always makes you smile. We may not be a very big world, and we may not be rich, and we may not be powerful, but you belong with us, and we all love you."

"Oh my God, David, could you be more sappy?" John sputtered with laughter. How could he even take it seriously?

"Shut up, you need to hear this." He grabbed John's face in his hands and wouldn't let him move away. "We'll buy them drinks, and we'll tip Billy too much, because that's all we can do to spread today's good fortune. We'll share it with the people who treat us like we belong. And fuck the rest of the entire God damned world." And those were true words. The people David had spoken, they were John's family, his tribe.

One day, all reality aside, they'd all be free. Right?

"Coz, what in the world would I ever do without you?" John pulled David into a rough hug, not a sentimental hug that might set him off, but a friendly hug.

"You will never need to find out," David said. "I will be right here with you until the day you die."

"I guess I can't ask for much more than that."

They finished the walk across the bridge, and somehow, it didn't hurt nearly as much as John had expected.

Michael perched on the bridge, high above the young men, his fingers gently brushing the cooling metal between his bare feet. The echoes of David's last words stung his heart. They were so much truer than John suspected. Before moving off into the Ghetto, David glanced over a shoulder and met Michael's gaze. For a moment, the boy's mask dropped and revealed the horrible pain hidden from John, from everyone but his guardian.

David knew what lay around the corner. He knew how much it would hurt. He knew no one could stop it.

There was a saying among the humans: truth hurts.

They had no idea whatsoever how right they were.

"So what do you think?" Jamie relaxed into one hip of the suit Joanne had loaned her. Please, don't let Tracey laugh.

"Holy wow, Jamsie." Tracey's eyes grew huge. She flashed a big thumbs up, and her hologram played a fanfare. Balloons, confetti, and streamers cascaded down the screen. "Oops!" She waved a hand to kill the trumpets. "Sorry. Forgot I had that active." The balloons bounced around near the floor.

"It's not too much?" Jamie turned to the hologram she used as a mirror. She'd followed Joanne's instructions to the letter, from her mascara to the number of buttons to leave open on her blouse.

"No. Seriously. It's perfect. Look at me." Tracey waved her hands. "Over here."

Jamie complied and settled into her hip again. Joanne had said it would look sexy but relaxed.

"You brought out your eyes." Tracey made a very frank perusal. "But not so much that you look like you're trying too hard, and the suit? Power. The skirt is amazing on you." She nodded. "I'd give you another thumbs up, but the balloons get on my nerves."

"Thanks." Jamie sucked in a deep breath.

"So. . ." Tracey folded her arms. "The new look. This is for. . .?"

"Truth?"

"No, coz, lie to me." The arms traveled to Tracey's hips. "What the what?"

"I'm suddenly playing with the big kids, right?" Jamie sat against her dresser. "We all are. I think that drive the guys found is the real deal."

Tracey laughed.

"Thank you so much." Jamie's friend mocked her ambition? Really?

"No, no. . . you look perfect. Very professional." Tracy waved a hand. "Here I am thinking you were after a boy, and you *are*, but, you know, the big boy himself. Makabee. I'm laughing because I may technically be an adult since I hit the big one-eight, but you are decades beyond me, coz. And it's funny because you're more likely to get your boy than I am mine."

"What?" Jamie hadn't heard about a boy. "Who are *you* after?"

"You cannot mock me." Tracey looked away for a moment, and the edges of the screen glowed red.

"Yes, I can. I'm actually rather good at it."

Who the heck could Tracey want?

"Fine. Let me ask you a question." She took a deep breath. "Do you think Barry's a womanizer?"

"Barry?" Jamie's heart thumped in her chest. Shock didn't cover it. "You're interested in *Barry*?"

"I know." Tracey paced, and the hologram followed her movements. "He'll make it with anyone in a skirt under the age of, like, a hundred—"

"And doesn't mind doing so where we all can watch." The fact that some of her friends had no qualms about who was around when they made it still freaked her out, all attempts at worldliness aside.

"I know." Tracey clenched her hands into fists and shook them. "Total womanizer, but he's just. . ."

Barry was just the most gentlemanly, flamboyant, and sensitive guy they knew. He would tell you his deepest secret and cry at puppy videos. He'd also punch out anyone who said a cross word to you.

And he was easy on the eyes.

"He's also the sweetest guy you know," Jamie said at last.

"Yes." Tracey's face filled with hope. "So you don't think I'm insane?"

"No, I don't." And she wasn't. Tracey was pretty, smart, and one of the least annoying girls Jamie knew. "And he's not a womanizer. He's just. . . easy. I hear him talking to John and David. I sincerely believe he thinks he's going to marry each and every one of those girls he makes."

Which was also true. He had a reputation now, and girls went after him because he was a sure thing and, from all reports, ridiculously good at what he did. He was also completely and irrevocably out of Jamie's league. Unfortunately.

"He just wants to fall in love," Jamie muttered.

Tracey squealed in delight and clapped her hands. Okay. Maybe not the least annoying girl Jamie knew after all.

Someone pounded on the door.

Jamie jumped. "Who is it?" No reason to stress, really. The parents were out for the evening.

"It's *just us*." David over-pronounced the words to make them sound like Jamie's online handle. How did he always know when she was on the net? Okay. She had a chance to show them her new image. She put one hand in her pocket.

"Come on in."

The door opened.

"Hey, sis. Hey, Tracey." David and John peered in, secret agent style, with David directly above John. "You about ready to go? We'll be downstairs."

"Where is everyone?" John asked.

"Church," Jamie and Tracey choroused.

"Bonus." John swiped the brim of his fedora.

"We should leave a note," David said. "You promised."

"Fine." John's face didn't seem nearly as annoyed as it should. What had happened there?

The boys slipped away and closed the door.

"Seriously?" Jamie muttered. "They didn't even notice?"

"They're your brothers, girl," Tracey said. "You could be dressed in a dominatrix outfit, and they wouldn't notice."

"Fine." Jamie hated them both. "See you there." She waved her hand to disconnect the line before Tracey could say more.

She opened the door and clacked into the hallway. She loved the sound the heels made on the wood floor.

"Boo!"

Jamie literally jumped. David and John leaned on opposite walls, arms and ankles crossed, fedoras half-covering their faces.

"Hey, dollface," John said with his horrible impression of a gangster accent. "Has youse seen a dame name of Jamie hereabouts? She looks kinda likes youse, but not nearly so yowsa-wowsa va-va-*voom*." He shook one hand as if he'd burned it.

So they *had* noticed.

"You bastards." She smacked them both with her clutch purse. "And thank you."

John ran a thumb across the brim of his fedora and checked out the party. The music pushed his pulse faster. The bassline rattled the stones in the pile beneath his wingtip Oxfords. Lasers flashed across both platforms and holograms masked the ceiling over the central trench with a sparkling canopy of stars, meteors, and dragons.

"Dragons!" Jamie grabbed John's hand and pointed. "They're using my numbers! Mine! Can you believe it?"

"You hit the jackpot, Jamsie!" John recognized the serpentine movement of her app.

"Woohoo!" David grabbed her other hand and held it over her head.

She laughed.

John looked across her and met David's eyes. Their little sister was growing up. She was a genius with the numbers, and the fact that Babylon had stolen them for the light show was a huge coup for her. People up and down the coast knew about the parties held in this abandoned subway station.

The music cut out, everything except a single woman's voice, high and angelic. All movement slowed to a near standstill for eight beats, and the dragons slithered together and started mating.

"Okay, I didn't program that part of it." Jamie looked away. She'd only been coming to the parties for a couple of months now. Like John and David, she was a bit of a late bloomer.

John took advantage of the moment to scan the platforms for his friends. The right-hand platform held the bar and tables. Billy served drinks, as always. He spun a bottle in each hand while keeping time with his hips. Tonight, the trunks he wore for a uniform were dark red.

The left-hand platform was the dance floor, already filled to capacity. Finding Barry and Noah in that group would be impossible—whoops. There was Barry, anyway… and there was Tracey on her knees. Well, that was a new development.

"Couldn't take the time to find a mattress?" David's voice teased, but it drew John's attention to the central trench that ran from their feet to the opposite end of the space. The tracks had long ago been covered with mattresses and cushions for rushing and making it.

The music jumped in again, the crowd cheered, and the party

roared back to life. Lasers spattered the platforms with fireworks then met in the center to form the word "Babylon" in giant, flashing letters.

The crowd roared.

Jamie squeezed John's hand and tugged him down the rubble that blocked the party from the subway tunnel. If the party were raided, the Dicks had to clamber around a giant pile of rock while everyone scattered out dozens of side tunnels.

As he stepped carefully around the slack-jawed, sprawling rush junkies, John glanced up to see if Joanne was working her cage. Ten of them hung from the ceiling above the central trench where pros danced and hooked. The only folks with money to climb the ladders were usually rich crackers from the other side of the bridge slumming it with the Ghetto rats for a thrill.

She worked her usual spot at the very center of the party. The balding, fat man behind her had the vacant stare of someone coming down from rush. Well, as long as he paid well.

John waved and caught her eye. Her face lit up when she spotted him. When she saw David, she smiled even more. She glanced at her trick and crossed her eyes briefly before throwing her head back, shaking out her hair and calling out a string of Spanish nonsense words.

John laughed. "Joanne's here."

David looked up.

John waited for it.

David's face lit up when he spotted her then changed to a very surprised expression. He looked back at John with daggers in his eyes.

"You might have warned me."

"Oh crap." Jamie threw John's hand away. "I am never going to get used to that."

John chuckled and waited for the inevitable punch to the arm from David. Joanne liked both guys because they weren't always trying to make her the way the others did. John suspected David had a bit of a crush on her, but it was one of the few things his cousin wouldn't talk about. Ever. Probably embarrassed at just how far out of his league he'd be. Joanne had politicians and minor net stars as customers.

"Coz, why don't you ask her out?" John threw an arm around David.

David elbowed him. "I'm not going to dignify that—"

"See, that's how I know you have a crush on her."

"I do not."

"Well, then tell me who you do have a crush on, and I will leave you alone with your unrequited love." John patted David's back and released him so he could pick his way over passed out rush junkies.

David grabbed his shoulder. He pointed with his chin.

Rocky lay a few feet away grinning at the stars overhead, hands moving slowly above him.

David scowled and knelt down. Jamie sighed and crouched nearby.

"Why don't you head over to the bar," John suggested. "Billy's there."

Jamie shook her head while David tried to revive Rocky. "I want to find Tracey first."

"No, you don't."

She opened her mouth.

"You really don't," John insisted. "Not just yet. She's with Barry." He raised an eyebrow. "*With* with."

"Drinks it is then." Understanding lit Jamie's eyes. She ran off.

"Are you in there, Rocky?" David helped Rocky to his knees.

"He has time left." A hand tugged on the sleeve of John's jacket. A little Black girl with blonde hair looked up with all seriousness. Jesus, she couldn't be any older than Layla, and she was already dealing rush?

"Come out of it, coz." David had both hands on Rocky's face. "It's not safe in there."

"Shit." Rocky's eyes cleared. "What the hell?"

"I think he's had enough for tonight." John looked at the girl.

"No refunds." The girl turned away, crouched down and pulled a jack from a woman's neck. "Time's up, lady." She lifted the edges of her skirt with dainty fingers and stepped over the unconscious woman.

"Can you stand?" David had an arm around Rocky now.

"Give me a minute." He shrugged out of David's hands. "What the hell? I had time left. I paid for that." He made a grab for the data drive in David's hand. A data drive?

"Jesus, Rocky, you installed a port?" John asked. Only hardcore junkies had themselves wet-wired. Most used a wireless halo.

"It's for work." He touched the back of his neck and scowled. "I run data for these guys."

"The DIs are still in the Ghetto." David rose to his feet. "It's not safe to spark out."

"You're not my father." He pushed to his feet.

David stared at him.

"Man." Rocky seemed to realize he sounded like a kid. "You cats know how to ruin a party. I'm out of here."

"Rocky." David took his arm with one hand. "Just go home and sleep it off tonight."

"I feel fine." He pulled out of David's grasp. "Wait a minute. I really feel fine." He scowled at David. "What did you do?"

"I just woke you up." David held his hands up.

"Whatever." He brushed past John and headed toward the exit.

John watched him go. "He'll just go over to the Temporary Building."

"At least we tried." David broke the data drive in half.

"You think he really uses the port for work?" They made their way over to a ladder barside.

David climbed up first. "Even if he does, it's probably not for anything we want to know about." And that was saying a lot.

Jamie sat at the bar sipping a drink, her back very pointedly to the dance floor. Two glasses waited on the bar beside her.

"How's my favorite family?" Billy reached across the bar and kissed John. "Still causing trouble I hope?"

John felt the heat rise to his cheeks. He fought the urge to adjust himself more comfortably.

"Of course," Jamie said. "We blew up Grand Central Station just this morning."

"You should have seen the mushroom cloud." John made explosion noises and pulled his hands apart. "A thing of beauty."

"Speaking of beauty..." Billy winked at Jamie. "Looking extra, extra, hot stuff."

"Thanks." She blushed.

"What do we owe you?" John took his drink.

"For getting that line to move faster?" Billy winked again. "First drink's on the house."

"Thanks." John blushed again and ducked his head

"If only I weren't a married man." Billy blew John a kiss, then turned his attention to David. "You too, sexy quiet one." He reached over the bar, but he only kissed David on the cheek. Well, he likely flirted with John more because he tipped better. With the Senator's cash burning a hole in John's pocket, Billy was certain to make a killing tonight.

Over on the dance floor, Barry jumped up and down, waving.

John waved back. . . then spotted Noah.

"Man, he *really* needs to find a mattress." John jabbed a finger several times at Noah, then at Jamie beside him.

Barry's eyes opened wide, and he elbowed Noah, who scowled, then followed Barry's pointing finger. He looked directly into John's eyes, then glanced at Jamie. His eyes sprung wide open. Jamie was like a little sister to both of John's best friends.

John shook his head and leaned closer to Jamie. "It'll be safe to dance in five, four, three, two. . ."

Noah and the girl he'd been making moved off to the trench to finish their business, and Barry flashed a thumb's up with one hand. He held Tracey's hand in the other. He kissed her knuckles, and she smiled as they made their way to the bridge that crossed the divide.

"One."

The music changed. The Hitchcock theme cut in with a crazy swing remix. Lots of trumpet and clarinet with a hardcore back beat.

"Perfect timing!" Jamie sucked down the rest of her drink. "I love this song." She jumped off her bar stool and kissed John's cheek. "Ghetto swing rocks the planet." She kissed David's cheek. "Less sex, more violins."

She ran off, latching onto Tracey and dragging her back over the bridge that crossed the trench. Tracey waved at John, just a trace of embarrassment in her eyes. The way Jamie pulled her friend close, she had to be asking how she'd hooked up with Barry.

"Looks like Barry has a girlfriend." David's smile seemed wistful.

"At least for tonight." John sipped his drink.

Jamie grabbed Barry, who spun her a few times and dropped her into a dip. Okay, Barry would take care of her while John and David imbibed a bit more liquid encouragement. They'd been coming to parties at Babylon for almost two years now, but John still felt protective of Jamie. She had tech genius, but she didn't know a lot about some things. Like guys.

"It's not as if we know so much more than she does." David's voice in John's ear startled him.

"I thought I was a manwhore." John sipped his drink.

David smiled. "The manwhore virgin."

"You know she'd hit the parties on her own if we didn't bring her with us." John watched her dance with Barry and Tracey, both of whom were stripped to the waist now. The moves were sexy, but not too sexy.

Noah and his date joined the trio, and Noah introduced the girl, who shook hands politely then moved off into the crowd.

Noah stared after her helplessly.

"Demolished." John sipped his drink.

Addison watched Senator Chase fuck a whore in a cage. He wouldn't have guessed that blowhard had so much stamina. He was also pretty spry for a fat, old man.

"So. . ." The man across the table drummed his fingers impatiently. "Why are we *here* exactly? Seems an odd place for a meeting."

The go-go fag with their drinks allowed Addison to keep McCarthy in suspense. Two drinks hit the table, and the bartender turned to go.

"Hey." McCarthy stopped him with a wad of cash between two fingers.

"Thank you, sir." Bright blue eyes flicked Addison's way so briefly he'd have missed it had he not been looking for it.

"For both of us." McCarthy favored Addison with a predatory grin. Stupid men loved to impress colleagues by flashing money around, even when it was obvious they hadn't been expected to pay in the first place.

"Excuse me." Addison caught the young man's attention with his own wad of cash.

The bartender had natural blond hair and a perfect body that the tiny red shorts did little to conceal. There was only one reason an Aryan like him would live in the Ghetto. He took the money from Addison and slipped it into the waistband of his shorts without looking at it.

"What can I do for you?"

"You know a lot of these kids, right?" Addison turned his attention to the dance floor across the trench. "Part of the job?"

"I know what they drink, mostly."

Addison smiled. It was a smart answer, but also obviously a lie. He'd been watching the way the kid flirted and chatted with his customers. The better he knew them, the more they tipped. Or perhaps it was the other way around.

"The young lady at the end of the bar. Red dress." Addison had picked her at random. "What does she drink?"

"Whiskey sour." The bartender smiled. "With mushrooms."

Addison smiled back. "Make her one for me?"

"Of course, sir." His obvious relief that he hadn't been asked for information told Addison he must have information he knew would be dangerous to his clientele.

Addison nodded, and the bartender dashed off.

"She's a lovely one." McCarthy steepled his fingers with a smug expression that told Addison he thought he now knew the reason for their meeting place. Idiot.

"If you like hookers." Addison opened the satellite app on his cell but didn't activate the hologram.

The map of Babylon filled with red dots that showed him every chip in the place. At full scale, the screen resembled a beehive. He zoomed in. He zoomed in again so he could match the path of the bartender to the movement of his dot on the cell. He tapped the dot and the screen opened the bartender's file.

"Well, I thought so," he said.

"You thought what?" McCarthy asked.

"I figured he had to be queer." Addison showed him the tablet. "Blond? Blue eyes? In the Ghetto?" He set the tablet down between them. "Husband and kid. Must be pretty principled to end up here rather than find a fake wife somewhere out there." He tapped the screen back to the chip tracker.

McCarthy shifted uncomfortably in his seat. Addison tapped on a random dot. The screen had a name and nothing more.

"Not even a God damned number for this one." He tapped another. It came up just as empty. "Well, that's a coincidence. Two in a row that haven't been updated?"

"We lost most of the data in the Makabee virus," McCarthy said.

"But if you'd gone door to door immediately afterward and swabbed them the way you were told, I'd have a complete record." Addison closed the tablet and folded his hands on the table.

"They're just a bunch of Ghetto rats." McCarthy leaned closer. "What difference does it make?"

"I'm trying to find a terrorist cell hiding with these Ghetto rats." Addison held himself perfectly still. "If you'd done your job ten years ago, my job today would be as easy as shooting fish in a barrel."

"How was I supposed to know?" Apparently, McCarthy was going to try to blow it off as unimportant. Wrong move.

"You weren't supposed to know." Addison pulled out a cigarette. "You were supposed to do your fucking job."

"And who are you to tell me my job?" McCarthy rose. "You're just some flunky for Dickerson."

Addison inhaled and tapped the tablet. The hologram popped up with a very clear video of McCarthy making it with a Black prostitute.

"I'm also the man who has about ten hours of similar footage with a bevy of hookers."

"Is this blackmail?" McCarthy went pale and waved a hand through the hologram to dispel it. He took his seat.

"Call it incentive. I need you to form a large enough team to swab the cheeks of everyone in the Ghetto in a week."

McCarthy laughed. "That would cost millions."

"You can pay for that with the money you're making here tonight."

"What does that mean?" McCarthy squinted at him through the smoke. "What does this party have to do with me?"

"You run it. You get kickbacks from the bar, from the cages, from the white noise."

"That's ridiculous." McCarthy slugged back his drink.

Addison tapped his tablet again. A series of charts and graphs appeared, all of them detailing the profit and loss for the Babylon events. Pierce was quite good at his research.

"How the hell—" McCarthy rose to his feet. "How the fuck did you get those files?"

"*That* is who I am to tell you how to do your job." Addison inhaled. "I have clearance that would make the president jealous."

"Fuck you."

"Not my type, now sit down before I have one of my fifteen undercover DIs put a bullet in your head."

After a glance around, McCarthy sat.

"Good." Addison settled himself more comfortably. "Now, you're going to do as I asked, and you are going to fund it personally with your exquisitely laundered money so there isn't a trail even my assistant can find. You're going to do it fast, and you're going to do it quietly."

The bartender appeared with new drinks. He took the old glasses.

McCarthy emptied his glass in one swallow and didn't even pretend he needed to pay Billy. Addison held out a large bill.

"Thank you, sir." The fag disappeared.

"If you'd done your job the way you should have," Addison pointed out, "neither of us would be in this predicament you've created."

"It'll bankrupt me." McCarthy glared. "You have to know that."

"Oh, I'm very aware of it. But it's that or I not only show that video to your wife and have you imprisoned for any of a dozen laws you've broken, but I'll also find a porn star with the world's biggest cock to rape you both."

McCarthy grabbed the edge of the table.

"And he'll make sure to leave her pregnant."

McCarthy leapt up and threw the table over. He pointed his gun at Addison's forehead. Gasps sounded around them, and the crowd made room. Apparently, no one wanted blood stains on their party clothes.

Addison held McCarthy's desperate glare. Would a bullet to the head kill a man so quick he didn't feel it? He'd have Pierce look that up if he had the chance.

The gun wavered.

The fact that none of the event's official security made a move proved beyond a shadow of a doubt that McCarthy was their boss.

He spat at Addison and holstered his gun. The spittle hit Addison's shoulder. He ignored it.

McCarthy stalked off without a word.

"I told him I fucked his sister last night." Addison regarded the curious crowd. "Who knew he'd be the jealous type?"

Nervous laughter rippled across the platform, but the party returned to normal.

"I am so sorry, sir." Billy appeared to reset the table. "Let me get you another drink."

"Not necessary but thank you."

The go-go fag wiped a towel over the table and retreated with the empty glasses.

Addison surveyed the crowd. For all he knew the little biological freak was right there with him. In shooting distance.

John recognized the guy in the Armani suit as the Dick from the street the other night, the one looking for a mouthy Ghetto rat in a synagogue. He turned to ask if David recognized him.

David sat hunched on his bar stool, staring into an empty glass. Yep. Must have.

Billy pressed between them and dropped two glasses and a wet towel on the other side of the bar. He smelled of musky cologne and sweat.

"Who's the Armani?" John asked before Billy could dash off.

"No one you want to know." He met John's eyes with fear in his own. He leaned closer. "If you knew, he'd kill you."

"Doesn't seem the type to do his own killing." John thought about the old crazy the younger guy had killed, but half the reason he kept talking was to keep Billy close. The man really *was* sex on a cracker.

"You'd be surprised." Billy grabbed a clean towel and dashed off.

David stared at John with half a smile. "Manwhore."

John almost spat his drink, but at least David had stopped brooding.

The Armani rose and moved toward the rubble at the end of the platform.

"It's the guy." John scooted closer.

"I know it's the guy."

"What do you think he wants?"

"How would I know what he wants?"

"Sometimes you know stuff."

"And sometimes I don't." And there he was, back to brooding.

"How's yer hammers hanging, old sweats?" Barry grabbed John, lifted him off the floor, and kissed him.

"Hi Barry, nice to see you, too." John tasted whiskey. "But stop pulling your vocabulary from the net." He ruffled his friend's unruly black curls. Shirtless and glistening with sweat, Barry was a perfect statue cut from marble.

The Greek god furrowed his brows and nudged John, indicating David with an exaggerated sidelong glance. David stared at the Armani, who now stood atop the rubble watching the dance floor.

John pressed close. "Armani on the rocks."

"A new drink?" Barry did a double take.

John laughed and pointed with his chin. "The Dick from the other day is over there on the rubble."

"Oh!" Barry mouthed the words, *mouthy Jewish guy*.

John nodded. Barry raised his eyebrows and lifted one finger. He settled beside David, who had turned his attention to his drink again.

"Find the meaning of life in there?" Barry swirled his finger in the glass.

"Not yet, but I will." David almost smiled.

"So you can tell us what it is about this guy that kettles you, or I will be forced to blow you publicly." Barry poked David's cheek.

John choked on his drink.

"Yeah." Barry's brow furrowed. "I don't think that saying's going to catch on no matter how many A-list actors say it." He dropped an arm around David and pulled him close. "Tell me your deal with this guy, or I will embarrass you publicly." He pressed his lips to David's ear. "This is a party, coz, and you aren't even drunk, yet." Barry had no boundaries whatsoever.

Beyond them, the Armani picked his way around the rubble at the end of the tunnel. David continued to sulk.

"You leave me no choice then." Barry sucked in a deep breath and spun around to include the entire platform. "Ladies and gentleman, boys and girls, as well as everyone within and outside those parameters. . ."

David grabbed him from behind and clamped a hand over his mouth. Barry bent forward and flipped David completely over his back, snatching at his jacket, slowing him as he fell in a pile at Barry's feet. He took David's hat and dropped it onto his own head, looking down with his hands in fists on his hips.

"I may be drunk, my good friend, but you still can't surprise me." He hauled David to his feet, then spread his arms wide with a clownish grin. "Ha-cha-cha-cha." He engulfed David in a bear hug. "It's a party, coz."

"I just feel the weight of the world once in a while." David took him in a headlock.

A shiver ran across John's neck, and he looked up. The Armani stood framed in the light of the exit tunnel. He stared at David and Barry. Then his eyes shifted, and he met John's gaze. He smiled, nodded, and touched the brim of his hat before disappearing behind the rocks.

Blast it. Getting that man's attention could *not* be a good thing.

David and Barry danced Ghetto swing, and David's smile melted John's concern. He looked so much better when he smiled.

"Sorry about the gloom." David grinned. "It's all typical teenage angst bullshit, I guess." He pushed Barry away.

"Ahhhh, Teenage Angst Bullshit," Barry proclaimed dramatically with one hand in the air and the other tugging on a suspender. "Teenage Angst Bullshit? I know the cure for that!" He turned to get Billy's attention.

"And this one's on you for sweating all over my nicely ironed shirt." David poked him in the side.

"Right on ya." Barry giggled like a little girl.

While Barry ordered, David caught John's eye. He smiled a real smile, the honest one when it was just the two of them hunkered in the moonlight in their room talking into the wee hours of the morning.

"Sorry."

John shrugged and shook his head. David had no reason to apologize. David's eyes grew brighter. They flashed. A laser must have hit them or something.

Addison strode down the abandoned subway tunnel. That was them. Absolutely. He passed Pierce, who talked to a clutch of DIs. He grabbed his assistant's jacket and dragged him away so abruptly that Pierce dropped his cell. The hologram flashed and winked out.

"He's here." He held Pierce's coat in both fists. "I fucking saw the little bastard with my own God damn eyes."

Pierce's eyes opened wide, and he seemed to forget about the cell.

"The Indian half-breed, too. I'm sure of it. I looked right in his face, and it was like looking into that motherfucking redskin's eyes, I swear to God." He pushed Pierce away. "Ha!"

"What do we do, sir?"

A good question. Stumbling onto them was a fluke. No way would he allow anything to blow this.

"Contact the DIs. Get them spread evenly around the platform at every side entrance. Once they're in place, we'll send them all a photo of the science project and tell them to kill every fucking Ghetto rat at that party, but I want that little bastard alive."

"Alive at all costs?"

"Alive if we can." Shit. "But if he's dead, the body better damn well have recognizable DNA."

Pierce cleared his throat.

"What?"

"I believe there are a few fairly important—"

"Kill them, too," Addison insisted. "If some stupid politicians are dumb enough to show up here instead of throwing a party in their own God damned mansions, they deserve whatever happens to them. Even you can afford a whore who makes house calls."

"Very good, sir."

John's heart raced the pounding drums.

The booze in his veins upped the ante.

At some point, his shirt, jacket, and hat ended up in a pile with David's. The lights and lasers spun him dizzy. He danced with Tracey, until she took control and twirled him away so she could dance with Barry again. John laughed, crashed into someone and hung on to keep from falling.

"John!" It was David.

"David!" John laughed and kissed David's cheek as his cousin held him close and turned them both in pivots to the end of a swing song. "Yee-ha!"

The music changed, and John pulled back enough to focus on David's face. Nope. Too much liquor in his system to focus. David's face kept dividing in two, so John grabbed it with both hands to keep it together. He chuckled. David's face couldn't actually split in two.

The new song was slower, more dangerous, darker. David slowed their movements. John followed with his hips. He threw his arms over David's shoulders and let his head fall forward onto David's sweating chest. David's scent was almost as familiar as his own. It was the smell of safety and comfort. He smelled like home. And armpits.

John chuckled and looked up into David's eyes, hoping some kind of joke came to him when their eyes met.

Stars filled David's eyes. More stars than John had ever seen.

John shook his head, and David's eyes returned to normal. A reflection from the hologram? It had to be.

"You okay?" David asked.

"Okee-dokee." John let his head fall back and relaxed his knees, his arms slack at his sides.

David grabbed John's belt loops, keeping balance for both of them. Wow, drunk! As they moved together, David's bare skin slid against John's. His hips shifted against John's. Wow, sexy.

What the what? Too wow drunk!

John hauled himself upright and dropped his hands on David's shoulders to steady himself and move away. "I think I need some air. . ."

David's eyes fell away into vast chasms of darkness.

The sounds of the party receded, as if everything had dropped under water, *and the endless void of David's eyes drew John in.*

Stars spun and swirled. There in the center shone a single nova brighter than the rest. David's heartbeat filled John. He felt it in his bones.

He floated in star-filled space.

John closed his eyes and shook his head to clear it.

When he opened them again, *he and David stood across a stream in a rocky desert. The sun beat down on them like it wanted them dead.*

David's skin was dark and creased. His hair hung long and shaggy to his shoulders. A thick beard covered his face.

"Why are you afraid of this?" David spoke in a voice so much deeper than the one John knew.

John stepped away. He couldn't breathe.

He couldn't take his eyes from David's face.

He stumbled. . .

And Babylon came crashing back. The music pounded so loud it hurt his ears. The floor jumped and shifted under his feet. The cries of the dancers sounded like screams. Wait. They *were* screams.

The floor danced under his feet again. An earthquake! John tripped and fell on his ass. Pebbles rattled on the bare concrete.

David stood over him with the hologram of a galaxy over his head. He was eighteen again, without the beard. He held a hand down to John. But what the hell had he seen in David's eyes? Stars? In his eyes?

John scuttled away, turned, and pushed to his feet.

Rather than the pandemonium he'd expected, the party just cranked up a notch, as if a minor earthquake was part of the entertainment package. The tremors subsided, and the screams returned... but joyous now. They'd survived.

A hand grabbed John's arm. He spun. Barry.

"You okay, coz?"

"Drunk. Way too drunk." The floor swung out from under his feet.

"Whoa there." Barry's arms wrapped around John and supported him. "Earthquake's over, my friend."

"His eyes." John latched onto Barry's arms. "Did you see his eyes?"

"Yeah, there's something about him these days, isn't there?"

That's not what John meant. His heart wouldn't slow down.

Jamie appeared at his other side. She still wore her shirt. Good.

David pushed through the crowd toward him.

"Maybe you should be telling *him*. . ." Barry patted John's chest with one hand.

Then the lights went out. All of them.

Shrieks filled the darkness for ten seconds then emergency lights flashed on. Screams turned to embarrassed laughter. The hologram above them stuttered with static.

Across the platform, the few dancers with cells hauled them out, and the holograms sputtered the exact same static as the ceiling.

"Oh, shit." Jamie gathered everyone they knew. "This is going to get weird folks. I hope to God you turned off your cells before coming out tonight."

The static above them flashed white. Dozens of scrolls appeared above them. All the holograms on the cells across the dance floor showed the same image.

"It's Makabee," Jamie said. "A new virus. He set it to piggyback the next earthquake alert."

"That is *wacky*." Barry whooped and gave Jamie a high five. "How do you even know this?"

"A girl has to keep a few secrets." She settled into one hip.

The scrolls opened.

The amendments. Every agent's cell had popped up a hologram with a different amendment on it. Freedom of speech. Freedom of religion. Freedom to bear arms.

"Motherfucking Makabee!" Addison shouted. It had to be him, or them, or whoever the fuck Makabee really was. "How bad is this?"

"I don't. . ." Pierce's face turned gray in the emergency lights. "It's not good, sir." He held up a cell. "I'm not connected to any public server. This signal is our own motherfucking satellite. He's in there, too."

The fourth amendment scrolled over the open parchment.

Had Addison ever heard Pierce curse before?

"If he got his virus onto *this*?" Pierce shook his head.

"Just fucking spit it out."

"Every single database in the country could be erased."

That wasn't possible. It couldn't be. Addison's blood ran hot.

"Tell me we have our shit backed up on fucking paper somewhere."

Pierce shook his head.

"Fuck!"

The men stood around waiting for orders. Addison had no time to think. They were there. He was so fucking close.

"Go. Kill them all." He pointed. "Now. Kill them or truss them up like Christmas turkeys. Leave a few for questioning."

Shit. They looked confused. A siren sounded. An alarm that the party was being raided. Fuck!

"Go!" Addison shook an arm. "Kill them! Kill them all! They are terrorists who would rape your daughters in their beds."

The men moved. They ran.

He needed information. Pierce was useless without his precious net. Who would know more about the people at that party than anyone?

Wait. One man there had information.

Cool water flowed over Addison. He headed to the bar.

"Come on, Pierce. I think I need a drink."

A raid siren screamed. Everybody froze.

Then all hell broke loose.

"Dicks." Barry shoved John into motion.

The sirens burst through John's drunken fog. The adrenaline didn't hurt. People ran every which way, pulling on clothes, some of them not bothering. John felt his shirt and coat pressed into his hands. David, his face worried but not because of the Dicks.

"Come on." John threw an arm around him and pulled him along. "Just teenage angst bullshit." There would be time for all that later.

David nodded.

Where was Jamie? Right behind. Okay. And the others? Already moving. They shoved through the mob to the ladder directly below Joanne's cage. She held the door open and waved them up. John drove his visions aside as he pushed David's ass so he'd climb faster.

"Go!" Joanne passed him through the cage and up a second ladder into the ceiling. She unhooked the ladder and let the cage drop. She gave John a push to hurry him through the hatch and followed quickly behind.

The crawl space above the tunnel was dark and cramped. Shouts and sirens followed them even after the hatch closed.

A sudden light startled John.

"Someone detach the cage." Joanne flashed the light around

and dug into a stash of clothes for a pair of jeans. "We aren't safe yet." She pointed at a latch on the floor as she grabbed a t-shirt.

Jamie pulled the latch. There was a long squeal of metal then shouts and a loud thump that rattled the tunnel.

"Who do I have?" Joanne flashed her light from face to face.

Barry and David were there, of course, and Jamie. Noah had made it, thank God, and Tracey. The light lingered a moment over the little blonde girl who worked the white noise. It barely paused on the face of the middle-aged cracker who must have been Joanne's trick. "Okay folks, we should—"

Gunshots exploded over the sounds of the sirens.

Everyone jumped.

"Follow me." Joanne squeezed to the front.

"Are you okay?" David grabbed John's neck as he passed. His eyes were dark and human.

"I'm fine." John grabbed his wrist. "Let's just get through this."

David nodded and moved him along. Of course, John had to go first. David would always have his back.

Billy grabbed the latch on a trapdoor behind the bar, but strong hands stopped him.

"Hey there, Billy. I'd like a word with you before you go." It was the Armani who'd pissed off Mr. McCarthy. Shit. He knew Billy's name. That was bad.

"What do you want?" Billy tried to keep his voice steady. "We need to get out of here."

"These are my boys." The man pulled out a cigarette and lit it. "They won't bother you while you're with me."

Oh shit, that was bad, too.

Dicks filled Babylon, more than Billy had ever seen in one place. They shouted at the customers who hadn't escaped fast enough. They grabbed people and threw them to the floor, beating them. There were local cops, too, but something was different. They wore the uniforms, but most of them had to be Dicks. He'd never seen so many cops.

Shots rang out. Holy shit.

Half a dozen bodies fell. Screams once again filled Babylon.

"Oh shit." Billy shook. "This is bad."

The Armani smoked his cigarette as peaceful as could be.

"Oh shit, oh shit, oh shit, oh shit. . ."

The guy stood there, smoking, waiting.

"What do you want?"

"Why don't we start with a bottle of gin?" The man held out a hand.

Billy took a bottle from the bar with trembling hands and passed it over. The Armani took the bottle, checked the label and winced.

"This is the cheap stuff, Billy." In one swift movement, he smashed the bottle across the side of Billy's head.

When Billy could see again, he lay sprawled across the bar on his stomach, alcohol burning his eyes. Strong hands held him in place, a couple of Dicks must've joined the Armani.

Across the platform, a Dick beat the head of some junkie who screamed and screamed until his skull split open and his brain sprayed the concrete. The Dick kept pounding.

One of them pinned Billy's left arm behind his back, and someone held his right hand flat on top of the bar.

The Armani flicked his cigarette to the floor and stared down at Billy with nothing in his face. No pleasure. No horror. Nothing.

"What do you want?" Billy was too afraid to struggle. "Just tell me what you want!"

"Do you know why your hand is on the bar, Billy?" The Armani touched the back of Billy's right hand with the tip of his index finger.

Billy shook his head.

"That's the hand that will guarantee your honesty."

Sobs bubbled up from Billy's chest.

"Do I make myself clear?"

Billy nodded. Tears and gin blinded him. A muffled, far-off explosion rattled the bottles. Billy winced. When he opened his eyes again, the Armani's face peered at him from inches away.

"The teenage kike." The man stank of cigarettes. "The kike with the gypsy and the spic who looks more like a redskin. What's his name?"

"I don't know who you're talking about." What the hell was he saying? "I don't know."

"Wrong answer." The man pulled away and Billy felt cold steel pressed against his index finger for one brief moment before a blast of pain tore through his hand.

Billy screamed. He struggled to pull his arm away. The hand on his neck pressed down so hard he could barely breathe. He coughed.

"Let's try that one again." The man's lips whispered against his ear. "A little more politically correct perhaps. Jewish kid, eighteen, wrestling around with a Gypsy Muslim and a teenage Tonto. . . maybe he says he's Mexican. They came in with a pretty White girl."

Oh shit. Billy stopped struggling. He couldn't inform on his favorite family. Compared to the rest of his regulars, those kids were so innocent. So kind.

"You know who I'm talking about, now?" The man's breath stank of stale smoke and disease.

"Fuck you." Billy braced himself to die.

"Wrong answer." The man pressed his gun to Billy's wrist.

Bam! Billy screamed again. Please God, let him pass out or die.

"This can take a very long time." The man spat the words directly into Billy's ear. "Or we can get it over quickly and get you to a doctor while you still have a hand to jack off your husband." He dropped his voice to a whisper. "His name's Matthew, isn't it?" He kissed Billy's ear. "Matthew. Matt, Matty, Matt, Matt, Matt."

The world fell silent. The guy knew his family.

"And what about Nora?"

The only sound Billy heard was his own heartbeat.

Not his daughter. Please, God, not his daughter.

"Who is the Jewish kid?"

"David." Billy closed his eyes and prayed for death. He prayed this monster would leave his family alone once he had what he wanted. "His name is David."

"David?" The man yanked Billy's other arm out from behind his back and held it down on the bar. "You wouldn't be lying to me would you?"

"No!" Billy screamed. "David." His voice faded to a hoarse whisper. "His name's David." David would get away. They'd all get away from this madman. They had to.

"I guess David makes sense. Now give me a last name. Something tells me in the New Jerusalem here, there's a lot of guys named David."

"I don't know!" Billy struggled against the Dicks. "He never told me his last name. Nobody here uses last names!"

The men holding him pulled him away from the bar and then slammed him back onto it. There was no getting away. And if they killed him, if they didn't get what they wanted from him. . . What would they do to Matthew? To Nora?

"He has a sister Jamie and a. . . and a. . . brother, no! A cousin. . . John!"

"First names don't mean shit, cocksucker!" The Armani slammed Billy's arm against the bar and squeezed his forearm with a grip like a vise, pressed the gun against the joint where the palm met the wrist. "Say goodbye to Rosy Palm and her five ugly sisters unless you come up with a last name!"

"I don't know!" Billy screamed, thrashing, terrified and blind. "I don't know!"

"Say goodbye!"

"I don't know!" Billy shouted it again and again. His shouts turned to sobs as the man released his arm and took a step away. Billy wept into the sticky wood of the bar. "I don't know."

"I guess you're probably telling the truth." He dropped the gun to his side. "Back off."

The men released Billy. He pulled his ruined arm to his chest and held it tightly with the other. He leaned against the bar. Would they leave his family alone? Would they leave him alive? If they did, could he warn David and his family in time?

Would they ever forgive him?

Billy wiped his face and looked out across the platform. The siren had shut off. Bodies lay strewn across the concrete. Sobs and whimpers filled the air. Dicks walked through the bodies, scanning chips.

"You sure you don't know a last name?" the Armani asked.

"I don't know." Billy fought the urge to vomit.

The gun flashed up.

Bang! The concussion blew out the back of the bartender's skull and tossed his body off the bar to the floor. Addison stared down at the go-go fag's body. He hadn't known enough. Damn it. Maybe, *maybe* with the right algorithm he could match the names. What a fucking waste of time. He shot the body again and again. Fucking Makabee. He'd been so close.

"You okay, boss?" some idiot asked.

Addison shot the nosy DI in the head. Another body for the cleanup crew.

"Anyone else have a question?" Addison demanded.

Pierce stood a few feet away. Their eyes met. They were so God damn close to retrieving that little bastard. So God damn close. They'd worked this fucking case together almost twenty years.

For the very first time, Addison wanted to talk to Pierce. Maybe have a fucking beer and curse Makabee until they both felt better. Isn't that what people did?

What the fuck did Addison know about what people did? He looked out over the platform. How many bodies would he need to justify this time? Wait. Maybe there was still a chance.

"How many holes to the surface are there?" he asked.

"Not a lot, sir." Pierce didn't squirm under his gaze. Never had.

"We have napalm?"

"Better than napalm, sir. Much better." Was that a smile?

Addison holstered his weapon and pulled out a cigarette.

Pierce held out a lighter.

Yeah. Fuck talking.

Addison lit up and headed for the exit. "Roll it in."

Periodic gunshots and screams echoed through the service ducts as John followed Barry's butt in a bewildering maze.

Only Joanne knew the route. She'd kept it secret, which made sense. That way she could never be left behind. If only she knew they'd never do that, but she hadn't grown up with them, and she was older. She'd had a rough life.

John bumped into Barry's thigh. The caravan had halted.

Voices reached them from below. Close. Lights flickered through a nearby vent. Two local cops crept through the subway tunnel, rifles up and ready. The lights strapped across their chests cast confusing shadows on their faces, but John recognized the voice of Noah's father instantly.

"We aren't going to get any sleep tonight," Jonas King said.

"I'm telling you. . ." The other cop was a cracker, and he looked nervous. "If those assholes go from house to house taking swabs of every Jewish kid in the Ghetto, we're going to have another riot."

"What difference will it make?" Jonas' voice stayed low and gravelly. "They don't want us around."

"No?"

"Nope, this shit belongs to the DIs. They want us to stay way the hell out of it. I say they want to give me the day off and start a riot, let'em." His voice faded as they made their way around a corner. "There sure are a hell of a lot of the bastards, though."

What an asshole. John hoped Noah could keep it together. He hated his father so much.

The group waited in silence for a minute, then Joanne opened the vent, and the caravan crawled down into the open passage: a junction of five tunnels littered with broken crates and subway debris. Shredded cables crisscrossed the space. The faint light from Joanne's lantern cast crazy shadows.

One tunnel grew teeth and opened like a cavernous mouth. . .

John jumped back into Noah, who grabbed him. "You okay?"

"I'm fine." The tunnel was just a tunnel. John had to keep it together. He gave Noah his attention. "Are you okay?"

"Fuck him." He spat. "You can't pick your parents."

"Righteously spoken." Barry squeezed Noah's shoulder.

John sympathized. A lot of folks in the Ghetto gave Noah crap because of his dad, like he had any control over the man.

"How do we get to the streets?" Joanne's trick asked. He seemed uncomfortable with so many Ghetto rats near him. "Is there any way out of the Ghetto from here?"

Everyone stared at him. He expected them to tell him their secrets? What an idiot.

"Shhh." Joanne touched his lips with a fingertip. She handed out lights from a pack. "I heard about the Ghetto sweep earlier this evening. A client heard rumors but didn't have a go date. I doubt he suspected it would be this soon. I'm pretty sure the Dicks'll start about an hour before sunup. It's easier to catch everyone asleep in their beds."

"If they're starting at sunup. . ." Noah's face lost all expression, carved in onyx. "We have a couple hours to get info out to the people." He stared directly at David. "Unless they have the entire DI, FBI, and CIA, it'll take them all day to sweep everything. We can seriously fuck'em up." He smiled. "As usual."

A distant, muffled explosion echoed through the darkness. Everyone dove for cover. Another quake? All the lights snapped off, plunging the tunnel into blackness. No one even breathed.

Nothing happened. No aftershocks.

No explosions near enough to matter.

"I can get you to the surface." Joanne relit her lantern. "But I'm not sure that's a good idea for everyone."

"Who are they looking for?" Jamie pushed forward.

"I don't know for certain," Joanne said. "What I heard was they were going to go door to door, scanning chips, swabbing, and rebuilding the database. But he let it slip that they're really looking for a Jewish male between sixteen and twenty." Joanne stared at David.

"But why?" Jamie twisted the flashlight in her hands. "Why pick on Jewish men?"

"I told you, I don't know," Joanne insisted. "They're looking for someone in particular."

Barry was the one who said it. "A mouthy Jewish cat in a synagogue."

"What?" Jamie shone her light directly in his face.

"Something we overheard." Barry touched David, whose eyes were shadowed. "There's a Dick looking for a troublemaker."

Jamie scoffed. "That could be any of us."

"Young Jewish *dude*." Barry was emphatic. "He said so."

"The Dick was at Babylon." John held David's eyes. They didn't react. "I saw him." He didn't want to admit the next part. "He saw us, too. I'm certain."

David's eyes didn't change. What did that mean?

"What?" Barry paced. "Burn it."

"Why would they want you?" Jamie pushed into her brother's face. "You're nobody. You torqued off a Rabbi? Big deal. You do that every day ending in Y."

All eyes turned to David. He was the only Jewish guy there.

"I can't be in the Ghetto for this sweep." David turned to John. He needed help. He couldn't do what needed to be done alone.

Well, John had his back.

"We'll go out to Venice," John said. "I know a few places on Makabee's map. We can find them without a cell."

"Cells!" Jamie held up both hands. "Don't turn on your cells until I send you the patch to protect you from the scroll virus. It's on my system at home."

"Scroll virus?" Joanne's trick had his cell out. It was dead.

"Sorry, sir. You're screwed. Time for a new one." Jamie turned to John. "Venice? Seriously? For how long?"

"We have supplies in the tunnels." John held David's gaze. "We'll find an air pocket and hole up for a couple of days." They'd need to be underwater so no one could find a heat signature and to hide their chips.

"With aftershocks?" Jamie shook her head. "I don't like it."

"I don't either." John held Jamie's gaze. "I'd rather be out there helping you guys if there's a riot. But you heard Joanne. David needs to hide."

Jamie worked it through her stubborn head.

"And you need to make sure the rest of the family knows what's about to happen." John took her hand. "It's time to step up little sister and do what the big kids do. You get word out to the Ghetto. If anyone can find a way to work around the virus, it's you. You're Justice, right?"

"Fine. You're right. I'm a freakin' genius." She looked around. "If this goes full scale riot, we're all screwed." Her eyes fell on Joanne's trick. "I'm sure Mister. . .?"

"Smith."

Jamie rolled her eyes. "I'm sure Mr. Smith would like to go home to his wife."

Smith opened his mouth to speak, but Joanne shook her head and touched his lips again.

"I'll get him to the street." Joanne turned to the little girl. "I'll take you, too. What's your name?"

"Lilith." She strapped her light to her forehead. "I can find my own way. I know where I am." She ran off.

"Jamie?" David's voice was small. "I need you to tell our parents about the Dick. They'll cover for me."

Jamie nodded.

"Tracey, can you go with Jamie and watch her back?" David asked.

Tracey agreed. She kissed Barry and moved off.

"Take care of each other." Jamie hugged John and David.

"We always do." John kissed her cheek.

The women ran off.

"Me and Barry'll hit the streets." Noah stepped forward. "Door to door if we have to." He held up an open palm to David. "We need to let people know about this."

David slapped his palm. John did, too.

"I know you just want to go out there to search for hidden treasure, you blasted pirate." Barry grabbed John. He hugged David, then he and Noah ran off together.

"I love y'all." Joanne clucked her tongue and took David's face in her hands. "You almost make me feel like part of a family."

"You are part of the family." David hugged her fiercely. "You just saved us all."

"One day I swear you'll save the world." She touched his face and moved a bit away then led Mr. Smith down a side tunnel.

"I guess that settles it." John watched the last of the lights rattle away. "Let's leave vapor trails."

"There's something I need to do." What Noah needed to do, he had to do alone. He wouldn't drag Barry into his father's bullshit. He pulled up short and stopped his friend.

Barry arched an eyebrow.

"It'll just take a few minutes, and I'll catch you up topside."

"I'll help," Barry offered.

Noah shook his head. "I need to do this on my own."

Barry crossed his arms, scowling.

"Five minutes, I swear."

"I swear too, motherfucker, but it don't mean I speak truth."

He stared at Noah for several seconds. "Fuck." He shook his head. "Fine, but I'll be damned if you get away from me without a hug."

"Yeah, yeah, yeah." Noah grumbled, but he allowed Barry his affection and thumped his back once or twice for good measure. "Get on the streets. There's work to do."

"See you in the funny papers." Barry disappeared into the darkness.

Noah slipped through the tunnels quickly, aiming directly for a junction he knew his dad would hit. Slipping his miner's lamp into position, he pulled out a can of black spray paint and went to work.

"Stupid old man," he muttered. "Let's see what your buddies think about this piece of information."

A light hit him from behind.

"Hold it right there." His dad's voice.

A gun cocked and Noah froze.

"Hands up."

Noah complied.

"What the shit?" He must've read the message. A hand grabbed Noah's arm and spun him around. "Noah?"

His dad grabbed the spray paint from Noah's hand, grumbling and muttering under his breath. He looked his son up and down, took in his bare torso and sweat-stained slacks.

"You were at that party." Jonas shook his head. "You stupid, stupid punk. You're lucky you didn't get killed." He pushed past Noah and started spraying over the message.

"*I'm* stupid." Noah took a few steps away from his father and looked around to see if his old man had any backup. Didn't seem so. "You know they're killing people at parties, you do nothing about it. . . and *I'm* the stupid one." The tunnel was deserted. "Where's your partner?"

"They needed him somewhere else." His dad stepped back and checked his work.

"The White man was needed somewhere else?"

"'Officer Jonas is. . .' what exactly?" He tossed the can aside.

"A fine upstanding citizen." Noah hooked his thumbs in his

pants and faced his father, feet wide apart and hips forward. "Isn't that what you want everyone to think?"

"Yeah, I'm positive that's what you were going to write." Jonas snorted. "You love your old man so much you want to advertise for him."

"You only got one thing right in that whole sentence," Noah said. "You're an old man." He spoke again before his dad could hit him. "Rocky was there, too." He said it plain, as though he wasn't worried about his brother. "He was rushed out in the middle of the tracks like a landed trout." He knew his brother had made it out long before the trouble hit, but his dad didn't know that. "So if they were killing people—"

The back of his father's hand hit him so fast he didn't see it coming. He didn't blame the old man either. He'd meant to provoke him. It wasn't a hard hit.

"You know when they don't need you anymore, they're going to throw you away." Noah wiped his mouth with the back of his hand. His father hadn't even drawn blood.

"I guess I just need to make sure they need me."

What was that sound? It wasn't an explosion. Noah had once thrown an old spray can into a fire to see what it'd do. It didn't explode. It just sucked up the fire and blew it out. It was that kind of sound. More like an implosion. It came from both directions

His dad's face turned gray, and his eyes opened wide in disbelief.

A cool wind pulled at them from both directions at the same time.

"The White man was needed somewhere else." Noah closed his eyes and turned his face to a sky he'd never see again. Good thing Barry had that hug to remember. Things like that were important to him.

The manhole covers blew fifteen feet into the air, lifted by columns of plasma. Addison covered his face with one arm and turned away. Even a few of the ordinarily macho DIs called out in surprise.

By the time Addison looked again, the plasma had already been sucked back into the sewer tunnels and the manhole covers were ringing and clanging on the pavement.

"That'll do it, sir." Had Pierce even looked away? "As fast as the plasma was sucked back in, we blew a hole into the subway tunnels. Plenty of oxygen for the fire." He glanced at his wristwatch. "And. . . by now anyone down there is extra crispy."

"I had men down there." McCarthy sounded pissed.

"And now you don't." Addison walked into the antique electronics store he'd commandeered.

Pierce followed him and took his place at an old-fashioned computer. The equipment was safe because it hadn't been online in decades, but it was so old Pierce had had to jerry-rig pieces together to make it function in the first place. How the hell did that dot-head from India make any money from such shit? Well, everything old was new again, after all.

"Get me the president," Addison demanded. "I need helicopters and enough firepower to sink this island into the Atlantic for good."

Ruth lay awake, listening to the far-off sirens. The quake had been small enough, and Bo had already fallen back to sleep, bless his heart. The holograms above her played out their programs in the early morning hours.

Layla had slept right through the rumbling.

The other children were out in the world somewhere.

Well, Naomi had asked them to leave a note.

That's what she'd found in the boys' room: *Dancing at Babylon, getting our exercise.*

She'd had to ask Bo what that meant then wished she hadn't done so. At least she knew they weren't hurt. If they'd been injured in the quake, she'd have known.

Her dreams that night had been horrible. She'd seen Addison. In her very own kitchen. With a gun. The gunshot that woke her had been the start of the quake. Then she'd found the boys' note.

Well, no point in waking Bo with her tossing and turning. Her husband sprawled on his stomach, snoring. No point in lying there either.

Naomi was awake and already resetting the store. Ruth might as well help and wait for the children to return.

She slipped her bathrobe over her nightdress then passed through the workshop and into the store. As expected, Naomi had all the lights on. She swept the remains of a glass lamp. She didn't even look up at Ruth's entrance.

"The lamp was an embarrassment, anyway." Naomi looked up. "Don't tell Bo I said so."

Ruth smelled coffee and made her way to the pot while a siren wailed in the distance.

"I spoke with Zack yesterday." Naomi set her broom aside and picked up her coffee mug. "He told me to be strong, to wait just a little while, and we'd be together again."

"Zack came to you?" Ruth asked, missing the rest of what Naomi had said. They'd never had a visit from him before. Why now?

"To my room," Naomi said. "He was with Gabriel."

"Gabriel?" They'd had no visitors in so long. But something was wrong. "He's. . . all right, then?" And what was he? A ghost?

"He's wonderful." Naomi's eyes twinkled in the dim light. "He's. . ." She faltered. "He's perfect." She smiled a warm, gentle smile and shrugged innocently.

It was an expression Ruth hadn't seen in years. Her heart jumped as she remembered the first time she'd seen that look on her cousin's face.

Ruth had been all of eighteen. She'd known her parents would be furious once she worked up the courage to tell them about Addison's project. She'd had no idea how Bo would react. The last thing she expected was Naomi flying out the front door, engulfing her in hugs and kisses like a little girl.

"I've seen an angel!"

"So what's wrong?" Ruth sipped her coffee.

Naomi's face darkened.

"You had dreams," Ruth said.

Naomi nodded.

"Me, too." Ruth's hand shook, and she set the coffee cup on the table. She had enough of a mess to clean up without adding a broken cup. "It's been so long, Naomi."

"You almost started to believe it was *all* a dream, didn't you."

"Yes."

"Me, too." Naomi turned her cup. "What did you see?"

"He's back." Ruth shuddered. "I saw him in our kitchen with a gun. Either he's found us, or he will very soon."

"We've grown too comfortable." Naomi refilled her cup. "I hardly remember what to do."

"I doubt that's true." Ruth watched the sun warm the windows. "We'll know what to do when the time comes."

"We need to tell the children everything." Naomi started opening the shutters.

Ruth nodded. "They need to be prepared."

"Should we wake them?"

"They're out somewhere."

Naomi stiffened.

"The boys left a note, just like you asked."

"Be careful what you ask for." Naomi pursed her lips.

The sirens drew closer.

"I wonder where they could be." The rattle in Naomi's voice proved the tenuousness of her newfound strength.

The shop door banged open, and both women jumped. Jamie caught herself with one hand on the doorway as she swung inside, panting. She glanced around.

"We have to get the store boarded up." She closed the shutters Naomi had just opened. "Dozens of Dicks are on the streets."

Jamie's friend Tracey snuck inside and waved meekly.

"We had to detour and double back so much I wanted to scream." Jamie fought with a reluctant latch. "They're doing a sweep, and everyone expects riots all day long. We have to get things locked up."

"What the fuck are you talking about, Simon? I need copters scrambled *now*. I need this place erased." Addison gripped the old-fashioned telephone in a white-knuckled fist.

"Are you listening to yourself?" The president's voice was surprisingly clear over the ancient land line and infuriatingly calm. "I can't just blow Staten Island out of the water without provocation, Ghetto rats or not."

"Provocation? They're rioting in the streets." Even inside the little store, Addison could hear the shouts and gunshots.

"You started that riot, Stuart."

"No one needs to know that." If only his hand circled that fat bastard's neck instead of the cold, black, ancient phone receiver. "We can spin this to make it their fault."

"And that's fine, that's fine, but that sort of story takes a little time to figure out."

"I don't have—" Addison forced himself to stop screaming. "He is here. Now. Given a little time, who knows where he'll be?"

The line fell silent for several seconds.

"You need some space to clear your head," Clement said.

"Jesus fucking Christ, Simon, if you do this to me I'll—"

"You'll do what, you cuntlicking son of a bitch?" Clement shouted. "Don't forget who I am!"

How could Addison forget? The bastard reminded him every five minutes. He forced himself to breathe and held his tongue. Clement was as ruthless as Addison, and he paid all the fucking DIs. One word and they'd be only too happy to put a bullet in Addison's

178 J o h n   R o b e r t   M a c k

head. He'd done as much to three of them that night. Three? Four? Whatever.

"Are you breathing, Stuart?"

Addison sucked in a deep breath. A cigarette appeared, already lit, in Pierce's fingers. Addison took it.

"I'm breathing, Simon." Addison drew on the cigarette. "What would you like me to do?"

"Well, now, isn't it nice when we can have a civil discussion with no one needing to kill anyone else?" He chuckled.

If Addison found a way to do it, the smug bastard was dead.

"I have a copter on its way to pick you up," Clement said. "We're moving the Nevada operation to DC."

"But. . ." Holy shit, he *would* kill Clement. He forced his voice to stay calm. "While I understand that this move has been in the works for some time, is this the best time for it? Right. . . now?"

"We-e-ell, with all this internet nonsense to deal with, it makes sense. If we're rebuilding all those damn databases anyway, you know?"

Addison couldn't speak. With the fallout from the Makabee scroll virus, it was the absolute worst time to move their operations to the city.

"What's the real reason, Simon?"

"I just want to get you the hell out of that ghetto before you create a bigger mess than even I can clean up." Clement chuckled again. "You realize you killed two senators in that damn party?"

"So?"

"See, that's why I want you to come visit me in DC, Stuart." More God damned chuckling. "Perspective. Don't worry. I'll get you what you want. But first, do this little favor for me."

Addison couldn't speak.

"Pretty please?"

Clement's fake Southern accent made Addison want to shove a baseball bat so far up his ass he choked on it. He took a deep, deep breath. If he left now, it was over. They'd disappear... again. He had them.

"Of course, Simon," Addison said, as much calm in his voice as he could maintain. "You are the boss, after all."

"And don't you forget it." Yeah, so much for the accent.

"However. . ." Addison had one chance.

The silence stretched out.

"However?" The accent made a comeback.

Addison had one card to play. One. Once. If he played it now, he'd have to start from scratch finding blackmail material on the president, and the man was far too good at hiding things, now. Not so much thirty years ago, before he knew he was going to be the president of the USA and the head of the UCA.

"However, I think you can find better people to facilitate that move," Addison said, "and I think I need to head this operation myself."

"I don't really care for your tone, Stuart." The president laughed.

"You also won't care for the world to see the video of your dick up the ass of a fourteen-year-old virgin," Addison said.

Silence greeted his comment.

"Although the face you made when you shot your load would likely win an award somewhere." Addison might as well enjoy the moment. "Of course, the fact that you beat the life out of her because she wouldn't stop crying means our market would be a bit limited."

Pierce's face showed nothing. Addison probably shouldn't have played that card with his assistant there, but what the fuck? He'd wanted someone to know he had that video for thirty years.

It was priceless.

"It's on the original cell," Addison said. "Never copied."

"How the fuck do I know that?"

"Because this is me." Any number of caustic names could be applied to Addison, but Simon had to know that, in something like this, he would never lie. It was the kind of thing Addison's life depended on, and his life was not something he would squander.

"You promised the cell was off." Clement's petulance would've been comical in a different world. Poor baby.

"Glass houses, Simon. You beat a fourteen-year-old blonde-haired blue-eyed virgin to death after sodomizing her." Addison swallowed. "Do we have a deal? I get carte blanche in this fucking ghetto, and you get the cell."

And Addison lost his Get-out-of-Jail-Free card, damn it.

He met Pierce's eyes. The man had to be wondering how many videos his boss had of him. They could've filled a library.

"All right, Stuart, you unconscionable fuck." The president's voice was quiet and beaten. "You get this one. I get the cell, and after that I will own your ass."

"I understand."

"If you ever get around to fucking anything, you cunt-sucking repressed—"

Addison slammed the receiver.

"Fuck!" He smashed the phone again and again. He cursed and screamed. "I wanted to save that fucking video!" He shouted at the top of his lungs. "That fucking lunatic needs to die!"

The door opened.

Pierce started to move… but hesitated. Smart man.

"Are you okay—" said some stupid Dick. Addison grabbed him by the front of his shirt and slammed the entire phone into his face.

"I didn't want to waste that fucking video on something like this." He slammed the phone into the Dick's face again.

Pierce closed the door.

Addison followed the body to the floor and slammed the phone into the bloody, torn skull. Straddling the unconscious form, he smashed it's head again and again. He pounded the phone with all his strength, and when the Dick's skull was nothing more than a smear on the concrete with a few fragments of bone scattered around, Addison sat up, breathing heavily.

He dropped the broken phone to one side.

He rose to his feet.

He kicked the lifeless body in the crotch.

Fucking Simon. He thought he could take Addison off his own

project? The Project he'd fucking created from nothing for the fucking Pope and realigned for the UCA? Fuck that.

Fuck... that...

Simon thought he pulled the strings. Really?

Fuck that, too.

Addison would be done with the Project when *he* was done with the Project. Fuck anyone else. The Project was *his* project.

His fucking Project.

Fucking *his*!

Fuck.

Blood covered him from head to foot. He panted and wheezed, trying to get his breath.

"Fucking worthless. . ." He looked up.

Pierce stood nearby with a suit draped over one arm. He also held up a first aid kit.

Addison sucked in another breath, shaking out his battered hand.

He met Pierce's eyes.

Nothing. Good.

"I hope you brought towels." Addison yanked off his tie, pulled his shirt out of his slacks, and kicked off his shoes.

Michael crouched atop the highest point in the Ghetto, the tower that David and John used to enter the subway. Fires burned. Smoke rose into the sky. Sirens cried alarm.

"An earthquake?" Raphael's voice dripped disdain. "Not very subtle."

"Neither was Chernobyl."

Raphael opened his mouth, then closed it. "Touché." He tucked his arms into the sleeves of his robes.

"I haven't caused an earthquake in a long, long time." Michael smiled.

"Well, we gave up all the smiting eons ago."

"I kind of miss the smiting," Michael admitted.

Another fire broke out.

"Are you sure it was worth it?" Raphael asked, but his tone wasn't accusatory.

Was it? Without the earthquake and the virus it had triggered, David would be in Addison's hands. Michael closed his eyes and followed the threads of time.

"He'd be dead, Raph. Without the earthquake, he'd be dead." The scene Barry caused had surprised Michael. It had drawn Addison's attention too early. Michael had had to improvise.

"Most likely true," Raphael acknowledged. "Otherwise. . ."

Otherwise Michael would be in serious trouble. How many had died to save David? How many more now that Michael had changed things? He didn't follow the lines. He didn't want to know. He'd spend eons enough feeling guilty after the fact.

Smoke rose from the city.

"I do miss the smiting." Back then, Michael had had direct orders almost every day. More than anything, Michael missed the Father. He prayed he'd made the right choice and that the Father would approve.

"Sweep?" Ruth set her coffee aside and exchanged a worried glance with Naomi.

"The Dicks are going door to door," Jamie told her, "taking swabs and reading chips of all Jewish guys under twenty. David and John are hiding out until it's over." She finished with the shutters and grabbed the bar for the door. "David told me you'd understand why and said you'd know how urgent things were." She dropped the bar into place.

"Where are the boys now?" Ruth needed her daughter to slow down. She grabbed Jamie's arm.

"They're hiding out in Venice. I don't know where." She pulled against her mother's hand. "We need to move, Mom."

"Just keep breathing." Ruth traded glances with Naomi. The Dicks had to be Addison and his flunkies. How had they found her family? "The shop just needs the last shutters closed and locked. Did David say who was doing this? Or why?"

"David didn't know anything about it. It was Joanne and. . . and. . ." She looked out the window at the rising sun. "Blast it." She addressed her mother directly. "I need to get online in my room, and. . ." She glanced from Naomi to Ruth. "Just follow me."

Jamie broke Ruth's grip and rushed up the stairs, dragging Tracey with her.

Ruth ran after, with Naomi a step or two behind.

"Okay, look," Jamie said, "I was down in the tunnels at a party with David and John, and you can ground me from here 'til Doomsday, but you said you'd be okay with it if I was with David. . ." She burst into her bedroom and rushed to her dresser, her flurry of energy so rapid, Ruth couldn't find a point of entry.

"Busted." Layla rubbed sleep from her eyes. "Told you so."

"The Dicks came through." Jamie pulled out a cell. "There was gunfire and explosions, and we overheard these two local cops. . . One of them was Noah's dad? It's going to get ugly."

She tapped the cell, and its hologram jumped to life. Jamie's fingers flashed through the images. She froze. She looked up at her mother with a fierceness Ruth really didn't like.

"People are going to die if I don't do this, Mom." Jamie waved both hands in a complex gesture like a magic spell, and the room filled with enormous images.

"What in the world?" Ruth jumped back with a gasp.

"I'm a lot better at this that I let on." Her hands fluttered through the screens and a keyboard appeared. She typed so rapidly Ruth could hardly follow the movement.

"Texting?" Layla rose from bed and took Ruth's hand. "What century is this?"

"I need to multitask." Images flashed around Jamie. "I need to patch my system and set up immunization for when you guys turn on your cells."

"Can I make pictures?" Layla took Tracey's hand.

"Sorry, Li'l Bit," Jamie said. "I need to see who survived the Makabee scrolls."

"That's a new virus, right?" Ruth understood that much, at least.

"Oh my God, have you not been online at all, tonight?" Jamie glanced up with utter scorn. "Yes, the latest virus wiped out. . . Holy Mother Bell, it wiped out half the country this time. I need to find a safe server to get word out to the Ghetto."

"When did you learn to do all this?" Ruth was astonished. When had Jamie grown from pretty holograms to hacking national servers?

"What do you think I do in here all the time?" Her hands flashed and the images swirled.

"When we were girls, it was Skyping about boys and uploading selfies." Ruth watched the flurry of images. She glanced at Naomi, who shrugged.

"What century did you grow up in?" Jamie worked the hologram. "Selfies? Mom, don't ever use that word again if you have any self-respect." Her voice dropped a bit. "There you are, you sneaky. . ." She glanced at her mother. ". . .guy. What the heck is skyping?" She typed: *Ghetto Rats attend. Dicks on the lookout for a male Jewish cat 16-20.*

"Where did you get this equipment?" Ruth asked, fairly certain she already knew.

"Barry has the world's best connections." Jamie kept typing: *Going door to door. Don't know who they want.*

"The projectors fell off a truck, I'll bet," Ruth said.

"How'd you guess?" Jamie asked. "Hey, when the government steals from us, it's acquisition."

Beware the smoking cracker in an Armani suit. That's all we know.

No, no, no, no...

Ruth couldn't breathe. Her daughter kept talking... but Ruth didn't hear a word of it. She touched the screen with a finger right where the last line had been written. The image shimmered.

"What does this mean?" But Ruth already knew.

"The lead agent smokes like a chimney," Tracey said.

"Speaking of adults living in the last century," Jamie tossed in. "Doesn't everyone know that smoking kills?"

Naomi's hand touched Ruth's shoulder.

"It might have been nice to have a little more notice." Ruth had just dreamed it less than an hour ago.

"Oh, wow!" Bo's voice in the doorway sounded excited, but still sleepy. "That is a stellar. . . *wacky.* . . hologram. Where'd Barry steal it?"

"Is there any chance you can be their father and not the fifth child for one morning?" Ruth's jaw clenched.

His eyes opened so wide, she thought he might tear up on the spot. His arms crossed over his bare chest.

Even Naomi seemed startled.

Ruth sighed. At least he'd put on sweatpants and not just boxers. She moved closer and put her arms around him.

"I'm sorry. There was an earthquake, Addison's in the Ghetto, riots are about to start, and our boys are off hiding in Venice somewhere." She kissed him. "I haven't had enough coffee."

"Oh my God." His entire body stiffened in her arms.

"Jamie." Ruth knew the drill. "Get the word out as fast as you can." Wait. "What about your other friends? They must have been out with you. Are they okay?"

"Barry's already online and going door to door. He lost touch with Noah, but *he* probably ended up needing to handle Rocky." Jamie actually smiled. "Thanks for asking, Mom, but too much of the net is down for me to know."

"That's a good thing." Bo spoke quietly from the doorway. "Having the net down hurts Addison more than it hurts us."

"Addison." Jamie stopped her work and faced them. "You keep using that name. Who's Addison?"

"You know what?" Ruth moved toward the door. "We have work to do. We'll figure out who knows what once we're safe." She dragged Naomi and Bo with her. "Get the word out. We'll secure the store." She stopped to touch Tracey's arm. "Can you get the shutters on the windows up here? Layla can help."

"Of course." Tracey squeezed Layla's hand.

Ruth turned to her elder daughter one more time. "Make sure you tell Tracey's family that she's safe."

"Got it." Jamie went back to work.

"It's started." Ruth hurried down the steps with Naomi and Bo. "He's closing in. We have to make a decision."

"We can't let them see us." Bo closed and locked the higher windows.

Metal rattled distantly as someone closed the shutters upstairs. Sirens screamed nearby.

"There's no time to get away." Naomi said. "We can't leave the boys, and if we're caught in the street, we'll be questioned, and that's it."

"We can't just ignore someone at the door." Ruth peered out through the slats. Their street was still quiet but that meant nothing. "They'll force their way in and once they scan our chips. . ." Or swab them. Even a stray hair would reveal them to Addison.

"I always thought we'd have more warning, more time to prepare." Bo sucked down coffee.

The girls ran clacking down the stairs into the shop. Where'd her daughter get those heels? Or the suit for that matter?

"Upstairs is secured." Jamie double-checked the front door. "What do we do?"

What should they do next? They couldn't leave the boys. Could they hide out in Venice, too? No, that was ridiculous.

"I mean, what do we tell them about the guys?" Jamie put her hands on her hips. "Is David really in danger? What the what?"

"We can't answer the door," Ruth said. "They're looking for *us*." She rose to her feet and took Layla's hand, leading her to the back of the shop.

"Holy crap." Jamie let out one short laugh. "David said this was all about him. But it can't be." She shrugged. "Can it?"

A nearby explosion rattled the windows. Layla shrieked, and Mom dropped to one knee to hold her. She stroked Layla's hair and kissed her forehead, and, even though she was all of eight years old, Layla let her mom treat her like a little girl. Just this once.

"I can't see anything except smoke." Dad peered between two metal slats. "But I think it's the synagogue."

Mom left Layla on her own to look outside, too.

"Oh my God." Aunt Naomi sat on the stairs.

Layla sat beside her. She pulled her nightgown down around her feet and tucked the edges under her toes. She understood about the sweeps, but her parents' reaction seemed extreme. The police had made sweeps before. This time was different, somehow.

"Again, I ask, what do we do?" Jamie stood her ground near her friend, Tracey. As often as Layla teased her big sister, because that's what little sisters were supposed to do, she couldn't deny her sister's strength, speaking up against their parents like that.

Okay, the important thing was that Mom and Dad would have some kind of plan. They always did. That's what parents did. But no one said a word. The adults stood there, eyes wide and mouths open, like big suffocating fish.

Layla closed her eyes to do some deep thinking. Closing her eyes always helped.

In her mind, she saw two men, men in uniforms, men who wanted to find David. But why David? No, the *why* didn't matter. The question was what to do about the strange men. And then, suddenly, the answer seemed obvious, but would any of them listen to her? Why should they? How did she even know what to do? And why was she so certain?

While the adults exchanged frightened glances, Layla rose to her feet and hoped her voice wouldn't break. She held the railing for support. Jamie could be strong? So could Layla.

"I have an idea.," she said.

Everyone turned to her.

"You have an idea?" Dad asked.

"I have an idea." She worried the cotton of her nightgown with one hand while she pulled herself together.

"All right, sweetie." Dad didn't even glance at Mom or Aunt Naomi for approval. "Tell us your idea. We're all ears."

Special agents Lander and Curtis stood at ease, hands folded together innocently over their groins like fig leaves, trying to seem as harmless as possible, doing their level best to ignore the sirens. Lander felt like a Witness in a cheap, blue suit, white shirt, and red tie.

The smoke from the synagogue rose over the house across the street. Blast it. That kind of violence could start a full-scale riot. So far, the people in this neighborhood had been peaceful. Well, that's why Lander had chosen to start there. He'd worked the Godforsaken place ten years and knew the complacent neighborhoods and the troublemakers.

"What's taking so long?" He turned back to the current address. The explosion may have panicked the family. "Check the files."

Curtis pulled out his cell, called up a screen, and flipped through a couple thousand files, finally settling on the address of the shop where they waited. He showed the screen to Lander: two males age eighteen, one with a Jewish father. Probably hiding. Damn it. Maybe they'd realized the sirens meant trouble.

They'd probably have to force an entry. It would be the first time that night. All the other families were so surprised they'd acquiesced without hesitation. Looking like the class president and dressing like Witnesses probably helped.

The chains on the other side of the door rattled, settling Lander. The sirens were too close for his comfort, and the explosion at the synagogue had been only a few blocks away. When he'd called in to see what *that* was about, he'd been told that the Rabbi refused to let anyone into the synagogue to check for hiding boys. They'd had to blow the doors open. Riot squads headed that way.

Lander had nothing against necessary violence, but he didn't like being in the middle of full-scale riots. He very nearly had himself appointed to the governor, which meant he'd be able to ride out the last ten years until retirement behind a nice comfy desk. He didn't want to take any unnecessary risks during his last few weeks on the streets.

The barred and shuttered door opened a few inches, but there was no one there. What the hell?

"Who is it?" a tiny voice asked.

Lander looked down: a small, dark-haired, Jewish girl sucked on a thumb, holding the hem of her nightgown in her free hand. Well, entry would be easy, after all. Kids always respected an authority figure.

He dropped into a crouch and smiled his most paternal smile. She reminded him of his youngest granddaughter, and, for a moment, he wondered what she was doing in the Ghetto. Then he brought himself back to the moment. She was Jewish. His granddaughter was Italian.

"Hi, there," Lander said. "Where are your mommy and daddy?"

The little girl looked at him with unblinking eyes for a long time before speaking around her thumb.

"Daddy's in LA selling stuff," she said, "and Mommy's at the store with her boyfriend."

Lander exchanged a look with his partner. He hated the way these irresponsible Ghetto parents left their kids to fend for themselves. Apparently, Curtis agreed.

"He's gay," the little girl said, startling Lander.

"Who is, darling?" he asked.

"My daddy. That's why Mommy has a boyfriend." Even though she took her thumb out of her mouth, her speech was still slurred. Her eyes seemed glassy, too. Looked about seven but talked like a four-year-old. He couldn't believe someone let her answer the door after that explosion.

"Where are the other kids?" He stroked the girl's hair, pushed it behind one ear for her.

"At school."

Lander nodded with satisfaction. Someone would get photos at the school, but something else bothered him.

"So, who's watching you, darling?" he asked.

The little girl regarded him stupidly.

"Who else is here?" he tried.

"No one." The thumb found her mouth again. "Mommy's gonna be back quick. She said so."

"When did she leave?"

The little girl shrugged. "I can't tell time."

Lander rose to his feet. "I want to take a look around, just in case."

Curtis nodded. He always did what Lander suggested. It made him an ideal partner.

"Can we come in and take a look around?" Lander shouldn't care about this girl, but he wanted to make sure she wasn't living in total squalor, and they should at least wander through in case anyone asked.

"Mommy said no one comes in." She shook her head far more than necessary.

"What's your name, darling?" Lander smiled his most endearing smile.

"Mommy said not to say."

"Give me the tablet." Lander kept on smiling and held a hand to Curtis. His partner hesitated but gave it over: two underage females. This one was eight. He scanned her chip to confirm her ID. "Layla?"

Her eyes opened wide.

"Are you eight years old?" Lander thumbed through a few folders.

"It says that?" The girl stepped away from the door to peer at the screen.

Lander called up a hologram and handed the tablet to her. She stared at the images with the closest thing to interest Lander had yet seen. The thumb came out of her mouth and the index finger of that hand poised at the image. She looked up at Lander with wide eyes.

"Go ahead."

The little girl smiled and started pressing icons, immediately engrossed. When Lander rose and motioned for Curtis to follow, she moved quietly out of the way for them to pass. Perfect. Lander patted her head as he stepped through. Idiot child.

The place was some kind of furniture store, but the stock was straight out of *Alice in Wonderland*. What the hell was any of this stuff? Tables? Chairs? Okay, Mad Hatter. Whatever.

Hmm. The shop had some kind of kiln in one corner going strong, throwing off Lander's readings. He motioned to Curtis, and they wandered around the room.

As soon as the men turned their backs, Layla swiped through pages on the screen Lander had used to bribe her. Keeping one eye on the two agents, Layla poured through information, sticking with the screen so they wouldn't see her actions in the hologram.

For her and Jamie, the files contained scans, ages, schools, names, approximate descriptions... but for her brothers? Nothing. Were all the birth certificate files except hers deleted? Apparently. David's birth certificate file said, "Lost in Fire," which made no sense at all. She opened her mother's file. The first entry started only thirteen years before: "Previous records lost to Makabee II."

Layla had heard of the virus. Makabee was friends with Jamie, or something like that. She worked with him.

According to the record, Layla had the only complete file.

The sound of a curtain being drawn aside shocked her. Her grip on the tablet tightened.

The two FBI men searched the closet that backed against her father's huge kiln. Only a thick curtain covered the closet, and it was empty… but the back wall opened like a door onto the crawl space where her family had crammed together to hide behind the kiln which radiated enough heat to cover the signatures of anyone hiding there, but if the agents suspected anything and ran a chip scan, they'd be discovered.

"Can I make pictures?" Layla waved the tablet in the air wildly. She made sure to hold the screen with the thumb she'd been sucking.

What had she seen in *that* habit when she was little? Her thumb tasted like dirt.

Lander turned to her, and his eyes opened wider as he moved quickly and took the tablet from her gently, but firmly. He took one last look around the room and crouched down to her level.

"Does your mommy leave you alone very often?"

"No." Layla pretended to be alarmed by the question. "Just today. David needed medicine at school." Would they realize she had changed her story?

"That's the Jewish boy." Curtis leaned over Lander's shoulder.

"Mm-hm." Could Layla find a way to convince them to leave? "Mommy needed to get him medicine at school because he's Jewish. That's what she said."

"On her way to school to warn the boy?" Lander looked over his shoulder at Curtis. "Seems suspicious."

Curtis tapped his partner on the shoulder and nodded his head to ask Lander to step away, but Layla could still hear them. They likely thought she was too stupid to understand, at least that was her hope.

"You sure you trust this kid?" Curtis asked.

"She's retarded." He bought her charade. Good. "She probably couldn't lie if she wanted to."

Layla stared at them, her face a carefully blank mask, her mouth open.

"She's just afraid her mom's in trouble for leaving her here alone." Lander waved at the door. "Let's get over to the school."

Curtis wiped the tablet screen, frowning.

"See you around, kid." Lander moved past Layla and patted her head as if she were an obedient pet. He made his way to the door with Curtis following in his shadow, still wiping the tablet.

"Good-bye, Mister." Layla closed the door and locked it fast, her hands shaking. She peered through the crack between the heavy shutters to make sure they really left.

The two men hurried down the street away from her home.

"Wow." She wiped the damp thumb on her nightgown. Her plan had worked! Incredible. She rushed across the room to the closet. She rapped out the signal her father had given her: seven quick taps, then three slow, then seven quick again.

"They're gone," she said. "It's safe."

The back wall of the closet slowly swung towards her, and her father's face appeared uncertainly from behind it. His hair dripped with sweat and lay plastered against his face. Hiding in there must have been horrible. Her father's face was drawn and pale.

"It's okay. They're really gone." She grabbed his hand and pulled him out. "They went to the school to look for David."

Dad glanced around the store, then turned and motioned for the others to follow him out.

"It's okay." Layla felt giddy now that the scary part had ended.

Everyone emerged from the crawl space like scared little kids, soaked with sweat, hair and clothes plastered to their bodies, her father's bare shoulders glistening. They blinked in the bright, fluorescent lights, eyes darting around the room. Her parents' eyes were guarded, and their embrace seemed almost frantic. Aunt Naomi looked as if she were about to faint.

When Bo looked at Layla, really looked at her and saw the fear in her face, he gave Ruth a squeeze that told her they had to be parents, first. They could be terrified later, on their own time. Their little girl had been so brave, had likely saved all their lives. It was time for the adults to step up. The immediate threat had been averted, and they'd purchased valuable time. Now, they'd be able to sit down and formulate some kind of plan.

Ruth loosened her hold on him. She gave Naomi's hand a squeeze.

"Sorry, girls, we didn't want to scare you, but those men want to hurt us." Ruth faced the girls squarely.

"But why?" Layla wiped her hand on her dress.

"What did they say?" Bo touched her hair and faked a smile.

"They thought I was stupid," she said.

"Why did they think that?" That was not what he had expected.

"I figured they'd believe me better if they thought I was too dumb to tell a lie, so I hammed it up." She shrugged. "They bought it."

She told them what had happened while they hid in the crawl space. Incredible. Impressed didn't even cover it. How had she thought of all that?

Bo picked her up and spun her around until she was so dizzy she laughed. Maybe he'd help her relax if he convinced her the entire episode had been like a game.

"But, Dad, why are they after you?" Layla asked when her feet were on the floor again. "What did you do?"

Bo knew her world was topsy-turvy, but he couldn't bear to have his children wonder whether their parents had done something to deserve a search.

Everyone gathered in the middle of the room, and Ruth raised an eyebrow, asking if she should take this one. Bo nodded. So did Naomi. And how much information should they give?

Ruth looked from Layla to Jamie to Tracey, the last of which meant she couldn't say everything that needed saying.

"We didn't do anything wrong, girls." She weighed her words

carefully. Bo squeezed her hand to tell her he trusted her judgment. "A very important man broke the law many years ago and blamed us for his crime. People believed him."

"What did he do?" Jamie's voice seemed uncertain.

"He killed your Uncle Zack." Naomi stood near the stairwell, holding the banister tightly in one hand, but she held her shoulders square and strong. "He killed your Uncle Zack and blamed us for it."

The girls exchanged a very puzzled glance, but all eyes fixed themselves on Naomi. After checking with Bo and Ruth, she took the ball, stepped closer to the others, and released the banister.

"Dickersons thinks *we* murdered him, and they think this for no good reason except that a very important man said so," Naomi said. "The man named Addison."

"But what does that have to do with the riots?" Jamie asked. "And what does that have to do with David?"

Ruth had nothing to say.

Jamie's face fell. "Why the hell do they want David?"

Naomi turned to Bo and Ruth. David was their son. Revealing anything about him was their call. Dear God, what could Bo possibly say?

"What did he *do*?" Jamie demanded.

"He didn't do anything," Bo said. "He's just a victim like the rest of us."

An explosion shattered the front window.

Bo's world filled up with light and heat and pain.

Layla screamed.

With the net up and running again, Addison had the Air Force on one line, and the local police on a second. Hell, he had seven lines open and trusted Pierce would make sure no one heard anything they shouldn't. He had helicopters lined up to incinerate the entire island. Media outlets were on hold to blame the entire debacle on Makabee.

During a lull, while they waited for some general to confirm just how many megatons of munitions they could deploy, Addison looked over at Pierce. His jacket, shirt, and tie had been discarded, and his undershirt was stained with sweat.

Addison still wore his suit. His image appeared in every conversation. Pierce regularly ran to the other side of the store for side research, but his contacts didn't have a dress code. His movements were small but intense as he manipulated the screens. His eyes darted from image to image. His breath huffed out in quick, shallow bursts.

"You have a hard on for blowing this island, don't you?" Addison was amazed he didn't see tenting in his assistant's slacks.

"Pardon me?" Pierce looked up in shock.

"I can tell. I know that face" Addison chuckled. "You are absolutely boned up with all this, aren't you? You look like a teenager with his first hooker."

For one of few times since he'd known the officious freak, Pierce had nothing to say.

"I wasn't criticizing." Addison chuckled. "It's good to enjoy your work."

Someone knocked at the door. What the hell? His men wouldn't disturb him. The first corpse would have taught them that lesson.

Pierce shook his head and shrugged.

Addison moved to the door while Pierce slipped his gun out of the holster.

Opening the door a crack, Addison found a long-haired blonde woman with the blackest skin he'd ever seen.

"What do you want?" he asked.

She looked directly into his eyes. "If you blow up the island tonight, you'll never catch your science project." The Australian accent took a second to decipher. How did she know about the Project?

Addison glanced at Pierce, who had his weapon ready. Addison pulled his own piece out of his holster.

"Hands where I can see them," Addison said.

She complied.

He opened the door all the way, and the woman brushed past him. The four men standing guard looked at him as if they had no idea that someone had just waltzed past them to knock on the door. What the fuck?

"Let's cut the bullshit, Stuart. You know there are powers deeper and far more powerful than anything you choose to acknowledge." She wore a dark grey suit, her hair tied back in a ponytail. Tall, late twenties, athletic figure. The way she carried herself, she had to be some sort of assassin.

"Now that you've sized me up," she said, "can we get on with me helping you avoid the greatest mistake of your career?"

She was good. Maybe too good?

"You have a speech," Addison said. "Make it."

"Your target has already escaped into Venice. He's safely tucked away under a hundred feet of water." She puttered with circuit boards on a table. "Feel free to firebomb the city. All you'll do is break his ties to the region by killing his family and giving him every reason to flee the country. I hear Canada is lovely this time of year." She dropped the circuits back into a box and brushed her hands together.

"You speak of powers." Addison said.

"You couldn't have bribed your tiny-dicked president if he didn't answer to someone more important." She leaned against a dusty display case.

"The American people?"

She burst out laughing. "Please. He's as concerned about the opinion of the American people as you are your assistant's opinion of my tits."

Amazing. Whoever she was, she had to answer to someone higher than he'd ever imagined. His joke to Pierce about erections flickered through his head.

She smiled as if she knew his thoughts. All the better.

"If this conversation goes that high up," Addison asked, "why is Pierce here?"

"If I'm going to fuck you, Stuart, I figured you'd want an audience." She glanced at the assistant, still smiling.

No. That was Simon. . .

She winked at Addison.

Wait. Was she literally reading his mind?

"Tell me what you know," he said. "Please."

"I already did. That's it. If you firebomb this city to kill this kid, you'll fail." Her smile promised him she'd fulfill every possible fantasy he'd ever had. "Today."

That one word spoke volumes.

"Tomorrow?"

She shook her head. "Wait three days."

"Three days? Isn't that a bit Biblical?"

"Do you even know these people you're trying to kill?" She pulled a flask from a jacket pocket and suckled it. "Of course, three days. Then he will rejoin his family in the Ghetto, where you can pick him off like farmed prey."

"Why would you tell me this?"

"I want you to get him." She said it as if he were stupid. She handed the flask to Pierce.

"You?" Addison said. "Not your boss?"

"Do what you want." She glanced from one man to the other, then moved so close to Addison he could smell her perfume. Jasmine. She leaned closer. "But you shoot your load too soon, and no one gets satisfied."

Should he stop her? Could he?

She left.

Addison sucked in several raged breaths.

Pierce cleared his throat. He held up the flask.

"Run it for prints and DNA," Addison said, "not that I think you'll find anything." He couldn't tear his eyes from the door. "Well, now we've seen each other with hard-ons. Get me anyone on the line who might be able to corroborate what that bitch had to say."

Pierce nodded and set to work.

She strolled past Addison's men and around the corner into an alley. Once away from any cameras or prying eyes, she allowed herself a very satisfied smile. Addison had been everything she'd expected. And the minion? Priceless. She wanted the minion for one of her own.

"Master?" Speaking of minions, Lilith stared at her quizzically a few feet away.

"What?"

The minion looked her up and down.

"Oh. Right. I forgot." She shook her hair out, and it pulled up shorter and straight. Lighter, too. She shook out one leg so it lengthened and thickened, the trousers and shoe adjusting as necessary. She stepped up onto it and shook the other leg to match.

"I thought those two would respond better to your shape, so I borrowed it. Hope you don't mind." She made a tiny jump, and the shirt fell flat over his chest. His suit bled to white.

"Although. . ." He coughed with the change in his vocal chords. "Although with Addison, it's really hard to say."

Lilith cleared her throat.

"What?"

"You have a little bit of me stuck to your face, master." She tapped her nose. "Sorry, but it's unsettling."

Lucifer rubbed his hands over his face, changing it to the one he'd been using as his default for the last few thousand years. His skin paled to a sun-kissed bronze. He'd worn this form when Michael cast him out of Heaven, so it had sentimental value. When Lucifer drove a dagger through that fucking slave's heart and fed his entrails to pigs, this face would be the last thing Michael saw.

"Why do you go through the whole messy process anyway?" Lilith asked. "You could just. . . transform."

"I know," he adjusted his clothing, shifting his package to a more comfortable position. He unhooked his bra and maneuvered it from under his shirt through one sleeve. "For the same reason I just did that." He held up the bra in one hand. "Ta-daa. It's fun."

Fun was something those bastard slaves to the Father didn't understand. The desire for fun separated *him* from *them*.

He sent his sight into Addison's room. The monkey had his assistant verifying the intel. Good. Lucifer's interference had worked. He couldn't see the future the way some of the Father's slaves could, but he had his spies in their ranks, and they all talked.

The angels had started meddling? Fine. Lucifer knew a thing or two about meddling. He'd heard they were counting on an air strike. Why? Who knew? Who cared? They wanted an air strike, he'd cancel it. Why? One reason. Fucking up their plans was fun.

None of it really mattered. The final battle was predestined. It would happen. He and Michael would meet on the field of Megiddo, and only one would walk away. That's what mattered. All their pointless machinations to attempt the salvation of the flea-bitten monkeys from the coming apocalypse mattered not at all. Of course, every step he took to frustrating their doomed plans would be. . . what was the word? Fun!

He and his minion shifted to his Manhattan townhouse. When he'd been cast out of Heaven, he hadn't been given a lovely fire and brimstone realm of his own. He'd been cast down to Earth, the home of the fucking monkeys that'd ruined everything in the first place, so he'd had to find a number of homes among the flea-biters.

The atheists had nailed it. Hell was, indeed, on Earth

A faint blue glow woke David from a deep, dreamless sleep into a damp, chilly world. John lay curled up with him against the cold.

Raphael stood over them, his face disapproving as always.

David rose to his feet, hugging himself and pulling his rumpled suit coat closed. No matter how well they'd tried to keep their clothes dry, hiding out in Venice meant everything stayed damp.

"Why are you here?" The angel's voice echoed around the enclosed space.

David glanced down at John's sleeping form.

"He will not awaken." Raphael folded his arms in the folds of his robes. "Why are you here?"

"I'm here so Addison doesn't find me." David wanted dry clothes to wear. He hated feeling cold. Stupid mortal body. "That isn't part of the plan, is it?"

"Neither is this little jaunt with your cousin."

David felt his face grow hot with anger. His heart sped up.

The angel suspected he was hiding John away to save him from his fate.

He stared directly into Raphael's glowing blue eyes. When David was a little boy, the icy depths of those eyes had always frightened him into obedience. He wasn't a child anymore.

"This is the most logical place to hide." The chattering of his teeth subsided. "Even if Addison calls in an air strike, his bombs won't reach me here."

"And when do you plan to return?" Raphael asked.

"Don't worry." He spoke through clenched teeth. It was the only way to keep from shouting. "We'll be back in time. I know what has to happen. I have no intention of changing things." But could he? He'd never tried.

"What if I don't believe you?"

That was it. David had had enough. "What if I don't give a damn what you believe, anymore?"

Raphael tried to speak.

"Three days," David preempted. "Give me three days of peace with him. I know what has to happen. I understand that it is necessary. For the sake of all that is holy give me three days to say goodbye to the best friend I have ever had. . . will ever have. From here on in everything sucks for the rest of my life." He tried to hold back the tears, but they rolled down his cheeks all the same. "I lose so much, Raphael. May I please have three days without you breathing down my neck?"

"It will be so." Gabriel's voice startled David so much he jumped and coughed.

He turned to her.

"Thank you." He coughed again.

"I think—"

"We all know what you think, Raph." Gabriel pulled out a white handkerchief and wiped David's face. "We always know what you think. You never shut up about what you think, do you?"

David's heart slowed down. His lungs hurt less.

"I am against this." And Raphael was gone.

"Always has to have the last word, that one." Gabriel patted David's cheek and stepped back. "If you look behind the pile of bookshelves there, you'll find a door. The room on the other side has some dry linens and blankets to keep you warmer." She winked.

In other words, there was *now* a door behind the fallen bookshelves. But John had helped him explore the room. How would he explain—?

"You hadn't shifted that pile, yet." She smiled. "It's a hospital, David. They have linens in closets in hospitals." Her smiled broadened. "Well, they do now."

"Thank you." He was afraid to say more, afraid of what he might admit. Would even Gabriel understand why he wanted this time with John? Of everyone in his family, why did it have to be John who died?

As if reading David's thoughts, she looked down at his cousin. "You realize this is only going to make it all the more painful when he dies."

"I know."

"I'm not criticizing." She looked up again. "Raphael has never incarnated. He doesn't understand love or family, not really." She smiled. "I do."

She'd had children of her own, once upon a time. David remembered them vaguely now that she'd mentioned family. Like so many of his memories, the images felt like they belonged in a dream.

"Enjoy your three days, David, although some of that time has already passed." She folded her hands. "I will do what I can to keep the world from falling apart while you're gone."

"Thank you." He wiped at his face with the back of one hand.

"Wait a while before you thank me," she warned. "Sometimes we should be very careful what we ask for. Sometimes we are doomed to receive it." She left. Darkness swallowed the room

John muttered in his sleep.

David shivered. Stupid mortal body.

The Ghetto did not sleep peacefully. Thousands of feet—some in timeworn shoes, some in slippers, many simply bare—pounded, padded, and shuffled through the midnight streets.

Voices whispered questions without answers, faces blurry and indistinct.

A young man, chocolate skin and long, kinky dreadlocks—Rocky—pushed through the crowd to the Temporary Building.

The building stood tall and broken against the smoke-filled sky, reaching up with naked girders from the highest floors. Inside, the rumble of bass and the blaring of trumpets drowned out the sounds of the passing crowd. Rush junkies young and old layered the concrete floor, lost in an oblivion so deep they didn't notice the alarms downloading into their brains piggybacked on the electronic hallucinations.

Rocky forced the seductive whispers from his mind. Not now. This was too important. But just a few minutes couldn't hurt. . .

"No. . . I need to go. . ."

The little Black girl with a halo of blonde hair appeared out of nowhere in front of Rocky, holding out a headset for him. He brushed past her and picked his way across the floor, bee-lining his way to Barry, who was making it with Tracey in the corner.

Rocky grabbed Barry's shoulder, which earned him an angry glance. Sirens cut through the bass and the trumpets, nothing more than an unusual addition to the music until Rocky's frantic shouts connected the sounds to their purpose.

Barry stopped what he was doing, his gray eyes wide and frightened. He

apologized to Tracey, and they all ran up the winding stairway. The walls opened around them, letting in the night, drowning them in the sound of the sirens and a canopy of unnaturally dark sky.

Joanne stood on a rusty girder with her back to them, one arm wrapped around an upright beam and one shaky hand pointing. Fires lit the skyline where she pointed, and silent helicopters raced through the smoke. The four of them huddled together, convinced they watched the end of the world.

An obscene flash of light swallowed the church in the center of the Ghetto.

A moment of absolute stillness enveloped the world. . .

. . .then the Temporary Building jumped six inches to the right.

A supernova flared, igniting the sky with fire.

Joanne grabbed Barry—who suddenly stood on empty air—and she screamed when her arm caught his full weight.

Rocky felt his chest hit the girder—he grabbed blindly, felt his hand touch slippery metal, saw a blur of movement as someone fell past him. He hung, suspended by the burning fingers of one hand and watched the building next door tremble, catch fire, and collapse into itself.

The fireball consumed them.

John awoke screaming in the darkness. The air stifled him, a tremendous, crushing weight with terrifying blindness. When hands touched him, they burned, and he lashed out wildly. His fists connected with flesh and struck again and again.

"No fire!" he screamed. "No fire!"

He had to breathe. He had to.

The fire and death melted into the darkness and the cold.

"For Christ's sake, it's only me!" David. That was David's voice.

John stopped striking out and felt the wall solid against his back. Cold. His breath came in short, quick gasps so harsh they hurt his throat. He huddled in the darkness, knees pulled up to his chest. The stale air tasted like sulfur. Cold. A light flashed on, blinding him. He lifted his arms to protect his face, and he shouted again.

"John. You're safe. No one's dead. It's a dream."

The light picked out gurneys and medical equipment. They were in the flooded hospital in Venice, another air pocket Mackabee had detected, but this one checked and abandoned as nothing important. The gurneys vanished into darkness as the beam spun across the dusty room and settled on David's worried and dirty face. He crouched a few feet away, nursing a bleeding lip with the corner of a blanket. Holding the lamp over his head, he leaned against a pile of linens they'd found in the next room.

"See? It's just me. It was a dream." The light cast vicious shadows. "You're okay."

Demons leapt and danced.

A cold shudder swept through John, head to toe. He snatched a couple of dry blankets from the nest they'd made and wrapped them around his body. He wiped his sweat-soaked face. Their damp clothes hung along the room divider.

He focused on David, who set the lamp on the floor. John stared into David's eyes. Who was inside them? His best friend or that vision from the party? Would he lose himself in a field of stars?

His stomach convulsed, and he doubled over, trying to vomit. Nothing came up.

David scooted closer, rubbed John's back with one hand.

John's stomach settled. Some of the panic faded.

"I'm fine." With a deep breath, John wrapped the blankets around himself and settled against the cold wall. He ran a hand over his hair. "It was. . . it was really messed up." He couldn't clear his head.

"What do you mean?" David asked.

Your friends are all dead. Fire burned them all.

John leapt to his feet, wrapping the blankets tighter. He paced the room that had been their refuge since the party at Babylon, the cold of the linoleum strange against the memory of flames.

The dream meant something. It was a vision. It wasn't just a dream. Nausea touched his stomach again. The air felt thick and hard to breathe, as if it had turned to poison.

John grabbed an air canister and released oxygen into the room. The canisters were their lifeline. As long as those lasted, they could stay hidden.

But should they? Were their friends in danger? Should they help?

"John. Talk to me."

He shuddered and found David's face again. Blood dripped out of his nose. Wait a minute, John had awakened lashing out. How many times had he struck?

"Oh, Jesus." John dropped down to sit cross-legged. A nervous twinge tickled his stomach as he took David's face in his hands. "I'm sorry, coz. . . I. . . it was horrible. . . I didn't. . ."

David shook his head to say no apology was necessary. He understood.

John took a deep breath, not certain whether his trembling was from guilt or the dream or the vision in Babylon. What if David's eyes turned to stars again? Had John been that drunk? He turned his cousin's cheek to the light. Blood trickled from his lip.

"I'm sorry." John dabbed at it with the corner of a blanket. Except for the fat lip, his face was unharmed. "Where'd I get you?"

"Don't worry about it." David pulled his own blanket tighter around his chest. So he'd been nailed there.

John pulled David's arms away to reveal several large red welts on his chest. John winced. That would leave a mark.

"You've got a heck of a left hook." David smiled, but there was more pain than humor in it. In the dim light, David seemed a million years old.

And his eyes. . . dark chasms.

"I'm so sorry." John stared at David's chest.

"I know."

John closed David's blanket, holding it by the edges for a moment. He forced himself to look into David's eyes. They were dark, but that was just because the light sucked. Then something flickered deep inside them.

John scooted backward.

David blinked and the light vanished. Had it been there?

"What was that?" John demanded.

"What was what?" But David's voice told John he knew.

"Don't," John insisted. "Don't lie to me. What I saw at the party, it was real, wasn't it?"

"What did you see?" His voice was small and frightened.

"I said don't lie."

David curled the blanket tightly. He muttered something John didn't understand.

"What?"

"I told you I was a freak, too." Fear filled his eyes. *Will you reject me now?*

John ran his hands over his face. He wanted to trust David, but there was so much he wouldn't explain. And what about their friends? What about the nightmare?

"Our friends are perfectly safe right now," David said. "Anything that was going to happen is over, now." His voice stayed quiet, like a frightened little boy's. "We don't need to go back, yet."

"How do you know that?" John asked.

David leaned against the wall. He didn't speak.

"How do you know any of the shit you know?" Anger grew inside John. "And don't tell me you just know shit."

"I told you." David stared at the floor. "It's my gig."

"David!" John wanted to smack him. "You're going in circles. You know more than you're telling me, and you know how you know. Why are those men out there fucking with the Ghetto?"

Silence filled the room as thick as the air.

"I told you the Dicks are looking for me," David said.

"Why are they looking for you?" John leaned forward. He needed to see David's face.

David studied him. "These questions have something to do with your dream, don't they, and with what happened at Babylon?"

"I have no idea *what* happened at Babylon." John rose to his feet. "I got sucked into your eyes, and it was like falling through an entire blasted galaxy." He swung back to David. "What the hell was that?" He stepped closer.

David stared at him, and his eyes didn't fall away into chasms.

But maybe John almost wished they would.

David cocked his head to one side in a familiar movement.

John sighed deeply. "And leave my aura out of it."

"The fact that I can see your aura is part of it." David pushed to his feet. "How can I leave it out?"

John backed up to lean against the opposite wall.

"Tell me about the dream you just had." David paced.

John snorted. "And there he is with the redirection again."

"No. Tell me your dream so I can tell you if it's something you have to worry about." He faced John. "Please, John, it's how I talk. You know that. I need a starting point. Please?"

He seemed so genuine. But he hid so much.

John closed his eyes and pulled in a deep breath.

"Something terrible happened." He let the feeling tighten his chest. He saw the explosion again.

"What?"

"I don't know." But that wasn't true. Somehow, John did know. "Someone's going to kill the Ghetto. Or maybe he already has."

"The faces," David urged, "think about the faces."

John saw Barry's face... and Rocky's... all their friends.

"But who was it really?"

The faces changed. John looked harder.

"Was it the future or the past?" David asked.

John saw the Ghetto rats streaming through the streets, a flood of humanity. But the faces changed, the clothes aged, and the streets became the hard-packed dirt of a desert village.

They ran screaming through the streets, and the helicopters faded away. It was horses, horses with soldiers in armor and swords. The blades of the copters became swords they whirled through the air over their heads.

They trampled the peasants underfoot.

They slaughtered the innocents looking for a single man: David.

Their blood ran like water over the thirsty sand.

And then it was Dicks, in uniform, and people kneeling in a dark red street. A helicopter overhead, and a large, lopsided man cut down with a whip.

John fell on his ass with a gasp. His stomach jumped, and

David held a bucket out for him just in time as the spare rations he'd eaten leapt from his stomach like a living alien presence.

"Oh, fuck, that hurts." John puked again.

David's hand on his back calmed him.

John sat back, and David handed him a bottle of water.

John drank, rinsed, spat, and drank again.

"What was that?" He retrieved his fallen blankets and wrapped up tightly. He took a deep breath. "The nightmare had our friends in it, Rocky, Barry, Joanne. But just now, it's like it all changed and it was the past. Or the future? But they were after you. Always, you..."

No, that wasn't right. Not just David.

John, too.

Where did that come from?

"Us. . . they were after us?" John said.

It all jumbled together.

"Calm down," David said. "Breathe."

"What? Why?" John studied David's face. Fear. "What the hell are you so afraid of? How the fuck do you know so much? Why the hell should I breathe and relax?"

"Because that's what works for me, damn it!" David's outburst surprised them both. He rose. "I'm sorry. This isn't. . ." He met John's gaze.

"I'm sorry." He breathed deeply. "These dreams you have, it's the future, it's the past, it's the present, all jumbled together. I see things, too. You know that. I've learned to control it, to sort through all the confusion to figure out what's important. You weren't supposed to see these things."

His voice sounded so different. Lower. Calmer. And his eyes were so deep. John almost felt them tugging at him.

"You need to be calm to figure out what's symbolic and what just is what it is." David stared down at John. "I wanted us to have a few days away from it all, to just be friends, without all this. . ." He sighed. "Without all this."

"What *is* all this?"

David stared at him a long time without speaking.

"You understand it all," John said. "I know you do. Why won't you tell me?"

"They wanted *me*, John. The Dicks." He spoke so quietly John wasn't certain he'd heard him correctly. "They were after *me*. You're right about the past. Thousands died." He stopped and looked at the floor between them. "Many, many people have died because of me. I can't tell you why."

"You mean you don't know?" John asked.

"No. I mean I can't tell you." David sat again, his eyes frightened. John had rarely seen that. "Trust your dreams. They speak the truth. You have a gift." David shook his head. "I'm not sure why. If I'd known you were going to have these gifts, I'd have told you about all this sooner. You're going to need your gifts in the days to come. Don't ever distrust them." David drew in the dust with the tip of one finger. He looked up and held out his hand. "Aren't you cold?" His face was guarded, but gentle and afraid. His eyes were wet, deep pools of pain. "Please, John. I just want us not to fight."

John took David's hand and lay with him, wrapped in their blankets.

"These guys aren't really Dicks." David sighed deeply. "It has to do with the UCA."

"The what?" John asked.

"The UCA. They work for Clement."

"Why the hell does Clement want you?" John sat up. It had to be some kind of put-on.

"It might be the UCA now, but it was the Vatican who started the whole thing. Pope Pius." David sighed and sat up as well. "It's a long story. And I can't tell you a lot of it right now, and you need to trust me that I'm not being an asshole. I'll tell you what I can, but you have to trust me that you aren't ready to hear this, yet."

"Not ready?" John fought to control his voice. Was David trying to Sunday school him?

"Bad phrase." David closed his eyes and made a frustrated face. "Look, this is hard for me." He opened his eyes. "I've never lied to you—ever, and I don't want to lie to you now, but if you try to make me tell you everything, I'm going to have to lie to you because I made a promise to our parents that I wouldn't say anything to anyone until they said so."

John clenched his fists at his sides. So their parents had known about this Vatican thing all along and had kept it from him, too?

"I didn't know you were involved like this." David knelt there; he scared out of his mind. "I swear to you I never imagined you'd turn out to be a freak like me." He shook his head. "I don't even know how that happened."

"So what can you tell me?" John forced himself to calm down. He pushed to his feet and wandered over to the wall.

"It started before we were born," David said. "My mother was part of a Vatican project. Pope Pius wanted to bring the fundamentalists into the Church. The UCA was gaining momentum. Our parents thought they were serving God, but the Pope was insane, and these private interests stepped in. . . Shortly after I was born, our parents ran away."

He stopped, and John turned to see why.

"The plane crash that killed your father wasn't an accident." Tears ran in smudgy streaks through the dirt on David's face. He swallowed hard and continued. "He was protecting us, diverting attention while you and I were brought to safety. They shot him out of the sky over a Nevada desert and blamed his death on our parents. We went into hiding. Our parents eventually brought us to New York and lost themselves in the Ghetto, praying they wouldn't be found. It took eighteen years, but they finally found us." His gaze dropped to the floor.

John's head swam. Everything David said was insane, but John still knew it was all true.

"When did they tell you this?"

"They didn't need to." David shook his head. "Years ago, they tried to decide whether to say anything, so I saved them the stress and told them I already knew." He looked down at his hands. "I know so many things." He looked up at John. "And the people who made me want me back before I start telling people what I know."

"What *do* you know?"

"More than you can possibly imagine."

His face was so serious that John had to laugh.

"I know it sounds insane," David said, "but look deep inside yourself and tell me you don't believe me, that you didn't already know all of this before I said it."

And he was right. Somehow, John knew it was all true. It was like watching a video he'd already seen but only remembering it as it happened.

"If you're involved, then there are things even I don't understand." David's brow furrowed. "Maybe you are a part of the project, too, a part I never knew about. Maybe they made us both." He shook his head and shrugged. "I can't think of another explanation for your visions."

"What are we then, David? What did they do to us?"

David didn't answer.

John could make the next step on his own.

He had dreams and visions, now, but it went farther back. He'd always known what David thought, in a way that went beyond sharing a room. And David had always known things, been able to sense things.

Pieces fell into place. A single word leapt into his mind.

"Prophets." It was the only word that fit. "If it was the Pope who started it all, it has to be something like that. They made us into prophets, didn't they? How?"

"Prophets aren't made, they're born." David's eyes held all the stars and planets.

"But why did they do that? What's the point of it all?"

"This is where you get really mad at me and want to hit me again, for real this time." David's eyes grew dark.

"You mean you're not going to tell me?"

"That's what I mean." His face showed nothing, now.

"God damn it, David!" John turned away and banged his fist on a nearby table. The broken glass rattled. He took a deep breath and thick air caught in his throat.

He coughed, tried to keep himself calm. "Why tell me part of this but not the rest?"

"The Armani."

What the what? John turned to David and flailed his frustration.

"The two men we saw looking for a mouthy Jew? The guy at Babylon? His suit's an Armani." David rose to his feet.

"I remember the guy."

"He's the reason I was so quiet last night. I knew he'd spot us and that there was nothing I could do to stop it. His name's Addison." Addison. Right. The scary, blond cracker had called him that.

"I need to talk to my parents," David said, "to find out what we're going to do about him, then, once we get our plans made, I promise, I *promise* I'll tell you everything. I promise. Please don't force me to make a choice between my loyalty to my parents. . . to our parents. . . and to you."

If it affected the entire family, why was David the only one who knew about it? If John was involved somehow, didn't he have a right to be *involved*, too? Right now? What the hell?

"John..." David said quietly. The warmth in his voice compelled John to face him. "Our family is in a lot of danger. I need to know you'll trust me. Our lives depend on it." His eyes had that wise, mature look that sometimes infuriated John and other times melted his anger completely.

"I should trust you?" John tried to keep his voice level. "I just found out we're all involved in some top-secret project that made me a complete and total fucktastic freak. That someone is out there trying to kill me, or capture me or something, and that I wouldn't even know about this now if my inner freak hadn't made a surprise appearance." He shook his head. "Oh, and you don't trust me enough to tell me the most important part."

Nope. The quiet voice wouldn't work.

"Why the fuck did they do this to me!" John shouted.

So, no. He didn't trust David right now.

Michael watched the argument from a corner of the room. John wasn't likely to notice if he accidentally walked through the angel, but Michael always found that sort of thing unsettling.

"We should go back." John dropped his blanket and pulled on his trunks.

"What? Why?" David moved closer to John. So much for quality time together. Disappointment blew off David in waves.

"Where should I start?" John turned on his cousin. "The one guy I've always trusted, who I've never lied to about anything? He's been keeping the planet's biggest secret from me for, oh, I don't know, David, just how long have you been hiding this from me? Our whole lives?" He gathered his things and shoved them into packs. "I don't really want to be alone in this cold, suffocating room with you right now, and I figure you need to talk to our parents before you can tell me what the hell is going on? Fine. You can't talk to them here."

"But once we leave—" Regret filled the words as they left David's mouth.

"Once we leave here *what?*" John spun to face him.

Once they left, John's time was up. None of them knew how fast his end would come, just that every thread in the fabric of the future spun out to the same conclusion. And once they left their sanctuary, it could happen at any time.

"Jesus Christ, are you listening to yourself?" John scoffed. "No wait, you *can't* listen to yourself because you're not *saying anything!*" He wiped an arm over his face. "I've trusted you my whole life, and you've done nothing but hide things from me." He wiped his arm over his face again. "Blast it, I will not cry." He shook his head. "I don't even know who you are right now."

"I'm just me." David seemed so small and broken. "I'm just. . ."

Michael raised a hand in warning.

David glanced up at the movement. He hung his head.

"You're just what?" John demanded.

"I'm just. . . really sorry."

"Yeah." John strapped his packs into place. "Yeah, you are. Really... sorry." He strode to the door then stopped, his back to David. "Are you coming? We're safer together."

At least, John hadn't lost all reason.

David looked up at Michael, who motioned for him to hurry. Pain filled his young charge's eyes, rendering him so human.

This was what the heavenly host cherished, what drove the demons mad with jealousy.

Humanity. Human pain. It was madness.

David quickly gathered his things. They *were* safer together, and John needed all the safety he could get. Not that it would help.

"Tell me one thing," John said quietly, still not looking at David.

"What?" David met Michael's gaze evenly should he need Michael's silent advice.

"Should I be scared?"

David's eyes closed, and his cheek twitched. He swallowed deeply and blinked back tears. He shook his head and wiped his face with one hand. With a deep breath he met Michael's eyes again.

"Yes. You should." His heartbreak poured out of him so completely, Michael was glad John had his back turned.

"Okay, then." John nodded. "Let's go."

John ignored David as best he could while they swam through Venice and into the subway. How could David have kept something so huge from him forever without John noticing something? Had there been clues? Should he have known?

When John extinguished his light and prepared to surface at their usual spot, David touched his arm, holding him back. He shone the beam of his flashlight up to the surface of the water where something floated in the water above them. . . many somethings. . . so many somethings they completely blocked the surface.

What the hell? John pointed his light, and it flashed on a tiny open eye. He pushed himself away from the things, grabbing David.

Dozens of eyes glinted in the flashlight beam, along with the tails and little clawed feet of thousands of dead rats. They'd have to push through them to leave the water. John's skin crawled. He tugged on David's arm and pointed down a side tunnel.

David nodded.

Training his light all around to keep from swimming into anything dead, John led the way to another exit. The trip took an extra hour, but it was worth it to avoid the rats. They weren't a good sign. Something bad had gone down. Something very bad.

When they reached the Dresden platform, the sight was exactly the same: thousands of dead rats covered the surface from wall to wall. Shit. Apparently, rats blanketed every possible exit.

David jabbed a thumb upward. "We might as well go ahead and climb out here."

The sound startled John. It was the first thing either of them had said since they'd left Venice. He examined the bloated carcasses. How many diseases did they carry?

"Might as well." More than ever, John wanted to get out of the tunnels altogether and see what had happened in the Ghetto.

The bloated, furry bodies bumped against his head first, then his shoulders and chest. He shuddered and worked hard to breathe steadily, refusing even to look at the dead animals as he pushed his way through to the surface.

A thick, gray smoke filled the air. It coated the walls a sooty black.

David swept away enough of the rats on the ledge to climb out.

John followed his cousin, who gave him a hand up. He searched the blackened walls and the scorched bodies of the rats.

"We should leave the masks on," David said.

John agreed. "They firebombed the tunnels." He worked hard to control his voice. Had their friends escaped in time? Had Jamie?

"It's just like the vision I had. It happened."

David didn't say anything.

A lump grew in John's throat and not from the sight of the rats. How many of their friends had been caught in the blast? Was the Ghetto worse?

"Come on." David looked just as worried.

John grabbed his arm. "I'm still pissed at you, but this is more important than the fact that you're an ass pony." He squeezed the arm. "Truce for now?"

"Truce." David worked hard to keep his face blank, but John could see the hope.

They hurried into the tunnels.

When John found the first human body, David barreled directly into him. Was it a man or a woman? Charred down to the skeleton, the body lay curled up in a fetal position. It smiled a Cheshire grin of yellow teeth and blackened gums. Its eyes were empty sockets, its arms crossed against the side of its face. John felt drawn to it, pulled by an invisible thread.

John and David crouched together.

"You think it's someone we know?" He reached out one tentative hand, let it hang in the air for a second, debating, then touched the papery skin on the thing's left ankle. Skin fell away into ash.

A roiling wall of fire surged through the tunnels directly at her. She fell to her side and covered her face with her arms. There wasn't even enough oxygen to scream. A searing blast roasted her skin as it crashed over her, blowing her long hair out behind her as if she were caught in a hurricane. . .

John fell to his knees. David curled an arm around him.

"She was a woman."

David nodded.

"I don't know who."

David shook his head. "I never get used to seeing these."

For a moment, John forgot his anger and didn't dislodge his cousin's arm.

David led him away from the corpse.

John kept his face turned to it even as he walked away from the thing that had once been a person. . .

Had the same thing happened to Joanne? To Jamie? He turned to watch the path so he could hurry.

David's arm dropped away as they ran through the tunnel as quickly as they could. Visibility was so low they sometimes felt blind. The other bodies they simply ignored. No way to identify them, anyway.

By the time they reached the tower, John was nauseous from the bitterness of the smoke in spite of the masks and rebreathers.

They climbed to the roof.

The sky glowed pink.

John belly-crawled across the tile and the bird droppings, startling a flock of crows into flight. He and David huddled against the ledge that ringed the roof.

Slowly, afraid of what he'd see, John lifted himself high enough to peer over the ledge.

The sun rose brilliantly over buildings that seemed normal, as if nothing had happened.

Where was the smoke damage and scarred brickwork? Why weren't the cars lining the streets pushed over or crushed?

"Didn't anything happen?" John asked. "Am I missing something?"

"Look." David pointed down at the empty alley below them. "The garbage is gone."

John hauled himself up so he could look straight down into the alley. David was right. The trash had vanished.

"What about the tunnels?" John asked. "Wasn't there a riot?"

David shrugged and shook his head. Seriously? With everything he knew, this was a surprise to him? David rolled his eyes. He'd been with John the whole time.

They ripped open their packs and pulled out their clothes.

Thirty seconds later, the rooftop was deserted.

Bo worked silently on Dr. Sung's table. A mosaic illustrated abstract fish in vivid green and blue and gold, the symbols of his childhood worked into the motif. The tiny tiles sparkled like glass. He bent over his work, carefully gluing the tiles into place with a surgeon's precision, pulling different colors from the pockets of his coveralls, wiping excess glue onto his bare arms and chest. So far, this piece had taken him three weeks.

The doctor paid him the absolute maximum anyone was allowed to earn when they lived in the Ghetto, and from the size of the tips his wife had reportedly handed the guys, they planned on finding ways around the earning caps. Bo wanted to do his very best work for them.

If only Bo had seen the guys after their return. The doctor's wife had been very curious about them, and he'd love to know how they'd gotten along. Jamie had told him about the tips. The message he'd received in the original purchase order had commented on the symbols he'd used in Mabel's patio furniture, so he made sure all three figured into this design as well.

"Pretend it's a secret code," the message had said, "and hide them in the design. My boy will think it's clever."

Ha. If only she knew. The symbols *were* a code. . . well, as much of a code as he and his best friends had thought up as five-year-olds. Bo set the last piece of the open circle that Dave Sato had chosen for his symbol.

What had happened to his friends? They'd said very rushed goodbyes before Bo and his family left Wisconsin forever, and he'd always been afraid to look them up. Surely, Addison had all his old friends monitored. Even a search on Dave or Joey's name could be traced back to the source.

Well, in his small way, Bo could honor their friendship with his work, even if the only one who enjoyed it was the son of a wealthy doctor.

He wished *his* boys would return. The first day had passed quickly as he helped handle the riot and subsequent cleanup, but Bo hadn't slept a wink that night. Ruth kept reassuring him that she would know if something bad had happened, but he wouldn't relax until he saw them with his own eyes.

He'd set up a workspace in the shop where he could watch the door. The light sucked now that boards covered the holes left by the explosion that had taken out the front windows, but he'd set up clamp lights to compensate.

Barry had tried to check in Venice for the guys, but the tunnels seemed impassable. With Noah missing as well, Barry had been frantic, so if a way in existed, he would've found it. Now that the riots had dissipated and Addison had apparently withdrawn for the time being, why would the guys stay away? Maybe they couldn't find a way back.

No. That didn't worry him. David could always find a way back. Bo was afraid the guys hadn't stopped in Venice at all but had kept going. Sooner or later, he'd wake up and David would be gone into the world. As close as the guys were, more likely than not, they'd go together. His only consolation was Barry's insistence that all their hiding places were too far under water to connect to the net. If they'd left the Ghetto for good, they'd have contacted someone. Bo kept telling himself that.

Jamie insisted that her setup was advanced enough that they could reach her without detection.

He adjusted his glasses on the tip of his nose and explored the nearby lamp he was sculpting from the glass globes the guys had given him. It still looked like a pole with a bunch of doorknobs stuck into it. Ugh. He was too distracted to be creative, and the room was too dark. He could work on the table because he'd finished the design and could fill in the blanks in his sleep.

He bounced one of the globes in one hand while he…

Pounding footsteps on the sidewalk outside caught Bo's attention. With the door open, he heard every pair of feet, every bicycle, every voice as it approached, only to face disappointment when someone else crossed the open doorway. He had to stop getting his hopes up and focus on his work…

Then two young men appeared as silhouettes in the doorway in the early morning sunshine. Bo held his breath. They careened into each other and piled through the door. Bo let himself breathe again.

His boys were home.

"Dad!"

"Uncle Bo!"

Bo barely had time to get to his feet before they dropped their bags on the floor, threw themselves at him and latched on. Bo held them with an arm apiece and kissed both grimy, sooty faces. They were damp and smelled of salt and smoke and two days without a shower, but they felt strong and solid in his arms, each babbling a mile a minute.

"What happened, Dad? Is everyone all right? What happened to the windows—?"

"We thought the whole place would be a cinder, but the garbage is gone—?"

Their voices overlapped as they plied him with rapid questions. John's were to be expected, but David's surprised Bo. He finally silenced them both by cupping his hands over their mouths.

"If you'll be quiet for a moment, I'll tell you what happened."

With a final squeeze he released them. Now that they were home, exhaustion hit him with a wave of dizziness. He chose a chair away from the piece in progress. As expected, the moment Bo was seated, the guys jumped up onto a nearby table, David with his foot on Bo's knee. Once again, Bo reminded himself how lucky he was.

"I can't explain it," Bo said. "The Dicks started a sweep, and when Rabbi Kaufman wouldn't let them in the synagogue, they blew the doors with explosives."

The boys exchanged a concerned look.

"Hundreds of people came out with clubs and baseball bats and guns even and started moving on them. People threw pipe bombs at the agents near the synagogue." He gestured at the plywood covering the front of the store. "One idiot dropped his."

"Was anyone in the store?" John asked. "Was anyone hurt?"

"Everyone in the family is fine. We got lucky." Bo would never forget the second fireball he'd seen in his lifetime. "Scrapes and cuts for all of us. Your mother may have a hard time hearing for a few days, but nothing serious."

"So why isn't the Ghetto a cinder?" John asked.

"I don't know," Bo admitted. "They spent an hour going door to door—"

"Wait, did they come here?" David asked.

"Yes." Bo had no idea how to explain what had happened. "Layla saved the day, and I'll tell you that story later…" How could he explain the rest? It made no sense. "But just when everyone poured out of their homes for a riot, the Dicks backed off."

Bo had his theories, but how much did John know? What had David told him?

"They had serious artillery, and we would've been massacred. They even had copters, but as soon as the violence started, poof, the Dicks climbed into their trucks and took off. Everyone stood around asking themselves why so few of us died."

"What about the garbage?" John asked quietly.

And what the heck about that?

"After the almost riot, Dickersons issued a formal apology on the net and promised to raise the standard of living in the Ghetto." Bo ran a hand through John's dirty hair. "They made up some crap about Clement not knowing how bad things had gotten, how fortunate the drug bust—"

"Seriously?"

"A drug bust?"

"Yeah, that's what they called it: a drug bust. They said it was fortunate the Dicks found out what a lousy job the local government was doing. It's like they expect us to believe Clement didn't know everything." He scoffed bitterly. "Yesterday, dump trucks came through and collected all the garbage. No one trusts it, though. Over a hundred people died and dozens are still missing. . . including Noah and his dad."

"Noah?" The boys shared a look of dismay that surprised Bo. Didn't David already know?

"Barry and Jamie are checking into it." He squeezed David's knee. "We hope he's in custody. Maybe Jonas is trying to teach him a lesson?" He remembered a bit of good news he could share. "Jamie, Rocky, and Barry got out for sure. Barry's helping. So is Tracey."

"Joanne?" David asked.

"She's fine."

"There's a bartender," John asked, his face turning red. "His name's Billy. I don't know his last name."

Bo thought through the names he knew but came up empty. "Sorry, son. I just don't know." But he'd have to find out more about why it made John blush.

"What's your theory?" David asked.

What? David must know that Addison was in charge of the situation. Asking to speculate in front of John meant something had changed.

John bristled as if noticing Bo's hesitation. Damn it. The young man stepped away completely and crossed his arms over his chest. David rolled his eyes, as if this were one more in a line of protests on John's part. He threw an arm around John's neck and tousled his hair.

"Don't." John elbowed him away with a vicious look.

David held John's stare, but his face filled with pain.

"I told John about Addison, Dad." He turned to look Bo squarely in the eye. "It's kosher."

"My theory?" Bo relaxed. The fact that David mentioned Addison specifically told Bo what John didn't know as well as what he did. "He's trying to flush us out. He knew we were in *this* ghetto but couldn't pinpoint us exactly. If there'd been a full-scale riot, we'd have escaped in the confusion." The rest scared Bo. "I'm not sure about the garbage, though. My guess is he wants to flush us out, let us think we have some space, so we make a break for it. Maybe even convince us he's been reprimanded."

Would the next part go beyond what John already knew? The guys stared at him with wide innocent eyes. If only they were still little boys Bo could protect. He hated saying what came next, but they weren't boys anymore, were they?

"We think they're going to take the whole place apart, one brick at a time, until they find us, and they don't care who gets caught in the crossfire." He watched David's face, but his son's calm demeanor told him he could say what he wanted. "The official word is the Dicks uncovered a Mafia-style drug ring dealing white noise, prostitution, and body parts. I mean, they've known about all that for years, but they choose right now to do something?" He noticed the guilt on their faces. They didn't know Jamie had already spilled her guts about the finer points of their nocturnal activities. Bo had had time to adjust.

"They're saying the ring's headquarters was in the Ghetto. That's why they did the sweep, to try to get info on this Jewish mafia they've invented."

"But Noah saw his dad's records." John threw his hands up in disgust. "The guy in charge of the local Dicks runs the whole thing. Some ass pony named McCarthy."

"I know all that," Bo said, "that's why we think. . . we think they're setting us up. They make this big show of trying to do right by the Ghetto rats finally, in spite of this big Jewish mafia thing, so if we don't make a break for it, they can wipe out the whole Ghetto and blame it on the ungrateful Jews with their illegal mafia in spite of the Dicks' good will."

"This guy would destroy the entire Ghetto just to get us?" John's face had fallen completely blank.

"He's already done worse," David said. "Remember what I told you about your visions?"

Visions?

"Oh, praise the Lord!" Naomi's shout from the doorway distracted Bo, along with the clatter of canned soup hitting the floor.

"Thank God." Ruth steadied herself against the door jamb with one hand.

David rushed to them. After a moment's hesitation, John followed. Before the guys could bend to retrieve the groceries, Naomi grabbed each of them and held them tight for a quick hug and a kiss on the cheek.

"When did you get back?"

"Just a minute ago, ma'am," John answered.

David picked Ruth up in his arms and swung her around. Her feet hung a good three inches from the floor. Bo sighed. When had that happened?

"See, husband?" Ruth turned to Bo when her feet returned to the floor. "I told you they were all right." She cupped both guys' necks. "You had food?"

"And you're both okay?" Naomi finally let them pick up the tin cans and ripped paper bag. "Of course, you're both okay. It was just a shock to see you like this." She turned to John. "I knew you'd take care of each other." She rubbed a black streak on his cheek with the thumb of one hand. Uncharacteristically, he allowed it.

Ruth hurried to Bo and sat in his lap, hugging him.

"What should we do next?" David asked, disrupting the moment.

Bo winced when he saw the expression on the women's faces. If John was upset by something he thought they knew, how would he react? Naomi only glanced at John for the briefest second before he suddenly and roughly passed the groceries to David and stomped over to the stairway. So much anger had suddenly written itself across his face. What did that even mean? Why was he so angry?

"How did I never notice this shit? You are so obvious." He kept his back to them, one hand on the railing. What did it mean? "I know there's some big secret you know that I don't, so I wish you'd quit with the meaningful looks and secret glances." His voice dripped sarcasm, and he favored David with a dark glare. "Just tell me to go upstairs and take a shower, which is what I'd pretty much like to do, anyway."

"John." David hurried over and touched his cousin's arm.

"You have this great big secret that involves me, but you won't tell me." John yanked his arm away, more anger clouding his eyes than Bo had seen in years. "You know what? Fuck all of it."

"We're in a lot of danger." David stepped back. "I really need you to trust me. Please."

A veritable panoply of emotions washed over John's face. He struggled and almost spoke twice but stopped himself both times. He set his jaw in an expression of defiance Bo knew only too well. The next statement would not be pleasant.

"I don't give a damn about your stupid secrets." John looked around at the pained faces, then settled on Bo's. "You want to know *my* secret?" He closed his eyes, and his brow furrowed.

Bo felt a gentle probing in his mind, something he hadn't felt in almost twenty years. Not since...

Do you hear me?

Bo gasped. No. It wasn't possible.

"Yeah, Uncle Bo, it *is* possible." John opened his eyes and stared directly at his uncle. "Surprise! I don't know how, but I know exactly what you're thinking. I guess *both* of your sons are freaks." He turned his vicious glare on his mother. "If we're part of some fucking science project, who the hell is my *real* father, anyway? I might as well..." He waved at Bo, then stared hard, his eyes both wet and angry. "I always wanted you to be my dad. I did. I've always loved you that way. Always. I have. But now?" His eyes chilled to ice, and Bo's heart broke. "Who cares if I'm in the middle of it, right? Who cares about my stupid visions?" He waved at them dismissively. "Have your stupid meeting without me. I'm going to take a shower."

He thumped up the stairs without looking back.

David started up the stairs.

"Don't." Naomi laid one hand on his arm. "Don't offer him something you can't possibly give him."

"I need to talk to him." David pulled away, and anger flared in his eyes. "I don't want him to be mad about this." Had Bo seen a literal flash of light?

"If you go to him, now, he'll expect you to explain everything." Naomi crossed her arms, letting David mull that over. "So if you don't intend to spit out the whole truth just yet, you need to let him work through this on his own."

"He's so angry with me." David's voice sounded broken. He stared at the hallway above, his pain a rough stain across his face.

Upstairs, John started the shower.

"He has every right to be," Naomi said. "At all of us, especially if he's having visions."

David turned to Naomi suddenly, as if surprised and annoyed by her candor. . . but a quick response seemed to die on his lips. He looked up the stairs again.

"He's having visions?" she asked.

"I don't know how." David turned to Naomi. "Do you?"

"I don't." How could she not? How could she not know that her own son was involved in the Project? How could David not know? "I didn't know." Naomi met met Bo's eyes. "What he said. He heard your thoughts?"

Bo nodded.

She crossed her arms and stared at the floor. Then her eyes abruptly opened wide, as if she'd just had an epiphany. She looked over at Ruth and shook her head. She hadn't known, but she'd just put the pieces together. She fought for composure and turned to David.

"Do you understand why he's upset with you?" she asked.

"No, Aunt Naomi, I don't." He looked at her. "Isn't that bizarre?"

"Sometimes the people closest to us surprise and confuse us the most." Naomi placed her hand on his arm again. Amen to that.

"I'll go talk to him." Bo patted the table with one hand.

"I appreciate the offer." Naomi waved him down. "He'd likely take it better coming from you. . . but I'd like to talk with him myself. It's about time I had a chance to talk *with* my son instead of *at* him." Without looking back, she passed David and climbed the stairs.

Bo stared at her until she disappeared around the corner.

"What's going on?" he asked his son.

David gazed up the stairway. His shoulders rose and fell as he rolled them twice. His shoulder blades pressed like wings against the fabric of his T-shirt.

"Why is he so angry?" David turned to face his parents with tears pouring down his face.

Bo's heart tightened in a knot. David was a sensitive young man, yet the strong emotions always confused him.

Ruth went to him, reached up to take him into her arms.

"No!" He moved away, glaring at her with his hands in fists at his side. "Why is John so angry? Doesn't he trust me?"

Bo couldn't tear his eyes from David's tears. Fear and anger fought for control of his son, holding him in a tornado of uncertainty.

"He's angry because he's young and confused," Ruth said. "With everything going on, he doesn't know who to trust. He's always trusted you, David, and now there's this secret you never told him. It scares him. He might find out he can't trust any of us, and we're the only people he's ever trusted. Imagine how scary that would be. And he's started having visions? And he can see our thoughts? He must be terrified, and fear is a short trip to anger."

"Why does it hurt me so much?" David wiped his face with his shirt and made an almost animal noise. He turned back to the stairwell and hit his own chest with a white-knuckled fist.

Bo flinched at the thump. It had been years since David had hurt himself, but it'd been years since he'd felt so much, too.

"Here," David said. "It hurts here." He thumped his chest again.

Bo moved to Ruth's side and laid an arm around her shoulders.

"You forget sometimes how much I don't understand," David said. "You're so used to thinking of me as the Son of God, you forget that I'm just a messed-up teenager, too." His gaze settled on the staircase. "You forget how much I don't remember. . . how small I feel."

He pressed his fists into his stomach, and Bo drew every ounce of strength from his soul to let his son work through it on his own.

"It hurts me here." David looked down at himself. "I still don't understand why that happens, after all this time, why my stomach hurts when. . . when I'm afraid." He sucked in several deep breaths. He turned to face his parents, calmer, now. "Isn't that funny?" He rolled his shoulders then wiped his face once more. "Your suspicions are correct, Father." He used that deeper voice only the adults heard. "Addison knows we're in the Ghetto, but he hasn't found us. I'm not sure why he pulled the Dicks out. That was unexpected. Now, he's waiting for us to make a move." His eyes wandered down from the ceiling to rest on his parents. "We need to wait and pretend that everything is normal. We can't let anyone know how scared we are."

David was frightened? That worried Bo more than anything else.

"What can you see?" Ruth asked David, squeezing Bo's hand. "Naomi and I had dreams about Addison."

"Someone is going to die before this part of it is over." David set one hand on the railing.

"Do you know who?" Ruth's arm slipped around Bo's waist.

"Do you really want to know?" David stared up the stairs.

Ruth's body relaxed against Bo as she shook her head. There were some things better left unknown.

"I have no idea how John's visions fit into any of this." David stared at his hand for a moment. "The flesh gets in the way."

Ruth shuddered against Bo's side. The first time David had told them that, he'd been five years old. Bo had no memory of what had started it all, probably some fight with John over a block of wood.

David threw a hysterical fit, an absolute frenzied tantrum, screaming about how much his stomach hurt and his chest and his eyes, and why couldn't he see what was going to happen, and why was he going through all this again?

He'd ranted things Bo hadn't even understood. . . but the anguish in David's face? Bo couldn't remember what had upset the boy, yet he remembered the pain in his face. He'd had nightmares about that day, about David's pain and the fear beyond panic and the anger at his own limitations. All those things together on the face of a five-year-old had terrified Bo.

"It's this." The boy had held his hand up for his parents to see. He shook his hand in their faces. "This!" His voice was hysterical and high. "The flesh gets in the way!"

He scraped the back of one hand as if trying to scrub off the skin, rubbed it obsessively, screaming the same thing again and again. And then he'd stopped speaking English. Bo had never figured out the language. He'd tried to hold the boy down until he regained control of himself, but David had broken away.

He'd made a mad dash for Bo's work counter, grabbed one of the Exacto knives lying there, pressed a hand onto the counter, and stabbed the knife into the back of his hand with all his strength. The blade had gone all the way through.

Bo could still hear the sound of David's screams.

Who knew that much blood could pour out of such a tiny hand? Bo shuddered at the memory and forced himself back to the present. David had survived eighteen years, now, yet some concepts still eluded him. He might be a genius, but he still struggled with his feelings.

And Bo was no genius. How could he help his son who was also the Son of God?

"We need to keep waiting." David's voice startled Bo after such a long silence. "It's not time, yet."

"David." Bo's voice caught in his throat, and he had to cough before he continued. "We're going to be okay." He held out a hand. "John will get over it. People get mad. They get over it, too. He won't stay mad at you."

"You think so?"

Bo nodded and gestured for David to take his hand, which his son did, and Bo reeled him in. Ruth held him as well. David often forgot how much he needed that comfort. Bo smiled. His son often forgot how much his parents also needed it. David relaxed and leaned against them. He felt bony and fragile in Bo's arms.

"You are both very good to me," David said. "Addison chose well."

Bo could tell he'd be all right because it was a joke.

"I should take a shower." He moved away from his parents. "I love you both." His eyes were deep pools of wisdom and concern. He turned and ascended the stairs very slowly.

"We love you, too," Bo answered for them both. "So we continue to wait," he added once David had gone.

"We're good at that." Ruth squeezed him. "Don't worry. Once things start rolling, I'm sure our patience won't get much of a workout." She looked up the stairs. "It hurts them so much more when they fight these days, husband. I sometimes wonder what it means."

Upstairs, when Naomi reached the door to John's room, she looked around at the things he shared with David. How did they know what belonged to whom? Everything mixed together. Dirty clothes littered the wooden floor among piles of books.

Naomi picked her way over the debris, found her way to the side of John's bed, flipped the blanket over the bare mattress and lowered herself delicately, hands folded in her lap, to wait.

She hadn't been in the boys' room for over a year. Wasn't that strange? The holograms that covered the peeling paint of the walls had changed from wild animals and world maps to swing bands and ads for videos. Near the window lay a guitar the boys shared. The closet door stood open, its contents spilling across the room. Both beds were unmade; the dresser drawers lay open and overflowing.

Snapshots at the head of John's mattress hovered near the wall above a small projector. Naomi leaned closer. Some of the faces she recognized as friends the children brought home from time to time: a photo of John riding piggyback on their dramatic friend Barry, who always insisted on kissing Naomi's hand and opening doors for her. She'd pegged him right away as a troublemaker sucking up, but he seemed harmless enough. He'd worked very hard to find the boys these last few days. She should let him know they were home.

Jonas' older son appeared in several shots, as well as Joanne, who had unceremoniously announced her job as a prostitute one afternoon at a church picnic. A photo of the church youth group hovered there, a whole mob of kids piled together on a couch, and one photo of a little boy Naomi had to mull over to recognize.

She gently brushed the image to expand it. He sported a space helmet and brandished a bright blue light saber made from a wooden stick and some tempera paint. He wore a jumpsuit—with patches and insignia sewed onto it to resemble a flight suit—and shiny, black cowboy boots. He also wore a serious expression to show that he meant to kick some serious alien butt.

Naomi chuckled at the memory of her son on Halloween after his seventh birthday. She'd helped him with the costume, sitting at a table in Bo's workroom sewing the patches while John painted the wooden stick. They'd worked quietly side by side, John occasionally making suggestions for the placement of patches, Naomi complimenting her son's work.

She smiled at the memory of the two of them wandering the streets panhandling for candy. Her cousin's family had been away for some lost reason, and she and John had spent that Halloween on their own.

But John had climbed into trees until she shooed him down. He'd menaced the neighborhood kids with his play sword until Naomi told him to behave. There'd been millions of normal childhood antics she'd curtailed out of fear, fear that he would grow up and never fulfill his purpose, or, even more probably, that he would.

Zack had had a purpose that had taken him away from her.

Feeling eyes on her, Naomi looked up. John stood silhouetted in the doorway, clutching a towel around his waist. When he stepped into the light of the bare bulb that hung from the middle of the ceiling, he wore the same determined expression as the boy in the photo. His eyes were exactly the same—deep and furrowed with thought—but he was so much taller and more solid. His hair stood up all over his head.

The hand that had brushed the photo floated down to her lap as she gazed at her son. Was he waiting for a lecture, feet wide apart? When had she become so horrible?

"I'm sorry," she said.

The lines on John's brow deepened.

"For what?" His stance didn't change.

She pushed up from his mattress and gestured at the photo. It rose and separated itself from the others.

He took a few steps toward it.

She straightened her skirt nervously.

"For being so harsh with you all your life."

He bent over the picture for a long time.

"John. . . when your father died, I didn't know what to do. I lost my faith that day, and I've been scared every day for the past eighteen years. I've been very unfair to you, and I'm sorry I didn't see that sooner. You were a good boy, John. You've always been a good boy."

John scowled. No wait. That didn't help.

"A good *man*. You've grown into a good man."

He stood in the middle of the room, bowed over the photo, gripping his towel tightly with one hand. A toe on one foot scratched the ankle of the other leg. He looked up at her with confusion written as deeply on his face as determination had been painted there a moment before.

"What changed?" he asked.

How in the world could she answer that question?

"So much." If she'd been accustomed to standing in her own son's room, she could've used the time to think about what to tell him, how to tell him.

"I'm not putting you off." But so much *had* changed. "Finding out that you have. . . visions? Dreams? I don't even know what you have. It surprised me. When I saw your father the other day—"

"My father? He's dead." John's eyes were guarded.

His eyes were always so guarded

"I know that,' Namoi said.

"You said you saw him."

Well, there was a starting point anyway.

"You want me to tell you the truth? You're not going to believe the truth. These things have been secrets for so long because we didn't think you could possibly believe us, but you need to understand that I believe it. As far as I'm concerned it *is* the truth." She breathed. "You have visions, now. Can logic explain that?"

"Can you?"

"No." That was the truth, too. "I can't." She had her suspicions but nothing certain.

"You were involved in some secret government project to make your kid a freak, and you have no idea what they did?" Suspicion colored his voice a dark and ugly tone. So much anger.

"I wasn't involved in the project; I swear to you." Just how insane was she going to sound? "Let me get it out. It's not going to make any sense, and I know that, so please just let me tell it."

He nodded.

"I couldn't conceive," she told him. "And your father was infertile. We'd tried for years, but every doctor we knew told us we'd never have children of our own." She leaned against the dresser. "Then we found ourselves at the most advanced obstetrics and genetics lab on the planet. We begged Addison to help us. He even agreed to do it."

"So, what, he slipped the freaklazoid genes into me when I was in some test tube?"

"That's the part I don't understand." And she truly didn't. "It never worked. They tried. They failed. I'm going to assume you don't really want the reproductive details."

He shuddered and shook his head. So, still enough of a boy to be embarrassed about that sort of information.

Before Naomi could continue, footsteps on the stairs distracted them both. David. He walked past the open doorway, pulling off his shirt on his way to the bathroom.

Naomi noticed for the first time that her son stood there in only a towel, and she had trouble focusing on him. Ever since he'd grown into such a tall, young man, seeing him undressed made her uncomfortable.

He seemed suddenly awkward as well, so she wandered toward the door as he crossed the room to his dresser.

"A month later, I was pregnant." She kept her back to him and absently pretended to study one of the many hologram posters. "Addison swore it had nothing to do with his efforts." She traced the signatures of a band called Dance Monkey. "Maybe he lied."

"You didn't wonder at the time?"

Should she talk about the angels? No. Not right now.

"I did. But I honestly thought you were a miracle. A gift from God." She crossed her arms. "That's what your name means. Gift from God. I suppose that sounds foolish to you, but it's the truth." How much could he understand? "I was almost thirty years old and had spent ten years trying to have a child. When I held you in my arms that first day?" She still felt a lump in her throat. "I didn't ask a lot of questions. I loved you so much. I still do. Even if I show it poorly."

No. She wouldn't break down. That would be unfair. Manipulative.

"Then your father spoke to me a few days ago," she said, "and told me that everything is going according to plan."

"What plan?"

"God's plan. I know how cozy and comfortable that sounds." Did he even believe in God? "Faith is a mysterious thing. Without it, the world is a frightening and dangerous place, but with it, everything makes a certain kind of sense."

"That's what people say about sparking up. . . about rush."

He had to be testing her, expecting her to change back into the mother he knew if he pushed a little.

"Sometimes I think it's the same thing."

John pulled on a dress shirt. She sounded like a vastly different person, but could he really take down any of the walls he'd spent so much energy erecting against her judgments and smothering? Especially now? His image in the mirror gazed back at him with an acidic stare.

His mother stood by the closet with her back to him, waiting for him to cover himself.

Why was he self-conscious in front of nobody but his own mother? He focused on his reflection and tried to soften the hardness in his eyes then tucked in his shirt.

"You can turn around."

She did so.

They watched each other in the mirror.

She seemed to wait for him to ask the next question.

"How did Dad die?"

His mother looked down. He could tell it was one of the questions she'd expected.

"He died so that we might live," she said. What did she mean? She stood silently for a moment, eyes closed, face full of memories. "We were at the compound in Nevada. We stole a plane and were about to escape when your father saw incoming fighters on the radar." She obviously assumed he knew far more than he did. "We weren't going to make it. Your father insisted I take you into the mountains in the jeep while he acted as a decoy. I thought they'd force him down and take him back to the compound." Tears ran down her face now. Her voice was soft. "They shot him out of the sky, and, by the time they realized he was alone in the plane, we were gone." She closed her eyes and shuddered. "Not a day has gone by that I haven't seen that flash of light. . ." She opened her eyes and wiped her face. She looked at her son. "You have his eyes."

"I do?" The words caught in his throat.

"So handsome. . ."

So much of her story confused John, but it agreed with David's explanation. Maybe John didn't want to know the truth. . . so then why was he so mad that he hadn't been told before? His emotions made no sense at all.

"I don't know why you have visions. Truly I don't, but. . ."

When she smiled, she looked ten years younger. "But I'd like to think it's because God has a wonderful plan in store for you as well."

"As well?"

The shower stopped.

"Go to him." His mother startled him. "He needs you. Lord knows he'd never show it, but I think he's afraid."

"Afraid?"

"He's never been good with emotions." She fixed the collar of John's shirt. "He doesn't understand them, and he's afraid of them. You've always been much more honest about your feelings. Help David stop being afraid of his. Emotions are what make us human." She smoothed his shirt out across his chest. "Can you tell me about your visions?"

It was strange to be so close to his mother. She wore lilac perfume. The scent reminded him of a time they had been much closer. He looked over at the photo of himself, a space ranger grimly facing his destiny.

"I see the future sometimes. Mostly bad things. I saw them firebomb the tunnels before it happened." How bizarre that these things had become so easy to say. "And I can read minds."

"I'm not sure what these visions mean." He'd never seen her smile so much. "But I think it's wonderful that you have them. I think you just might surprise a lot of people."

Wow. She thought the damn visions made him special?

"If I thought I could make up for all these bad years with one sappy emotional outburst, I would do it." She tentatively ran her fingers through John's hair. "But I don't think it'll really help. . . I love you, and you *are* special. . . to me at least. . . and. . ." She hesitated. "We aren't going to keep secrets from you anymore, but this isn't the kind of story that comes out all in one piece."

A short, soft burst of song floated from the bathroom, some song by Cole Porter. What the hell was it called?

"Go talk to him," his mother urged.

"Is that part of God's plan, too?" John asked, trying to seem a little less serious and intense.

His mother smiled. "Yes, I think it is."

"I don't believe in God, Mom." He didn't say it to hurt her, and his pronouncement might not even be even true, but she needed to know how hard this was. He needed to know she accepted him now, just as he was, no matter what he believed.

"You don't need to." She took his hand. He almost pulled away instinctively. "I think it's safe to say He believes in you. Very much." She chuckled and shook her head. "Now stop being so bullheaded and go talk to David."

John nodded and moved to the door. He stopped there and turned to her. A huge knot filled his chest, but he forced himself to say, "I love you, too, Mom."

"Thank you." Tears brimmed her eyes.

He didn't want to see her cry, so he padded down the hall to the bathroom and stood outside the door for a long time.

He lifted his hand to knock... but couldn't do it.

Come on. . . knock on the damn door.

He loved his family. David most of all. . . but all the lies, the confusion. His father was some kind of hero from an adventure video? And David had eyes full of stars. What did that huge vortex of emotion in John's chest really mean?

God damn it.

The cell in his pocket vibrated.

John snatched at it. Anything to distract himself.

Jamie. A text? *John. Glad you're okay. Tell David to answer his God damned cell. Huge favor. I left my lunch on the desk in my room. Please, please, grab it and bring it to school for me? Starving.*

Okay. So many strange things about that, but he could translate fairly well. He hurried down the hall to Jamie's room, glad to have a reason to avoid dealing with David. He slipped through the door and, sure enough, as soon as he approached the desk, her amazing hologram system kicked on. Jamie materialized in front of him. An icon told him it was a recording.

"So I'm trying this new app. Do I look 3d? Or just normal boring 2?

Holy wow. She was such a geek.

"Well?"

Crap. It was interactive, too.

"It looks pretty 3D. Nice job."

"Sweet." The image smiled. "Thanks. Okay, I'm so stoked you made it back safe and look forward to all your tales of exciting adventures. . ." She *so* didn't want to hear them. ". . .but Joanne found us a serious mission. The real thing. I'm not going into details here, but trust me, you want in. David, too. Get your skinny butts to Radio Shack at high noon. Love you."

And it cut out abruptly. Good old Jamie. Always the most logical one in the family. Radio Shack was an electronics antique store that fronted a high-end tech dealer. The owner worked on the Pipeline, and Jamie got a lot of her equipment through them. Well, it might be more honest to say they told Barry what to steal, and Jamie got her fair share of the booty because of her mad skills.

John pulled out his cell. He opened the text message and tapped the screen.

"Message reply," he said. "I found your lunch. On my way."

The cell beeped.

John shoved it into a pocket.

David would be dressing in their room by now.

He could pick him up on the way.

Yep. He could do that.

Except that. . . no, he couldn't.

John hurried to the stairs.

David had lied to him his whole life.

So had their parents.

What the hell was he supposed to do with that? What he would do was help Jamie and Joanne with a mission for Mackabee because that would be simple and clean and distracting. He'd do something good and true with people he trusted, who hadn't lied to him about. . . pretty damn much everything. He sent a message to Barry.

John met Barry outside his apartment building. They rarely hung out at Barry's place. His parents didn't approve of "those damn Jewish Christian friends of yours who should know better." They neither understood nor approved of anyone who practiced the Christian faith inside the Ghetto. Barry had given up explaining years before. All the sleepovers had been in John and David's room.

"Glad you're not dead!" Barry's hug lifted John completely off his feet.

"Me, too."

"Where's David?"

How to answer that one.

"Lover's quarrel?" Barry struck a stupid pose.

"Knock it off, coz." John punched his arm. He still hadn't worked through his feelings since the party at Babylon, and the whole point of the mission was to avoid all that. "Any chance I can just say we were stuck in one room together for too long and have you leave it alone?"

"No."

Of course not. Fine. He started toward Radio Shack. The streets seemed so much wider than they had with garbage piled along the sidewalks. Since the only working vehicles in the Ghetto were Dick cars and things like buses, pedestrian traffic ordinarily spread across the roads.

Folks seemed jittery. Tense. So was John.

But what could he say? Barry knew him almost as well as David, and John had never lied to him, either. He just wasn't built that way, but how could he explain it to Barry when he didn't understand it himself?

"Waiting." Barry nudged him.

"We hid out in that hospital we found last month." John stopped and faced Barry. "Nothing eventful, but I found out there's some big fucking secret David and our parents have been keeping from the rest of us, and I'm really cheesed off about it, and David gave me just enough info to piss me off more rather than less, and until I get them all to just fucking lay it on the line, I really don't want to talk about it, but I don't really know how to hide anything from you, so can you please just let me pretend that the only important thing going on is this mission? I really don't want to talk about it, but I don't want it to be weird, either."

Okay, that'd been really fast.

Barry seemed to process it. He shrugged and started down the street again.

"Noah's missing."

"Shit." The bottom fell out of John's chest. "That's right." How self-absorbed could he get? "I'm sorry."

So Barry told John what he knew, which was about what Uncle Bo had already said. The cops weren't saying anything, but Rocky insisted that the old man must have Noah locked up somewhere to teach him a—

"If he's dead, it's my fault," Barry blurted out, stopping in the middle of the street.

"What?"

"He had this thing he wanted to do," Barry said, tears filling his eyes. "I didn't want to let him go alone, but he insisted. Said it would only take a minute." He wiped his eyes with one sleeve. "I shouldn't have let him go. I should have made him leave with me. If I hadn't let him go. . ." He wiped his face again.

John grabbed him.

"No, I don't want—" Barry tried to shrug away, but John held on. A second later, Barry returned the embrace and his shoulders shook. "I killed my best friend."

"No, you didn't" John held him tighter and stroked his hair. "We don't know anything for sure yet."

I'll be damned if you get away from me without a hug. . .

Oh God, Barry's last words to Noah?

"No matter what, it wasn't your fault, and you made sure he knew you loved him." He took Barry's arms in his hands. "Don't mourn him until we know. We don't know, yet."

"We don't know, yet." Barry's face twisted with so much pain, but he nodded.

"We don't know, yet."

"It could just be his prick dad fucking with us all."

"Exactly." He wiped Barry's face with his sleeve.

It earned him a chuckle. "Coz, you're going to get snot all over your shirt."

"Like I never puked on you."

"Well, there is that." He wiped his own face and forced a smile. "Let's go do some good."

"Let's do." He turned Barry and aimed him down the street, slapping him on the back—

Foom! A familiar pair of men stood back-to-back as the plasma hit them from both sides. They vaporized.

Noah and his father. That's who he'd seen in his vision. John couldn't breathe. He choked.

Barry tried to turn around, but John held both shoulders with all his strength and kept his friend moving forward. He couldn't let Barry see his face.

"Keep walking," John insisted, praying with all his might it sounded light.

They were dead. Both of them. John knew it. Knew it for a fact as certain as the color of Barry's hair. Noah. Dead. So many others. Dead. He had to get a grip. He had no way to explain how he suddenly knew. With everything else, he didn't want Barry to freak, to think John was lying or rushed out. He had to keep moving. They had a mission. They didn't speak a word the rest of the way.

Radio Shack was an electronics thrift store full of castoff cells, cut-rate tables from five years ago, and antiques Jamie was certain couldn't work anymore. What would be back-compatible that far? And why were discs over four inches across called compact?

But everything from the last century had become popular again. Nostalgia ruled. Whatever. The store's name was a joke about some electronics business that went under before her parents had been born. She picked up a pair of glasses. They seemed ordinary enough.

"What are these?" she asked Daksh, the owner of the place.

"Ah, those were a fad for about five minutes over fifty years ago," he said. "They have a screen in one eye that showed the net."

"And?" She didn't see the point.

"And that is why I have a box of them in the backroom," Daksh said. "They were more of a joke than data spheres."

"Data spheres?" Jamie caught the glass globe tossed her way. "Never heard of it." She held it up to the light. Pretty colors. Something about it seemed familiar. But where would she have seen something like that?

"You'd not likely have heard about most of the things in my shop." The man chuckled. He did that a lot.

"Not about the crap up here, anyway." The shop was empty but for the two of them.

"Well, I do need to keep up appearances." Again with the chuckling.

Daksh ran most of his real business through the backroom he'd mentioned. He gave Barry and a few others intel on what to steal and where, helped them gain access to the very best shops in cracker town, and his gatherers kept a few special tidbits as payment. That's how Jamie had what was, in all likelihood, the best hologram projection system on the market. Barry knew she'd make better use of it than he.

And she did.

The shop's bell tinkled.

"Kiss, kiss." Joanne, carrying a rather overstuffed duffle bag, made her way to Jamie's side, kissing both of Jamie's cheeks.

Would she notice her attempts at disguise?

"Good." Joanne grabbed Jamie's chin and turned her face back and forth. "Cracker trash trying to look older and sexier but failing. I'm impressed."

Nice. Nailed it.

"Oh God, please tell me the makeup is intentional." Joanne's fingers gripped her chin.

"As if I'd wear anything this trashy unless it was part of a disguise." Jamie swatted Joanne's hand away. She'd spent an hour with a net tutorial to copy Neve Kristian's style. The singer's music was worse than the makeup, but it was all the rage in cracker town.

"No boys, yet?" Joanne dropped the duffle to the floor.

The bell rang.

"Speak of the devil," Daksh said.

John and Barry. What about David? Whatever. Since John had shown up, David had to be fine. Thank God. Jamie would never admit it in a million years, but she'd been worried as hell. Keep it cool.

"Glad you're not dead." She nodded casually.

"Me, too." John swept her up in a hug that lifted her off her feet.

"Okay, put me down before you drown me with your tears." She pounded on his shoulders. "We have work to do." She had to make sure they took her seriously, but she secretly enjoyed the affection.

"Not 'til I get a big wet, sloppy kiss." John pulled her closer.

"Ugh!" She pushed him away. It was something her dad always did. Cute, but seriously? How old were they?

"Is this all of us?" Joanne asked, taking control.

"All operatives present and accounted for, sir." Barry gave her a sharp salute.

Joanne stared at him darkly for a moment.

He blushed and shrugged.

"We can use the backroom, Daksh?"

"You can use whatever you want, *parvati*," he said.

She kissed his cheek. Everyone around Jamie was so damn affectionate. Ugh. The four of them moved into the back room. Barry carried Joanne's duffle.

"Okay, folks. This is the real deal." Once they were behind closed doors, Joanne opened the bag and rummaged through it. "I have a date with someone so high on the Dick's ladder, he can shake hands with the president barefoot. We need blackmail footage."

Holy crap! When Joanne had told her this was a serious mission, Jamie had had no idea it was *that* important.

"I see you understand how vital this is. Good." Joanne looked them each in the eye. "That data stick you guys found? It was a good find. I can't tell you what was on it, but I was asked to include you. . . well, and David, but whatever, because Makabee was *that* impressed."

"Wait." Jamie had to know. "Really? Makabee himself? The real deal?"

"If you still doubt how highly connected I am, why are you here?" Her eyes screamed annoyance.

Oh. Crap. Jamie needed to shut up.

"Good." Joanne rummaged some more. "Jamie and John will dress as hotel staff." She threw them green uniforms. "You will pretend to take care of the garden outside the window of the mark's room." She tossed a different uniform to Barry. "You are the pizza delivery boy who will show up should I need your assistance."

Barry started unbuttoning his shirt, and Jamie felt the heat rising in her cheeks. "Um. Kinda one room-ish here."

"Like you've never seen me naked?" Barry said.

"We live in the same house," John reminded her, kicking off his shoes.

"A gentleman turns his back, *gentlemen*," Joanne said harshly.

The guys turned their backs, and Jamie did the same.

"I'm wearing boxers today for God's sake," John muttered.

"Shush you," Joanne said.

"What about you?" Barry asked.

"I need to turn my back?" she asked.

Barry scoffed. "What's your disguise?"

"For this job," Joanne said, "I was in costume when I stepped out of the shower."

"I hear that," Barry said, and Jamie could almost hear the inevitable high five the guys would share.

Honestly, what in the world did she see in that boy?

After they changed, Joanne lifted a device. . . some kind of hypo.

"This," she said, "is something you need to take to your graves. It removes chips without rendering them inert or in any way interfering with their operation."

What the what? How was that possible?

"Holy wow!" John peered closer. "Where'd you get that?"

"Where I got it is irrelevant. That it works is what matters." Joanne passed the device across Jamie's body with one hand. Her other hand held her cell with a holo screen open. An outline of Jamie's body appeared with a red dot flashing at her right bicep. "This should be easy. Hold out your arm."

Jamie complied. Since the uniform had short sleeves, she merely tugged the fabric a bit higher.

"This is going to hurt a little." Joanne passed the tip of the device over Jamie's bicep a few times, until it beeped and flashed a red light. She pressed the tip against Jamie's skin. "Don't move."

It dug into her arm. Holy crap!

"A little?" Nope. She wouldn't flinch. It dug around. "Okay, officially *not* a little." Blast, that hurt!

The device retracted from her arm, and Joanne pulled it away. The hole in Jamie's bicep was barely visible, but it bled freely.

"It needs to take a bit of the tissue with it." Joanne held the tip of the device to a little grey box. "To fool the chip into thinking it's still inside you." She handed Jamie a can of adhesive bandage, then cracked open the box and popped out a tiny black disc. She attached a silver chain and handed it over.

"My chip's in that?" She took the bracelet.

"Yep." Joanne dropped the box into a waste basket. "Wear it at all times when living your normal life. Showers, sleeping, whatever. Anyone who scans you will have no way of knowing it's not inside your body." She held out a jewelry box. Inside lay an identical bracelet with a white charm.

"That's your mission bracelet," Joanne explained. "It emits a generic signal that reads as a slightly wonky chip. If you're just walking down the street, Dicks will shoot you in an instant if they can't read anything, but they usually don't waste their time on a fuzzy chip unless they're bored. If you pull a mission like today with no chip at all, they will not stop until you are dead. Remember that. Having the chip removed does not make you invisible. It makes you a target."

"Next?" She turned to Barry with a big smile.

His chip had lodged, of course, in his ass, and he dropped his pants around his ankles before Jamie could turn her back again. Damn him, why did he need to be such an exhibitionist? She could only hope the heavy makeup hid her glowing cheeks.

"Can you make it hurt extra?" she asked. The high-pitched yelp that followed made her smile. "Thanks."

"No problem."

John's chip? That presented a problem.

"Uh-oh." Joanne held the device over John's sternum.

"What?" John peered at the holo screen. "I can't imagine Jamie has an issue with me taking off my shirt."

"No more jokes." She stared at the screen and ran the device up and down John's torso. "Lose the shirt."

John and Barry exchanged a serious look, and John unbuttoned.

"What's wrong?" Jamie asked.

Joanne shook her head. Her eyes were wide, and her lips tight.

"What's wrong?" Jamie demanded.

"John may not be able to do this." She pulled the device away and stared him in the eyes. "It's in the middle there. Somewhere between a wobbly grey thing and a wobbly purple thing."

"I thought you said no jokes," Jamie whispered.

"I'm not joking." Joanne held up the device and pressed a button. A short, metal whip with a tiny claw at the end snaked out of the tip and flashed around. "It has a sensor that leads it to the chip. In your arm or in your ass it can't do any damage if it has to dig around a bit."

The whip slipped back into the device with a *thwip*.

"But I'm not a doctor." She waved at the image of John's torso, rendered in much higher resolution and much more detail. His heart beat visibly and his lungs expanded and contracted. As Joanne had said, the chip lay between two wobbly bits just below John's heart.

"You need a doctor that can actually direct the probe," she said. "Someone who can make sure it doesn't slice through anything vital."

"What's the worst that can happen?" John made a dismissive noise, playing the strong man as usual. Idiot.

"It can graze your intestines," Jamie told him, "opening a hole that pours partially digested shit directly into the same place your heart beats."

His face turned pale. He looked at Joanne, who nodded.

He set his jaw. Oh, Lord no.

"Do it."

"You ridiculous child!" Joanne said.

"I know you think you're invincible—" Jamie slapped her hands over her face in disgust.

"No!" Joanne screamed.

Jamie pulled her hands away from her eyes. John stood there with the device against his side, his eyes closed, his face a grimace of pain.

Joanne shoved Barry away.

"No!" When Jamie lunged for John, Joanne held up a hand. "If we pull it away once he's started it's almost guaranteed to kill him."

"Oh, if the probe doesn't..." Jamie clenched her fists at her sides. "I just may do it anyway."

John's face tightened into a grimace of pain.

"Okay, this is ten times worse than I could have possibly imagined." He forced a very fake smile, but his eyes stayed tightly shut.

"No deep breath," Joanne said.

"Can't... do... it... anyway."

The device flashed green and beeped. Seriously? Just that?

"Fuck us all," Joanne shouted, "it worked,"

John yanked the device away and held it out to Joanne. His knees wobbled, but Barry seized him before he fell. Barry sprayed adhesive with one hand and lowered John to his knees with the opposite arm. John had both arms around his friend, his teeth still clenched.

Jamie snatched the cell from the table and examined John's readings, but the charts remained blank without the probe.

As soon as Joanne had John's charm separated from the device, Jamie grabbed the probe and waved it across John's body.

A new scan appeared. It didn't mean anything to Jamie.

"Cell," she asked, hoping the damn thing was set to voice commands. "Does the probe detect internal bleeding?"

"Negative. Bleeding limited to patient's epidermis."

"Any internal damage?" Jamie blew out her held breath.

"Negative. Probe removed foreign object without damaging any internal organs."

She handed the medical device to Joanne, planted her foot on John's chest, and shoved him over onto his ass.

"What the hell?" He toppled onto Barry.

"If you ever do anything so God damned stupid again, I swear I will kill you myself!"

"Jamie—" John jumped to his feet.

"We all thought you and David got yourselves killed out there." Her hands shook, and she couldn't stop it. "And now? You do this stupid stuff, and I can't—" She pulled an arm back and made a fist to stop the shaking. Her heart pounded in her chest. "People died yesterday." She would not break down. She would not let them see her like that, but he could've just all of a sudden out of nowhere been dead. God damn *dead*.

"You treat me like a little kid, like I need protecting, and then you go and do something God damn stupid and pointless like *this*?" She swallowed down the lump in her throat. "Who the hell is protecting *you*?" Both hands tightened into fists. "Who?"

They stared at her, open mouthed and silent.

Blast it. She'd made an idiot out of herself. All her big talk about being an adult and ready for real missions, yet the first time her cousin risks himself, she breaks down like a little girl.

"I'm not a—" No! She wouldn't say it. If she said it, it only proved that she was. She stormed out of the backroom and into Daksh's shop, hiding in a corner so he wouldn't notice her.

John couldn't move. He felt Barry's hands on his torso, felt them checking the adhesive.

Joanne moved to follow Jamie into the shop.

"No." John held up a hand. "I'll talk to her." He took his shirt from Barry and patted his friend's shoulder. "She has a huge crush on you, coz. You should stop flashing your ass unless you mean it."

Everything inside him hurt. That probe may not have left any permanent damage, but it sure as hell had taken its own sweet time.

"Jamsie."

Jamie stood in a corner with her back to the door. She wiped her face and turned to him. Ah, nuts. He'd made her cry.

"I'm sorry." Why had he really done it? "She was honest with me. Joanne told me exactly what could happen."

"She was honest about the fact that it could kill you, so you just had to give it a try?" His cousin's face wrinkled in confusion. "In what universe does that even make sense?"

Her words were so logical. As always. She didn't know how angry John was about all the secrets. She didn't know how much David and their parents had lied to them. And this was not a good time to tell her. Also, not likely a good time to say he'd just spilled the beans about her crush.

How to give her some consolation? With David, or Barry for that matter, he'd just give them a big hug and a kiss on the cheek and all would be forgiven. Jamie wasn't like that. She needed it to make sense.

"I'm sorry," he said. "I didn't want to be left out. I was afraid Joanne was about to tell me to sit this one out, and I couldn't bear the thought of you going on a mission like this without either me or

David to back you up. And I know that's bullshit, that you're smarter than either of us and just as ready for this mission. But I still need some time to believe that, okay? We're family, right? Will you ever stop seeing me as the annoying big brother who always steals the last of the oatmeal before you can get to it? Or who runs through the house in his underwear chasing David with a plastic sword?"

She actually smiled. Good.

"I still see you as the little girl who cried because Natalie Goldstein stole your Legos in the fourth grade, and I know that's not fair of me, but I was the one who went and got them back for you."

Jamie worked so hard to hold back the smile. She even hid her mouth behind one arm. Then she smiled. Then she laughed.

"She only gave them back because she felt sorry for me having an older brother who was so easy to beat up." She laughed all the more.

And that was exactly why he'd picked that story,

Uff! She smacked him in the middle.

"Seriously, John," she chided. "You aren't invincible. That was dumb. You're going to get your fool ass killed one of these days."

"Actually, it was Barry who had the chip in his ass. Not me." Heh.

She punched his shoulder.

"You saw that, right? When he flashed his ass?"

She punched him again.

"Did you notice he doesn't have tan lines?"

"La, la, la." She shoved her fingers into her ears and headed for the storeroom. "I do not want to know what you boys do out in Venice when I'm not around."

John sighed as the door swung shut behind her. The pain in his stomach had already begun to subside. He'd been damn lucky. He probably needed to watch stuff like that. It wasn't like he had guardian angels watching his back. He straightened his shirt and returned to the backroom for the rest of the briefing.

An hour later, John skirted a swimming pool sculpted to look like a pond. The grounds had been modeled after the forest in *A Midsummer Night*. A waterfall spilled into a natural pool edged with flowers and shrubs. Guests lounged and swam and paddled up to the bar. A small sign warned that after dark, fairy folk could be seen on the garden paths. Most likely holograms. Ironic, but John still wondered if they could keep the uniforms and check it out.

He ducked into the locker room and grabbed a stack of towels from a shelf. He and Jamie had been told to kill time blending into the surroundings, so they'd become invisible, like part of the well-manicured garden. Back on the pool deck, he slapped on his friendliest smile and offered a towel to a pasty white woman.

"I'm fine, thanks." She cringed then smiled to pass it off.

John smiled again in spite of the sudden desire to hit her. He offered the towel to the pasty white man across from the woman. He raised a hand and shook his head.

Seriously? They wouldn't take a towel he'd touched? Had to be a coincidence. He wandered around the pool, glancing up at Jamie. She handed a couple of towels to a mother and daughter. They smiled and thanked her.

Okay. So the pasty white couple was a fluke. He offered a towel to a kid climbing out from the waterfall.

"Thanks!" The kid took the towel and ran off.

Okay, see? John was just being para—

The woman who grabbed the kid had to be his mom, if the matching red hair was any indication. She snatched the towel away and dropped it into a nearby garbage can.

John couldn't move. He had to clench his jaw to keep from screaming. He spotted Jamie again. If anyone treated her that way, he'd have to. . .

Jamie held her last couple of towels over her chest as she laughed with a pair of pasty guys. Both dark-haired and muscular.

Good looking in a scary cracker sort of way. Jamie's eyes opened wide, and she covered her mouth with one hand. She was flirting? With them?

A cold sweat broke out over John's skin.

Holy wow.

She looked just like them. He glanced around. A wide circle of space had formed around him, as if none of the guests wanted to accidently breathe the same air.

Across the pool, guests brushed close to Jamie. Not bumping into her, but not avoiding her either, the way they'd avoid John. Or David. Or Noah.

Who was dead.

John ran a hand over his head and forced the lump out of his throat. He'd never noticed it before. She looked just like them. The boys laughed and chatted and one of them touched her arm. With the waterfall in the background, it was a scene from a video. Especially with Jamie's pop star makeup. She was the poor girl from the wrong side of the tracks who would find love and fortune by the end of the story.

How had he never noticed that before? And she looked just like his mom, like Aunt Ruth, too. Why the hell were they even in the Ghetto? Why didn't they all just join the blasted UCA and be done with it? They were Christians even.

Because of him. And David.

His mom had let herself get stuck in the Ghetto so he wouldn't be taken away and shuttled off to Texas. Aunt Ruth had stayed for David. And Uncle Bo. Hell, Uncle Bo was Jewish, but his parents hadn't practiced. He didn't have any reason to stay in the Ghetto, really. He could have pledged to the UCA.

And John's dad, the big Cherokee man who'd let himself get blown up to save his son, to save John. He hadn't needed to do that.

All those people doing things they didn't need to do to save him, to protect him. Him and David.

John had never realized just how much his mom had given up. For him.

The boys took the last of Jamie's towels and draped them around large, pale shoulders.

John dropped his onto an empty lounge and headed away from the pool. He couldn't stand there with all those people who wouldn't take a towel he'd touched, with his cousin, a girl who was more like a sister, who looked just like them, who could laugh and joke with them.

John would never be like them. Never. He was. . .

What the hell was he? He dropped onto a park bench and ran his hands over his head. Damn it.

John looked up.

The biggest wolf he'd ever seen stared directly into his eyes.

John couldn't breathe.

The huge animal sat against the building in a strangely vacant spot, a stretch of wall where the shrubs and bushes had been removed recently, exposing the scratched and dirty bricks. The animal stared directly at John, rose to all four paws and trotted toward him.

John sat up and looked around. Did no one else notice the giant killing machine traipsing across the garden?

"John?"

He looked over.

"What's wrong?" Jamie stood right there, concern in her face.

"Dog." He pointed.

"Where?" She glanced in the right direction, looked around. "Behind the bushes?"

The huge beast padded between two little kids throwing a ball back and forth. The ball passed right through it. No one noticed.

No one could see it. No one but John.

"Yep. It just ran behind the bushes," John lied quickly.

"John?" Jamie sat beside him on the bench.

He turned to her, despite the enormous dog that padded up to them and sat at John's feet. It couldn't be real. It was another vision. Another reminder that John was a freak. He'd be damned before he admitted it to Jamie.

"What's wrong?" She took his hand. "Are you mad about how

I reacted at Radio Shack? You have to admit, it was pretty boneheaded of you to take that risk." She squeezed his hand. "But I'm sorry I freaked out. That was so little kid of me."

The wolf whined.

"No. I get it," John said. The wolf that no one else could see leaned forward and licked his hand. John closed his eyes. It wasn't real. That scratchy, wet tongue, it wasn't real.

"Then why the hell did you do it?" She shoved him, and he used the recoil to pull away from the wolf.

It was gone. What the hell? John looked around, but it was gone.

"Well?" Jamie stared at him as if he'd sprouted antennae.

How could he tell her the truth?

"You could leave the Ghetto, you know." It was the only thing he could think to say.

"What the hell, Major Non Sequitur?"

"You could leave—"

"I heard what you said. I just can't believe you said it." She leaned close so no one would hear. "You actually think I want to be like them? I saw the way they treated you."

"You wouldn't have to be like them," John said, thinking about Senator Sato. "But you could get out. Have a normal life."

She had that look again, as if he'd just sprouted antennae.

"What?" he asked.

"You fathead. You just shoved a whiplash razorblade into your gut but think I could go skipping off into cracker town and leave my family behind, why? Because I look like them?"

Where was all the anger coming from? Oh. Only one place possible.

"So you've thought about this before," he said.

She snuffed and opened her mouth, probably to yell at him. Then she closed it. Stared at him a few more seconds then sat back.

"I figured out I was different by the time I was five." She stared at the crackers playing in the garden. "Why do you think I always have a dark tan? I hope everyone in the Ghetto will stop staring, stop muttering, 'What's the cracker doing here?' or 'Go back to cracker town, Whitey.'" She shook her head. "On the net I can use an avatar that looks however I want her to look. I can be a Nubian Princess or a Mayan King. No one knows how I really look. That's one of the reasons I love the net."

Holy crap. "I had no idea."

"Right, because I'm going to go around whining about discrimination." She snuffed again. "Me. With what I see and hear every day." She shook her head. "If the Dicks had fire-bombed a party here in cracker town, heads would have rolled. Maybe even literally. In the Ghetto? They convinced half of us it was our own fault. So many people want to be accepted they'll believe anything."

The clock on her wrist beeped. What a weird place for one, but they had to go low tech for this mission. Low tech gadgets that had no online connection would just register as part of the background EM field.

"Almost time," she said. "You ready for this?"

John glanced around. No vicious killing beasts.

"Let's piss off some crackers," John said. Then he froze.

"Oh my God, don't you dare get all careful around me, you dumb Injun." Her wrist clock beeped again. "Whoops. Gotta go."

They moved to the window of the room where Joanne engaged in they knew not what with a client at the top of the food chain in the government. As they reached the window, Jamie hesitated.

"What?" John asked.

"Well, if we just go crawling into the bushes, it'll look, you know, like we're going to, you know?" She punched his shoulder. "That may be all well and good for you and David, but—"

"What the hell?" John punched her shoulder.

"What?" She rubbed her arm. "You two pull this espionage shit all the time. I'm new." Oh. That was all she'd meant.

"Sorry." He grabbed her and dragged her into the shrubbery. "So they think we're a workplace romance. Deal." It wasn't like anyone would mistake them for relatives.

"Ew."

Michael stepped aside as John and Jamie hurried past, which was when he noticed Raphael.

"You appeared to him as a wolf?" his brother asked. "How old are you?"

"Well, I'm immortal, so technically, I'm ageless, which means I am both an infant and also an old man."

"I know what you're doing." Raphael was not amused.

"Do you?" His anger radiated out and knocked down a planter and a small child.

"Yes, I do." Raphael scowled.

"We're on a bit of a deadline, brother." Michael reined in his emotions. "John can't hold this grudge indefinitely. He needs to realize his foolishness."

Raphael folded his arms into the sleeves of his robes. He remained silent.

"What?"

Raphael sighed. "It happens tonight."

"Really? All of it?" So soon. Michael had hoped he might have more time.

"Yes." Raphael turned his attention to the cousins hunkering down below the window. "By the end of the night, the future I have seen becomes inevitable."

"All of it?" Michael watched the young man hiding in the bushes.

"Why aren't you with David?"

"I am. We're at the town meeting with his parents," Michael said. "It's this little thing they invented in the twentieth century called multitasking."

John sat with his back against the wall, watching the ancient tablet in Jamie's lap. A camera on the window ledge above fed video into the tablet via a physical wire. The system was about as low tech as he'd ever seen. They couldn't take the risk that video streamed wirelessly would be intercepted. No way to intercept this dinosaur. No wonder they'd needed actual people to handle the filming.

In the room behind them, Joanne straddled a man in a gimp suit who was tied spread eagle to the bed posts. The man's face was hidden behind a black mask and a ball gag.

"How are we supposed to identify the mark in that get up?" John asked.

"Wait for it."

A second man entered the frame, shirtless and barefoot with his back to the camera. He drank some kind of cocktail and watched the show.

"That's our mark."

He moved closer to the bed but kept his back to the window where Joanne had left a corner of the curtain turned back. He drank his drink and watched the show quietly.

John shoved in the ear plug. He didn't say anything. The only sounds were Joanne's fake pleasure and the occasional gurgle from the gimp.

"Face the camera," Jamie muttered. "Face the camera."

"Because looking at curtains is so much more interesting than what he's watching." They'd have to wait until he made another drink or decided to move around the bed for a different view. "Might as well get comfortable. This could be a while." He pulled out the ear piece. Faint sounds of kids playing in the pool reached him.

He peered through the bushes. Nope.

No sign of the ginormous wolf.

"Did our folks tell you exactly why David and I went into hiding?" he asked.

"Sort of. Dicks are looking for them, they said." Her voice was both excited and irritated. "Dicks looking for our parents, right?" She shook her head, her skepticism obvious. "They told me this guy named Addison killed your dad." She stopped and laid a hand on John's knee. "Oh, crap, you already knew that, right?"

"Is that it?" John's heart thumped in his chest at the things he might need to explain to his cousin.

"Why? Is there more?"

Tons more, but Jamie would never believe the supernatural aspects. Like enormous friendly wolves.

"Yeah," John said. "Addison's not really a Dick. That's just some kind of cover. He works for the UCA or something."

"As in the president?"

"Clement hisself."

"Why in God's name would the president be after our parents, or David for that matter?" She snorted and played with the tablet.

"I don't know." John couldn't look at her when he said it. She'd think he was psychotic if he told her that he and David were some kind of twenty-first century prophets. At least David had told John he was holding back. He hadn't lied.

John grabbed Jamie's hand. "Once they get us all together tonight, they're going to spill everything they know."

"I'll believe that when I—hey, our mark just came over to the window to make a drink."

John looked down. "Holy shit."

Addison's hired gun! His face was unmistakable. And he was talking. John plugged in the earpiece. Latin?

"*Deus meus, ex toto corde poenitet me omnium meorum peccatorum.*" He poured a glass of blood red wine.

"What's he saying?" Jamie asked.

"Because I speak Latin." Too bad they couldn't use their cells to translate.

"It's Latin?"

"Sounds churchy." John shrugged. "Isn't all churchy stuff Latin?"

"*Eaque detestor, quia peccando. . .*" He held the glass up. "*Non solum poenas a te iuste statutas promeritus sum.*"

Some kind of blessing?

"Why'd you say holy shit?" Jamie asked.

"It's him. He's one of the guys looking for David, for our parents."

"Really? Coincidence much?"

She was right. John didn't like it.

Pierce finished his prayer of contrition and drank the wine.

The offering on the bed mumbled something through the gag.

"What did he say?" Pierce asked.

"He said he's going to cum, I think."

The whore was so beautiful. He'd seen her in the tunnels before they'd burned them all. He'd known then he had to have her even though she was colored. He moved to the foot of the bed where the offering's head lay, a belt already around his throat. "*Súscipe, sancte Pater, omnípotens æterne Deus, hanc immaculatam hostiam, quam ego indignus famulus tuus offero tibi.*" He continued the offertory prayer as the man began to writhe in the final seconds before ejaculation.

"Holy Father…" Pierce wound the belt in one hand as he finished the prayer. "Please accept this, my offering, for the sins I am about to commit."

He pulled his gun and held it to the woman's head the same moment he yanked hard on the belt to tighten it around the offering's throat.

The woman stared at him with wide, wide eyes.

"Stop making him, and I shoot you in the head," he warned her.

She moved again, fell into rhythm. The man writhed under her as much as he could considering the restraints. Oh yes, strangulation could be quite pleasurable. The man's movements quickened as he suffocated and ejaculated at the same time.

The woman closed her eyes.

Pierce gave the belt one more hard yank, and the man seized. Pierce had seen that happen before. If the man released his bowels right there, Pierce would have to take the woman on the floor. Time slowed down in that amazing way that was almost as good as sex.

Pierce ached with excitement.

A loud pounding on the window!

What? Who?

The curtain stood open a crack. How had he not seen——?

Pierce released the corpse and shot the window. Six shots in a circle so he could throw a chair through it.

Someone banged on the door.

A set up.

Pierce shot into the door, a straight line from floor to ceiling so he'd hit the target whether he stood, crouched or sat.

The prostitute screamed and rolled off the corpse and onto the floor beside the bed. She had to be part of it. He shot through the bed until her scream cut short.

Reloading the gun, he rushed to the window. He grabbed a chair, threw it through the tempered glass, and leapt through the opening.

He'd seen a camera. That was his priority.

A glimpse of foot disappeared over the edge of the roof.

Damn Ghetto rats always took to the rooftops. Fine. He jumped into the nearest tree and climbed, tapping the subcutaneous release at his wrist for adrenal boosters. At least he'd have the element of surprise.

He reached the roof and spotted a girl racing across it.

He fired at her and missed, but she ducked behind an AC unit, so he'd slowed her down.

Barry crouched against the wall trying to get his breath back after taking two slugs to the chest. Thank God for Kevlar.

The pizza lay strewn across the sidewalk. What a damn waste.

The sound of crashing glass moved him. He slid the keycard over the sensor, threw the door open, and dove behind the nearest chair. Bright light poured through the shattered plate glass.

The curtains blew inward.

"He's gone." Joanne's voice brought him to his feet. "But I don't know for how long."

She lay on the bed in a pool of blood.

The cat in a gimp suit didn't move.

A device flew at Barry. He caught it.

"I want footage of me here with Carlos." She held a hand to her side where blood poured freely.

"You've been shot." He moved closer.

"Focus, Barry." Her steely eyes stopped him. "Film. Now. So I can try to stop the bleeding."

He held the cell up. The screen was set to record. He hit the red button.

"Okay. Good enough." She rolled onto her back with a can of adhesive in one hand.

"Let me help."

"No." She pointed at the low dresser. "His briefcase. There. It's loaded with electronics. Scan it with that."

"But you've been shot."

There was so much damn blood.

"And Carlos here is already dead." She sprayed adhesive onto her own side. "Put the cell on top of the case. If I bleed all over it, he'll know we copied his data."

Barry held the cell over the briefcase.

"Pocket rocket," Joanne said, and a holo screen popped up over the device. "Scan all contents. Use any and all necessary force."

It beeped. Joanne rolled to her feet with a grunt and pulled a dark, mud-colored caftan from her duffle. She pulled it over her head, and the colors should diffuse any spots of blood that might show through.

"You expected to get shot?" Barry asked.

"Didn't expect it." She pulled her hair out and shook it back. "But my costume didn't allow for Kevlar, now did it.

"I guess not."

"What?" She frowned. "No jokes?"

A dark spot formed on the dress.

"No jokes, Joanne. Not today."

Her cell beeped. "Unable to retrieve data."

"Damn." She held out a hand. "Let's hope Jamie and John have better luck."

"Can't we just take the briefcase?" Barry handed her the device.

"It's probably rigged to explode if it leaves this room."

"Oh." Barry took a step away. "Let's get you to a medic."

Up on the roof, gunshots drove John behind an air conditioning unit. When he'd been sure the Dick was going to kill Joanne, he hadn't been able to stop himself from banging on the window to draw attention. With the Dick giving chase, Joanne had to be safe.

Okay. New plan. Time to worry about Jamie.

His cousin skidded beside him, her eyes wide, but she didn't reprimand him for going off script. Apparently, she'd been as certain of Joanne's imminent danger.

"Grapnels," he said, and she yanked one from her belt and attached it to her wrist.

They'd seen holographic maps of the motel and surrounding buildings. An exit plan had been loosely discussed. They should have cover to the stairwell, a small aluminum building that thrust up from the roof.

"Go!" He dragged Jamie up and across the gravel roof. She'd run the drills on the Temporary Building, but how would she react in the real world?

Shots rang out, but they hit far and wide. Pierce must be trying to scare them. Had to be.

John grabbed the doorknob on the door to the stairs. Locked. Blast. He shoved Jamie around the corner to the far side of the little shack.

The sound of crunching gravel drew closer.

Okay, the motel lobby had a lofted ceiling, which meant an angled roof about ten yards away and ten feet up with a big sign at the bottom of the slope. Decent cover while they scaled the roof.

"Get behind the sign." John ran ahead to show her. He shot the grapnel for the vertical support at one side. He yanked his arm back to tighten the spring then hit the winch, bracing his shoulder.

Whoosh! He soared through the air up to the pitched roof, landing at the edge of the sign. He rolled behind it, grateful it was made of heavy metal. He released and retracted the grapnel as Jamie rolled up to a knee beside him and bullets sprayed the sign behind them. She jumped, but she'd made it so far so good.

"I'm a ladder." John dropped onto his stomach and spread his limbs.

Jamie climbed him, and her feet stretched to her toes on his shoulders. "I can't. . . quite. . ."

John lowered into his knees and pushed up onto his toes.

"Got it! I'm a ladder."

And John scrambled up to the peak, hoping Pierce would need time to get that high. In the motel room, he'd been shirtless and had no sign of a grapnel. Hopefully, he hadn't thought to grab one as he gave chase.

John scanned forward. What did they have?

A short sprint to the edge of the roof, then empty space.

A road sign advertising donuts.

High rise apartments on the other side, partially blocked by the road sign.

John closed his eyes for a second, visualizing the holograms.

"This is going to be tricky," he said. "Do exactly what I do."

He leapt to his feet and sprinted to the edge of the roof. As the edge approached, he heard Jamie's steps behind him. Shit. He'd hoped she'd watch the whole—

He hit the edge and leapt as hard as possible, shooting the grapnel for the top half of the metal road sign.

It caught fast, and he swung down, directly at the space below the sign.

The moment the line hit the bottom edge of the sign, it yanked John hard and threw him high into the air beyond. Thank God for physics.

He released the line and spider-monkeyed as he soared toward the balcony railing. The moment he hit the railing, he grabbed on with all four limbs. Whoof. The impact knocked the wind out of him, but he grabbed on tight as he heard Jamie call out.

"Don't close your eyes!" he shouted.

That was the biggest mistake newbies made.

She hit the railing a bit lower than John had. He grabbed a fistful of her shirt as she bounced off the metal pickets, giving her just the extra second she needed to latch on.

That was the second biggest mistake newbies made, letting the impact bounce them into the air.

They scrambled over the handrail and behind a patio bar, peering over the top of it.

Without a grapnel, Pierce couldn't possibly follow them, but they needed to stay behind cover since he was a good shot. From the perfect circle he'd blown in the window of the motel room, he likely—

There he was, running toward them along the steel pipes that connected the road sign to the lamp posts on either side. How the hell had he reached that? And right behind them? Still no sign of a grapnel.

"It's okay," John muttered, "there's no way he can—"

He sprinted the last few steps flat out.

How could he possibly stop in time?

He didn't.

Pierce soared through the air, arms and legs pinwheeling.

"No fucking way!" John pushed Jamie up onto the bar. "Next balcony up! Go, go, *go!*"

As John boosted Jamie to the balcony above, he glanced down.

Pierce latched one hand onto a picket of the railing two floors below, looked up, and met John's astonished eyes.

"How the blazes did he do that?" Jamie asked.

"Go, go, *go!*" John shouted. No time to waste! A man who could make that jump was likely to be a fast climber, too.

They reached the next balcony and climbed up onto the handrail. John boosted Jamie to the edge of the next floor.

Shit. How many more floors to the roof? Would Jamie last that long? How high was the building? John had been running the rooftops for several years. He barely felt winded, but Jamie struggled to pull herself up.

John chanced a glance down as he boosted her.

Damn it. Pierce was only one floor below.

John shoved Jamie to the next railing then shifted to stand to one side on his balcony. He balanced on the balls of his feet on the handrail, lowered into his knees, and leapt with all his strength, catching the pickets above in the middle.

He needed to get ahead of Jamie. She wouldn't be able to pull up on her own this time, and it was the last chance. Pierce would catch them before they made it one more story.

Hopefully, the patio doors were unlocked or at least breakable. Going through the building instead of over it was a huge risk, but Jamie wouldn't—

"John!" she screamed.

Pierce had her by one leg.

"Kick him in the head!" John dropped onto the balcony floor.

She kicked, but he just grabbed that foot and used her like a ladder, climbing up to her waist.

No time to think. John had tried insane moves at the Temporary Building. Time to try one for real.

He grabbed a picket with one hand and planted the other on the handrail. He kicked up as hard as he could to set himself in a solid handstand over the railing. Then he contracted his abs and pushed up with both arms.

He dropped feet first.

Jamie screamed.

John landed on Pierce's head and grabbed for the pickets with one hand. He snatched at Jamie with the other.

Pierce grunted.

John kicked down hard with his heel, landing the blow above Pierce's ear.

The man grunted again, let go, and fell backward into open air without a sound.

"Get over the railing," John shouted. "He still has a gun."

They dragged each other over the railing, onto the balcony beyond, and dropped to the floor.

No gunshots. Not a sound.

"What the hell was that you did?" Jamie's entire body shook. "That was completely insane. Again."

"Shut up," he muttered. "It worked. We're both alive. We do shit like that all the time at the Temporary Building."

"How the hell are you still alive." Then her voice rose to a shout: "Shit." Then even louder, "Shit! Shit! Shit!"

What now?

"He got the camera," she said. "I clipped it to my waist."

"What?"

"The camera." She closed her eyes tightly. "The whole blighted reason we're here. He took it." She wore a mask of anger and embarrassment.

All that danger for nothing. Unless. . .

"There's no way he survived that fall." John peeked out between the pickets. He scanned the street below. Nothing. No body ground to pulp. No crowd of shocked bystanders. Nothing.

"How the hell?" Jamie had poked her head through the pickets beside John. "What is he?"

"He must be enhanced with genetics, or drugs, or cybernetics. He's some kind of super-agent."

It was the only answer. The entire project had to do with genetic tinkering. It only made sense they'd fiddle with their own assassin, make him stronger, more durable.

"He must have grabbed onto a lower railing." Jamie jumped to her feet and hurried to the patio door. It slid open easily. "Apparently they don't worry about locking their doors this high up."

"We'll need to make sure Barry knows about that." John hurried to join her.

He didn't feel the humor but didn't want Jamie to see how upset he was. After all that work. After letting that man in the gimp suit die. They had nothing to show for it other than possibly leading that Dick one step closer. What the hell was he, that man who wanted them dead? And how much more was he now determined to kill them?

John raced into the backroom of Radio Shack with Jamie. Shouts and screams of pain and panic greeted them. Joanne lay struggling on a table, screaming profanities and bleeding while someone hovered over her with a tool similar to the chip-extracting device.

Barry and Daksh held her down. Blood covered them all.

"What the hell?" Jamie ran to Joanne's side.

"The Dick shot her," Barry said. "She said it was no big deal."

John hurried to Barry and helped him hold Joanne. He also circled Barry with one arm.

"She probably didn't feel it right away," Jamie said.

"What?" Barry stared at her wide-eyed.

"Not my information to give." Jamie shook her head.

But John understood. Joanne's former rush habit had many consequences, one of which was that her nervous system periodically stopped working, and her body fell numb. Getting shot was the kind of thing that would trigger the numbness.

She screamed. Loudly. Getting the bullet removed, apparently, had jump-started her system. Then she fell still, but not unconscious. Her eyes stayed open and flicked back and forth, but she didn't move. Super creepy. Was it some kind of seizure?

"Quick," Jamie said. "Get the fucking bullet out of her *now*."

The guy, a medic? went to work.

Joanne sucked in a deep breath, perfectly calm. She smiled.

"*Renich Tasa Uberaca Icar, Lucifer,*" she said, as if that was a perfectly normal thing to say.

Silence filled the room.

"What. the *fuck*. was that?" But Barry held her all the tighter.

"Got the last fragment," the stranger said. "Closing up." He ran something over her abdomen, then backed away.

Joanne fell limp and closed her eyes.

"She's just unconscious." The stranger felt her pulse. "Probably for the best."

Jamie grabbed a sheet and threw it over Joanne. Everyone else stepped away.

"It's the rush," Jamie said, hanging onto Joanne's hand. "It messed up her brain. Who knows what kind of crap got uploaded into her head."

"Okay, spectators need to bugger off." The stranger pulled off his gloves.

"Blast that and burn it." Jamie glared, obviously not letting go of Joanne's hand.

"You okay?" John pulled Barry into a corner of the room. "You get hit?"

Barry yanked off his shirt. Two bullets had embedded themselves into the Kevlar vest.

"Jesus shit." John reached forward to touch them but stopped.

Barry yanked off the vest. Bruises purpled his chest. He poked at them. "Hurts, but no big." He grabbed John's arms. "You? Jamie?"

"We're fine." But shit, he had to admit it to someone. "We lost the camera, coz."

The whole purpose of the mission. They'd boondoggled it.

Shock filled Barry's eyes, then understanding.

"That guy wasn't normal." He squeezed John's arms.

"You have no idea."

Barry raised an eyebrow.

John opened his mouth to spill it all. Of course, he did; he trusted Barry like family. Hell, Barry *was* family. Then John stopped. What did family mean, now?

Anything John knew, he knew because of his family's big secret. What could he say without betraying that? Fuck.

"Sorry." Barry's eyebrow lowered, and he tried to move away. "Didn't mean to pry." John held him fast. Covered in Joanne's blood, how could they lie to each other?

"What do you know?" John asked.

"Guy named Addison trying to find your family." Barry scanned John's face. "Lots of danger. Jamie thinks its bullshit."

Said like that, it all seemed so simple.

John had lied to Jamie so easily. But David had never lied. He'd told John what he couldn't say, but he'd never lied. As much as John held anger for his lack of info, David had never lied.

John had to stop lying.

"We're in a world of shit, my friend," he told Barry. "That brush ape who shot Joanne—he wants to get to David. Probably me, too. And he has some massively bioengineered upgrade that lets him leap tall buildings in a single bound."

Barry's eyes opened wide.

"I can't tell you more, and it's not because I don't love you and think of you as family. It's because I don't believe half of it myself... it all seems like bullshit, and I don't know what the blight it is." He held his friend at arm's length. "Our folks are going to explain it all to us tonight. As soon as I understand it, you will be the God damn first person I tell."

Barry stared at John for a long time, then nodded.

John was about to release him.

"Noah's dead, isn't he?" Barry held John's arms even tighter.

What the hell? He knew? John gulped, and a huge lump leapt into his throat. What was he supposed to say? He couldn't breathe.

"Don't you dare lie to me."

How could he?

"How did you know?" John asked.

"So... I'm right?" Barry sucked in a breath.

"I'm sorry," John said. "I couldn't tell you. I didn't know how you could possibly believe me."

Barry went weak in John's arms, and they fell to their knees.

"I'm so sorry," John held Barry as tightly as possible. "I'm so sorry. I just found out."

Jamie appeared a few feet away. She pulled back at the sight of Barry's weeping.

"Joanne's okay?" John pushed everything else aside.

"She will be."

"Good," John said. "That's good."

"Um, John?" Jamie's face said something had to be wrong. "I checked on the net. We have, like, a thousand messages." Understanding of Barry's pain seemed to war with her need to be logical. "I'm sorry to interrupt."

"What's wrong now?" Barry rose from John's chest and wiped his face.

"There's a meeting at the church." She held up a hand. "Not the religious kind. It's like a town meeting. Everyone wants to fight back."

"Fight back?" What the hell did that even mean? "Against who? The entire government?"

"This is going to suck, guys." Jamie spat it out quickly. "The list of casualties was released. Everyone who died in the tunnels." She stared at Barry.

"Say it," Barry insisted. "I already know."

She did a double take. "Noah and his dad. Ten other Ghetto cops. Over a hundred names. Billy, the bartender at Babylon." She shook her head. "Pastor Sue."

"What?" John couldn't hold back his shock. "Pastor Sue?"

"She was down there trying to minister to the rush junkies. It was the final straw." Jamie held out a cell. "I think the Ghetto's going to war."

"Oh, sweet Baby Jebus," Barry muttered. "It'll be a slaughter."

"Stay here with Joanne." John grabbed Jamie's wrist. "We'll be in touch."

The view from Addison's patio showed the entire garden, now, all the way to the fucking pool. He snubbed his cigarette on the railing and flicked the butt.

How long was Pierce going to stand in the doorway? Didn't he know that Addison's earpiece had reported his presence the moment he entered the room?

"Sir?"

Addison smirked. Two minutes. Must be embarrassed. Good. Addison needed a laugh. He dropped his hands to the railing.

"Anything interesting?" He already knew the basics but assumed there were pieces of the day Pierce had managed to keep to himself.

"I've worked for you a long time now, sir." His voice seemed amazingly steady considering what he needed to spit out. "And I've never let my personal life interfere with my job."

"And I give a shit about your personal life, why?" This would be fun.

"There was an incident today, sir, while I was off-duty. . ."

"I don't care what you do when you're off duty. Strapping hookers into a sling again, were we?" The silence was delicious. Slowly, Addison turned to face Pierce, who stood just inside the room looking shocked. "Or was it the other way around?" He waved the younger man onto the patio.

Pierce complied but remained several feet away.

"Do you actually think there is anything about you I don't already know?" Addison looked out over the garden. "As far as you're concerned, I am God. All-seeing and all-fucking-knowing."

Pierce cleared his throat. "I guess that makes this a little less embarrassing, somehow." He held out something in a plastic bag.

"And this is?" Without moving to take it, Addison smoked.

"A video camera with voice and DNA samples you need to see."

That's the piece Addison hadn't known.

"The video itself is of a rather personal nature, sir, but I knew you wouldn't want me to tamper with the equipment in any way." Pierce seemed to weigh every word.

"So some hooker videotaped you fucking." He turned to face Pierce directly. "Again, why do I give a shit?"

"It's them, sir. Mary's children. They mention you by name."

This time it was Addison's turn to fall speechless. After a moment's hesitation while he made sure he'd heard Pierce correctly, Addison flicked his cigarette away, grabbed the plastic bag from his assistant and hurried into the motel room. He crossed to his table and dumped the camera out of the bag onto the glass, tapping an icon in one corner. Immediately, a holographic screen popped up.

"Scan and upload all files. Also, scan for organic matter."

"All the relevant data's already been processed." Pierce joined his boss and tossed a data stick onto the table. "I wanted to make sure I was right, so I didn't waste your time."

"You mean you wanted to make sure there was a real need to let me watch you blow your load."

"I didn't. . ." Pierce coughed again. "Sorry."

The video played.

"This is a lot tamer than I would've expected." Addison chuckled. "You even fuck her?"

"If I may have the controls, sir?" Pierce shifted uncomfortably. "There's nothing in the video itself you need to see. It's the audio track."

"I'll be the judge of what's important—oh. . . hell." He chuckled again. "I was wrong; you *have* managed to keep one or two things from me." He rewound the video. Played it again. "Latin?"

"Sir. . ." His voice was practically a whine.

The voices of the kids videotaping his pervert assistant told him exactly why Pierce was willing to humiliate himself.

"Did our folks tell you why David and I went into hiding?" a boy said.

David. The name from the go-go fag.

"Sort of," a girl replied. "Dicks are looking for them, they said. Dicks looking for our parents, right? They told me this guy named Addison killed your dad. . ." She stopped suddenly, and Addison almost choked. "Oh, crap, you already knew that, right?"

"Is that it?" the boy asked.

"Why? Is there more?"

Addison hit an icon on the table to freeze the image at the moment Pierce strangled the whack job on the bed.

"Sir. . . I really don't think. . ." Pierce shifted uncomfortably again.

"No, sometimes you don't." He gestured to enlarge the center of the screen, which seemed to make Pierce even more uncomfortable. "Separate foreground from background," he instructed the computer. A miniature hourglass told him the machine was working so he turned to Pierce. "You said DNA?"

Pierce nodded.

Addison tapped the table to grant access to his assistant. While Pierce brought up the DNA files, Addison manipulated the video.

"Remove background," Addison said. The image of his assistant and the couple on the bed vanished, replaced by a fuzzy reflection in the window.

"Oh my God," Pierce muttered.

"Capture similar data across the entire video." The computer needed four seconds. "Cross-reference all images and enhance." A dark, teenage boy and a fair-skinned girl stared back at them from the screen.

"That's them," Pierce muttered.

"Run images against the project database." Even without Pierce's DNA data, Addison immediately knew whose kids these were. He gestured to highlight both pairs of eyes. "Find closest match." The computer needed only a second. "Display."

The two photos the computer showed were entirely expected.

"The spitting image of their parents," Addison said. Was it time? Yes, it was. "Get me the Pentagon. It's time to blow this island off the map."

People were already shouting by the time John and Barry reached the church. The volume pulled the two friends up short as soon as they entered the foyer. Barry snaked an arm around John's shoulders, and their eyes met. This meeting would suck for so many reasons.

Barry's face was tight and scared. He obviously didn't want to lose it in front of everyone. John pulled him into a tight embrace.

"We need to do this for Noah," John said.

Barry nodded into his shoulder, then pulled a bit away. He gestured with his eyes to the right. Ah. Tracey

"I should let her know that Jamie is all right."

"Go check on your girl, Romeo." John kissed his cheek.

Barry managed a smile but moved off wordlessly.

John stepped into the sanctuary.

Several neighborhood leaders stood near the altar with a familiar White cop at the microphone.

The folks there weren't just the church members. This meeting was for everyone in the Ghetto.

"...explain to my daughter why her father is dead?" The speaker in the middle of the floor was Matthew, Billy's husband. "What do I tell her? My husband was just doing a job down there, the only work he could find, and there was nothing illegal about it."

John recognized the man at the microphone: Jonas' partner, the one John had seen with Noah's dad in the tunnels. The cracker.

"I know this isn't what you want to hear, Matthew, but the fact that he was out working after curfew made it illegal."

John had never heard such a stream of profanity in the church before, and two men had to restrain Matthew from climbing over the pew.

John's mom stood with Uncle Bo and Aunt Ruth on the other side of the sanctuary. No way to reach them.

"What about *my* husband?" A woman's voice rang out over the hubbub. When the crowd recognized Noah's mom, the tumult died.

"What about my husband?" she repeated.

"In any drug bust of this size..." The cop at the microphone fidgeted. "There's always the risk of collateral damage—"

"Collateral damage?" She walked up the center aisle and space opened for her. "Jonas is collateral damage? You can look me in the eye and say that? You?"

The man looked down.

John couldn't listen to them. It was too close to Noah. He backed up several steps, then fled the sanctuary and maneuvered through the crowd into the foyer, where people huddled in small groups discussing the debate raging inside.

Where was David? Well, there weren't any kids around, so David was most likely watching them. He was usually "invited" to look after the kids because he asked controversial questions. Today his questions would likely start a riot.

Mouthy guy in a synagogue. It kept coming back to that. If David knew someone wanted them, why didn't he just keep quiet?

Because he couldn't help himself, blast it.

John poured a cup of coffee as the voices in the sanctuary rose to shouts again. He needed to find David and a quiet corner somewhere to talk about their fight that morning. Was it still the same day? Jesus. So much had changed in one day.

John wanted to tell David about the wolf Jamie couldn't see. He also needed to apologize for freaking out that morning. He closed his eyes and sipped coffee. David hadn't lied to him the way he'd lied to Jamie and Barry.

The volume in the church rose as the arguing spilled into the lobby.

John took another sip of coffee and listened to snatches of conversation. The people here seemed genuine... genuinely pissed. Well, didn't they have reason to be?

He closed his eyes and inhaled the sweet smell of coffee and doughnuts. The violence and stench of the Ghetto seemed miles away. If he let himself, John could almost pretend that the whole country was like this, with people from every spectrum of the rainbow all sipping caffeine and sugar, that most of the country wasn't trashed out and dying, that the ocean wasn't slowly swallowing the only part of the city where his people could own property.

His people. Who were his people, exactly? The "us" of the Ghetto and of the other ghettos tacked onto every major city in the country, contrasted against a gigantic "them" which was everyone else in the country.

He listened to the voices around him, to the quiet conversations, whispered and angry, to the louder arguments from the sanctuary.

He opened his eyes *and saw blood, a sea of blood that engulfed the church. All around him, people drowned in a red sea, reaching out to him with grasping arms, pleading to him with empty eyes, crying out to him with silent, gaping mouths....*

"John?" someone said.

John gasped for air and nearly dropped his coffee. Who had said his name? Everyone in the foyer stood where they had been moments before.

No blood. No dying, drowning people. Another damn vision.

"Earth to John."

A voice behind him. He spun.

"You okay?" Barry, hands in his pockets, regarded John with one eyebrow raised in a characteristically bemused manner.

"Yeah, fine." John gulped another swallow of coffee. Lies spilled out of his mouth so easily these days. "What's up, coz?"

Barry moved closer, leaning against the wall shoulder to shoulder with John, nodding nonchalantly at an older woman who passed them.

"I bumped around on my cell, and there's a tribute at the Temporary Building tonight." Barry took John's coffee and sipped. "David asked whether you were still mad at him."

"I'm not." John sighed.

"You want to take a few minutes to talk about it?"

John was about to answer an affirmative when he noticed his mother across the lobby.

She drank coffee in a tight circle of women. Tension ran palpably through everyone.

"Not right now, coz," he said. "Maybe after tonight."

"Uh-oh, you're scoping. What's he look like? Is he hot?" He tried to follow John's line of sight.

Annoyed again, John glanced into Barry's bright, mischievous eyes and forced himself to return the joke. "I wish... How 'bout you, big guy? You know I've been hot for you since the first time I saw you naked in sixth grade gym class."

"You know you'd be the only guy for me if I was into guys." He kissed John's cheek.

"Yeah, yeah." John pulled away from the kiss and pushed Barry's face to the side. "You keep saying that."

What was it about Mom? What had changed?

She met his eyes, nodded, and waved.

John waved back.

"Uh-oh." Barry seemed to notice the exchange. "Mom's on the warpath?"

"Actually, no. She's been cool since we got back from Venice. We talked this morning."

"Really?" He was surprised. "Talked? Like... talked?"

"Yeah. Something changed. I'm not sure what. It's all this great big mystery right now." He heard the cryptic in his voice again and thought about David. Here was Barry, John's best friend outside the family, and he couldn't tell him anything.

Barry leaned against John's shoulder, his brow furrowed into little lines of concern, his eyes bright and attentive and brown.

"You know, my man, I think I *could've* fallen for you." John deflected his friend's concern with a joke. "You've got beautiful eyes when they're all concerned like that." He wiped a hand over his friend's face.

"Aw shucks, Virginia..." Barry used his best southern accent. "I bet you say that to all the boys." He leaned closer. "But you better be careful David doesn't hear you say that. He might get jealous."

"What the hell is that supposed to mean?" John's face burned.

"Deep breathing, coz." Barry held his hands out, palms forward. "It does wonders. T'was only a jest."

"Sorry." John forced himself to relax. "It's been a long couple of days. I'm sorry." He pulled Barry into a hug. "I'm just..." Another lie leapt to his lips. "I'm just declassed about Noah." He squeezed. "I should in no way take that out on you."

"No pasta." Barry squeezed him back. "You sure there isn't something maybe you need to talk about that doesn't have to do with the Dicks?"

"It's nothing like that." John nudged him. "There's nothing like that between me and David. I tease him about Joanne, but I don't think he's ever really been interested in anyone."

"He hasn't?" Barry lowered his voice. "Please don't slug me, coz, but I don't think you're cooking with gas on that one."

What the heck did that even mean?

Barry rolled his eyes. "I must beg to differ with you."

John stared at him. The implication was obvious. What? The idea that David might be interested in John as something more than a brother sent chills all over John's body.

"We're cousins." What was up with the lack of conviction?

"*Second* cousins," Barry corrected. "Bo isn't your Uncle; you just call him that."

"You're nuts." John shrugged the idea away. "David's my best friend. The cat's like my brother, okay?"

"Okay." Barry backed away. He seemed to decide this was a bad time to push his point. "So we're set for tonight, then?"

John scowled. "Temporary Building after dark. We'll be there." The annoyance rattled away in his voice. Damn. "I'm sorry. It all sucks."

"Namaste." Barry clapped his hands once then spread them open again, palms upward, backing away with a bow. "We'll talk later, my good friend." He pointed at John's coffee cup and made a sign for John to take another drink. "You can never have enough." He moved away, noticed Uncle Bo in his path. "My good man." He hugged John's Uncle.

"I'm so sorry," Uncle Bo said.

"Thank you." Barry moved a bit away. Patted Uncle Bo's chest. "You are the best of us. Truly." He dashed off.

"Enough what?" Bo asked.

"Caffeine." John felt guilty, as if Uncle Bo had walked in on something obscene. "I'm being cranky."

And now it was Uncle Bo's turn to hug John. Apparently, a horrific tragedy meant lots of hugs. Not so bad a thing.

"Have you talked to David?" He held on. "I know this morning was hard on you guys."

"I haven't." He maintained his grip for the comfort. "I hope he's here."

"He's with the littles," Uncle Bo said. "Of course."

"Uncle Bo?" John had to ask... what? What could he ask? There was no way he could ask what had leapt into his mind. Quickly, he redirected. "You know what's up with my mom? I mean, besides this big secret and all. She seems different, somehow. She really listened to me this morning, and she said some bizarre stuff."

"I'm not sure, to be honest." Uncle Bo moved closer and let one hand rest on John's shoulder. "I talked with her, and she's sincere. She really means to change. Hell, she really *has* changed." He pulled John close one more time. "But we're all talking tonight, and I'm sure we'll figure it out then." He paused. "You worried?"

"Just curious."

"Understandable." He held John at arm's length. "We'll talk about everything tonight, I think. I'm sorry we haven't been able to tell you all along."

"It's okay. I think I understand, now." Counting off all the lies he'd told so far that day, John gave Bo a squeeze.

"If I get any information about your mom, I'll be sure to pass it along, though you might try asking her yourself." Bo ran a hand through John's hair. "Just a thought."

With too many concerns bouncing through his head, John rolled against the wall, felt the gentle grind of plaster against his shoulders, then wandered and down the hall that led to the kids' wing.

The excitement of children's laughter and clapping replaced the sounds of adult conversation. John ran one finger along the wallpaper, printed with rainbows and clouds in this part of the building. Week after week, John noticed how clean the place was. Even the police and hoodlums had enough respect to leave the church alone so there was enough energy and time left to make actual improvements.

The carpet under John's feet was new. He could smell the glue.

As he rounded the corner, the children's voices broke into song, led by David's emerging baritone that hardly ever cracked, anymore.

"Jesus loves the little children, all the children of the world..."

John leaned against the corner, hands in his pockets, legs crossed at the ankle.

The kids sat in a circle in an open space covered with rugs and filled with educational toys where several hallways met. David often brought mats or pillows when he told stories. They swayed back and forth as they sang, David in the center, sitting cross-legged with a dark, curly-headed girl in his lap.

Wait. John recognized her. She was one of the two sisters to whom he'd thrown his money. Well, she seemed happier, tonight. All the little ones did.

John liked to watch David with the kids. He wasn't so good with kids, himself, didn't have the patience, didn't really know how to get down on his hands and knees and talk to them at their level without talking down to them.

One of the kids started clapping and David joined in and encouraged the others. Soon, they all made enough noise to wake the dead. Then the song ended.

All the bright eyes fixed on David's face, waiting for his next words. David seemed lost in their world, the tiny microcosm he created for these tykes, and his eyes shone, and his gestures swept the room, and his voice rose and fell like a song.

Every sentence or so, he ran a hand through his hair.

A few of the kids had picked up the mannerism.

Warmth swelled in John's chest. For a few minutes, he managed to believe he was merely proud of his cousin, but Barry's words evoked a litany in John's head.

He'd never consciously thought about David *that* way, but now that Barry had put the idea in his head, he found himself obsessing.

Was David *maybe* interested in him? It's not something Barry would make up. Though John tried to push the concept out of his thoughts, they brought a flush to his face he could not deny.

What *were* his feelings for his cousin?

Second cousin…

Shit. They were friends… Best friends… That was all…

There could be nothing else.

Were they even related? Would John find out that this experiment meant he wasn't even *related* to David?

"So who does God love?" David spoke loudly.

"ME!" all the children answered.

"Yay!" David cheered. "And who else?"

A chorus of voices answered:

"My daddy!"

"My mommies!"

"My teacher!"

"He loves my dog, Scooter!"

David acknowledged all of them, nodding and smiling and laughing.

Then one kid said, "He loves everyone!"

And another replied, "Mommy says he doesn't love the Pope."

"And not President Clement!"

Laughter filled the space, but David's face had lost its smile.

As the children noticed the change, they all fell silent.

"God loves them, too." David spoke quietly. "Even bad people, God loves."

"That's not what my daddy says."

"For God so loved the *world* the Bible says. It doesn't say, 'For God so loved *some* of the people.' So God loves *everyone* in the world."

"Even bad people?"

"Lots of people you'd think were the best people in the world used to be what your daddy would call 'bad,'" David said. "Lots of the disciples went to prison, even, and lots of Jesus' best friends were what everyone would have called 'bad people.'"

The kids grew quiet.

"I know it's difficult, but we need to pray extra hard for God to love the people hurting us, so maybe they'll realize what they're doing is wrong."

"You mean they'll stop sending the police to wreck my mom's store?"

"We can only keep praying…"

"You shouldn't fill their heads with that garbage," a low voice said from nearby. All eyes looked up to see an older man John didn't recognize. "We should be doing a lot more than praying."

David turned to the newcomer, and that was his ingratiating face, the one he used when he knew he was about to get really pissed and wanted to avoid showing it. One eyebrow raised in an arch and the smile on his lips was gloriously plastic. Excellent.

"I think it's important for them to know that God loves all of us, even folks *we* don't like so well." His vocabulary was simple enough for the kids to follow the conversation, but his tone had changed completely.

"A lot of their parents think differently."

"I bet President Clement would agree with those folks." David cocked his head and smiled. "He doesn't think God loves *us*."

John sucked in his breath with a low hiss. Two points for David.

The man scowled more deeply, but John missed his response because an arm dropped around his shoulders. Barry. Of course.

"So David's causing trouble again." It was more a statement than a question.

"It's his love-your-enemy thing."

"Who's winning?" Barry asked.

"Who do you think?"

A couple more of the adults had wandered over. Wait. More

than a couple. A sizable group had moved from the sanctuary to the children's corner. One by one the children slunk off.

David shifted into a different mode, unfolded from the floor and moved to sit on the art table. He always sat during a debate, said he didn't want to shift nervously from foot to foot and that he appeared more relaxed when sitting.

"I agree that we need to fight back," David said. "For God's sake, I live in this hellhole, too. But the folks on the other side of the bridge are still children of God. If we start dictating who God can and cannot love, we are teaching our children the exact same hatred that drove us into this Ghetto."

Ah damn, that's not what they wanted to hear. Most of these folks weren't even Christian.

Several people told David what he could do with God's love. Which, of course, pissed off the Christians since they'd offered the church for this meeting in the first place.

"Look at my own mother," David offered, gesturing at the edge of the crowd where the three parents huddled. He turned on his extra calm face, the one he used when he realized he'd just stepped into it deep.

Aunt Ruth startled as every eye turned to regard her.

"And my Aunt."

John's mom scowled. For once John had to agree with her. Was this really a good time to draw attention?

"From all appearances, they should be on the other side of the bridge with the rest of the crackers."

All three parents seemed shocked at his use of that word.

"But they got themselves thrown into the Ghetto with the rest of us, why?" He scanned the crowd with his earnest eyes. "Because they love their children more than they value their freedom." He pointed at the cracker cop. "And Officer Wilkins here could probably get a much better beat to walk, but he keeps his job here, with us, helping us keep the peace."

The look on the cop's face told John that maybe he couldn't get a better beat, but he appreciated the vote of confidence.

"I understand your anger," David said. "I'm angry, too. I lost friends." He glanced at Mrs. King. "Family. Noah was my brother as much as anyone." He shrugged. "But what's more important to you? Vengeance. . ."

A number of people shouted agreement.

". . .or keeping your children alive?"

The crowd murmured.

"Who would we rise up against? My parents? Officer Wilkins? The men and women at the guard station? The shop owners on the other side of the bridge? What good will that do?"

"It'll show them they can't just troop in here and kill us."

"But they can!" David's voice rose and his eyes grew cold. They sent a thrill down John's back, and he couldn't convince himself it was just a feeling of pride. Jesus Christ, was Barry right?

"If we riot in the streets, what are they going to do?" He rose to his feet and stood confidently. "They'll send in copters. They'll sit up there in their giant glass tower, and they'll drop bombs on us without losing a single night's sleep."

The murmuring seemed to sway to David's side.

"So what do we do then, if you know so much?" someone shouted.

"We mourn." David let all the angry energy drain away. "We hold our loved ones close. . ." He met John's eye. "We hold our loved ones close," David repeated and sat on the desk. "And we wait until all this anger drains away. Then we come back here, without the anger, and we figure out what we *can* do." He met John's eye again. "Together."

Warmth swelled in John's chest. He'd always believed that just meant he was proud of David, but Barry's words kept repeating in his head. He'd never consciously thought about David that way before, but now that their friend had shoved the idea into his head, he found himself obsessing.

What were his feelings for his cousin?

Shit... were they even related?

At exactly that moment, David raised one eyebrow, still

speaking to the crowd with his words but his face spoke to John, whose heart suddenly beat painfully in his chest.

It was like they stood alone in that room. Together.

David's face asked John if he was still angry.

John shook his head.

David smiled and nodded, saying he understood. He glanced over a bit, most likely at Barry. He lost his smile. His face offered Barry his condolences.

John closed his eyes and took three deep breaths to calm himself. He counted to three and opened his eyes. . .

He floated weightless in the sanctuary of St. Matthew's.

Sunlight, filtered all the colors of the rainbow, played in restless waves around him. A school of silver dollars flashed and glittered as they scattered to the shadows in the corners of the church.

The water sparkled. The scenes in cut glass moved with life. Mary and Joseph struggled against the heat of an Egyptian sun. John the Baptist blessed the newly converted, awash in the River Jordan. Simon and Andrew cast their nets over the rising tide of the Sea of Galilee.

An image of Jesus teaching the little children called to John.

He looked up and met John's curious gaze.

John flushed.

Jesus beckoned him closer.

Without hesitation, John lifted his arms and threw himself forward through water that surged past him like a great wind.

He closed his eyes and glass shattered around him.

Hot, white light burned through his closed eyelids, scorching his eyes.

The light consumed him.

The light shattered him like glass.

The light released him.

He opened his eyes, gasping. Sweat stained his shirt. He could smell it on himself.

"You sure you're okay?" Barry asked.

"Fine." John stepped away and leaned against the wall. "I'm fine."

"Go back to your homes." David's voice distracted John from

the insane vision. "Mourn those we've lost and hold tight to those you still have. Wait until a day when the cameras aren't focused on us, when the entire nation isn't watching us to see what we'll do. We riot now, and Clement will say we've proved his point, and he'll send in the copters."

The nation was watching them?

Holy shit. Yes. At least three news crews filmed David's words.

What the hell was he thinking?

Addison would find them for sure now.

Unless. . .

Unless he'd already found them. Unless it was too late, and David knew it. With all those cameras on their family, Addison couldn't just steal them away in the night without questions being asked. Maybe hiding out in plain sight was all they had left.

And if no one gave Clement an excuse to simply wipe the Ghetto off the map, then maybe they could slip away quietly once the fury died down.

Brilliant. Two points for David.

Someone tapped his shoulder, startling him. Jamie.

"So David's causing trouble again?"

"Joanne's okay?" John asked.

She nodded. "Sent me to see what's going on."

"It's his love-your-enemy thing," Barry said.

"Who's winning?"

"Who do you think?" Barry answered.

John pressed close to him, his lips an inch from the ear away from Jamie. "You really think David has feelings for me? I mean, you know, *feelings*?"

He pulled away just enough to see Barry's eyes.

"Only one way to find out." Barry seemed to think so.

Oh, crap. John couldn't do that. He couldn't just *ask* David.

"Find out what?" Jamie asked.

"Nothing," John said quickly.

One more lie.

The crowd dispersed.

Bo had one arm around Ruth. Naomi stood with them across the street from the church where the people trickled out and hung around in groups. The last of the reporters spoke with David. The rest had cleared out fairly quickly, most likely losing interest since David had avoided a riot.

Should Bo be proud of his son or terrified?

"You see it, don't you?" Naomi asked. "The way the crowd listened to him. The way he maneuvered them. You see it in him."

Bo saw. Today was his first glimpse into how it all started. How it must have started two thousand years ago.

A few people heard him.

They believed.

They told others.

"But it's way too soon," Ruth said matter-of-factly.

"Too soon?" Bo raised an eyebrow.

"Okay, fine." She made a noise. "I know the Bible isn't a roadmap of how things are going to go for us, but he's still so young."

"He's not a child anymore." From Naomi, the words surprised Bo. "None of them are." She met Ruth's eyes. "Not like you were." She turned to watch their children who were no longer children.

Bo followed her gaze to the cluster of John, Jamie, and Barry. They certainly seemed like adults, the way they watched the crowd, commenting and studying, like they were working through strategies.

"I was even younger than them when it all started for me." Ruth squeezed Bo's arm. "For us. We were both so young."

And Naomi was right; they'd been so much more naïve. The world had seemed simpler. They'd had no reason to mistrust the men who promised they'd been picked to help save the Earth from a coming apocalypse. Funny. Addison had spoken nothing but lies, but he'd turned out to be right about so much, anyway.

John threw an arm round Barry, laughing, and tapped his chest with a fist. The young man winced, and John lifted his hand, as if remembering an injury and apologizing.

Jamie grabbed Barry's shirt. The normally uninhibited young man prevented her from baring his chest. The way he looked around told Bo he needed to hide something. How had he been injured? Well, Bo would likely hear all about it that night.

"David bought us a little time," he said, still watching the trio of young people as they closed ranks. "But I think we need to get everything into the open."

"I agree," Naomi said. "There's a memorial at the Temporary Building. They'll want to go to that, but afterward—"

"Afterward, we tell them the truth." Ruth turned and fidgeted. "Now, where's David gone? We need to get out of here."

"He's probably making sure the little ones find their parents," Naomi suggested.

So… back in the building. Great.

"I'll find him and drag him away." Bo released Ruth.

"Just don't give him an opening for the 'seeking him in his father's house' joke," she said.

Naomi rolled her eyes. "It stopped being funny when he was thirteen."

Head down and arms hanging, John watched the water pool at his feet because the tub drained too slowly. He wiggled his toes and splashed the puddle. For ten whole seconds, he lost himself in the relaxing spray of water across his shoulders.

He was part of some secret religious experiment. His family might have to flee murderous Dicks. His father had died in some heroic effort to save him. He had feelings buried deep down inside that he wished would stay buried.

Just a regular day at the office.

The idea that his dad had been some kind of hero kept niggling at John's brain. He rarely thought about the man who'd originally given him life. After so many years, he hardly seemed like a real person.

But could John make that kind of sacrifice?

Could he be a hero?

He turned away from the showerhead, arms folded across his chest.

What to do about David.

John rubbed his head briskly and the water flew. They'd spent a night in the hospital, curled up together for warmth and comfort, making up songs, whatever they could do to avoid worrying about their friends and family.

In one sense, it'd been like old times. They'd shared a bed for years and thought nothing of it. They'd only stopped because John had feared what people would think about two teenagers in the same bed. David had never worried about it.

Maybe because he liked it?

Like liked it?

The tightness in John's chest tugged a bit lower. He grabbed the shampoo and lathered his hair, scrubbing and scrubbing his scalp.

What were they going to do about the Dicks?

Their parents most likely wanted to run away. But where would they go? Another ghetto? Another country? Would they even be able to stay together? Separating the families might be safer.

John stopped scrubbing.

What if they *did* separate the families? Where would his mother take him? Would he ever see David again? A dark chasm opened in his chest at that thought.

No. They were adults. Their parents couldn't just tear the family apart, anymore. No matter what happened, he would stay with David. Nothing would separate them.

Yeah, because that didn't sound like hopelessly romantic pining. Shit.

He grabbed the washcloth and scrubbed his arms and legs. He scrubbed his face and gargled.

The doorknob turned and someone bumped into the door.

John jumped so hard he choked, slipped, and nearly fell. The soap shot out of his hands, rebounded against the curtain, and slid around the porcelain at his feet.

"John? Isn't that you?" David rattled the doorknob. "Why is the door locked?"

"I'm in the shower." John grabbed at the showerhead to keep from landing on his butt. He winced at how lame his words sounded.

"So? You never lock the door unless you're taking a dump."

A locked door was unusual between them. John turned off the water and stepped out of the tub before he killed himself.

"So I locked the door, today." He cringed at the annoyance he heard in his tone.

"O-kay." Confusion filled David's voice. "So unlock it, doofus."

"Yeah, sure, what do you want?" He tried desperately and unsuccessfully to keep his voice steady while he toweled off at record speed and jumped into his slacks.

"You okay?" David rattled the doorknob again.

"Yeah, sure." He unlocked the door and opened it. "You just scared me. I slipped."

"Sorry about that." David stood there with his arms crossed, and he didn't seem very sorry. More like suspicious. Conversations while they shared the bathroom were so common they barely rated comment. Why the locked door all of a sudden?

"What's up?" John grabbed the rest of his clothes and the wet towel, trying his best to act nonchalant.

He hurried past David to their room.

"I talked to our folks," David explained. "After you, me, and Jamie get back tonight, we're all going to sit down to explain everything. They want us together to get it out at once."

"Okay, great." He pulled on a T-shirt, keeping his back to David. What might he see in John's eyes?

"I'm sorry I've kept this from you so long." His voice grew softer and sort of guilty. "You have every right to be pissed at me."

"David. . . no, I'm not pissed, anymore." John pretended to go through their dress shirts in the closet. "I talked to Jamie this afternoon. I told her about Addison, that he works for the UCA, but I couldn't tell her anything else. . . about the prophet thing. . . and there was a wolf—"

"A wolf?"

"I know, right?" John turned to him without thinking. "Big fucking wolf, and this kid's ball sailed right through it like it wasn't there." He lifted a hand. "It licked my hand, but no one else could even see it."

"Are you okay?" David's eyes filled with concern.

How had John never noticed just how amazing those eyes were?

"I'm fine." He turned back to the closet. "Jamie didn't see it either. I had to pretend it wasn't there. I was afraid she'd think I was psycho." He chose a shirt at random and slipped into it. "I guess I understand what you meant, now. I mean, wolf? What's up with that?"

David remained silent.

"I'm sorry I went off on you this morning," John said. "At least you never lied to me." He had to be wrong about the time. "Jesus, was it just this morning?"

"Yes, it was."

John fussed with his cuffs.

"John?"

John knew what he was going to ask without needing to peek inside his mind.

Could he peek inside David's mind? No. Who knew what he might find there?

"Why won't you look at me?" David asked.

John's mind spun. What could he say? The truth was too frightening, and David would see right through any lie he might say.

"And why was the door locked if you're not mad at me?"

"I was naked," John muttered at last.

"So?"

"So nothing." Heat burned John's face.

"I thought you weren't mad at me?" David's voice sounded so sad.

John couldn't stand it. He turned around.

His cousin had his hands shoved deep into his pockets. He searched John's face for an explanation. His eyes were so confused.

"I'm not mad at you, coz. I'm just worried. . ." He couldn't stop the lie. "People are talking about us. . . like, Barry even, and I just think we should be careful before everyone starts to think. . ." He couldn't say it. He was too afraid. . .

Afraid that David would feel the same way. . .

Afraid that he wouldn't?

"Think what?"

"That we're not just friends. . . not just family." The words felt like acid on his tongue.

David's brows knit together.

"I just think we should. . . that maybe we should cool it on the affection. . . that we're a little too close, or something. . ."

Even as the words came out of his mouth, he wanted to take them back. He didn't believe them, didn't even know why he'd said them, except that telling David anything else terrified him. His cousin's face remained blank.

"I'm not mad at you." If only adding that could erase everything else.

"Why do you all of a sudden care what anyone else thinks?" David's voice was quiet. "They've talked about us as long as I can remember."

"What? No, they haven't."

"Are you that clueless?" David looked at him like he was dumb.

Apparently, he was. About so many things.

"As long as we know what we mean to each other," David continued. "Do you really care what anyone else says?"

"Right." John wanted to ask what they *did* mean to each other, but the words wouldn't come out. "As long as we know what we mean to each other."

"Exactly." David seemed to be satisfied with that.

Which meant what?

"So. . ." David moved to the dresser and opened a drawer for socks and underwear. "I heard about the mission today."

So the discussion was over. Problem solved as far as David was concerned. What did that mean?

"You saved Jamie's life, coz." His eyes looked proud. "I'm seriously impressed."

Coz. So they were cousins. Friends. Fine. Friends could be good. Right? A pit opened up in John's chest and swallowed him.

"Hello?"

"Yeah. . . right." John's hands trembled. "I'm a big hero who lost the camera. I didn't save Jamie. He wasn't after her."

"What?"

"Why don't you go take a shower." John couldn't look at David, anymore. Couldn't be in the same room. "We need to get ready for the. . . the thing."

"Right." David hesitated then crossed the room to grab John in a tight hug. John had to force his arms to touch David's back.

"I'm glad you're not mad at me." He punched John's shoulder. "And that you don't care what other people think."

David pulled away, smiling, and ran from the room. His scent lingered. John knew David's scent. Because that was the kind of thing roommates knew about each other.

Damn it.

He was in love with David. He had to admit it. Barry was wrong though, damn him. David didn't feel the same way. The way *that* tore a hole in John's heart was the final proof.

If John wasn't in love, why would it matter?

Safely alone in their room, he slammed the door and leaned against it staring at the floor. He wouldn't let himself cry. He ran his hands through his hair, breathing heavily. A hologram hung in the air in the middle of the room.

The Halloween photo.

John stared at the studied determination in the little boy's eyes then looked up. The same expression glared back at him from the mirror, the same fierce look he'd given to the camera by pretending he was a brave, threatening warrior on a quest to save a princess.

Princess. What a laugh.

He rubbed his head again with one hand. He had to be a freak in every single way. He was a gay Ghetto rat. Cherokee. He had visions and read minds. He saw giant wolves that didn't exist. And now, on top of everything else, he'd fallen in love with David.

Just another day in paradise.

"It'll work out." He spoke quietly to the boy in the image. "Just keep telling yourself that everything will work itself out." He wiped his arm over his face to kill the tears. "Just keep telling yourself that."

In the hallway outside the kitchen, Jamie considered the door her cousin had just closed rather too quickly and loudly. She leaned against the door jamb drinking Coke from a plastic bottle, arms crossed. She turned her head and glanced at the bathroom door.

John and David had acted weird all day, especially John. He was quiet and withdrawn, which was more David's trademark than John's.

He'd even been withdrawn during the mission. What was up with that? Was it really all the secrets their parents had kept? What had happened in Venice?

"Jesus loves the little children." Layla sang quietly in the kitchen.

Jamie leaned back to watch her sister rolling cookie dough on the flour-covered table. Flour covered her arms and face as well. Her fragile voice sounded angelic.

"You notice anything strange about our brothers?" Jamie asked.

Layla kept singing, which meant she'd noticed. Anything but a direct "no" from Layla meant "yes."

"What's up with them?" Jamie glanced from one closed door to the other.

"Isn't it obvious?" Her tone dripped superiority. Wow. That was surprisingly direct.

"Isn't what obvious, oh Great Fount of Knowledge?" Jamie turned to her sister who was still bent intently over her project.

"What's going on with John and David, dummy." Layla made a big deal out of sighing and rolling her eyes but managed to keep focused on the cookie dough, which she now shaped into perfect circles with a cutter.

"Okay, Great Fount, what's going on with them that I, in my stupidity, have not been able to ascertain?" Jamie took a slug of Coke and shook her head. She sometimes enjoyed her little sister's attempts at adult mannerisms.

"John's falling in love with David and is afraid we're all going to freak out about it." Layla finally looked up at her sister.

Cola spewed from Jamie's nose with her laughter. She coughed and sneezed and grabbed a towel to wipe her face.

"Laugh all you like." Layla cut cookies.

"And where did you get this preposterous idea?" Jamie wandered to the table.

Layla cut cookies.

"It never crossed your mind that it might have to do with the Dicks and having to move away and all that nonsense?"

Layla just kept cutting her cookies.

"Come on, L'il Bit. Where'd you get that crazy idea?"

"I see things."

Jamie finished her soda and tried to put the facts together in some way that added up to the same answer her sister had found. Layla might be extremely perceptive for an eight-year-old, but there was no way she could be right about this one. Everyone knew that John was gay and that was perfectly normal. . . but David. . . Well, David never talked about falling for anyone.

Jamie froze for a second. Maybe there was a reason he never talked about falling for anyone. She ran through all the jokes David and John had suffered over the years, jokes about how close they were.

"But David's not gay, is he?"

"I didn't say anything about David's feelings, did I?" Layla finished placing the cookies on a sheet and looked up at her sister again. Flour covered her nose, rather ruining her attempt at mature ennui.

"I guess I always assumed he was asexual." Jamie couldn't keep herself from laughing. "He's the only eighteen-year-old I know who doesn't talk about sex all the time. It's like he's a monk or something."

"He reproduces by budding, like amoebas." Layla laughed, too.

"Have you ever heard him talk about a crush even?" Jamie set the bottle on the table, crossed her arms and sat back in her chair.

"Poor John," Layla said. "What's he going to do?"

"I'm still not convinced about that, either. I think John's just bent because David was in on this whole mystery our parents got themselves into and he wasn't included."

Layla dropped another ball of dough on the table and picked up her rolling pin. She hummed again which had to be her way of saying, "We'll see," without saying anything and starting a fight. She seemed very sure of herself.

Bo stood at the platform all the way out in Lincoln with a box leaning against his leg. Even broken down, an iron table covered in little shards of glass became damn heavy after a long trip. With all the trouble the guys had had with the porter, Bo had decided to keep the table with him on the train where it had been kind of a pain.

He glanced around the busy platform. Lincoln didn't have a curfew. Bo had forgotten about that. He'd assumed the place would be deserted. Maybe slipping out for one more big payoff hadn't been such a good idea.

All the pale men and women in their fancy clothes gave him a wide berth. He'd worn sweats and a tank top for the heat. That had been a bad idea.

Where the heck was Dr. Sung? The emails had been desperate. Some sort of party had been planned, and they really wanted to use the new set. Quite the compliment, but Bo had wanted to wait at home for his kids to return from the memorial. More zeros than Bo had seen since entering the Ghetto had changed his mind. And now he stood on a busy platform with no idea about whom he should expect.

He checked his cell. His curfew had been lifted for the day, just as the guys' had. How a doctor did that, he'd never know. Had the guys ever told him what the wife did? They hadn't really talked since the guys' trip.

So much had happened.

Wait. There. Older Asian man. Had to be the doctor. Dragging the box with him, Bo made his way to the old man's side. Rather traditional robes. Whatever.

"Excuse me," Bo asked. "Are you Dr. Sung?"

"Indeed, I am not." The little man looked up at him with the bluest eyes Bo had ever seen.

"Oh, sorry." He'd made a lame supposition.

"I hear we all look alike," the man said with a faint smile.

"What? No, it's not that." Well, Bo had certainly stepped in it. "I'm sorry. I'm in a hurry." He took a breath and looked around. "I'm sorry. He told me he'd meet me here."

"Perhaps, we were meant to meet here instead."

"Oh." Bo hadn't thought to ask. "Did the doctor send you?"

"Indeed, he did not." The man didn't move at all. It was creepy. Was he even breathing? "When your burden is heavy, perhaps speed should not be your first priority."

"Right now, my first priority is getting back to my family, sir." Bo searched the platform. "And I can only do that if I find the doctor."

"There's another one of us over there." The man pointed at an Asian woman at the end of the platform. "If it's not me you seek, it's bound to be her, isn't it? How many Asians can you fit on the head of a pin?"

Real people spoke like that? Bo's invoice flashed green, and the woman looked over. Bingo! And now he could get away from the creepy old man, too.

"Thank you for your help, sir." Bo picked up the heavy box. Hopefully, the woman had a car nearby. He hadn't counted on needing to carry his burden all the way across the station.

"Joseph," the old man said. Really? Now what? "To those who must carry the heaviest burdens, the most assistance is given."

"I see." Holy fortune cookies. "Thank you." He shifted the box to his shoulder. No. That wouldn't work. "Speaking of burdens? This box is really heavy."

The man nodded. Finally.

Bo headed toward the woman. Wait a minute. What had the old man called him?

"Joey?" a familiar woman's voice said. "It really is you."

Bo turned. The Asian woman hurried toward him.

"Mrs. Sato?" Bo's arms went weak, and he almost dropped the box before he could lower it.

"I just knew it had to be you when I saw those symbols in Mabel's table." She folded her arms and cocked one hip in a way that flooded Bo with memories.

"I can't believe it's you. Here. Now." Bo had experienced any number of coincidences in his life, but this one rated near the top.

"When I met the boys the other day?" She pressed her hands together and touched her mouth. Her eyes grew moist. "Well, David looks just like you. I'm sorry to drag you all the way out here so late, but I just couldn't wait one more day to see you myself. Dave is going to be so excited."

"Dave?" Bo's vision blurred. He wiped his eyes. "Dave's good?"

"Let's get that table out of your arms before you drop it." Mrs. Sato smiled and grabbed Bo's shoulder. She led Bo across the platform, and the crowd melted out of their way. Huh. The stares and whispers didn't seem to be about him anymore. Was Dave's mom someone special?

Michael watched young people streaming through the streets to the large unfinished building that was, in some ways, the heart of the Ghetto. John, David, and Jamie made their own way there as well. Michael closed his eyes and checked the future.

No. Not that one. Or that one. He tested one possible future after another. Dozens. Hundreds. Millions of possibilities. They all intersected here. In this building. Tonight.

"There are some things we must accept on faith." Gabriel touched his arm.

"And there are some things we are meant to change."

"No, Michael," she said softly. "Not us. We don't change things."

Well, one brother had made some changes eons ago.

"And look how well it turned out for him," Gabriel said.

Lucifer had changed the natural order and had been expelled.

"I will not change things," Michael told her. "I know my place."

"You know your destiny," she reminded him.

He did. For Michael, all roads lead to Megiddo. For John, all roads led to that unfinished building.

"But you may very likely walk away from Megiddo," she said. "You may defeat Lucifer." She drew her hand away from his arm. "John cannot walk away from here."

"Is there a reason you feel the need to badger me with information I already have?" He watched the trio below, pointedly avoiding his sister's gaze. "I thought that was more Raphael's role."

"For you." She extended a hand into his line of sight. It held a single white lily. "I'm sorry for your loss."

He took the flower, mostly because she would depart once she'd completed her task. After she left, he dropped it to the rooftop at his feet.

"Would you cool it?" John bent his knees and sidestepped yet another of David's attempts to jump on for a piggyback ride.

David dashed off, swung around the nearest pole and up onto the metal railing that fronted the nearby apartment building. Everyone else on the street walked in rather somber silence. They were on their way to a memorial for the dead, for God's sake.

"What's his everlovin' deal?" John muttered while David balanced on top of a fire hydrant.

"With everything going on, who can tell?" Jamie said. "Maybe he's just venting stress."

"Because this is his usual way of handling stress."

"You sleep with him, cousin o'mine." Jamie shook her head. "You tell me."

What the hell?

But no. . . She had to mean they shared a room. Nothing more. Crap. A day ago, he wouldn't have even thought that. Now? Hopefully, she hadn't noticed his shock.

David grabbed him around the neck and ruffled his hair.

"What the shit?" John shoved him off.

David stared at him quizzically for half a second before running off again. What. the. hell? John was jumpy enough without David acting batshit crazy. He'd better reel it in before they reached the memorial where everyone would be grieving and somber... and where someone would notice how much he kept touching John. How had he never noticed just how much they freaking touched each other?

A sudden drumbeat started up. A throbbing bass line.

John stopped in his tracks. Jamie, too.

"Isn't it amazing?" David hopped to a standstill. "It's a Ghetto band named *Feast of the Apocalypse*. When they heard about the memorial, they canceled a concert somewhere north of here to show their support."

The music blared loud, angry, and violent. John took the few steps necessary to turn the corner and the Temporary Building appeared ahead, crowned with a halo of lasers and strobe lights flashing out every window of the tenth floor and across the scaffolding and girders above.

"Yes." David stopped in the middle of the road, a feral grin splashed across his face. He grabbed John's shoulders. "See? It's not about being quiet and sullen." He faked a sad face to mimic John's. "It's about yelling and screaming the pain away." He shook John. "Come on, coz. Let's scream 'til the roof blows off!"

A group of people John recognized from Babylon slowed to a standstill as they turned the corner. Their faces relaxed from sorrow into eager smiles filled with relief. They broke into a run. Others did, too. All the mourners turned a corner, saw the building, heard the music. . . and started running.

"Oh, sweet Jesus, I do not think I can do this tonight." John couldn't move. Too much energy. Too much grief. Too much. . . too much. . .

Too much David.

"Don't you get it, John?" Jamie turned to him, her eyes on fire. She grabbed his hand and dragged him forward. "If we can't fight back for our friends. . . the least we can do is shout down the moon."

David howled like a wolf, which sent a shiver down John's back. In the distance, a wolf answered the call. What the hell?

"Please, John?" Jamie tugged his hand. "Just for one night, can't we forget all the horrible bullshit in our lives and dance it to oblivion?" *I almost died more than once today and losing that damn camera was my fault. Mine.*

John blinked her thoughts away.

David grabbed John's other hand. Something about his pull couldn't be resisted, and John found himself moving, sliding into a run. Shouts filled the air. Jamie screamed with them. So did David. And they raced across the street.

They rushed headlong into the alley and waited their turn to climb the fire escape to the tenth floor. Banners and signs of support in the windows of the lower floors demonstrated that the current residents didn't begrudge the kids a night of bedlam.

Rocky greeted them at the entrance, and John caught his breath. How much pain must he feel? He grabbed John's neck and hauled him close for a rough hug. He seemed decidedly sober.

"Haven't touched a spark," he said as if reading John's mind. He released John and raised a hand with three fingers skyward. "Love you for attending. Memorial's over there." He pointed to one corner. "Keep it legal tonight, and if you jump in the mosh pit don't cry over broken bones. We're working through some demons."

Jamie and David embraced him, too.

"Hey. . ." Indecision worked its way across Rocky's face. "I want to do a service thing for Noah. Out in Venice. I know how much he loved it out there." He grabbed John's hand. "I know we're not that tight, but you were like his family, you guys and Barry. So I talked to my grandpa. He has a fishing boat." He squeezed John's hand. "Noah never took to it, but Gramps taught me everything he knew." He looked up, and his eyes burned with more sincerity than John had ever seen in them. "It'd mean a lot if you'd come out there with me."

"Of course, Rocky." David grabbed him and held on. "Just tell us when."

"Cool." Over David's shoulder, Rocky smiled. "That's cool." If Rocky could keep his shit together, maybe one good thing had come out of so much pain.

A crowd had built up, so he waved them on. As John ducked through the window, David smacked his ass from behind. John stood up abruptly and cracked his head on the window frame. Jesus, that hurt!

Jamie laughed.

John whirled around to yell at David, but his cousin was already shoving into the crowd.

"I thought we were going to cool it," John said angrily as he hurried to catch up. Not that David would hear his frustrated shout over the band.

Unbelievably, David turned back. He held his hands to his ears and shook his head mouthing, "I can't hear you. . . I can't hear you." The teasing raised John's temperature more than a few degrees, and he shoved people out of the way to catch his cousin, who saw what John was doing, made a foolish, excited face, and dashed away.

"Damn it!" John broke into a run. Part of him knew that David was playing, that he must be doing his best to cope with more emotional angst and crap than anyone had the equipment to handle. But another part of John, the part that had grown up with David and knew that sometimes the only way to get his damn attention was to smack him. . . that part won.

David stopped at the door to the stairwell and looked over his shoulder. As John nearly caught him, he yelped and ran up the winding stairs. John followed, pushing past irate bystanders until he reached the eleventh floor and ran into open air.

The cool wind and strobing lasers that greeted John at the top of the building only stopped him for a moment before he spotted David weaving around the steel girders and bits and pieces of wall that survived. They climbed up and down ladders, skittered across I-beams, and slid down chutes designed for construction refuse but relocated to serve as part of the training ground.

A shout of encouragement forced John to glance down at the doorway. Some of their friends had gathered there, eyes up, heads back, watching as John chased David through the flashing lasers, watching the game of tag as if John and David were monkeys in the zoo. They were a spectacle?

Then someone screamed. What the what? John looked forward.

David had stopped at the corner of the building, holding a vertical pole. John had too much momentum to stop.

They were so dead. . . but David dropped onto his stomach.

John caught the pole with one hand and swung out into empty space. The moment he felt air beneath his feet, he twisted, grabbed on with both hands, and swung completely around the pole twice, right over David's head.

Let it work! Let it work!

Centrifugal force swung him back to the I-beam the moment David leapt to his feet. The momentum propelled John into his cousin's open arms. John clutched tight to David, knowing what had to happen next if they were going to live.

David dropped backward, throwing John into a forward roll he could only control because they'd pulled similar maneuvers dozens of times. They'd run the playground so often they were practically an acrobatic duo.

Breathing heavily, grinning wildly, John popped to his feet and spread his arms in parody of a gymnast's dismount. Because that's what they'd done a million times before.

"Ta-fucking-daaaaah!" David shouted.

Their friends applauded.

"You should be a pole dancer!" Joanne called up, one arm in a sling.

John grabbed his cousin in a bear hug, adrenaline from the race stripping away all the stress and anguish until David chose that moment to kiss him on the nose. Shit. That's right. What would all that look like?

David pushed John's face nonchalantly and started back along the beam.

John took a second to catch his breath, but everyone just laughed and applauded and none of them seemed to suspect all the bizarre thoughts screaming through John's head. So. Fine. Play it cool. John followed David across the slippery beams, arms out at his sides like a tightrope walker. He looked up at the flashing lights and pretended he was flying.

Then his eyes dropped to the path directly ahead, where David's agile form skittered along the beam ahead of him. A lump caught in his throat that he had to swallow very hard to remove. How had David always been so blasted handsome and John never noticed?

Damn it, how was he going to survive the night?

Michael stood on a beam at the Temporary Building watching his son chase his charge across the scaffolding. Was there any way to avoid John's death? Did they really know? Was it inevitable?

Raphael appeared on the beam beside him. "You cannot change the course the Father has determined."

John and his friends scurried into the building with no idea the import of the evening.

"How do we know what course the Father has determined?" Michael asked. They hadn't heard from the Father in so long. How did any of them know his wishes?

"The humans must be allowed to make their own choices."

"I don't have the energy for a debate." Michael looked down at his companion's feet in bamboo sandals. He glanced up at the aged face. "If you're concerned I'll interfere, feel free to stay and guard me. We can watch the future unfold together." He turned his attention to the lights as they flashed and flickered. "Gabriel appears to know better than us how tonight will unfold."

"Father always did like her best." Raphael made a little noise in the back of his throat. Was that a smile on his lips?

"A joke, Raph? From you? At a time like this?" Michael shook his head and closed his eyes to turn his attention to the floors below them. "We'd better tell Lucifer to invest in parkas."

"Where's Barry?" John asked, back on the tenth floor. His friend had to be in a world of pain. A group had collected around John and David. Most of their closest friends.

Tracey pointed at the same corner Rocky had indicated, and there stood Barry. Ah, hell. He wept openly.

John made his way through the crowd with David at his side. A clear space surrounded the photos, flowers, and mementoes that covered the walls and the floor and several tables. So many memorials. So many dead.

A tree covered in photos of Billy stopped John. At its base, Matthew sat weeping, a half dozen friends holding him. A lump caught in John's throat. Billy had been a *good* man, and he was dead. How could that be justified?

John stepped past the grieving tree and looked over the familiar faces tacked to the walls. Hundreds of candles lit the display like an altar. Dozens of mourners huddled in twos and threes, weeping or simply staring at the flickering candles.

Barry stood alone holding Noah's old Teddy bear. Oh, damn. That bear had been a present from Barry when all of them had been five. Noah had carried it everywhere for a year. Toys like that were hard to come by in the Ghetto. Barry kissed the bear's head.

John and David closed on their friend as he placed the toy on a table with several photos of Noah and his father.

John touched Barry's shoulder. Barry turned to him, tears flowing freely down his cheeks. As soon as he recognized John, he hiccoughed loudly and fell into his arms. David held them both.

The band drowned out the sound of Barry's weeping, which had to be part of the reason for the music in the first place. Crying was easier if no one heard the sound.

John stared at the flickering candles over his friend's shoulder. All those people dead, killed by the Dicks looking for his parents. . . his family. . . for David.

Anguish filled David's face, and his tears were not only for the dead. He wept because it was his fault. If the Dicks hunting him had killed Noah and all those others while they searched, then David was responsible. John cupped the back of David's neck with one hand, and David looked into his eyes. John nodded to tell his cousin that if they were both a part of the Vatican project, then the responsibility belonged to both of them, and John would share the burden.

He pushed his face into David's hair. The scent overwhelmed

John. So much emotion flooded his body. How could he separate it all? He pulled away.

David stared at him with painful question marks across his face.

No. John had to be David's friend first, last, and always. His deeper emotions didn't matter. David needed his best friend. John wrapped one arm around Barry and the other around David, pressing his temple to his cousin's cheek.

Jamie latched on, as did Tracey and Joanne. Thank God she lived. John ran his hand through her hair. She sent him an air kiss.

A mob of people piled on top of them.

Then the music changed. It became less angry. More sexual. What would that do?

"I don't want to think anymore." Almost shyly, Tracey drew Barry out of the huddle. "I don't think you do, either."

Barry raised an eyebrow but hardly seemed inclined to turn down the invitation. He ruffled John's hair as Tracey led him off to a darker corner.

Others paired off as well and slipped into the shadows.

David held John to his side with one arm. If only the two of them could slink off together—

Shit! A hot flush broke out across John's face. He grabbed Jamie's hand and dragged her to the noise and the distraction of the mosh pit.

"Come on," he shouted. "I thought we were going to shout down the moon!"

Jamie yelled her approval. With David right behind, they dove into the flood of noise, lights, and sweating, jumping bodies.

The scene was completely different from a subway party. Everyone wore t-shirts and jeans or shorts, some of them shirtless because of the heat but without the sexual energy of Babylon. Here in the flashing lights, away from the dark corners, the dance was pure catharsis.

A hand grabbed John's shoulder, a tall red-headed woman in a bright white suit. Something about her sparked John's memory. Wait, hadn't he seen her at the bridge the day they went out to Lincoln?

She pressed something into his hand: a white flower made of folded paper.

She leaned in close to John's ear. "For you. I'm sorry."

He bent over the little flower, a lily. A memento for Noah?

The woman had already vanished into the heaving crowd, so John shoved the flower into his pocket and threw himself into the music, into the pushing and jumping and shoving. The anger and frustration of the music pulsed through a hundred bodies, but every time David pushed against him, John lost the moment. His cousin threw himself into the air, wrapping an arm over John's shoulders bouncing against him, pressing close, sweating and slick. . .

Christ, he'd never thought of David that way before, and now it was all he could think. He kept trying to move Jamie between them, but David maneuvered around his sister.

David ended up behind John, singing along, jumping up and down against John's back. Blast it. John shoved David into the crowd, where he stumbled and only managed to keep his feet because of the press of bodies.

"What's your problem?" Jamie smacked John's shoulder.

Oh. Fine. She had to get involved?

David laughed as if the aggression was part of the dance. He rushed John and shoved him hard. Seriously?

Okay. Fuck it. John was done. With a loud shout, he planted both hands on David's chest and pushed him as hard as he could.

David grabbed John's arm, and they tumbled to the floor together.

John went down swinging.

They hadn't fought in years, but the old moves returned quickly enough. They writhed like wildcats on the floor at the edge of the stage.

"I thought we were going to lay off the PDA!" John shouted.

"What?" David yelled back. "You said you don't care what people think!"

Blast it, every foot down there on the floor seemed to find John's ribs. Was no one paying attention?

John regained his feet, dragging David with him. Another shove pushed David against the edge of the stage, and he rolled onto it, dragging John with him. Twisting smoothly, David landed on top, straddling John's waist and holding him down on the stage with both hands.

"With everything going on," David shouted, "you pick now to get all weird and shit?"

"Me?" John shouted. "What the fuck?" David couldn't have found anything to make John angrier. With an adrenaline-filled twist, he threw his cousin off, rolled over a shoulder, and rose to his feet just as he saw, from the corner of his eye, David leaping at him.

"Fight! Fight! Fight!" Hundreds of the Ghetto rats watched and cheered. "Fight! Fight!"

The band had moved aside to give them the center of the stage.

John's world slipped into slow motion as David grabbed him and spun him so they stood face to face on the stage in a spotlight in front of the entire Ghetto.

Dozens of cells waved in the air above the crowd, recording.

Before John could react, David grabbed the back of his head with both hands, pulled him close, and kissed him full on the mouth.

"Tag, you're it!" He turned on his heel and ran toward the stairs.

John stood there in the most horrified shock he'd ever experienced. His face burned. His vision split and everything grew hazy.

Had he hated the kiss? No… but, yes! Not there! Not with the world watching on the net!

That's when he heard the laughter. Everyone laughing at him. At his stupidity. He couldn't even look at the crowd. He drowned in the laughter, furious at David.

The voices of the audience finally reached him.

"Fuck! Fuck! Fuck!"

The room spun twice around John. The lights hurt his eyes as the voices burned his ears. He had to get away. He raced after David, already on his way up the stairs.

The laughter fell behind as John sprinted through the space the crowd had made. He tore up the stairs, grabbed the rail at the first landing, and swung around the corner and up the next flight.

His confusion and the blood-red fury made it hard to hear.

His vision shrank to a tunnel.

He scaled the steps three at a time, slowly closing on David's retreating form, which managed to slip around each corner just as John reached it, infuriating inches beyond his grasp.

His heart pounded in his chest and throbbed at his temples. He could almost see the red of his own blood as the lights from the lower floors dimmed. The air tasted of rotten eggs.

When he reached the final flight of stairs, John flew headlong into the blazing cacophony of laser lights without bothering to wait for his eyes to adjust. He knew the construction zone too well to waste a second.

He had to reach David, had to find him to pummel him, to hold him down and beat him. . . or kiss him. He didn't know what he wanted to do, he just had to do something, to keep running and running until the adrenaline ran out.

David fast-stepped along the nearest I-beam on his way to the ladders. Swearing under his breath, John tore after him, the metal of the ladder rungs cool against his hands.

David laughed now. He looked down at John with a mocking smile.

John swore at him, shouted at him.

The catwalk on the twelfth floor took them in an ever-widening spiral from the center of the building to the very edges. Neither said a word. They ran harder; no one had followed them this time. They raced alone in the night air while their feet pounded the catwalk's metal webbing.

David grabbed a low beam and pulled himself up. Reaching forward with his momentum, he latched onto the next beam and the next, which led to another platform and there was a long jump onto yet another platform and then a leap for a horizontal pole and a swing that had to be perfectly timed to reach the next beam and then another stretch of catwalk. Up and around, down and back they raced while the pounding music boiled John's blood, and the flashing lights all but blinded him.

David reached the back corner of the building and launched himself through space, landing neatly on the slanted roof of the next building. He rolled over onto the flat roof beside it, sliding to a stop in a puddle where they had rescued Rocky just a few short days earlier.

John launched himself off the catwalk in hot pursuit and landed on the exact same spot as David—

But his right foot slipped. Shit.

John's leg shot out behind him, and he hit the slanted roof hard, landing on his chin and bouncing on his ribs. Bright stars flashed as the rough tiles scraped his side and his face.

He flailed blindly and grabbed for anything that might break his slide.

David's terrified shout reached him the same moment the roof slipped away.

Free fall…

The emptiness of space.

Then John's left hand snagged something metal. His fingers closed instinctively, but his body slammed into the side of the building with enough force to push the air from his lungs.

Fucking ow!

When his vision cleared, John hung by one hand from a gutter.

Wow. That had pretty much sucked. Ouch.

David lay stretched out on the flat roof where he might reach John without being pulled off. He'd have no leverage on the slanted roof.

John chuckled. Ouch, that hurt, too.

His friends had made that jump so many times, no one even considered it dangerous. How had he muffed it?

"Hang on, John! Hang on!" David screamed for help, but no one would hear him over the loud, angry music.

John glanced down. Holy Hell, that was a long way down.

Wow. He could actually die. For real.

He pulled with the one arm and swung his legs so he could grab the gutter with both hands, but the movement pulled the cheap aluminum half an inch away from the building, and the nails screeched.

The sound sent a shiver through John's body, and he missed. He swung again and managed to grab on with both hands, but the metal bent under his weight and movement.

John hung still for a moment.

Huh. What could he possibly do?

"Grab my hand!" David screamed, his eyes wide and terrified. Tears ran down his cheeks.

John closed his eyes and tried to breathe, but his chest was too tight to suck in any oxygen. He must have bruised a rib in the fall.

He kicked a foot up to catch it on the gutter. The movement bent the metal another half inch, and John missed it, anyway. Damn.

A strange calm filled John.

David would never want him, and the pain that stabbed John's heart told him just how badly he wanted David to want him. Maybe ending that pain wasn't such a bad option.

"I guess I found my way out of this blasted Ghetto, coz." He gave David his biggest smile.

"Take my hand!" David reached out to him, every muscle in his body taut. "I'll get a rope. . . I'll. . ." He sat up and pulled off his shirt, then lay on his chest again and swung the shirt at John like a rope. It brushed the gutter. David tried again but couldn't get the shirt to land near John's hand.

"It's okay, David," John said. "I think I'll just. . ."

"Shut up and grab the fucking shirt!" David screamed. "I will not let you die!" He pounded the roof with a fist. "Goddamn it, John, do not let yourself fall from this fucking building! There has to be a way!"

David's eyes shone wild. They filled up with stars. They reached out to John and held him, locked onto him... drew him inside. In the space between heartbeats, John fell into David's eyes.

There were galaxies there, and an ocean of space. . .

For a moment, the world fell silent.

David was terrified of losing John, could not imagine a life without John in it. His love filled John, flooded him.

David loved him, as much as he loved David.

John had misunderstood completely. When David had said they shouldn't care what anyone said, he'd meant it was time to admit their feelings.

How could John be so stupid? David had been manic all night because he thought they were going to finally shout their love to the world and damn the consequences.

How could John be so God damned stupid?

The screech of metal shocked John back to the real world.

The pain in David's eyes poured down his cheeks.

"Please," David murmured. "Please, John. Don't die."

"No." John couldn't do that. He wouldn't die and leave David alone.

Adrenaline filled his aching limbs.

One last time, David flung the shirt for John to catch.

John heaved himself up with all his strength…

He would do it…

He would grab the t-shirt and live…

And he and David…

He and David…

John grabbed for the shirt. . .

. . .and missed.

With a deafening shriek, the gutter pulled itself from the bricks and swung into empty space.

The motion churned John's stomach as he fell away from the building.

David screamed.

The gutter broke.

John fell.

Michael felt Raphael's hand on his arm before he'd twitched.

"You must not interfere." The grey head shook once.

Michael watched his son fall, not allowing himself the luxury of closing his eyes. He needed to witness John's end just as he had been there to revel in his birth.

The sound when John hit the ground was something Michael would remember for an eternity.

"No, no, no…" David heaved with sobs at the edge of the roof. "No, no, no…" He repeated the word dozens of times.

At first, his words filled with panic and desperation. Then they slowed. He grew calmer.

Had he accepted the inevitable?

He planted both hands on the gravel. He heaved a massive sigh, then pushed to his feet, staring directly down at the spot where John lay, broken and twisted and growing cold.

Then David's face lifted, and he stared directly into Michael's eyes. Michael felt his anguish like a blow to the gut.

David's eyes narrowed. Anger.

His hands closed into fists at his sides.

Would he jump? It was one possibility Michael had foreseen.

"No." He said it one more time, oh so quietly.

Then David vanished.

Just. . . vanished.

Raphael gasped. "Did you know he could do that?"

"I did not."

Rocky was right there on the damn sidewalk when John fell.

The sound of David's cries would haunt Rocky for years.

Then John hit the concrete with a loud crunch and spatter.

He bounced into the air, fucking *bounced*, and spun clean around in a spray of blood and guts… and… and… He landed on his side and lay still. Sweet Jesus. What the hell?

People screamed and rushed to get closer, but no one touched the body. They didn't need to check for signs of life. That cat was *dead*.

"Let me through." Was that David?

How'd he climb down so fast?

"David!" Rocky forced his way to him, grabbed him and had no intention of letting go. "He's gone, man. He's gone. You don't want to see him like that." He held David as tight as he could, but the cat didn't struggle, anyway.

"He's not dead," David insisted. "He can't be dead."

"You don't want to see him like that." Rocky had seen John's body hit the pavement, had seen the limbs loose and twisted like a pretzel.

And then Rocky saw it. . . in his mind's eye.

Noah and Dad stood back to back in the tunnel.

A soft wash of air hit them first.

Then fire like a living, breathing hungry animal ate them alive.

"It wasn't your fault, Rocky," David said quietly. "It had nothing to do with you."

Rocky gulped and swallowed.

It was horrible, but it wasn't Rocky's fault.

"I'm sorry about Noah." David's eyes filled with so much peace and strength that Rocky would do anything he asked. He cupped Rocky's face in one hand and serenity poured over him like cool water.

"I need to see him." David looked past Rocky at the twisted pile of flesh. "John isn't dead. He's only asleep."

The words sounded just as crazy as they'd seemed moments before, but Rocky stepped aside. The whole crowd opened.

Rocky followed in David's wake.

Michael and Raphael stood at the edge of the crowd.

Raphael stepped forward, but Michael laid a hand on his arm.

"It's not our place to interfere," Michael said.

"But he can't," Raphael said. "The consequences. . ."

For the first time in eons, Michael had no idea what the consequences might be.

Most likely, neither did Raphel.

That would be interesting.

Rocky's stomach quivered, but he held it down.

John lay on his side, part of his skull missing and his neck bent at a right angle to his shoulders. Dark blood covered the pavement in a growing circle around him.

"He's just asleep. . ." David knelt beside the twisted body, whispering the same phrase over and over. "He's just asleep. . ." He took the body carefully in his arms and rolled John onto his back, the dark blood covering David, too.

Blood poured out of John's mouth as his head lolled loosely to the other side.

Rocky closed his eyes for a second. That shit was just wrong.

David pulled John's head upright and managed to balance it so it stayed level. He laid the body flat on the pavement and moved from limb to limb, laying each of them straight, still whispering his desperate mantra.

"He's just asleep… he's just asleep."

Rocky wept silently. He didn't feel right interrupting, but David had to be out of his mind.

Covered in John's blood, David finished laying the body out then moved into place at his head, pulling John into his arms, resting the shattered skull against his chest.

John's eyes stared blindly at the crowd, one completely filled with blood.

"John?" David ran his fingers through John's hair. "It's time to wake up, now. It's time for you to wake up."

Rocky should have gone to David and pulled him away from the broken body. They could mourn together and maybe keep each other from going really, truly insane. But he couldn't convince his feet to—

Wait a minute. Was Rocky going crazy?

How the hell could David run his hand through John's hair? That whole side of John's head was gone.

"John." David said it more insistently, his voice a command this time. "You're just asleep." His voice had dropped an octave. "Wake up, now."

And John blinked.

Rocky jumped back a foot. What the what?

A unified gasp shot through the crowd. It had to be an involuntary movement, like a chicken with its head cut off. Right?

Then John blinked again... and again... and then he coughed.

He spasmed. He sat forward abruptly and dropped onto his hands and knees, vomiting blood and mucus onto the asphalt, blinking wildly as if the dim light hurt his eyes.

The crowd pulled away a step. People shouted.

"It's okay, John." David stroked John's back. "You're okay, now."

"David?" John rolled back and clutched David in a fit of coughing and frantic breath. David held him close and rubbed his chest until the coughing subsided.

John looked up at Rocky with terror in his eyes, at all the people standing there. . . then he turned to David.

"What happened?"

"You fell," David told him.

No one else said a word.

"I fell?" John looked up at Rocky again. "And. . . I'm alive?"

Rocky couldn't move. How the hell was that cat asking questions?

"I'm okay?" John turned back to David.

"You're wonderful." David nodded and wiped the blood and vomit.

John's face changed, became hopeful. He searched David's face for something, and Rocky didn't know them well enough to understand, but John must have seen what he wanted.

His blood-streaked face beamed with happiness. He threw his arms around David and held him close. They clutched one another there on the sidewalk, in the middle of an astonished, muttering crowd.

Rocky stared. Then it hit him. Somehow, impossibly, John was alive! What?

"Let me through, God damn it." Jamie's voice, loud and clear at the edge of the crowd, caught Rocky's attention. She pushed her way past a big man in a leather vest and shook off Barry's hand. "Let go of me. I want to see him."

More than a hundred people crowded around, with more joining every second.

That kind of attention couldn't be good.

People had their damn cells in the air.

Jamie burst through and stumbled into the empty space around those two incredible cats. She stood dumbly, staring at John and David, her face pale and confused and streaked with dirt.

"I thought you were dead," she whispered, then she shouted with joy and dashed across the space. "I thought you were dead!"

"I thought he was dead, too," Barry said quietly at Rocky's side.

"He was, man," Rocky said. "He *was*. Half his head broke off, Barry. I saw it. I was right here when it happened. I mean, I bet if we looked around hard enough, we'd find his brain bleeding in a puddle somewhere."

Barry grimaced. "That's a vivid image."

"It was gross. I'm serious. I cannot explain this one."

"John's alive!" Barry rushed forward. He took John's bloody face in his hands and kissed him on the mouth. "Don't you ever scare us like that again, you son of a bitch." He took John in his arms. "Your sister almost scratched my eyes out trying to get down here."

"He couldn't have been dead." Someone beside Rocky nudged him. "It must not have been as bad as you think."

"I saw it, buddy." He couldn't take his eyes from his friends. He had to swallow away a lump in his throat.

"Then how do you explain it?" someone else asked.

Rocky looked around. Dozens of faces stared at him. They could tell he knew the family, but if they wanted answers, he was the wrong cat to ask. If they couldn't tell a miracle when they saw it, he had *nada* to say.

A siren tore through the night sky. Rocky jumped. Everyone in the crowd turned, many of them ready to run. An ambulance screamed first, but a police siren quickly joined it.

"Wouldn't you know it?" Rocky muttered. "The one time EMS actually shows up."

"Your boat, coz." David, his face calm but deadly serious, grabbed Rocky's arm. "Please tell me you can get us out of here."

"Sure." Rocky thought about it for less than a second. His grandfather would kill him, but he couldn't say no. Something amazing had happened and Rocky wanted to be a part of it. "Whatever you need."

"His boat?" Jamie demanded. "What the blazes for?"

"We have to get out of here," David said flatly. "Now. Addison. He's fighting for an air strike, copters with missiles. This is the tipping point. Something like this will make it all happen."

"Something like what?" Jamie insisted. "What's to notice? Nobody's dead."

"Exactly." David turned to her with the oldest eyes Rocky had ever seen and grabbed his sister. "I need you to run home and tell Mom and Dad what just happened and tell them we need to get out of town."

"Out of town?" She pushed his hands away. "Now? Just like that? Where to?"

"I don't know, yet," David said. "I need to buy some time to think. Go get the family. Meet us at the dock. Bring as little as possible. We aren't coming back."

"Jesus Christ," Barry muttered. "Are you serious?"

David nodded once.

The sound of the sirens drew too close for comfort. Already, the shadier characters slipped into the shadows. A third siren joined the chorus. David was right. They needed to move.

"John was lucky. . ." Jamie made a noise of disgust in her throat. "Okay, *really* lucky, and someone somewhere must be watching out for him, but why would Addison care about that? And an air strike? How the hell do you even think you know that?"

"Dozens of people saw what happened, Jamie." David waved at the dispersing crowd. "They recorded everything. It's already on the net."

"So what?" Jamie looked from face to face.

No one replied.

"All this talk about Addison and secret government plots and blasted air strikes." Her face grew red as she shouted. "Why would anyone care about you? Or John? Why would anyone give a crap about what happened here?" She panted angry breaths. "What am I supposed to *tell* Mom and Dad, David? What do you think happened here?"

The sirens were too damn close, now.

A handful of people waited, ready to run, but Rocky could tell they wanted answers. Fine. He'd seen it himself.

"He was dead, Jamie," Rocky said. "John was dead, and David brought him back to life."

A squad car screamed around the corner.

"What the what?" Jamie shouted. "Are you mental?"

Red and blue lights flashed across the street.

"Go!" David shouted. "Leave vapor trails!"

Everyone jumped into action.

Barry dragged Jamie in one direction.

Rocky, David, and John ran off in another.

No one noticed the Asian man, hands in the folds of his orange and blue robes, silently staring at the spot where John had lain. When an officer knelt and picked up the bloody paper lily, Raphael's face grew pained and impatient. He looked away.

"What will happen now?" Gabriel asked.

Raphael shook his head. He had no idea.

"What do you see?" Gabriel asked.

"What do I see?" He searched for answers, but all he saw was emptiness and confusion. How could any of them have predicted this brash infraction on the part of the maybe Messiah? "I see nothing, Gabriel. This was not supposed to happen. John died in every conceivable future. He should not be alive. There is no way for any of us to know what happens next." He focused on his sister. She held a vase of lilies. Interesting. "Apparently, you know at least one thing that happens tonight."

"Indeed, I do." She shifted the flowers in the vase. "I don't think David's impetuous actions change everything."

Raphael closed his eyes. The threads of time rewove themselves into the future one tiny moment at a time. They twined and twisted and branched off.

There. Very soon.

"Ah," he said. "I see."

Interesting. So not everything had changed.

Addison's hands shook so badly, he shoved them into his armpits. Twenty holo screens played video from the "Memorial Day Miracle." Fuck. It'd already been named, and a new fucking holiday was likely in the works. How the hell had they done it? Little motherfuckers. The entire spectacle seemed impossible.

"Is there any footage of the transition from corpse to quid pro quo?" Addison demanded.

"Not that I've seen, sir."

"You can make a composite of what we have?" He tapped a screen and pointed at Pierce to send the data.

"Arrange all existing footage by timestamp," Pierce told the system. "Create composite video. Render 3D."

One hologram showed the half-breed hanging by one hand. Every single camera followed him down, but the image cut out after the body hit. Lots of video of the splatter of the corpse followed... but not one cell had had a clear shot of the... the... fuck... of the resurrection? Fuck. That's what they'd call it.

They all recorded the science project's cries of anguish, though, up on the roof.

Wah, wah, wah... Fuck!

"A fag," Addison muttered. "We made a damn fag? Clement's going to fucking love that." He made a mental note for an entirely new battery of tests once the current project moved to DC.

A second holo popped open. The mutilated corpse lay on the ground. The fag science project arranged the damn body.

Then the videos flickered. Static filled the screen.

"Every fucking video?" Addison shouted. "All of them?" The static faded and the gay boys sat there hugging. "Useless!" He picked up a chair and smashed it onto the table. All the screens derezzed.

"How the fuck did they do that?" Addison kicked the table.

"Makabee shut down nearly the entire grid a couple of days ago, sir." Pierce moved to a different table and waved a hand over the glass. "A localized white out would be nothing."

"Can *we* do that?" Addison asked. "Is our tech as good as that bastard's?"

"Do what exactly, sir?"

"Can we create a worm or whatever?" Addison waved at the screens. "Can we erase this from the planet? Can we make it go away?"

"Should be possible." Pierce started manipulating the screens. "Every cell is connected to the Dickerson servers in one way or another. Let me get our people on it."

"Do that." Addison wanted to light a cigarette, but his hands were almost out of control. He shoved them under his arms. "And then can we go back to blowing the fucking island off the face of the planet?"

"Yes, sir." Pierce turned from the screens. "We're just waiting for the missiles to arrive." He fidgeted. "Not much to do for a while." What the hell did he want?

"Just fucking say it."

"I haven't eaten in a day or so, sir." Pierce met his eyes.

"Jesus Christ, Pierce. You're allowed a fucking lunch break. Make sure the copters are set and go get a burger."

"Thank you, sir." He grabbed his coat. "All plans are under way." He hurried from the room.

Addison held his hands up. They shook and shook and shook. How long before his body destroyed him? And what was Pierce up to? He always ordered room service. Especially at times like this.

A dull haze choked the sky, blocking out the stars. Layla sat on the stoop outside her parents' shop, her hair hanging around her face in dark, sloppy curls. Her chin rested on her fists and her elbows on her knees as she stared at the sidewalk between her widespread feet.

Ants desiccated a spider in the shadow from the streetlight overhead. A distant police siren failed to distract her focused attention. The ants took the spider apart piece by piece and carried it away. Nearly a thousand of the little red insects swarmed over the shattered arachnid.

With a very deliberate movement, Layla lifted the toe of one shoe and turned her foot inward until it blocked the ants from her view, then she dropped her foot and pressed down hard.

A woman strode down the street toward her. Could it be Jamie?

Layla looked up. No, the woman sweeping toward her was too tall and carried herself like someone older than Layla's sister. As she drew closer, the overhead light caught long waves and curls of red that fell about her face and shoulders. She wore sandals.

The woman stopped directly over Layla. A light dusting of freckles ran across the bridge of her nose. The neck of her white Oxford lay open just enough for Layla to notice a silver charm. What was it?

Layla leaned back on her elbows. Something about the intensity of the stark, golden eyes said that the woman might be far, far older than she appeared.

"You're very beautiful." Layla spoke quite suddenly, but the woman didn't seem surprised. "What's your name?"

"Gabriel."

"Do I know you?" Layla cocked her head to one side and then the other.

"I don't believe we've met." Her hair shifted on her shoulders as if she were underwater.

"I'm Layla."

"Yes, you are." The woman crouched down so she was eye to eye with the girl. Her hands came out of her pockets and hung between her knees. How could she be so compelling and frightening at the same time? The light from the bare bulb overhead seemed brighter since her arrival.

"What are you doing here?" Layla asked.

"I'm delivering a message."

"Isn't Gabriel a man's name?"

"It's my name." She ruffled Layla's hair with one strong hand then rose to her feet. She had to be more than six feet tall.

"Who are you going to give the message to?"

"I've already delivered it." The light glinted on the charm at her throat.

"What's that?" Layla pointed.

The fingers of one hand touched the charm. "It's a trumpet."

"Are you a musician?"

"Among other things." She didn't shrug or nod or shake her head the way most people did.

"Like being a messenger?"

When would she tire of the questions? Most people did that, too.

"Exactly like that," the woman said.

"Are you in a band?"

"Of a sort." The woman shoved her hands into her pockets.

"Have I heard about you?"

"Most likely." The woman smiled.

Gabriel. In a band. Messenger. Could she be. . .?

The woman turned and walked away without looking back.

Layla chewed on her lower lip.

"Trumpet," she said, lifting her foot. A thousand ants swarmed into the space where her foot had been and tore apart the bodies of the dead insects.

"You didn't say it was a power hose." The water blasted cold, and it burst the air from John's lungs. He cupped his hands over his junk as Rocky sprayed the water up and down John's body.

The icy shower left John for a moment, and David yelped as it hit him instead. John jumped up and down on the wooden forward deck to warm up.

"You really think covered in blood and guts is a good way to try to sneak away?" Rocky sprayed the hose back and forth.

"But you don't have to enjoy it—" A blast to the face cut John short. "Quite so much."

"Oops." Rocky laughed. "Sorry about that."

What a liar! Finally getting used to it, John rinsed out his hair and wiped down his body.

"Cold, cold, cold." David worked the blood off beside John. He grinned.

John returned the smile.

"You look almost respectable, gentlemen." Rocky shut off the hose and dropped it to one side.

"Towels?" John hugged himself and jumped again. "Or blankets? Something?"

"Oh, right!" Rocky's grin changed to surprise. "Let me see what I can find." He dashed below decks.

"And hurry?" David encouraged. "Not everyone is as uninhibited as Barry."

"Huddle for warmth!" He threw his arms around David, and they jumped together. David's hand held John's neck and ran through his hair. John pressed his cheek to David's. There was that familiar scent again—

"Oh crap!" Heat filled John's face, and he abruptly turned his back to David. *That* hadn't happened before!

Feet pounded up the stairs from below.

"And I'm throwing them to you without looking," Rocky said.

John snatched the flying towel out of the air and rubbed himself dry, quickly securing the towel around his waist.

"Some shit's going to take a little getting used to." Rocky dropped an old t-shirt and a pair of sweats nearby. "Not that that's bad."

"Don't worry. It's going to take me a while, too." John kept his back to David while he scrambled into the clothes. How many times had he seen David naked? And you didn't share a room with someone all through adolescence without accidently seeing him aroused once in a while. But now? Totally different. John couldn't get his heart to slow down.

"I see y'all have a few things to talk about," Rocky declared. "I'm going to go down and clear some room for your family."

"Rocky," John called before he had a chance to disappear.

Their friend stopped. Waited.

"You're part of the family, too, coz," John said. "That you would do this for us without stopping for a second." He crossed to Rocky and hugged him tight. "Thanks."

"Hey, man, Ghetto rats need to stick together, right?" Rocky patted John's back and pulled away. Apparently, no one in the King family was accustomed to a lot of affection. "After what I saw?" He looked at David and peace flooded his face. "I'd follow you guys to the ends of the Earth."

He ducked below.

"He's completely clean," John said. "Has been since—" Holy wow! John pointed down the stairs and then at David. "He hasn't sparked up since you unplugged him at Babylon." He pointed down the stairs. "Did you do that?"

David smiled vaguely, wiping his hair with the towel. He wore a stained flannel shirt and ripped jeans. God, he looked good. The heat rose to John's face again.

David dropped the towel to one side and moved closer.

John couldn't move. This was the same person who'd walked up to John a million times. They'd held each other, slept in the same bed, even showered together. But this? John's heart pounded when David dropped hands on his shoulders. He had to swallow hard as David's hands moved up to John's neck.

Okay, that was it.

John leapt through the space, grabbed David's face in his hands.

He kissed him.

David met the kiss eagerly. His arms drew John closer.

They drew back an inch. Kissed again, but light. . . tender.

John stepped back.

David, too.

They waited.

A seagull squawked, and they both jumped.

Ha! They rushed forward into a strong embrace.

The world hadn't ended with a single kiss.

Deep inside, John had wondered if it would.

Ruth stood in the girls' room.

A huge map hung in the air.

"Well?" Naomi leaned in the doorway, a mug of coffee in both hands.

"Okay. I'm trying too hard." Ruth picked up her coffee mug and drained it. "Where do you think we'll go?"

"Most people have to settle for a strong feeling or a meaningful coincidence." Naomi sipped her coffee. "You usually get a road sign that says, 'Hey lady, this way for the road to God's Plan!'"

"I wish everyone would get home." Ruth tried to take a drink from her mug and found it empty. "I'm so anxious to do this." She waved the holo screens away and moved past Naomi to the kitchen.

"What do you think they'll say?" Naomi asked. "Do you think they'll believe us?"

"John shouldn't be a hard sell with the visions he's having." Ruth moved a vase of lilies from the counter to the table. "Layla has her own magic about her, doesn't she? I mean, not literally, but I think she'll accept it, too."

"Then there's Jamie." Naomi refilled her mug.

And then there was Jamie.

"Oh, I don't know," Ruth said, "if I were a teenage girl who didn't necessarily even believe in God, I'm sure I'd take it as perfectly natural when my parents said, 'Oh, by the way, your brother is the Son of God, now give him a hand with his bags, would you?'" She pushed the vase to the center of the table. "I'm sure it'll go great."

"You think Dr. Spock had a chapter in his book on this one?" Naomi pulled a flower higher in the arrangement.

"Chapter 7, raising the Son of God."

"Chapter 8, sibling rivalry with the Most High."

They laughed.

"I remember the first time I changed him." Ruth dropped her head onto her hands and listened to the hum of the refrigerator. "It was startling to me that the Son of God would poop his diaper like the rest of us."

"The flowers are lovely," Naomi said. "Where'd you find them?"

"I didn't." Ruth sat up abruptly. "I thought you bought them."

Naomi shook her head slowly.

"Gabriel?" Ruth's heart pounded.

They leapt to their feet, backing away from the table.

"What does it mean?" Ruth's chair tumbled to the floor.

"With Gabriel, it's almost always one of two things." Naomi still held her coffee mug, but now she clutched it to her chest like a weapon.

"Why do you suppose she didn't just come to us directly?" Ruth stepped closer her cousin.

"What was that you were saying about a road sign?"

The front door banged open downstairs, and they jumped.

Who could it be? Was Bo finally home?

"Mom? Dad?" Jamie shouted. "Aunt Naomi? Where the hell is everyone?" The sound of booted feet clomped on the stairs.

Someone was with her. Barry.

They careened into the kitchen and stood breathlessly in the door.

"What the fuck is going on, Mom?" Jamie's face burned red and frightened and angry, her hair a tangled mess.

Barry laid one hand on her shoulder, but she shrugged it away.

John relaxed forward against David's chest, arms around his waist, staring over his shoulder at the red and blue lights that flickered on the water in the distance.

"Do you know what happened to you?" David stroked John's back with the thumb of one hand. "When you fell. Do you understand what happened?"

"Rocky says I was dead." John moved out of David's arms to lean against the railing beside him. He looked down at the salty boards under his bare feet.

"But?"

"But that's not possible." But John's head had been smashed

to pulp. He'd seen the video. Seeing his own broken body had been freaking creepy.

"I need to tell you some things." David's voice was soft and afraid. "I need you to know who I am. . ."

"Who you are?"

"What I am."

The boats bobbed up and down in their moorings.

"I was dead." There. He'd said it. The tall masts shifted like porcupine quills. "I mean, really, totally, completely dead."

David nodded.

"How'd you do it? How'd you bring me back?" John yanked up his shirt. "My scars are all gone, too." As much as they ran the roofs and worked with Uncle Bo every day, John had had his fair share. "Every single scar is gone." He ran a thumb over his teeth. "The fillings even popped out." Wait. If *everything* had been healed. . . He pulled the waistband of the sweats away from his stomach. "Well, that's going to take some getting used to."

David chuckled. "I'm sure Rocky has a knife around here for skinning fish."

"Pass." John let the elastic snap closed. How had David done all that? What had that Vatican project done to him?

With a sigh, David dug in his pocket and pulled out a wrinkled dollar bill that he folded again and again.

"What does origami have to do with raising the dead?" John watched the wrinkled bill change into a paper bird.

"Blow on it." David held a paper hummingbird in his palm.

What the hell?

"Blow on it," David insisted. "And no jokes. It's too soon."

John smiled. Fine. He blew across the paper bird.

Nothing happened.

"Again."

So John blew again.

The wings fluttered quickly, and John jumped. What the what?

"One more time," David asked.

John hesitated. Not taking his eyes from the little paper bird, he blew gently across it one last time. The wings quivered once, twice, then they took up a crazed, steady beat. The origami bird lifted itself into the air and shook itself all over. Paper splashed from its body like water, and then, *bam*, it was a real, live hummingbird!

Its body glistened green with a flush of red at its throat. Its wings hummed as it darted around John, circling him three times then hovered in the air directly in front of his nose. The bird circled David three times then dashed off into the night. Just as suddenly as it had come to life, it vanished.

John's heart pounded in his chest. That hadn't been a trick, some sleight of hand magic with holograms. David had transformed a dollar bill into a living, breathing creature.

John believed what Rocky had told him. But it was different, seeing something with his own eyes, different from the video, even.

Videos could be faked.

David had brought John back to life. . . and John was in love with him, with the person who could do that.

"Who are you?" John asked.

"Who am I? What am I?" David smiled and stepped over to a rain barrel. "I heal the sick. I raise the dead." He knocked the lid off and took a beaten tin cup from where it hung on the side. He dipped the cup into the barrel and held it out to John. "Who do you think I am?"

Something dark and red filled the cup.

John grabbed it. He drank.

It was wine. Of course, it was wine. What else would it be?

"Jesus Christ," John muttered.

David laughed and laughed.

"What happened?" Ruth stared at her daughter, barely recognizing the angry, twisted face across the table. Something had gone terribly wrong with her children's plans.

"Don't change the subject," Jamie shot back.

"I'm not, Jamie, but you're scaring me. Why are you so angry?"

Jamie scoffed in disbelief. She folded her arms and stayed silent.

"Something happened at the Temporary Building." Barry's voice was unusually soft, and he watched Jamie the whole time. "A bunch of us saw it."

"Saw what?" Acid filled Ruth's throat. For the first time, she noticed Naomi at her side, lending her support without interfering.

"John fell," Barry said.

Naomi gasped. "What? Oh, my God!"

"No, no, no. . . he's okay." Barry stepped toward her, hands up, shaking his head. "He fell from the top of the building but he's perfectly fine. That's what we saw. . . what. . . happened. What. . ."

Ruth had never seen him at a loss for words before.

"John's okay?" Naomi asked.

Barry nodded.

"But how?" Ruth glanced at the vase of lilies on the table. Could they have arrived to foretell John's death?

"Go ahead, Barry," Jamie said sharply. "Say it."

"John fell from the top of the Temporary Building." Barry took a deep breath. "We all saw it. It's all over the net."

Naomi pulled out her cell.

"No." Barry touched her arm. "You don't want to watch it. Trust me. We all thought he was dead, but then David knelt down beside him, pulled him to his feet, and he was okay. He had a couple of scratches, maybe, but that was it. He's fine."

"David?" Naomi muttered.

"Oh, my God." Ruth's hands covered her mouth. It had happened at last. David had been forced to reveal himself in public. If it was on the net, Addison was already on his way or scrambling helicopters.

Where the hell was Bo?

"You know something about this." Jamie's voice was quiet and strained. "What is going on with my brother?"

Not with Barry there. No matter what.

"Where are they now?" Ruth asked.

"Mom!" Jamie shouted.

"Where are they?" Ruth demanded sternly. She had to get control of the situation.

"At the pier," Jamie muttered. "At Rocky's boat. We're supposed to get everyone and bring you there."

"Go to them," she told Barry to get rid of him so she could focus on her daughter. "Tell them we're on our way. Bo isn't here, and we need to wait for him."

"But—"

"There isn't time, Barry. Go."

"Jamsie?" Barry kissed Jamie on the forehead and ran his hand through her hair.

Her eyes darted to meet his. She squeezed his hand and nodded.

"Go," she said.

He ran for the door.

"Barry?" Naomi called, stopping him. "Give John my love. . . give it to both of them."

"I'll give them both a wet, sloppy kiss for you." Then he dashed away.

Jamie stood there, arms crossed defiantly. Waiting.

"Biologically, David isn't your brother." Ruth swallowed hard.

"What?" Jamie furrowed her brow and shook her head.

"David came from an embryo placed inside me by the Vatican in a lab in Nevada." Ruth poured herself more coffee. "He's a clone of Jesus Christ."

Well, all run together like that, it hadn't been nearly as difficult to say as Ruth had thought it would be.

"A clone." Jamie's tone stayed flat and restrained. "Of Jesus Christ."

And then she started shouting.

The train ran silently through the night, racing Bo back to his family. He stared at the screen of his cell as the photos flashed past: Dave and Vonna. God, Vonna? Those two had hated each other in high school. They'd actually come to blows at the wedding. Well, for those two that could've been courtship.

And a son. Gardner. Jamie's age, and quite the athlete from all the photos of him sparring and swimming.

Bo's reunion with Dave's mom had been short, but she'd transferred all those photos for him.

Bo with Dave and Joey 2. With Mary—No, *Ruth*. No, back then she'd been Mary. So damn young it made his heart ache. Bo in the overalls he'd practically lived in every summer. Everything had seemed simple. Perfect.

Zack and Sally before she'd been Naomi. She looked so much younger. God, the years had aged her most of all.

Even one baby picture of the boys. Back when they were still boys.

John would be thrilled to see photos of his father.

Although. Strangely, looking at the photo of Zack right there, John didn't look as much like him as Bo had thought. Zack was so damn big. His face stronger, harder somehow in spite of the huge grin he wore in every photo. Well, once John filled out, grew into his body... the resemblance would be uncanny.

Bo turned off the little device. How bizarre that his past had finally caught up to him right when his family was about to make a run for it again. Huh. The good part of the past caught up the same week as the bad.

He pulled a glass globe from a pocket and worked it between his hands. He'd found it lying on David's bed and brought it on the trip across town. Maybe his client would want them in future projects, but meeting an old friend from his past had pretty much emptied his brain of professional thoughts.

And Addison had returned. What in the world would they do about him? They had to run. Of course, they did. But Bo was growing a little tired of running and hiding. He and Zack had made plans to fight back. To expose the project to the world. Then Zack had died, and Naomi lost her faith.

And Bo had set aside those plans forever.

Well, maybe not forever. Maybe that's what they needed to do after all, tell the world what had happened in a fake military camp in Nevada.

John stared at David. This was him. . . well, Him. This was what He'd looked like two thousand years ago. Him. Jesus. It was hard to picture without the beard. But the vision he'd had... the vision of the two of them standing across a creek: David as an older man, grizzled, with a full beard.

Yes. John could see that man as Jesus.

"Do you believe me?" David asked.

John nodded, unable to speak.

"Are you afraid?"

Afraid of what? Of David? Of the guy he'd known since birth? How could he fear that?

John shook his head.

"You should be." David turned and looked out across the bay. Tiny ripples snaked across the water as something moved beneath the surface. "There was a time when this was enough." David's voice dropped deeper. "There was a time when the oceans were pure, and the land was a patchwork of grassy plains and brilliant mountains, and there was a moment when that was enough." He pulled a chip of wood from the railing and dropped it into the water. "And ever since. . . I've always wondered whether it was the right decision."

"The right decision?" John asked. "To make people?"

"People, nothing." David laughed. "I'm still not sure the birds weren't a step too far."

"How?" That was John's real question. He snaked an arm around David's waist to remind himself this was the same person he'd seen puke after too much vodka. "I mean the project makes sense, now," John said. "I get that. DNA lasts millions of years. Fine. But how do we get from a clone to raising the dead? Are you. . . are you God?" What kind of answer did John even want from that?

"I *was* God." David turned to contemplate the water. "I remember being God. I remember the stars." He looked up. "So many stars. But then I made myself a body, and my brain was far too small to fit all those stars into it." He looked at John. "So I forgot almost all of it. But there's a piece left, a tiny piece of God in here. I'm the son of God." He held John closer. "As soon as I was born, maybe before even. . . anyway, I lost my connection to all that. To God, to the One out there who runs everything." His brow furrowed. "At least, I think He's running it. I don't really remember, and Michael seems to think He's kinda MIA."

"Michael?" John could attach reality to names.

"The angel," David explained as if that were normal. "Well, archangel, really."

What the what? So much for grounding in reality.

"Do you have the least clue what's really happening?" David asked.

"To be honest, I don't." John took David's face in his hands and kissed him lightly. "Give me a couple of decades to adjust, okay?"

"I'll do what I can."

"Hey!" Rocky's voice called out from the far side of the bridge house. "Did I give you permission to come aboard? I do not recall giving you permission to come aboard."

Dear God, what now? John led David around the cabin where Rocky faced off against the biggest Indian John had ever seen. Who was he kidding? John had never met a real Indian in his life.

The stranger stood well over six feet tall and almost as wide at the shoulders. His inky black hair fell down his back in a braid. He wore jeans and a black, leather vest open across his considerable chest. His feet were bare. His eyes were a bright, piercing green.

"He says he has to see you," Rocky said sarcastically. "He says he knows where you're going."

"My name is Michael," the man said. "I was sent to see David and John safely on their journey."

"It's okay, Rocky," David said. "I know him."

John couldn't breathe. Did David really know this guy? In a life that had just turned upside down, seeing this huge man had to be the most astonishing thing, yet.

"Hello, David." When he smiled, the harsh craggy lines of the man's face shattered, and he looked like an excited kid. A really shredded, excited kid.

David leapt past John, and the man had just enough time to set his feet before David smashed into him and wrapped himself around his torso.

Michael folded his arms around David, lifting him effortlessly from the ground.

"I guess they know each other?" Rocky moved closer to John.

John glared at him. Who the hell was this guy, and how did David know a huge, okay, *hot* Indian, and he'd never mentioned it to John? Pissed off about the lie hit head on with the heat in John's face because David was still hanging onto the stranger.

John wiped perspiration from his forehead. He couldn't think.

David pulled away and led the man over to John by the edge of his black leather vest that had no shirt under it. David's eyes met John's, and he jumped a little. His face flushed.

"John." He held out his free hand, but John didn't move. David sighed and shook the hand. "Come meet Michael."

Reluctantly, John stepped forward. Twenty-four hours earlier, he would have been stoked to meet someone—anyone—who looked like him. Instead, he couldn't help wanting to hit the guy.

"John, this is *Michael*." David said with a wave of one hand.

Michael held out a hand for John to shake.

So. Michael. Sure. Whatever.

John looked at the hand then at David's expectant face then at the hand again.

Fine. He reached forward. Wait. He'd just heard about a Michael, hadn't he? The hand closed completely around John's.

And the world exploded.

Metal crashed against metal. Screams so loud John's ears must be bleeding. Bullets rattled the air.

A battle waged all around him, hundreds, no, thousands, no, billions of warriors in metal armor, no, leather jerkins, no, camouflage jackets and gas masks. Fighter planes and men on horses.

And there! Michael fell from the sky like a comet, his face drawn in anger, an enormous steel sword raised overhead in one arm, protected by torn and bloody armor.

A warrior raced past John to meet him. Tall. Blond. Handsome, yes, but he couldn't approach Michael's glory. They fell to combat with a vengeance.

The battlefield erupted and flew into particles.

John fell back on his ass.

It felt like a fucking alien raced its way up from John's stomach. He fell onto the railing just as vomit launched itself out of his mouth. Oh, *fuck* that hurt. A second alien, just as big, hurtled itself from his stomach. Where was that coming from? He hadn't eaten all day!

Then a hand on his back. David, familiar and soothing. A cup appeared in front of him. Water this time. John rinsed and spat, rinsed and spat. A second cup.

"Drink it this time." Rocky held the cup.

David rubbed his back again, and the horrible pain in his gut subsided.

"Thanks." John drank the water and sucked in deep lungfuls of air.

"Feeling better?" David asked, his hand running through John's hair.

Well, it certainly felt better than the freaking watermelon he'd puked up.

"Wait a minute." He took David's hand. "You've always done this. I get hurt. You touch me. I feel better."

"Is that a bad thing?" David worried about so much all of a sudden.

"No." John squeezed David's hand. "Just putting the pieces together." He moved in to kiss him, then stopped. Puke mouth. "How about I just say thanks?"

David smiled.

John shook his head and looked up. Michael perched on the top rail in a crouch, staring at John intently.

"What just happened?" John pushed away a couple of feet.

"I'm sorry, John." Michael raised his hands. "I didn't realize you were *that* Prophet. I should've. . . I didn't mean to. . ."

"*That* prophet?" John asked. "Which prophet?"

"David's Prophet. Capital P." Michael's voice had softened. "I was trying to find the pathways of the future. Possible futures. It's an angel thing. And we've kind of lost the ability. When our hands met, you created a pathway for me to Megiddo, one possibility for the end of time. I had not thought you could do that. I apologize profusely."

"I give him extra credit for using the word profusely in casual conversation." Rocky leaned back against the rain barrel.

Everyone turned to stare at him.

"What? I just want to make sure no one forgets I'm still here."

"How could we forget you, Peter?" Michael's smile faltered as he looked back to John. "You may have been a prophet before, John. Maybe a little p prophet. But now?" He shook his head. "I shouldn't tell you this, but I expect David will anyway, eventually, and it's likely easier for me."

"Tell me what?" John asked.

"You were not meant to survive the fall." He jumped down from the railing and rose to his full height. "You should be dead."

"When I saved you," David said. "It changed... everything."

"Everything?" John asked. That one word seemed so large the way David had said it.

David nodded. "I meant it to sound that big."

Jamie shouted for a solid minute. When she finished shouting, she stood still for a long time, breathing loudly, her mind a tornado filled with broken lumber.

The shouting had felt good.

Pounding the table had felt good.

Her mom breathed a heavy sigh and looked at Jamie's aunt.

"There was a piece of wood sealed in glass and buried for centuries in the depths of the Vatican," Mom said. "Tradition always maintained that that piece of wood was from the True Cross, where Jesus died. It was soaked in blood. . . human blood. Jesus' blood."

Jamie met her mother's gaze. All the anger and violence drained away, replaced by curiosity.

"How do you know it was really the blood of Jesus and not some first century Jewish martyr?" Jamie asked. "Thousands of Jews were crucified back then."

"She doesn't know," a man said from the hallway.

Something about the voice made Jamie's blood run cold. Her mom and Aunt Naomi rose to their feet even before he turned the corner where he must have been listening.

"That's where the whole thing falls apart, isn't it, Mary?" His southern accent made him sound so harmless, but Christ on a stick, it was him. The super-agent. The man who'd shot Joanne.

Ruth lay an arm around Jamie protectively and pulled her to her side. Fortunately, her daughter didn't complain.

"Hello, Jedidiah." Ruth kept her voice as casual as his had been.

"Hello, Mary." He moved into the room. "It's been a long time." He whistled. "You are as beautiful as ever."

She forced herself to smile. So he was *that* Jedidiah. The nice one.

"You seem to be keeping fit," Ruth said. His suit must have cost a fortune. His hat was the latest style. Playing God paid well then.

Jamie shivered in Ruth's arms. Did her daughter know this man?

"I'd offer you some coffee," Ruth said. "But we've run out."

Pierce shook his head, looking the place over. He nodded at Naomi. "Ma'am."

"Mr. Pierce." Naomi took a single step away from Ruth. "To what do we owe the pleasure?"

"Can't a fella just stop by to say hello?" Then he actually laughed. "I'm sorry ladies, it's just mighty strange being in the same room with y'all after so long." He pointed at Jamie with a grin. "And that one led me a merry chase across a few rooftops, I must say."

What in the world? First the ridiculous hologram system, now Jamie was running the rooftops?

No. No distractions.

"Did Mr. Addison send you?" Keeping her voice light grew more difficult. If Bo showed up, he'd be a dead man, friendly Pierce or not.

The agent shook his head, wandering around the room and touching things, picking them up as if this was a purely social call.

"I came here to see you, Mary."

"Me?" Ruth prayed Jamie would keep her mouth shut. He'd had a crush on her once upon a time. Did he still?

"Well, it's just that Mr. Addison is about to blow this entire island off the map." He said it as if talking about the weather. "And I thought I'd give you a chance to get away before everyone in a five-mile radius is incinerated."

"Well, Jedidiah, that's very generous of you." Think, think, think, dear God, think. "Should I get the family packed?"

"See, that's the snag I was afraid of." He clucked his tongue and moved closer. "There's no way I can sneak the whole clan under Mr. Addison's nose." He raised a hand as if to touch her. "Just the one however, I think I can manage. He doesn't know *everything* about me."

Don't pull back. Don't cringe.

He touched her hair. He leaned close and sniffed.

"Mmm, Mary. You always smelled so nice."

Jamie cleared her throat. "Why are you calling her Mary?"

Ruth closed her eyes.

Was she stupid? She had to know what kind of danger they faced.

"She doesn't know her own mother's real name?" He examined Jamie as if she were an enchanting flower. "What else doesn't she know?"

"Leave her out of this, Jedidiah." Naomi's voice stayed calm and flat.

His eyes darted to study her.

"She has nothing to do with this," Naomi insisted.

"You have no concept of who this involves, Sally." He turned his attention back to Jamie. "You never did."

As grown up as her daughter tried to be, Ruth could tell from the way she shook that this man terrified her.

"Well, if your momma doesn't want me to save *her*. . ." He tugged at a strand of Jamie's hair. "Maybe you'd like to come play with me."

Jamie fell still. She hadn't been shaking in fear, then. It had been rage. And this stillness, what could it mean?

Dear Lord, let her not have some kind of weapon on her.

"You know how I like to play, don't you?" Pierce twirled the strand of hair in his fingers. "We'd have no secrets at all."

Jamie's hand twitched against Ruth. It'd been between them the entire time, behind Jamie's back, and Ruth hadn't noticed it.

What in the world was she going to try? She held the girl tighter.

"Leave her alone," Naomi said darkly. "She's too good for a piece of trash like you."

The gunshot was so quiet, barely a puff of air.

The hand held out toward Naomi had fired before Ruth even saw the arm move.

A red dot appeared above the bridge of Naomi's nose, between her eyebrows, and a large red stain sprayed the cupboards behind her.

Her head snapped back, and she crumpled.

She must have known what he would do for an insult like that.

"Look what you made me do!" he shouted at Naomi where she lay in a heap. He looked up at Ruth, anguish in his face. "I'm sorry. She shouldn't have said that."

He stepped back, took off his hat and ran an arm over his face, shaking his head. How in the world could he think there was a way to salvage the situation, to convince her to run away with him?

Ruth squeezed Jamie, hoping to keep her daughter absolutely still.

Someone's cell vibrated.

"Dang it." Pierce held the gun out at Ruth and Jamie, yanking the cell from a pocket. "Yes, Mr. Addison?" And just like that he was perfectly cool again. The Southern accent had all but vanished.

"What the fuck are you doing in the Ghetto, Pierce?" Addison's voice over the cell brought back so many memories. "They don't make fucking burgers on this side of the God damned bridge?"

"The Ghetto?" Pierce's face scrunched up.

"You think I don't track every fucking move you make?"

Ruth slid her hand over Jamie's mouth. She'd take no chances. With that man on the line, anything could happen.

"Of course, sir." Pierce fell still again. "Tying up loose ends, sir. I got a call on my break. McCarthy hadn't sealed off all the tunnels. I thought he needed some personal attention."

"How many fingers did you need to break?" Addison asked.

"Just one hand, sir." Pierce's entire body relaxed.

"And the tunnels?" the older man demanded.

"Sealed off, sir." Pierce stared directly into Ruth's eyes, but his face remained a complete blank now. "Not a single soul will get off this island once they blow the bridge." He was trying to work her, and she knew it, trying one last time to convince Ruth to go with him. She couldn't. But if she said no, what would stop him from just shooting her and her daughter right there?

Ruth closed her eyes and held Jamie as tightly as she could, sliding her hand over her daughter's eyes. She shook her head. She couldn't go with him. *Please God, find a way to save my little girl.*

"Fine," Addison snapped over the open channel. "Then I need you to do something while I have you on the line."

"Right now, sir?" Pierce asked. "Shouldn't I get my butt across the bridge first?"

"Yeah, yeah, yeah." Addison coughed. "You can walk and talk and operate those damn holograms at the same time. I've seen you do it a million times. Now move."

Ruth opened her eyes.

Pierce's face twisted in pain.

"Please," he mouthed silently.

The gun had fallen away.

Ruth shook her head again. If Addison heard gunshots over the line, he'd ask too many questions, right? Pierce would get in trouble.

"I don't see your little red dot on the move," Addison said angrily. "Go. Now!"

Pierce huffed. He pointed the gun directly at Ruth's forehead. An inch away. He huffed again.

"Now!" Addison shouted.

"Sorry, sir." The gun fell away, and Pierce turned. "Stuck in an elevator. What do you need?"

Suddenly, he was gone.

Ruth glanced at the lilies on the table.

The flowers oozed drops of bright red.

"Layla?" Jamie took a step forward.

Ruth closed her eyes and reached out, then shook her head.

"Layla's safe."

The girl didn't even know what had happened. . . what had happened to Naomi. Ruth couldn't look down. If she looked down, she'd never get her children to safety. She led Jamie out of the kitchen and into the hallway.

"Pack a bag," Ruth insisted. "One bag for you and Layla. Keep it light. Pretend you're sneaking out for the weekend." She brushed the hair out of her daughter's face and forced herself to smile for Jamie's sake. "I don't want Layla up here again, so I need you to do this for me." She needed to keep her daughter moving until Bo returned and they could leave, and she prayed for Bo to hurry.

"We need to get word out." She followed Jamie to her room. "We need to tell everyone to get out of the Ghetto. Addison's going to burn it to the ground. I can't let him do it without trying to warn everyone."

When Barry reached the boat, Rocky and David spat bullets. John leaned against a rope, watching, periodically sneaking peeks at the top of the bridge house. Why?

Yowsa! Large fellow perched up there like a bird, crouched low, hands hanging between his feet, bare toes curled over the edge, staring out over the water with abject peace. Who the heck was he?

"But you've already stolen the boat from your grandfather." David's voice was controlled but declassed.

"That doesn't make it right," Rocky jiggered back. "I'm not letting you go off in my grandfather's boat without me."

"There is no way you'd be able to bring it back to him," David insisted.

Barry met John's eyes and nodded. John nodded back. Barry glanced from the big guy on the bridge house to John and back again, startled at the similarities. Why was a big Indian perched on top of Rocky's boat?

"You don't know that." Rocky crossed his arms. "I might could find a way to get it back to him."

"I don't know that?" David scoffed. "Of course, I know that!"

"Yeah. . . well. . . okay. . ." Rocky turned his attention to John. "He can't dump this giant thing on me and then expect me to go skating off into the night. Tell him, John. It isn't fair."

John held up his hands to keep from getting involved, then Rocky finally found Barry's eyes.

"Barry, my man! You are not going to believe what these two lovebirds are trying to do!"

But then Barry saw only David. He was taller. . . or maybe stronger. . . different. On fire.

"You really did it, didn't you?" Barry took David's hand.

David nodded.

"Wow."

David smiled.

"I have a message for you." Barry kissed them both, as promised, although not so much on the wet and sloppy side. Now that they were a couple that would feel a trifle active duty. "Your folks are waiting on your dad. They'll slide in as fast as possible once he's back."

"See?" Rocky slapped Barry on the back so hard he stumbled. "You have to wait for your family."

John shook his head and held Barry by both arms. He turned him to face the giant on the roof.

"That guy up there?" John pointed over Barry's shoulder. "Name's Michael. He's an angel sent to tell us we need to go with him and that no one can come with us."

"You're an angel?" Barry stared at the man perched above them.

The man looked down at him and nodded.

"Where's your wings?" It was all Barry could think to say.

Michael cocked his head to one side with his brows knit, then he smiled. He shrugged the vest from his shoulders and down his arms. He rolled his shoulders and closed his eyes.

The wings unfolded behind him out of nowhere, the wings of an eagle, but opened to a span of thirty feet. With the subtlest movement of his shoulders, Michael shook them out and flapped them twice. They rose and fell above him with strength and grace.

The air blew Barry's hair behind his shoulders.

The angel opened his eyes. They burned with supernatural green fire. The flames raced from his eyes, spun into a thin, bright circle around his head and traced every line of the enormous wings.

Barry couldn't breathe.

Michael was the most beautiful thing he'd ever seen.

Then the wings fluttered, shimmered, and folded in on themselves until they disappeared behind Michael's back. The angel shook himself, and the ethereal green fire flew from his body like water. He returned to his quiet contemplation of the horizon, his eyes once again dark chasms. He pulled his vest up over his shoulders as if nothing unusual had happened. His hands fell between his knees, lightly gripping the metal roof between his feet.

For a moment, no one spoke.

Barry found his voice. "Excuse me, cats, but holy. flying. *fuck*."

"I raised someone from the dead." David chuckled. "He's a showoff."

When Barry looked away from Michael and at his friends again, he felt calm. He shook his head and sighed deeply.

"Naomi said to tell you she loves you both."

"Mom," John said, as if making plans on the fly. The tone of voice was so familiar. "Barry, you know you've always been family." He included Rocky. "You too, now." He clasped his hands together. "I need you to make sure the rest of our family gets out. David meant it about the missiles. Copters are likely loading up as we speak. Make sure your folks get out, too, but please take ours with you." He glanced up at Michael. "They may not have angels guiding them."

The angel shrugged. "I can't see bupkis since David changed the future."

Barry laughed. Bupkis? An angel said bupkis? Wacky!

A lump caught in Barry's throat. He hugged David first. Then he took John in his arms and breathed in deeply, trying to hold the memory of his scent. He took John's hand, kissed it, and draped it around David's neck.

"I love you cats." He didn't want to make their departure any harder than it already was. It was time to go. "Hold each other to the snuggly out there. Right?"

"We'll find you," John promised. "We have an angel, now, right? We can find you wherever you go."

About that. Their angel... Native American angel? What the what? Barry needed attention. He held up a hand as high as he could.

"Why does your angel look like Tonto on steroids?"

John looked up at the angel.

So did David. Huh, so he didn't know, either?

The angel stared down at Barry.

He spoke not a word. Holy baby Jebus, he had eyes that scoped your soul.

Excelsior. Enough said.

"Say goodbye, coz." Barry threw an arm around Rocky's neck. "Tell them you love them."

Bo hurried through the Ghetto. Why were so many people out after curfew? And what did the whispers mean? Someone fell off the Temporary Building? Some kind of miracle? And copters on the way?

Bo's gut twisted. He broke into a run. It was happening. Now. Addison was making his move.

"You're going the wrong way, coz," a young man told him. "We gotta get out of here."

Damn. Bo turned a corner and ran into someone so hard he spun and fell to his knees.

"I'm so sorry," he said as a strong hand helped him up.

A woman's hand. Gabriel.

Bo froze.

"You." It was her. Tall. Red hair. Angelic smile and perfect composure in spite of their collision.

"Indeed." She released his arm.

"Who died?" Bo asked out of habit.

Gabriel frowned. "That's not why I'm here."

"Why *are* you here?" He could scarcely believe his eyes.

"You need to get your family to safety, Joseph." She glanced around. "And I'm afraid you might not have understood Raphael's message." She smiled. "He tends to be needlessly subtle."

"Raphael's message?" Bo looked around. Another angel? Where?

"He showed you exactly how to escape, Joseph," she told him. "If you can just remember, Joseph, the path he pointed out."

Why the hell did she keep saying his name like that?

Someone bumped into Bo, muttered an apology, and ran off.

Bo glanced around.

No Gabriel, but an increasing number of people hurrying from their homes.

"Blast it." What the hell had she meant? He hadn't seen another angel, had he? And *Raphael* was needlessly subtle? Bo ran. Maybe Ruth would be able to figure out what the angel had meant.

Layla sat on the stoop watching people pass. Jamie had run home with Barry and rushed inside giving Layla little more than a hello. He had rushed out a few minutes later without even glancing at her. Rude.

A frightening White man had come and gone without giving her a second look. When she'd heard him on his way out through the shop, she'd sort of melted into the steps, so he walked past without seeing her.

Most recently, her father had come home, stopping long enough to mess up her hair and to tell her they'd be out to get her in just a few minutes. Her world was changing, growing darker and brighter at the same time. Everyone around her, all the people who had come and gone during the evening thought she was too young to understand and too innocent to be troubled with the dangers and ugliness around her.

Something horrible had happened in their home that night, something ugly involving her Aunt Naomi and the frightening White man. Layla wanted someone to stop and tell her what was going on, but a part of her was still young enough to be too afraid to ask.

Sooner or later, someone would tell her, or, more likely than not, she would know on her own. She often knew things without being told.

"Hello, there."

Layla jumped. The voice was so close.

"I'm sorry, dear," said a tall man in a bright, white suit standing right at the corner of the stoop. "I didn't mean to frighten you."

How had he snuck up on her like that?

He stood very tall and had long, straight hair the color of autumn wheat, skin the color of bronze, and a neatly trimmed goatee and mustache. He was the most attractive man Layla had ever seen, but there was something vaguely frightening about him. He reminded her of the red-haired woman, Gabriel, whom she'd seen earlier. His suit was light and fit him loosely, and it was so bright she could hardly believe she hadn't seen him coming up the sidewalk.

"Are you a model?" she asked.

"Not at all." The man laughed lightly and shook his head.

"You look like one."

"Do I indeed?" He sat on the stoop beside her and folded his hands into a steeple on his knees. "Thank you."

"Why are you out so late?" Layla asked.

"I prefer the moon." He pointed at the sky. "She is much more forgiving than the sun."

"The moon set fifteen minutes ago," Layla pointed out.

"Indeed, she has," the astonishing man said. "I was heading home."

"Do you know what's happening to my family?" Layla looked down at her feet.

"Why would you think I know anything about your family?"

"Because you're not a regular person." She looked up at him with one eye closed. "You know things, don't you?"

"And how can you tell that?" The man leaned closer. He glowed.

Layla looked down at her feet again. People never asked her how she knew the things she knew.

"You're a very special person, aren't you?" The man bumped her with his knee. "You know a lot of things."

"Why are you here?" It was hard to keep her eyes off him. Looking away was physically painful.

"You tell me." He drew himself up for her perusal.

She gazed at him a long time, but everything inside him seemed completely contrary to what she saw in his mesmerizing face. Something dark lived inside him.

"Are you a bad man?" Was there another way to say it?

"No, no." The man chuckled, shaking his head.

"You aren't bad?"

"No." His eyes changed. They glittered in the darkness. "I'm not a man."

Layla shivered.

"Does that frighten you?"

Layla shook her head.

The gesture was a lie, and they both knew it.

"Why are you here?" she asked again.

He looked across the street with a sigh. When he looked back at her, he beamed again, all friendly, but Layla wasn't about to relax.

"I wanted to meet you." His answer, like so much about him, surprised her.

"Me? Why me?"

"Your family is much talked about in my little circle of friends and acquaintances." He looked right at her as he talked, and Layla relaxed. "Your brother more than the rest, I suppose, but you. . ." He touched her nose with one fingertip. "You are very important in your own way. I wanted you to know that, and I wanted to tell you myself."

Layla stayed silent, enraptured.

"When we meet again, some time from now, I want you to remember me, remember that I talked *with* you and not *at* you. Remember that I recognized your gifts before anyone else. And, most importantly, remember that there was a time when I was light and air and gossamer wings." He smiled and touched her nose again. "Can you remember that?"

She nodded.

"Good. I think it's time for you to go, now."

A noise in the shop drew Layla's attention for less than a second. When she turned back, the man was gone.

Where had he gone? She searched frantically up and down the street. He'd touched something deep inside her no one else had tried to find.

She jumped to her feet, ready to run if she saw him.

Then the shop door banged open, and her parents and Jamie rushed out to her, each carrying a heavy-looking bag.

Layla searched the street one last time. Where could he be?

Families filled the street, now, breaking the spell. Sirens screamed at Layla from every direction. Her parents grabbed her hands and carried her down the street with them, rushing into the growing crowd.

As she ran, Layla searched for a glimpse of the man in the white suit. For just a moment with him, she'd felt important. Just that one moment. She wanted to feel that again.

Her parents pressed tightly against her, and her father kept Jamie's hand, as if she were a little girl, but Jamie didn't protest. With all the pushing and running, if they were separated, they'd never find each other again, would they?

People called out. A little boy of no more than four stood on a porch by himself, crying. Two women reached for him as they passed and pulled him into the growing river, asking him who his parents were.

And then Barry and Rocky joined them in the rush. Barry kept shouting his parents' names, but they were nowhere to be found.

Joanne joined them, too. The growing family held together in the surging mob.

But where were John and David? Layla closed her eyes and reached out. A boat? Why did they get to ride a boat?

Oh. Well, she'd get to ride in a helicopter, so that was okay.

Her father snatched her up into his arms, and she opened her eyes. As they reached the bridge, the sound of sirens hurt her ears.

Layla went blind with hot white light for a moment.

She closed them for a single second to try to clear them.

When she opened them again, she could see so much more.

So much more…

The front edge of the human flood reached the checkpoints at the bridge and fanned out. Armed guards blocked the bridge that led to safety. Standing shoulder to shoulder, men and women stared impassively, holding automatic weapons across their chests.

The crowd hesitated. . . wavered. A few people shouted, telling the guards to stand aside, but no one seemed willing to make the first move. A clear distance of twenty feet lay open between the checkpoint and the crowd.

"Go back to your homes," a voice called over a speaker. "This island has been quarantined. No one is permitted to enter or to leave. Go back to your homes or face the consequences."

The crowd shuffled. Voices muttered.

The people who had spread along the banks of the river complained about being squashed against the fence. The distance between the crowd and the police shrank a foot or two.

That's when the gunfire began, the first shots fired over the Ghetto rats' heads, meant to scare them, to convince them to retreat, but the shots drew attention upward, to the sky, where a dozen silent black helicopters swarmed.

People screamed. They knew what the copters meant.

Death. Violent death.

The crowd folded in on itself as the leading edge drove away from the gunfire. Then an explosion rocked the concrete beneath their feet, and then another as first the churches and then the Temporary Building burst into flame and collapsed into rubble.

A dozen missiles exploded across the Ghetto. Panic spread through the crowd and turned it into a stampede, forcing the front of the mob into the buffer zone.

As the multitude closed the gap, the police opened fire. The victims in front had no way to flee. Hot slugs of metal ripped them apart, and the mob pressed back on itself and imploded. Thousands ran toward the bridge to escape the explosions and the fire, panicked by the smell of burning flesh and the screams of the dying, completely unaware of the danger at the bridge itself.

Hundreds pushed back, away from the vicious death spit out by the guards' automatic weapons. Bodies littered the pavement. A final surge from behind pressed the crowd against the fences along the river's edge.

The barrier gave out, dropping hundreds into the water in a single moment.

More bodies fell under gunfire, and the multitude split into twin streams that flooded into the river on both sides of the bridge.

Soon, the black waters filled with panicked and confused swimmers, struggling against the current and each other.

Police boats, screaming down on them from the opposite shore, opened fire.

Thick smoke filled the air, blinding everyone but the police who wore goggles and gas masks. They'd known what to expect. They'd been told to be merciless because they needed to protect the city from a disease-ridden, vigilante mob bent on riots and looting. It was up to the police to protect their loved ones and families on their side of the bridge.

The bridge exploded.

The heat from the blast brought Layla back to herself, and she cringed at the concussion, waiting to die. When flying debris didn't incinerate or crush her, she opened her eyes. Fire reached eager fingers into the sky over the entire island.

How had she gone into the water? She clung to her father's back, and they'd almost reached the opposite shore. How had they found the way?

"Layla!" A woman held her hands out from among the bushes, glowing all golden and red. Layla held her breath for one second, caught in that beautiful woman's face, then she groped forward, and her arms were grasped.

Her mother pulled her out of the water.

The redheaded woman, Gabriel, was gone.

Her father climbed up behind. He helped Jamie and the others out of the water. Then he scooped Layla into his arms, held her tightly, and carried her toward a nearby fence.

"I know a way under it," Jamie said.

Over her father's strong shoulder, fires consumed the only home Layla knew.

Gunfire kept up a constant rhythm. The screams were continuous. Explosions punctuated the general roar.

Layla's schoolteacher, Miss Havelock, was over there, somewhere. So was Ms. Schimmel and her wife. So many of her friends and their families. Barry's parents hadn't made it out of their apartment. If he'd gone back to them, he'd be dead, too.

Should she tell him? No. Not right then.

In the glare of the searchlights, broken and torn bodies floated in the water, thousands of them.

Mrs. King stared at the sooty clouds overhead.

Flames moved like living things, racing through the buildings and eating everything they touched.

Layla's family reached the fence and crawled through.

Pierce watched Addison for several moments before working up the courage to speak. His boss looked out through the windows over a garden where holographic fairies darted among the trees. A dozen holo screens lay open between them, but Pierce had muted the sound.

The operation was out of the old man's control for now. It was up to the warriors. The men who actually shot the guns and dropped the bombs. Men like Pierce. Addison just told them where to aim.

A warm, flickering light glowed over the roof on the opposite side of the garden. The island was a cinder.

Addison worked the fingers of one hand on the wrist of the other, clasped together behind his back.

Pierce coughed politely to get his boss' attention.

Without moving, Addison met his eyes in the reflection of the glass.

"Out with it," the old man said.

Pierce waved his hand over the glass table and the screens shifted.

"The science project and the half-breed stole a boat and slipped out to sea at o-three—at around three o'clock."

Data scrolled across the screens, but Addison ignored it.

"They managed to escape the police and coast guard ships," Pierce told him. "Our best guess is they're heading south."

"Your best guess," Addison repeated flatly.

"There were some serious storms to the North that probably would have swamped a small fishing boat, so we guess they traveled south. The Coast Guard is searching the coastline from here to Georgia."

"Guess," Addison repeated coldly.

Pierce had learned years before to make sure his boss knew exactly the accuracy of his information. His stomach had tightened when he'd said that word, but he'd have been in trouble if he'd exaggerated their chances.

"What other bad news do you have for me?" Addison asked.

"The family's gone, too."

Addison worked the wrist harder.

"And how exactly did that happen?" His smoldering quiet frightened Pierce even after eighteen years.

"They escaped the Ghetto and made their way to a sympathizer named Dr. Sung." He braced himself for the upcoming explosion. "Sung owns a small, private plane, and, as I'm sure you know, Joe learned how to fly. We assume they commandeered the plane and flew off in it."

Pierce didn't allow himself to react to his boneheaded verbal slip. Addison had flagellated himself a thousand times for letting Zack and his sidekick spend so much time with the pilots in Nevada. At the time, it had seemed a handy way to keep them out of the way.

The older man made a soft noise in this throat.

"Cruise missiles worked well enough last time." He reached for a cigarette. "So why is this an assumption? A private plane can only go so far." He raised his volume enough for the computer. "Map of the East coast, centered on my location." The map appeared. "Using data from recent flight plans, project possible distance of a small private plane." The map enlarged and drew a circle for potential flight distance. "Highlight all landing strips in the projected area." Red dots lit the map. "Access logs from all projected airfields."

Pierce closed his eyes. He already knew the "error" icon must be flashing.

"Do you know why I'm getting an error message?" Addison asked.

Pierce couldn't speak for several seconds.

"There are no airfield reports," he said at last. "Another Makabee virus hit half an hour ago. All data for the past week erased from every airport from DC to Maine."

"It hit just the airports in *that* fucking location," Addison demanded, "right after our quarry hijacked a plane?"

"Yes." Pierce relaxed into his knees and slowly moved his hand closer to his weapon.

"So you've spoken to and/or killed Dr. Sung?"

"We spoke with him," Pierce said. "He told us he gave them the plane under duress and insisted they would not tell him where they were going."

"Insisted. And you verified his honesty?"

Here was the worst part.

"Dr. Sung's wife is Senator Amanda Sato. We were unable to utilize the usual methods for verification."

"Sato," Addison said. "Why do I know that name?"

"She's a fairly vocal Progressive," Pierce explained. "We learned about the family's presence from an informant we have in her household." What he didn't add was that they'd likely end up in a federal penitentiary if they tried breaking any of her husband's limbs. The woman had her roots almost as deep as Addison's, just on a somewhat different tree. Possibly a different forest altogether.

Addison's long silences were worse than his tirades. Pierce comforted himself with the knowledge that his weapon was fully loaded and the safety off.

"So we just burned a city to cinders and killed thousands of people with no readily apparent benefit?" Addison asked.

"Yes, sir." There was really no other way to describe it.

All the screens derezzed. The lights went out.

Shrieks reached them from the darkened garden outside, but mostly of excitement.

Pierce swallowed. "I believe the Makabee virus has spread, sir."

Addison's lighter clicked. The flame showed a face as calm as Pierce had ever seen it. He lit the cigarette, inhaled deeply, and let the lighter go out. In the deep darkness outside, the dying fires over the Ghetto played across the smoke-filled sky.

"Get lost for a while, Pierce."

Pierce fled the room. Within seconds, the laughter of the motel guests was dwarfed by the sound of something like a desk thrown through a plate glass window. A string of emphatic cursing followed.

Water lapped against the side of the boat, dark and glassy, reflecting the light of a million stars. The prow cut through the glass, sending ripples over its surface. The stars danced.

The only home John had ever known was no more than an orange glow on the horizon. The Ghetto had been leveled, and John couldn't take his eyes from that fading light. All his life he'd wanted to escape that prison. But not like this. Not at the cost of so many lives.

"You're sure they're safe?" he asked. "Our family? John stood at the prow with David behind him, arms wrapped around John's stomach.

David squeezed him.

"As far as we know," he said. "They managed to get out of the city. Senator Sato gave them a plane."

Amanda Sato. Something bothered John about her, about the coincidence of it all.

"Who made it out?" he asked.

"Everything's cloudy," David said. "I'm not a research engine. That's. . ."

That's what a prophet was supposed to do. Right?

John pulled David's arms more tightly around his middle.

"How do I do that?" he asked. "How do I. . . prophet? Do prophety things?" What the hell was it even called?

"I don't know." David seemed slightly annoyed by the question. But how could he not know?

"Being human is complicated." David sighed. "It's hard to see sometimes, and I've never known the future one hundred percent."

"So you have no idea what happens next?" John turned and gazed into David's eyes.

"Everyone's in a panic," David said. "They're used to a certain. . . order." And by everyone he meant angels because that was normal, now. "They don't like uncertainty."

"So was it a bad thing, then?" John frowned. "Saving me?"

David pulled him close and kissed him, sending a spark through John's body. So much had changed. But was that a good thing? It felt like a good thing. The kiss ended.

"It was a very good thing." David smiled.

John felt the heat rise to his cheeks. "Even if it ruffled some feathers?"

David snorted and turned to watch the water. "I'm amazed at how quickly you've adjusted. Even the bad jokes are back."

"Don't worry. At some point very soon, I'll start screaming. I'd guess I'm still in shock. It doesn't seem real." He tried to believe that this person in his arms had actually made everything around them. The water, the birds, the air, the stars, but he'd watched David grow up, had seen him piss and puke and shit. How could he also be the Son of God? How?

"Don't ever get used to the idea." David pulled John's arms tighter about himself. "I don't want you to pretend that it isn't the most unusual thing in the universe to be in love with me." He kissed the back of John's hand. "Pretending this is ordinary will kill it."

John was in love with the Son of God, and an angel, wait, no, an archangel steered their boat they knew not where. Ordinary?

"No. No worries there. At least not today."

But he still wanted to know who'd made it out of the Ghetto.

He was a prophet, right? A prophet should be able to see.

He closed his eyes. Centered.

Uncle Bo climbed out of the cockpit of some kind of small plane, holding Aunt Ruth's hand. She passed him and led the others outside. Jamie, Layla, Barry, Rocky, and Joanne jumped down onto a hard-packed dirt road out in the middle of a nowhere filled with enormous trees.

They examined their surroundings. They argued.

Where was Mom?

Jamie pointed at the sky. A familiar black helicopter raced toward them.

Barry and Rocky ran toward the plane.

Jamie grabbed Layla and headed for the tree line.

Aunt Ruth shouted at them, gathered them together when the copter landed, dragged them into the terrifying thing.

She pounded on the door to the cockpit, opened it. No one sat at the controls.

The dark glass canopy flared brightly as the little plane they'd left behind exploded.

Boom.

John fell back into himself and emptied his stomach over the side of the boat. All he had left to vomit was water.

Why did propheting hurt so damn much? Was it because he'd never been meant to be one, a real Prophet? Was it all wrong?

David's hand on his back eased the pain. How had he never noticed how often his cousin did that?

"A copter," John said when he could talk. "A copter got them. We have to go help."

"They're fine," Michael said from behind.

"Fine?" John spun. "The Dicks have them."

"Amanda Sato sent the helicopter," Michael said. "Your family is safe." With his arms crossed over his chest like that, he didn't seem likely to be persuaded to change course.

"Her?" John asked. "How the hell does she have a Dickerson copter?"

The angel didn't move or react. Wow. He was such a stereotype.

"Shhhhh." David gently trailed his fingertips across John's face. "If Michael says they're safe, then they're safe. He can't lie."

"What? Seriously?"

"It's an angel thing." David smiled. "He can't lie, at least not to us. They can't lie to humans."

No. That wasn't likely to seem ordinary any time soon.

David laughed, and his eyes sparkled but only from the reflection of the light above.

...to be continued in *The Acts of St. Michael.*
Available soon on Amazon.

Afterward to the Second Edition

This letter was sent out as part of my promotional material.

RE: *Third Testament: The Gospel of John, 2ⁿᵈ Edition*
John Robert Mack
Zen Monster Press

Dear Person,

I started to research the life of Jesus in 1996 when my brother needed Bible verses to hold up his allied support of the gay community. I learned, as I studied, that what most of us are taught in Sunday School has little or no resemblance to the things the guy named Jesus would have said... even as recorded canonically in the Bible.

That was the beginning of my endless fascination with this thing that came to be called Christianity, which had an incredible influence on nearly all Western civilization but which very few people take the time to understand. Folks exist who want us to believe that Jesus would support a Prosperity Gospel where good people are rewarded with riches, that he would want everyone to own a gun, that he would hate immigrants. These people select a very few Bible verses to support their theology and ignore the rest of Jesus' words. So, I decided that if all those folks could expound the versions of Jesus they created in their own image, why couldn't I?

So I did.

In *The Gospel of John*, David is a hypothetical clone of Jesus in the year 2086, a version of the man modeled after my own ideas and frustrations and based on the scholarly writing of dozens of scholars, including you. [Personal note to each scholar.] Jesus' closest associates were fishermen, tax collectors, and, remarkably for the day, women. He touched lepers. He told a positive story about a good Samaritan. He hung out with the outcasts... with the downtrodden. He healed the sick without expecting payment, and he fed the hungry even if they didn't have proof of employment.

I recently published a second edition of the novel originally published in 2015. Why? I started the first draft of this novel in 1996 during the

Clinton administration and published the first edition at the end of the Obama administration. At both of those times, the idea of radical right-wing evangelicals taking over the government seemed absurd. The idea that People of Color could be forced into what are, for lack of a kinder word, internment camps, seemed impossible. Who would have guessed in 2015 that armed, anonymous men would be able to snatch People of Color off the street and make them disappear? The reality disgusts me.

I wrote this novel out of a fear that we would forget the past, that we would forget that in the 1920s there were more gay newspapers in Berlin than in New York in the 1990s when I began my studies.

And now it's 2025. I am disturbed by the fact that so much of what I wrote as Apocalyptic fiction has become reality. Ten years after I first published this novel, it is a thousand times more relevant. I have made changes for the Second Edition: in grammar, in clarity, and in pacing. I have not changed one iota of material to create a closer parallel to reality. I had no need. Anything like prophesy was an accident. I didn't mean to predict the future. I had meant to warn of the past. Who would have thought this reality was possible?

What follows is a sample of the novel. Attached is a PDF of the complete manuscript. As your own scholarly words had a tremendous impact on the finished product, I would be honored if you would read even a small sample and express your opinion. If you'd like a paperback copy to read, please send me a suitable address, and I will have one shipped directly from Amazon.

Thank you for taking the time to read this letter.

Any response, positive or negative, is welcome.

Sincerely,

John Robert Mack
www.JohnRobertMack.com
@JohnRobertMack on all social media.

Reading Lists

I have studied the life of Jesus, the New Testament, and the transition from Judaism to Christianity for 30 years. The following is an incomplete list of authors I recommend. I wrote a novel, not a scholarly treatise, but I desire to pay tribute to the scholars whose work created the foundation of the theology involved.

Nothing theological was invented by me. While I created the story and the characters from my own deviant imagination, every bit of theology and theory was based on the foundation laid by people far more knowledgeable than I.

I am not a Biblical scholar. I am not a theologian.

I am a student of the Bible and a novelist.

Suggested authors, in no particular order:

Bart D. Ehrman
Ellaine Pagels
Marvin Meyer
Craig A. Evans
C.S. Lewis
Michael Baignet and Richard Leigh
Peter Flint and James VanderKam
John Dominic Crossan
Marcus Borg
John P. Meier
Lawrence Schiffman
Morton Smith
Reza Aslan
The scholars of the Jesus Seminar
And many more.

To better understand the Bible, I have studied numerous ancient documents in translation. I once started to learn Latin so I could read some of the ancient writers in the original language, but then decided I'd also need to learn Ancient Greek, possibly Coptic… and that just seemed a bit silly for a novelist.

I did get a great Latin joke for my novel *Zen Monsters*.

I especially encourage folks to read about the Nag Hammadi texts. These are documents written in ancient times that were rejected by the orthodox Christians because they showed a completely different concept of Jesus. For them, "different" was "bad."

I disagree.

Suggested ancient material, in no particular order:

Tertulian

Justin Martyr

Augustine

Eusebius

The Didache

Origen

The Dead Sea Scrolls

The Nag Hamadi texts

Hildegard Von Bingen

Marcion

Josephus

Acknowledgements

First and foremost, thank you to my brother for all the encouragement over the years, and to his family for giving me a home while I tore this thing apart yet again. This would not exist without y'all.

Also, thanks to Marilyn Putriment, for saying, "If Jesus ever did come back, he'd most likely end up in the electric chair."

As usual, thanks to my editor, Lauran Strait for assaulting my prose with the dagger of Lucifer. Thanks also to Paula Hudson for important input and critique. Various versions of this also benefitted from input by Michael Khandelwal and the Muse Writing Center in Norfolk, VA, from Amanda Aksel of Elephantine Publishing, Jennifer Wenninger-Neidfeldt, the ladies of my writing group: Nancy, Jan, Mary, Donna, Lisa, Cecelia, Candance and Jean, some of whom had to really dig deep to help with this one because of the subject matter.

Special thanks to Dan Kowal for providing shelter while I fashioned the second edition.

Thanks to all! Damn, this project has been a part of my life for so long, I am certain to miss more folks than I mention. To anyone I have missed, my sincerest apologies. Feel free to email me with a reminder, and you'll make it into the next edition.

About the Author

John Robert Mack has struggled with the ways Christianity impacts our culture since he was looking for seminaries at sixteen... and a boy kissed him. These days, he's hanging out in Western North Carolina trying to make a living as a dance teacher, photographer, English teacher, and writer... and hoping to find another guy who wants to kiss him.

To find out more about him, check out his social media.

@johnrobertmack on all social media.

Interested in seeing what happens next?

Here is a sample of
The Acts of St. Michael
The second exciting novel in the
Third Testament series.

THIRD TESTAMENT
THE ACTS OF
ST.MICHAEL

JOHN ROBERT MACK

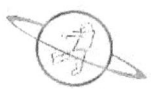

Zen Monster Press

In Memory of Joyce Marie Mack.
Mother.
Editor.
Friend.

Part One

The Nephilim were on the earth in those days—
and also afterward—
when the sons of God went to the daughters of men
and had children by them.
They were the heroes of old, men of renown.

~~Genesis 6:1–4

A pickup truck rattled and squeaked along a dusty road deep in the bowels of Texas. Ash filled the air from the dead cedar that had caught fire due to nothing more than the savage Texas sun. Since the drought of 2074, the entire state was a desert.

Michael crouched in the back of the truck, leaning against the cab, knees up, his massive arms resting on his knees. A reddish-grey cloud hovered over the road behind them where the pickup kicked dust from the caliche, a straight line that stretched from horizon to horizon, north to south. Nothing but rock and a few scraggly cacti filled the landscape from east to west.

His eyes locked on the two young men who lay sleeping, wrapped in a blanket for the comfort of it more than from any need for warmth. They were his responsibility now, these two, and he had absolutely no idea what would happen to them. The lines of the future continued their relentless twisting.

The planet would be destroyed by fire.

Mankind would experience a new Eden.

The pickup maintained its relentless bouncing and banging.

John kicked at the blanket until it twisted around his legs. He murmured and his breathing sped up. Sweat stained the pants and t-shirt he'd worn nonstop for two weeks.

Oh, yes. Sweat. Michael had to remind himself to do that. That's what bodies did. He didn't really have a body this time. Not a flesh and blood one. Not one that would sweat unless he made it.

John's eyes flicked under his eyelids. He'd been destined for a small part in the Father's final plan to redeem the world. . . to redeem the angels who had Fallen, but John had also been destined to die.

Two weeks after the fall from a twelve-story building had killed him, John lay in the back of a pickup with David, possibly the Messiah, who'd brought him back from the dead against all reason and advice.

No one had known he could do that, least of all David.

Michael smiled. He would cherish for all eternity the look on Raphael's face when David had translocated from the top of the Temporary Building to the ground below.

That had been the moment Michael had known. Had been certain: God's plan was more complicated than any of them imagined.

Michael shifted from foot to foot against the cab window like a bird in a black leather vest and jeans. As always, the angel wore a form and dress of the time. In this form, in this time, his hair was dark again and pulled into a braid. As always, he sported the body of a warrior.

John shifted in his sleep. His aura darkened. The dream was a vision, then, and not a pleasant one. He had few pleasant visions.

Prophets rarely did.

Michael peeked.

John stood on a mountain.

At the end of the valley, a brilliant twist of light and the land rippled like water.

The moon shattered, and heavy pieces fell and punched a mile into the Earth.

The valley split open like an egg, and red-hot molten rock poured into the sky, igniting the atmosphere and flash-frying the entire planet in a moment.

So, no, not a pleasant vision.

Michael watched John whenever he could. He never tired of it. The young man was a source of endless fascination. Like that, the way one foot twitched in his sleep. Always the right foot. Did that mean something? Why never the left?

John was much more than just another prophet to the warrior angel. Although John didn't know it, he was also Michael's son.

None of the Heavenly Host understood why Michael's child had lived. Truth be told, no one understood much of anything, anymore; all they had was guesswork. The Father had been quiet for so long, there were those who wondered whether He would ever speak again.

Not Michael. He kept his faith.

John had lived. That was enough. More than enough. It was a miracle. It had also changed the world in ways even the most profound of Michael's siblings couldn't understand.

Raphael had remained surly since proven wrong about the inevitability of John's death, so at least Michael had that to cheer him. The passive fortune cookie sayings his brother tossed around grated on Michael's nerves.

John rolled onto his side and curled up against David, muttering louder. He dreamed the dreams of a prophet who should have died.

The romance between the two young men had come as a bit of a surprise. It hadn't been as astonishing as David's ability to raise the dead, but it ranked close. The woman, Mary, had been a favorite last time. Well, even twins turned out different in that respect, and clones came from different wombs.

Clones. Such a complicated way to create a Messiah. Back in the day, God would simply speak the Word, and a world would pop into existence.

And what of the little one? Layla. The girl who had been destined to be David's Prophet, what would happen to her now that everything had changed?

So many things they didn't know or understand. Why wouldn't the Father simply show up and point the way?

At times, Michael felt as lost as the humans.

Brakes. The driver of the pickup, Domino, tapped the window behind Michael. The truck slowed and stopped.

Michael rose, turning forward, leaning on the cab. A scattering of clay and timber huts stretched out on either side of the road. Red dust blew through the air, catching up now that the truck had stopped.

Michael closed his eyes.

About two hundred lived in small homes, most of which had blankets for doors and open squares for windows. They had water from wells and, sometimes, electricity from a solar generator. Patches covered their threadbare clothes, but, considering the heat and the dust, they all kept remarkably clean.

Every hut had a tub or a shower, and the community maintained bathing houses and a sweat lodge as well.

So that much was the same this time.

Ten Native American's moved into position to meet the truck. None of them displayed the weapons they all carried: guns in the small of their backs. None of their faces exuded welcome.

"Interesting place for a village. What's it called?" John took a spot at Michael's side.

"Novida," Michael said.

"Seriously?" John scoffed. "Nobody here knows Spanish?" He explored the village with his eyes. "Or maybe they do. I'll assume no one has a cell for us to call our parents."

Michael frowned. They couldn't contact the rest of the family. The results might be disastrous. Michael had explained that several times.

"Are we there?" David asked, still on his back in the bed of the truck.

"We are," Michael said. "You should stay down for the moment."

John's eyes furrowed. So often with the distrust and belligerence.

"The Indian Nation has been isolated and persecuted even worse than anyone in the ghettos," Michael explained. "And for centuries. They're likely hostile to anyone who doesn't look like you or me."

"Is that why you look like you could be my Uncle Mike?" John's eyes relaxed.

"Michael," the angel corrected automatically. How long would it take John to stop using the nickname? "And Uncle. . . works. . . and yes, that's part of the reason, anyway." It was a better explanation than the truth. "We'll go with I'm your Uncle Michael."

John could never know that Michael was his father. Promising to keep that secret had been a condition of the angel's presence in his son's life.

The line of villagers stretched into a rough semi-circle at the head of the cab. One man stepped forward, tall, middle-aged, and lean, wearing a straw cowboy hat and a coyote's smile, a friendly expression that would likely turn into a vicious bite to the throat in a heartbeat. He was the one Michael needed to convince.

"He's not really that friendly," John whispered. "The smile's a fake."

Did he really think Michael hadn't already divined that?

"Sorry." John stared forward. "I forget sometimes." He'd likely need more than a couple of weeks to remember that his guide was an angel sent from Heaven. . . and John had been something of a leader among his friends. Giving over control was likely to take some time.

And maybe he shouldn't do that.

Since he'd lived, he was a Prophet, after all. Right?

So the big guy was an angel sent from Heaven. John got that. He had a direct line to unfathomable knowledge and a lot of power. Fine.

Did he have to act so smug about it? John had spent two years working missions for the Pipeline with his friends. He wasn't a total noob.

Domino, the guy who'd given them a ride, climbed out of the cab and dashed over to the man who had to be the village leader. A red cloud traced his footsteps. He spoke into the leader's ear. Ah, hell.

"Get up here, David," John muttered. "They know about you."

But David already stood at John's shoulder. What the what? Damn. Did he need to keep with the mind reading thing?

Michael raised a bemused eyebrow.

"What?" John asked him. "Did someone die and make you

God so no one else can take initiative?" Then John scowled at David. "And can you wait for me to ask, please?"

"Sorry, oh great leader," David said without the least trace of irony. "But someone did die and make me God." He met John's eyes. "You know... me."

Damn. It was going to be one of *those* days. Some days were all hugs and kisses. Other days. . . not so much. The leader stared at them without smiling while Domino whispered in his ear. Things could go from bad to worse.

"Please let me do the talking," Michael said. "I handled conversations like this before your species learned to speak."

Seriously? Did he really think. . .

A woman on the end of the line fidgeted and touched the back of her pants a couple of times. Yikes. If one of them had a gun, chances were, they all did.

John sighed. "All yours, Uncle Mike."

"Michael." Even slouching and leaning on his hands, the angel towered over John. He called louder. "I'm Michael. This is John and his boyfriend David."

Blast. Boyfriend. How would they react to that?

"I have no issue with the fact that you have a boyfriend." The leader laughed. "But I'm not thrilled with your lousy pale taste." He waved the driver away. "You gave Domino a lot of money for a ride out here into the lower intestine of Hell. Why here?"

"We need to disappear," Michael said.

John held his breath. Michael was admitting so much to people they didn't know. He seemed to bank a lot on the whole "enemy of my enemy is a friend" thing.

Especially to people with guns in the small of their backs.

Jamie checked the water supply. Low. Someone would need to take the cooler outside for more snow.

Cooler. Right. The temp outside had to be below zero: howling winds and three feet of snow. In their shed, the metal "cooler" was more a place for snow to melt over a fire so they could drink it. All they had was wood to warm them in an ancient stove thing, and the wood was fast running out. When it was gone, they'd all die.

Snow. She'd never seen snow outside video on the net. It'd always looked pretty. Sparkly.

In real life? Blast it and burn it, snow was *cold*! And it got into everything! Every time she left the shelter, it blew into her pants and up her shirt.

"We need to make a run?" Barry looked over her shoulder.

"Maybe later." She listened to the howling wind. "We should last until the wind dies down so we don't freeze completely."

Barry raised an eyebrow. Once upon a time, he'd have made some kind of smartass comment about his balls already being frozen. Instead, he shrugged and headed to his blanket beside Rocky near the corrugated metal wall. He slid down and wrapped in the blanket without a word.

Few of them spoke anymore. What was there to say that wouldn't start an argument? Everything started an argument.

The metal shed held out the howling wind but did little to keep the freezing temperatures at bay. After almost two weeks trapped together in the blasted Canadian tundra, would they simply freeze to death when the wood ran out?

Mom and Dad had given them such hope. Their old friend Senator Sato, a blasted *Senator*, had given them a plane to fly away from the Ghetto, and she'd sent a copter to take them to freedom in Canada. . . A Dickerson copter piloted by AI. Where the heck had she gotten *that*? And why did she leave them there? In the cold. In the dark. Alone. And no one wanted to accept that they were doomed.

No one except Jamie. She leaned against an empty supply table. Mom and Dad sat together in one corner, sharing a blanket. Mom's eyes seemed shadowed with stress. Then she looked up at Jamie, and the shadow lifted. She winked.

Yeah, keep pretending. Keep hoping someone would come into the middle of frozen Canada to save them.

Which would be the worse way to die?

She'd once heard that freezing to death was peaceful. You fell asleep and never woke up.

"It's a dinosaur." Layla's voice creaked a little. She'd hardly said a word in a week. Not since Jamie had yelled at her. Screamed.

Layla drew on the wall with crayons they'd found with the supplies. She'd already filled every scrap of paper.

Why had someone given them food and craft supplies, only to let them die two weeks later?

"Why's it have seven heads?" Joanne crouched beside her. "Hydra?"

"No. It just has seven heads." The girl stared at the drawing with one eye closed. She switched eyes. "I think it needs hats."

"Top hats," Rocky mumbled. He shifted, huddling close to Barry. Those two had formed an expected alliance. They'd both lost Noah, in some ways more a brother to Barry than to Rocky, the biological sibling. Barry circled Rocky's shoulders with an arm. Warmer.

"You can't go wrong with top hats," Jamie encouraged. Anything to fix what she'd broken.

Layla gazed at her with both eyes but nothing in them. She resumed drawing without another word. Burn it.

Barry caught Jamie's eye and shrugged as if to say her sister would come around eventually. He'd said so a dozen times. He'd forgiven Jamie. So had Rocky. Both of them thought their families were dead.

That was Layla's fault. She had made an announcement after some stupid argument between Jamie and Barry.

"Be nice to him," she'd screeched over their battle. "His whole family died!"

But she had no way of knowing. Well, she'd known a bunch of

stuff that maybe was right, stuff she shouldn't have known, but that was because she'd always been observant, had seen stuff no one else noticed.

"Did you see them in the river, sweetie?" Dad had asked.

Layla shook her head.

"On the street, somewhere?" he'd tried.

"The apartment burned." Her voice had been so quiet. And they'd taken it seriously, as if she were some kind of prophet or something, like somehow, she could know. It was stupid.

They all wanted to believe in angels and prophets and God so much because that was the only way they'd get out of the death trap around them.

Layla told Rocky his mom had died, as well. And everyone believed her. They'd all kept asking her questions about the Ghetto, as if she had any idea. But *everyone* was dead. All of them. Of course, they were. It wouldn't take a prophet to figure out that everyone they'd ever known had died horribly. What a nightmare.

"Oh my God!" Jamie had finally screamed. "Would you stop with the fucking baby prophet talk? She's just a stupid little girl. She doesn't know *anything*."

And Layla had stopped talking. Completely. She just kept drawing. Dinosaurs, today. And, instead of hats, she gave them scarves.

How could Jamie have been so awful? Maybe *she* deserved to die.

Joanne leaned against the table beside Jamie. She nudged her with an elbow and lifted her chin, her way of asking if Jamie was okay.

Jamie nodded.

With so many people in one room, privacy didn't exist. They'd managed to hang a blanket in one corner for the bucket they used, but, in all reality, the sounds and smells were almost as bad as the sight would be.

The dim, flickering light from the stove cast erratic shadows across the walls. They reminded Jamie of her final sight of the Ghetto as it burned and vast clouds of black smoke had risen into the sky, visible in the light of the fires. Black copters had circled the island like dirty vultures. How long would fires give her nightmares? The smell of burning flesh and plastic lingered.

When they'd first arrived, they'd tried to clean up as best they could, before they knew the water had to last, but without soap. . . the water only worked so well.

Joanne's presence gave Jamie a sense of peace. This woman worked on the Pipeline. She knew Makabee himself. Or herself. No one knew. Well, Joanne probably did, but Jamie could never bring herself to ask for any details.

Having someone who knew how to handle herself in a crisis was the only thing that had prevented Jamie from walking out into the cold and giving up. With Joanne there. . . maybe somehow. . .

Blast! What the hell was happening in the rest of the world? Who had died? Who'd lived? Had the other ghettos been attacked? Had anyone rebelled at long last? Or had the destruction of the Ghetto, the first of them all, had it squashed the Pipeline completely?

More importantly, what had happened to John and David? They'd been sent to escape in Rocky's boat. . .

. . .with an angel.

Blighted, stupid story. The guys' insistence that David had raised John from the dead sucked enough, but they also claimed to see this man unfold actual wings and stir up a halo.

Okay, from Rocky, no huge surprise. Who knew what apps still floated around his drug-addled brain, but Barry? Sure, he sampled the goods from time to time, but not enough for full-blown flashback hallucinations.

Jamie sighed.

Joanne nudged her.

Jamie rolled her eyes. It was like her friend knew what she thought.

Someone knocked on the door.

Wait. What?

Everyone jumped to their feet, so she hadn't imagined it.

Another knock.

Jamie started forward, but Joanne grabbed her arm.

They had no way to know who it was.

Dad slipped in front of Mom and held a hand out to Layla. The little girl's eyes had gone huge. She dashed behind her father.

Dad's eyes found Jamie, who grabbed Joanne's hand and pulled her to the back of the room with the rest of her family.

The boys shifted to stand in front of Mom and Layla. Dad tried to force Joanne and Jamie to the back, but seriously?

Jamie stood her ground, and Joanne scoffed, pulling the pistol out of her boot.

"We know there's seven of you in there," a man's voice called out, intentionally effected: low and spooky. "We can see the heat signatures. I want all hands up or we start shooting."

Oh blast, what should they do?

"And the one with the gun?" the deep voice said. "Drop it."

Joanne sucked in a breath.

Mom placed her hand over Joanne's and shook her head. They had no idea how many stood outside the cottage. One small gun wouldn't help.

Joanne placed the gun on the floor and slid it into a far corner.

"Who are you?" Dad called out.

"We have the same damn question," the man shouted back. "What are you doing on our land? Who the hell are you, and why did you tell us to come out here?"

What the heck did that even mean?

"We. . . we didn't…" her father said. "We were dropped off here in a helicopter. We don't. . . we don't even know where we are. This is your shed?" His eyes opened wide. "Do you know Amanda Sato? She brought us here… at least, I think she did."

Oh hell, why not just hand over their identity chips? What if it was Addison. . . or that freak of an assassin who worked for him?

Barry slammed a palm to his forehead. Even Mom rolled her eyes. Joanne sighed and raised a fist. The bracelet that held her chip dangled. She, Jamie, and Barry could all be killed just for having their chips removed.

"We really have options?" Dad whispered. "If Sato didn't leave us here on purpose, we're pretty much screwed." He had a point. "Hello?" He called out.

"Stay away from the door and keep your hands up," the deep voice said. "We're coming in, and we have automatic weapons ready to blow you away if anyone sneezes."

"Oh blight it, now I really need to sneeze." Barry snuffled.

Rocky nudged him.

Everyone huddled closer together against the far wall. Joanne pressed against Jamie's left side, Mom against her right.

"I love all of you." Dad touched Jamie's hair and kissed her head.

Others muttered similar sentiments.

Whatever. Jamie dropped one hand to the metal cooler because it was the heaviest thing in reach, and she'd already decided how to use the supply table as a shield.

The door opened, and wind swirled the snow into a frenzy.

The temperature plummeted.

Two people in parkas entered, their faces covered in masks.

They held huge guns, automatic spewers of death.

Oh, hell. The supply table would help not at all against those.

"How are we going to kill the Sato bitch?" Addison asked.

"Three assassins have failed so far," Pierce reminded him.

They moved through the antiseptic halls of the DC Project, and the dozens of underlings knew well enough to scurry out of their way as Addison stalked the corridor and his shadow kept up while monitoring three holographic screens above his tablet.

"Why is her muscle so damn effective?" Addison had asked the question a hundred times. "What is she hiding?"

"Apart from the fact that she appropriated a drone copter to ferry Subject Zero's family across the border?" Pierce folded the screens into one.

Unraveling the past connections between the Senator and the Project had taken five minutes. Her brat and his whore of a wife had grown up with the fanatical girl and her folksy husband.

Sato's *current* angle remained obscure. Okay, sentimentality was a common explanation, but something else was going on. Sato had far too many deep underground connections for a Senator and this grandstand stunt had exposed her. Until he'd started digging, Addison hadn't even noticed the woman's actions behind the scenes.

Was her entire career a ploy to infiltrate the deep underbelly of the government? If so, playing her hand to save her son's little friends had been an enormous mistake. She'd be under a microscope the rest of her life.

The only theory that made any sense was that she knew about the Project. That Makabee knew about the Project and wanted the little bastard for himself.

But that was impossible. No one could have leaked the information, anyone close to compromise was eliminated long before they could turn, and Subject Zero had fled in a completely different direction.

Unless an entirely new power was in play.

Fuck that idea. It made Addison want blood.

"And we haven't found her son?" Addison demanded.

"The Canadian government hates us unilaterally, sir." Pierce messed with his toy.

When the ghettos had opened almost two decades ago and a deluge of refugees slipped over the border, Canada efficiently granted them asylum, removed their chips, and created a mountain of red tape to hide them. Bastards. They'd even deleted their own records and started an entirely new database with all the refugees entered as existing citizens.

Addison and Pierce reached the usual door. The advantage of the DC Project was its smaller size. Addison didn't need to bake in the desert going from building to building. In DC, they had one connected facility. They also had fewer subjects to train. They'd started with twenty. They were down to seven, an annoyingly symbolic number.

Pierce closed his screen and tucked the tablet under an arm.

A green beam played over them both.

"Welcome, Mr. Addison," a calm male voice said. "I hope you're having a lovely day."

"We need to kill whoever programmed the doors," Addison said.

Pierce tapped the tablet.

"Any more on possible connections to Makabee?" Addison slipped through before the door had opened completely.

"If she is involved in the Pipeline," Pierce admitted, "she is better at covering her tracks than anyone we've encountered."

For a public figure to maintain a shadow existence in spite of massive scrutiny seemed nearly impossible.

Addison hated her. He needed to find someone to rape her and kill her husband. And her fucking son and his family.

All of them.

The colossal cock-up on Staten Island had changed everything. Addison vowed to kill anyone in his way without hesitation. Fuck the politically correct pussies who wanted him to "go through channels" and "get approval." Bullshit.

From this point forward, when someone needed to die, Addison would see them dead. In a world rife with disease and natural disaster, a few—or a few thousand—bodies could be explained away.

Failure? Not so easy to justify.

Addison hurried to the holding cells with Pierce a step behind. This part of the complex was decidedly less crowded. They passed through several checkpoints until they reached the causeway that overlooked the Project's living quarters.

Every time he'd visited during construction, the setup had reminded him of an observation deck overlooking racquetball courts. Here, each court was a concrete holding cell. Each held a bed, a dresser and now. . . one subject.

The subjects had been given private quarters for the first time. Each of the seven stood in the center of his cell with a nurse poking and prodding, taking baseline measurements so changes could be monitored as they acclimated to privacy.

They wore identical grey scrubs with a number clearly marked on the back and breast of their shirt so they could be identified.

1, 3, 6, 9, 11, 15, 19.

And they looked exactly like the little bastard Addison had seen in the subways of the Ghetto.

These boys had crew cuts that hid the curls, but they all had the same nearly black eyes, thick eyebrows. He'd recognized the brat in an instant... but he'd lost the little shit.

www.ingramcontent.com/pod-product-compliance
Lightning Source LLC
Chambersburg PA
CBHW071223250626
47163CB00001B/81